Kurthak seethed with fury at what was happening. Rage filled his mind, clouding his vision with red mist. The kender were grouped on the other side of the pits, in the shadows of the courtyards, laughing. Laughing at him.

His temper snapping, he threw his massive arms up over his head and howled. "Kill them!" he cried. "Take no prisoners! Kill them all!"

NOVELS

BRIDGES OF TIME SERIES

Spirit of the Wind
Chris Pierson

Legacy of Steel
Mary H. Herbert
November 1998

DragonLance® NOVELS

Spirit of the Wind

Chris Pierson

For my parents, Don and Jan Pierson—for encourage-ment, patience, and for always answering the phone.

SPIRIT OF THE WIND

Distributed to the book trade in the United States by Random House, Inc. and in Canada by Random House of Canada, Ltd.

Distributed to the hobby, toy, and comic trade in the United States and Canada by regional distributors.

Distributed worldwide by Wizards of the Coast, Inc. and regional distributors.

Cover art by Jeff Easley
First Printing: July 1998
Library of Congress Catalog Card Number: 97-062373

9 8 7 6 5 4 3 2 1

ISBN: 0-7869-1174-3

8390XXX1501

U.S., CANADA,
ASIA, PACIFIC, & LATIN AMERICA
Wizards of the Coast, Inc.
P.O. Box 707
Renton, WA 98057-0707
+1-206-624-0933

EUROPEAN HEADQUARTERS
Wizards of the Coast, Belgium
P.B. 34
2300 Turnhout
Belgium
+32-14-44-30-44

Visit our website at **www.tsr.com**

Prologue

The day dawned clear. The few ribbons of cloud shone gold as the sun pushed itself up over the horizon. It was not quite full summer, and morning's cool breeze bore the salty tang of the sea. Gulls shrieked and squalled as they dove into the water, coming up with gleaming silver fish that they swallowed in quick gulps. The surf crashed against the cliffs of the Goodlund peninsula, exploding in bursts of crimson spray.

In years past, before the world changed, superstitious folk had come up with many tales of the Blood Sea of Istar. Some said it was the blood of the thousands who had perished in the Cataclysm that gave the waters their sanguine hue. Others claimed the scarlet color came from a gateway to the Abyss itself, where the gods' fiery mountain had smashed the Kingpriest in his Temple. Those who made their living from the Blood Sea, however, had scoffed at such notions, calling them landlubber's nonsense.

Tuller Quinn had scoffed with the rest of them, over mugs of grog at the Jetties taphouse in Flotsam. "Blood indeed," he'd told his crew. "Soil's all it is—farmlands pushed under water by the Cataclysm. The Maelstrom keeps it all stirred up. It ain't blood, no matter what anyone says. It's just dirt."

Standing at the prow of the *Elchenior*, his ship, Tuller stared out across the waves, worrying—and thinking what a fool he'd once been to say that.

"Cap'n?" called Perth, his first mate. "The lads are ready to get underway."

For a moment, Tuller chose to ignore him. Perth cleared his throat and raised his voice a little. "Cap'n?"

"Aye, then," Tuller answered over his shoulder. "Full sails. We'll need the whole day to get back to Flotsam, if the winds don't pick up."

"Weigh anchor!" shouted Perth. "You heard the captain, you dogs! Quit lazing about and hoist the bloody sails! I've got a lass waiting for me in port, and if I have to spend another night aboard this tub, I'll flog the lot o' ye blue!"

Sailors scrambled, shouting and cursing. The *Elchenior's* green sails rose swiftly. Elsewhere, three bare-chested sailors strained as they pulled the ship's anchor up from the sea floor. The helmsman took the tiller, turning them into the listless wind to keep them in irons until Tuller gave the order to get under way. Within minutes, the ship was ready to sail.

Tuller continued to lean against the gunwale, his attention fixed on the sea.

"We're in shape, Cap'n," Perth declared, striding forward. His boot heels made an uneven rhythm on the deck—Perth had walked with a limp for years, ever since he'd caught a pirate's gaff hook in the shin. He'd done the pirate far worse. "Cap'n?" he asked again.

Still Tuller didn't answer. Perth stopped behind him and coughed loudly.

Blinking, Tuller turned away from the waves. "Sorry, lad," he said, chuckling ruefully. "I was woolgathering. Let's be off."

Perth barked curt orders at the crew. Men hurried to obey, and presently the *Elchenior* came about, her boom swinging as the paltry wind caught the sails. The ship began to move west, along the coast.

Tuller's weathered face tightened into a scowl as he gauged their speed. "Bloody weather," he muttered. "I don't remember it ever being so calm for so long."

"Or so warm," Perth agreed. "Winter's not even a month past, and already it's like high summer out."

For a moment, both men were silent, sharing the same

grim thought. The last time the weather had turned unseasonably hot, not two years since, the legions of Chaos had nearly blasted Flotsam from the face of Krynn—and then the Second Cataclysm had struck, and the gods had left once more.

Perth shook his head angrily. He wasn't a man who liked to hold on to thoughts for very long, least of all dark ones. "What were you thinking about, Cap'n?" he asked.

"Oh, the Blood Sea," Tuller answered. "It's still red, you know."

"I'd noticed."

The captain regarded his first mate a moment, then laughed. "Aye, reckon it's hard to miss, eh? But have ye wondered what it means?"

Perth's brow furrowed, then he shook his head. "Ain't given it much thought," he said.

"All right, then, give it a try. When you were young, did your da ever tell you why the Blood Sea was red?"

"Sure. It's dirt kicked up by the Maelstrom. Everyone who's ever set foot on a ship knows that."

Tuller grunted agreement, then glanced back across the deck. "Let the mainsail out a bit more!" he called. The sailors at the mainmast loosened the halyards, and another yard of sailcloth rose to catch the wind. Tuller nodded in satisfaction, then turned back to Perth. "Now think about that, lad. What happened to the Maelstrom?"

"It stopped," Perth said. "When the moons went away. Old Jig Rinfel told me he's been out that way, and the seas are calm now."

"Right," Tuller said. "And how long's it been since that happened? A year and a half?"

Perth counted on his fingers. "Sounds close."

"So—if it's dirt that makes the water red, what's stirring it up now the Maelstrom's gone?"

"Hmph," Perth declared. "Good point. It should've settled by now."

"And the waters should be clear." Tuller gestured at the crimson waves. "Which, of course, they're not."

Perth looked out across the water, pursing his lips.

"Then it isn't dirt after all? So what is it, then?"

"That's what I was wondering," Tuller answered.

The *Elchenior* was moving west now, so the two men stared starboard, out toward the open sea. After a few minutes, Perth shook his head. "Well," he said, "I can't figure it out. Don't see the point in dwelling on it, neither. My da told me once, 'This world's got mysteries man ain't meant to solve.' Reckon this is one of them.

"As long as there's still water, who cares if it's blue, red, or silver and gold? It ain't like ye're a wizard who's lost his magic, or—"

He stopped suddenly, his eyes widening. Tuller saw this, and squinted, trying to follow his first mate's gaze. "What's the matter?" he asked.

"There," Perth hissed, stabbing a finger north across the water.

"I don't see a damn thing," Tuller snapped. "You know my eyes ain't what they once were. What are you—"

Then he saw it too, and his mouth dropped wide open.

It was a red dragon, skimming low over the waves. Her scales were the same color as the waters, camouflaging her and making it hard to guess her full shape. She was huge, though, and she was heading straight for the *Elchenior*.

"Zeboim's twenty teats," Tuller swore.

A great cry rose as the crew spotted the dragon too. She was still half a mile off, but there was no mistaking her speed. She would be on top of them in moments. Sailors abandoned their posts, running every which way.

"Get back on those ropes!" Perth barked, storming across the deck. "Now, or a dragon's the least o' your worries!" Though his voice was as gruff as before, there was a new edge to it: fear.

Tuller looked down at his hands and saw that they were white from gripping the rail. He forced himself to let go, and ran to the stern. "Hard to port!" he snapped at the helmsman. "Come about now!"

It was ridiculous, of course. There was hardly any wind, and the dragon could have outrun a gale. Still, the helmsman leaned hard on the tiller, and the boom swung wildly. Someone screamed and fell from the rigging, splashing down into the water. There was no time to turn back or even to figure out who had fallen overboard. They were moving straight toward the rocky coastline now, the dragon on their tail. The wyrm gained on them steadily.

"We're gonna die!" shouted a sailor.

The dragon was five hundred yards away. Tuller could see her golden eyes gleaming cruelly in the morning light. Her enormous wings pumped hard, dipping into the water with each beat. Her tail lashed behind her like a whip.

Two hundred yards. Her cavernous maw, lined with stalactite teeth, yawned open.

One hundred yards. Smoke curled up from her throat.

"Grab hold of something!" Perth shouted.

Fifty yards, twenty, ten. Tuller closed his eyes and held on to the rail.

The impact wasn't nearly as strong as he'd expected. Rather than smashing his ship to flinders, it merely sent it spinning out of control, listing wildly to starboard. A great rush of wind knocked him off his feet, nearly hurling him into the sea.

Opening his eyes, he saw the mainmast was gone.

The deck was splintered and torn where the dragon had ripped the spar away. Several sailors lay bleeding on the deck, dead or dying. The dragon soared above and ahead of them now, the mast clutched in its jaws like a stick in a dog's mouth. The tattered green sail flapped in the breeze. Ropes trailed beneath the wyrm. Someone was clinging to one of them, cursing at the top of his voice.

"Perth," Tuller murmured dully.

Slowly, the *Elchenior* righted itself. Men jumped over the rails into the surf, screaming in terror. The helmsman let go of the useless tiller and drew a cutlass from his belt. "She's coming around," he cried.

The dragon banked sharply, the mast still clasped in her jaws, and soared back over the waves. Perth continued to shout as he hung from the trailing rope. Then the great wyrm shook her head, and flung the mast away from her. Tuller marked its path as it plummeted into the sea. Before the mast hit the water, the dragon turned back toward the ship, tucked in her wings, and dove.

The helmsman screamed, dropping his cutlass, and leaped over the gunwale. Tuller stood rigid, his eyes fixed upon the dragon as it streaked toward him like a falling star. Its claws stretched forward, bristling with talons the size of tree trunks. This time, Tuller didn't close his eyes.

The dragon's impact drove Tuller to his knees. Her claws closed over her deck and around her hull. Beside Tuller, a massive talon drove through six inches of wood like a spear through snow. The few men who hadn't abandoned their posts clung to the ship in abject terror.

Then the *Elchenior* took flight.

"Habbakuk have mercy," Tuller swore. He pushed himself to his feet and stared over the rail as the Blood Sea dropped away beneath them. The dragon's belly arched above the ship, a scaly roof. Her wings creaked as she climbed, turning inland. They passed over the rocky shore and the cliffs beyond, then they were flying over a rich, green forest. Wind rushed all around. Tuller Quinn, who had plied the seas all his life, fell to his knees and vomited.

At last, the dragon leveled off. There were clouds all around them, and the air was chill. Tuller lay on his back, gasping, looking up at the muscles that rippled beneath the wyrm's vast, scaly hide. The dragon laughed—a ghastly, grating sound—and let go of the ship.

Tuller screamed in mad, blind terror as his ship plummeted toward the woods below. It was a long fall, though, and his voice was gone by the time the *Elchenior* smashed through the treetops into the ground.

Chapter 1

"I am not making up stories," said Catt Thistleknot. The little kender's eyebrows knitted in vexation. "I did too see a boat fall from the sky last month."

"Of course you did," answered her brother Kronn, in a tone of voice that made him sound like the older sibling, rather than the younger. "It happens all the time around here. In fact, I hear it's supposed to hail dinghies tonight."

"Don't be sarcastic," Catt huffed. She pushed aside a low-hanging branch as she trudged through the undergrowth of the Kenderwood. "Are you sure you know where we're going?"

Kronn glanced at the tall trees surrounding them. "Of course I do. Father's map says Woodsedge shouldn't be too far from where we are right now." He examined a scrap of vellum and scratched his head, turning the map this way and that. "Of course, it'd help if it said which way's supposed to be north. . . ."

"Oh, good," Catt declared. "So we're less than an hour's walk from either Woodsedge or . . . Neraka, maybe?"

"Don't be snotty." Kronn studied the map a moment longer, then shrugged and tucked it into his belt. "Anyway, anyone can see that there's too many trees around here for it to be Neraka."

"Too many for a town called Woodsedge, too."

Glowering, Kronn started pushing through the brush again. Shaking her head, Catt followed. "We don't even know for sure that Father's going to be there," she complained.

"Merldon Metwinger said he was," Kronn retorted.

"Merldon Metwinger says his daughter married Uncle Trapspringer."

"It's distinctly possible," Kronn said. "Uncle Trapspringer is quite the catch, and I know for a fact that he's been married seven or nine times."

He stopped suddenly. Catt nearly piled into the back of him. "What—" she began.

Kronn pressed a finger against her lips. "Listen."

Catt cocked a pointed ear, her forehead furrowing. It was a moment before she heard anything but birdsong and whispering leaves. Then she discerned a new sound. A chorus of odd cries wafted through the wood, equal parts cackle and screech, accompanied by the rustle of something passing through the scrub. It was getting louder, moving toward them.

"What is it?" she whispered.

Kronn didn't reply. He crept forward, moving swiftly through the bushes. After about twenty paces, he looked back at Catt. "Come on," he urged.

Catt hurried to catch up with her brother. More and more voices joined the strange chorus. Kronn drew to a halt, holding up a hand to stay his sister. They hunkered down behind a lichen-dappled boulder. Catt started to reach into her belt pouch, looking for a stone to load into her hoopak, but stopped with her hand on the bag's clasp. Kronn hadn't yet reached for the chapak—a kender weapon that is part axe, part sling, and part many other things—that he wore across his back. Trusting her brother's instincts for danger, she hunched beside him, listening. The sound was almost upon them now.

"This is going to be good," Kronn murmured, now grinning mischievously.

"Blast it, Kronn," Catt urged. "What's going—"

Without warning, Kronn leapt up from where he crouched, yelling at the top of his voice and gesticulating wildly. Suddenly the squawk-screeches gave way to startled shouts, then laughter. Following Kronn's lead, Catt jumped up beside him, waving her arms and shouting even louder than he did. Shapes rose from the undergrowth around them—a score or more of kender children, all of them boys. They turned and ran away, shrieking with laughter.

Kronn gave chase without hesitation. Catt shrugged and followed, hollering all the while. They raced through the woods, but the children eluded them, vanishing among the ferns and shrubs. Kronn came to a halt and slumped back against a papery birch tree, holding his sides as he shook with silent mirth.

"What was that about?" Catt asked.

Kronn gave her an odd look, as if he weren't sure she was serious. Then understanding dawned on his face. "Ah," he said. "I guess you wouldn't know, being a girl and all."

"Know what?" Catt asked, frowning.

Kronn stroked his chin. "Well," he said, "today's the first day of the Harrowing festival, right?"

"Right . . ."

"So, every year on Harrowing, all the boys in a village get together and go goatsucker hunting."

Catt rolled her eyes. "Goatsucker hunting? Goatsuckers are just a Trapspringer tale."

"This from someone who's seen it rain boats," Kronn countered. "I know that goatsuckers don't exist. But all kender boys go out, sounding the goatsucker call, and after a while the adults head into the woods and chase them, like we just did. It's good fun," he added, pushing away from the tree. "Besides, if there's that many children around, we must be close to Woodsedge. But we shouldn't stay here long."

Catt raised her eyebrows. "Why not?"

"Well, usually during goatsucker hunting, the kids try to get back at the grownups for chasing them," Kronn said. "When they stop to rest, the kids sneak back up on them and—"

Suddenly, a small, brown object flew out of the bushes, hitting a tree just above Catt's head with a wet crack. Something slippery dripped into her long, black hair.

"—throw eggs," Kronn finished, then turned and bolted through the forest, whooping with laughter.

* * * * *

Catt's shoes squished noisily as she and Kronn trudged along the path through the outermost fringe of the Kenderwood. She picked bits of eggshell, sticky with albumen, off her favorite yellow blouse. The shirt was ruined, as were her nice red breeches, and there seemed to be more egg in her hair than there was hair. Her lip curled in disgust as she flicked the shell away.

"I notice they left you alone," she said grumpily, glaring at her brother.

Kronn winked at her. His bright green tunic and leggings were completely unbesmirched. "What twelve-year-old boy would chuck an egg at me when there was a girl handy?"

"Hmph," Catt grumbled. She reached into her blouse and plucked out a yolk that had slithered down her neck during the bombardment. Without hesitating, she lobbed it at her brother.

He ducked nimbly aside. "Watch it there, Catt. They probably have some ammunition left." He nodded ahead, where the boys they'd chased were skipping and jostling along the trail.

At last, they reached the tree line. The path led away from the forest, toward a small town perched on a clifftop overlooking the sea. Like most kender villages, Woodsedge was a mismatched jumble of buildings and towers. Surrounding it was a wooden palisade, hung with garlands of willow branches and white wildflowers for the festival. Ahead of Kronn and Catt, the children broke into a run, yelling and whirling their small hoopaks as they sprinted toward the gates. The guardsmen had to jump aside to avoid being run down.

"Hey, Giffel!" called Kronn, waving to the guards' leader.

The guard, a tall kender with a head of short-cropped,

bright yellow hair, squinted down, then smiled broadly.

Kronn ran forward, his arms flung wide, and he and the guard caught each other in a rough embrace that quickly turned into a wrestling match. Before long, Kronn found himself sprawled in the dust, Giffel's body parked on top of him. "Ow," he grunted. "Get off, you ox. Is this any way to treat an old friend?"

"It is if he just took your purse," Giffel said, pushing himself to his feet. He held out his hand. "Give it over, Kronn."

Sheepishly, Kronn handed the guard his money pouch, which he'd purloined when they'd hugged. "Can I have mine back, too?" he asked.

Giffel chuckled. He had, in turn, lifted Kronn's purse while they wrestled. He tossed it back.

"Giffel," Kronn said, rising fluidly from the ground. "You remember Catt, don't you?"

"Your sister," Giffel replied, grinning. "Of course. It, uh, looks like you found the goatsucker hunters."

Beneath the dripping bits of egg, Catt glared a fierce shade of red. Kronn chuckled.

"You here for the festival doings?" Giffel asked.

Kronn shook his head, his cheek braids flapping. "Not as such. We're looking for our father. Is he around?" He waved toward the town's open gates.

Giffel folded his arms across his chest. "I'm not supposed to say," he answered. "Kronin gave specific instructions not to let anyone know he was in Woodsedge."

"How specific?" asked Catt.

"Well, he certainly isn't at the hoopak-slinging contest."

Laughing, Kronn clapped Giffel on the arm. "Good fellow," he said. "I'm glad to see my father picked the right man to be candid with."

"Go on in," Giffel bade.

"Thanks, Giff," Kronn said. He and Catt started to through the gates, but he stopped and glanced back. "Will you be at the feast tonight?"

"Of course," Giffel replied, and slapped his belly. "Do you think I'd miss a free meal?"

"I suppose not," Kronn said. "I'll make sure Catt saves a dance for you."

Catt punched her brother in the arm. But as Kronn walked on, both Giffel and Catt turned quite interesting colors.

* * * * *

The kender, as a people, have surprisingly few heroes. It isn't that they are a cowardly race, of course. On the contrary, fear is alien to them. If he has good reason, a kender will practically march into Dargaard Keep, walk up to Lord Soth, and poke him in the eye without balking. It is, ironically, for this reason that they don't revere many of their own. What might seem a feat of reckless bravery to a human, a kender regards as no big deal. "I could have done that, if I wanted," is a favorite kender saying.

That doesn't mean the kender have no legendary figures at all. Over their history, a handful have proven sufficiently interesting to earn their fellows' esteem. The most famous of these is Uncle Trapspringer, whom every kender claims as a relative and close personal friend. There are enough wild stories about his adventures—and, frequently, gruesome deaths—to fill an entire wing of the great Library in Palanthas. The kender would swear up and down that each and every one is the complete and untainted truth.

There are certain legends of ancient kender heroes. Balif, the warrior who had fought beside the elven king Silvanos, was purported by some to have been himself born an elf. Rithel Stubbletoe, who'd defended the kender nation of Hylo, in the west of Ansalon, from an invasion by the expanding Empire of Ergoth, once broke into the Imperial Court in Daltigoth and made off with the Emperor's crown jewels. A young kender named Noblosha Lampwick was believed to have taken and passed the Test at the Tower of High Sorcery in Wayreth, though none of the wizards' records listed her name.

After the Cataclysm, the kender had gone for more than

three centuries without any new heroes. Recently, though, two of them had won that honor through their valorous deeds. One was Tasslehoff Burrfoot. He had broken dragon orbs, gone back in time and into the Abyss, and chatted with a number of gods—then, sealed his reputation by sacrificing his life to draw blood from the mad god, Chaos. Now, scarcely two years after his death, young kender often claimed their most prized possessions had been given to them by "Uncle Tas."

The other, relatively new kender hero was Kronin Thistleknot. Kronin was something of a special case, as his deeds fell somewhat short of his people's usual high standards. Sure, he had ruled Kendermore for an unprecedented twenty-five years before stepping down to let his daughter Paxina take over. And yes, he had killed the loathsome Dragon Highlord, Fewmaster Toede. There were already numerous versions of that victory. Only Kronin himself knew which was true, and he wasn't telling. But neither of these feats was what made him stand out above his kind. No, what drew the kender's attention to Kronin was that his deeds made him a hero among the other races of Ansalon. Elves, humans, and even dwarves revered him for his role in the Dragonarmies' downfall. It was only after nearly everyone else had honored him that the kender, deciding they must have missed something important, made him a hero by acclamation.

Thus it was that Woodsedge's town square was crammed with onlookers as a rare flesh-and-blood hero stepped up to the firing line of the slinging contest. Kronin was, by this time, eighty-six years old, his face a maze of wrinkles and his silvery hair almost gone. He hobbled as he walked, leaning heavily on his old, worn hoopak, and his favorite purple shoes were faded with age, but his eyes were clear, and his hand didn't shake as he delved into his belt pouch. Silence, punctuated by murmurs of awe, fell over the crowd as he rooted through the bag and started pulling out rocks.

He examined each in turn, eyeing it closely, then tossed

it on the ground. Finally, on the fourth try, he produced a round, smooth stone. The furrows of his brow deepened as he regarded it. Then he nodded and tucked it into the leather pocket on the forked end of his hoopak. He brought the weapon back, carefully poised.

"Ready," he said loudly.

The far end of the courtyard, beyond the spectators, was flanked by several small catapults. The machines were spread out at various distances, and each was cocked and loaded with a large clay disc. Now, at Kronin's command, the kender manning the closest one—only about thirty yards away—released the catch. The catapult's arm sprang forward, flinging the clay disc through the air.

Kronin concentrated, marking its flight, then brought his hoopak sharply forward, sending his slingstone flashing across the courtyard. It struck the middle of the disc, shattering it with a crash. Shards of clay rattled down on the cobblestones.

"Ooooh!" said the assembled kender. "Aaah!"

Kronin nodded in satisfaction, then rifled through his pouch until he found a second suitable stone. He loaded his hoopak again. "Ready," he declared a second time.

A second catapult, this one sixty yards away, let fly. He slung again, and broke the second disc. He did the same to the third, then the fourth.

Kronn and Catt elbowed through the crowd, making their way to the front. "How's he doing?" Kronn asked one of the officials, a bespectacled kender in a fancy, turquoise jerkin.

The official peered at him closely. "Four for four," he replied. Another crash, this one well over a hundred yards away, rang across the courtyard, and the official turned to see the pieces of yet another disc rain down on the ground. "Make that five for five."

Catt, who had washed and put on a clean yellow dress, raised an eyebrow. "Not bad, for an old codger," she mused.

"Kender never lose their aim!" Kronn said proudly. "Who's in the lead?"

Frowning, the official looked down at the slate he was using to keep score. "That'd be Yarren Ringglimmer," he said, nodding toward a red-haired kender at the edge of the firing line. "He hit six out of seven, but this last one's tricky. No one's gotten it yet."

"Really?" Kronn remarked. "Why's that?"

"Would someone please tell my son to kindly keep his voice down?" snapped Kronin as he prepared his hoopak for a sixth shot. "I'm trying to concentrate."

"Sorry, Father," Kronn called.

Kronin made a sour face, then peered straight down the courtyard. Two catapults, almost directly across from each other, remained unfired. Their operators stood ready, their hands on the release catches.

The crowd was completely silent. Kronin licked his lips. "Ready," he said.

Both catapults sprang at once, their discs arcing toward each other. Kronin watched them calmly, his eyes narrowing, then brought his hoopak sharply forward.

The slingstone tore through the air. The first disc was at the apex of its flight and the second had just begun to fall when the stone smashed through them both.

The crowd broke into laughing and cheering and clapping their hands. Kronin straightened his violet silk tunic and hobbled away from the firing line. Kronn and Catt hurried forward to meet him.

"Nice shooting, Papa," Catt said.

Kronin wrinkled his nose. "Child's play," he grumbled. "Hello, Catt . . . Kronn." He kissed her on the cheek, then clasped arms with his son. "Who told you I was here? That old fool Metwinger, I suppose."

"You suppose right," Catt said.

"Hmph." Kronin scowled, then glanced around. The crowd was starting to break up now. His eyes fixed on a nearby cluster of market stalls. "All right, then. There's a fellow over there selling cider. Fetch me a flask and some roasted acorns. Then you can tell me why you're here."

* * * * *

"Ah," Kronin sighed, his knees creaking as he eased himself down on the ground. He leaned back against a blossoming cherry tree, then kicked off his purple shoes and wriggled his toes as he took a long pull from his flask of cider. Kronn and Catt had traded a pocketknife and a copper saltcellar for the drink. "So, what trouble's your big sister in now?"

Catt blinked. "How did you guess Paxina sent us?"

"Please, girl," Kronin grumbled, rapping his temple with a gnarled finger. "Credit me with some brains. The problem with this hero business is that people always want something from me. I'm supposed to be retired, though you'd never know it. Trapspringer's ears, what is it this time?"

"Well," Kronn began, clasping his hands together, "Pax thinks we're going to be attacked soon."

"Again?" Kronin rolled his eyes. "Why bother me about it? Paxina didn't need my help keeping the Knights of Takhisis from killing us all, a couple years back."

"That was easy," Catt countered. "Relatively speaking, of course. All Pax had to do was get us to convince the knights we could be more useful to them alive than dead. It's different, this time; we're dealing with ogres."

Kronin's eyes flared. He plucked an acorn from the small bag his children had gotten for him, and popped it in his mouth. After a moment he spat out the cap and started chewing on the bitter nutmeat. "Well, that is different. How many?"

"Thousands," Kronn answered. "So far all we know is that ogres have been overrunning the villages of the Darly Plains. All sorts of human refugees have been coming through the Kenderwood. It looks as though the ogres have all banded together, and are moving steadily toward Kendermore. Pax thinks we're in real danger."

Kronn gave a low whistle. "I can't argue that. What does she want from me?"

"Help, Father," Catt pleaded. "We need help."

"I should say so," Kronin agreed. " You're going to need every bit of help you can get." He munched on an acorn.

Kronn knelt beside his father. "Well?"

"I'm thinking." Kronin frowned, chewing noisily. "I suppose Paxina wants me to come to Kendermore with you."

"She most certainly does," Kronn snapped.

"Well, then." Kronin stood with a sigh, raising his flask to his lips and drinking down the last of his cider. "I learned long ago that a hero ain't allowed to resign. Nor a father, I might add. We'll leave tomorrow. But for tonight, let's enjoy the feast, eh?"

* * * * *

By late afternoon, the catapults and debris had been cleared out of the courtyard and the large tables wheeled in, laden with more food than the entire village could hope to eat. Laughter and sumptuous smells filled the air as the kender gorged themselves on oven-hot herb breads, roasted rabbit and spring lamb, dandelion greens and pungent cheeses. Wine and ale, mead and cider, fresh milk and strawberry juice flowed freely. The feast finished with an array of puddings and cakes that satisfied the sweetest teeth in town. As the sun hung, swollen and red, over the trees to the west, many of the villagers stumbled off to sleep or passed out where they stood.

"If I eat anything else," Kronin declared, "I worry that the buttons might fly off my shirt and put out someone's eye." He patted his bulging stomach contentedly.

"I can never figure out where you find room for it all, Giffel," Kronn told the tall guardsman, who had joined them for the meal.

Giffel, who had exchanged his fighting leathers for a long red shirt and maroon trousers, was chewing contentedly on a lamb haunch. "The key is to pace yourself," he mumbled around a mouthful of meat.

"And have a belly the size of a kurpa melon," Catt added, laughing. Giffel blushed in embarrassment.

"Looks like the band's setting up for the dance,"

Kronn noted. He pointed at a raised platform across the courtyard. A group of musicians were milling about, holding an unlikely array of instruments: triple-necked lutes, bagpipes, xylophones, a great brass horn that was bigger than the kender who played it, and a contraption that appeared to be part dulcimer, part musical saw. They started to tune up, but there seemed to be some disagreement as to which key they should play in.

"Let's go someplace and talk," Kronn suggested. "Giffel, take care of Catt. You promised her the first dance earlier."

"Sure, Kronn," the guard said. He offered his arm to Catt.

She took it. "Just don't spin me around too fast," she said. "All that mead's made me a bit dizzy."

Kronin and Kronn watched the two of them walk off toward the musicians. "Remember when you were young, how he used to put salamanders in her boots?" Kronin observed wistfully.

"Of course I do." Kronn grinned wryly. "It was my idea."

Kronin returned his smile. "Come on, lad," he bade. "You're right. We need to talk."

* * * * *

It being a festival day, the palisade was largely abandoned. A few guards remained on duty, overlooking the town gates, but for the most part Woodsedge's walls remained still and silent. Kronin hobbled up the ladder to the catwalk, then sat down and leaned heavily against the battlements. Kronn came up after, and glanced up and down the palisade. There was no one close enough to hear. He turned to follow his father's gaze, north across the Blood Sea. There was a light chop on the water, whipped up by a wind that seemed surprisingly warm for so early in the year. The sky dimmed from sunset-red to twilight-purple, and stars began to glimmer beyond the clouds.

"Father, I'm sorry to be the one dragging you off to Kendermore," Kronn murmured. He reached in his pouch and pulled out a pebble that had caught his fancy when he'd spotted it in a streambed a few days ago. It had been splendid then, shining with bright colors, but now that it was dry it was just another gray, uninteresting rock. Kronn threw it, watching it sail over the cliff, into the surf. "I hate to interrupt your retirement."

"Bah," Kronin said. "Retirement's boring, and I'm looking forward to a good fight." He reached over and patted his son's foot. "Actually, I'm glad you and your sister were the ones who came for me."

"Catt was the one who offered to look for you, truth be told," Kronn said. "Pax sent me along for protection."

Kronin scoffed. "You're the one needs protecting!" He looked across the village, toward the town square. "Thousands of ogres," he remarked. "That should be interesting. Still, we've faced worse."

Kronn grunted noncommittally. In his father's lifetime, the kender had stood against the dragonarmies, the Knights of Takhisis, and the legions of Chaos. Still, something about this situation made him uneasy.

The sound of laughter and clapping hands rose from the town below, echoing weirdly off the walls of the town's randomly scattered houses.

"How's Paxina doing?" Kronin asked.

"Not badly," Kronn answered. "You must have rubbed off on her—she's a pretty good Lord Mayor. Better than I'd ever be, anyway, even if I did want—" He stopped suddenly, a deep frown darkening his face.

"Kronn?" Kronin asked. "What's wrong?"

It was a moment before the younger kender answered. His eyes focused on something far off, a flash of movement against the darkening sky. "Uh," he said, "have you noticed, there's an absolutely enormous dragon out there?"

"Really?" Kronin asked, glancing up at his son with genuine interest. "What color?"

Kronn squinted. "Red."

"Oh," Kronin said, nodding sagely. "That's just Malystryx—or Malys, as folks around here call her. Don't worry about her. She turned up about a year ago—has a lair at Blood Watch, apparently. Caused an awful row among the humans, but she leaves us alone. Usually she just circles, but every now and then she puts on a show out over the water, too. A few weeks ago she picked a whole sailing ship up out of the sea."

"She did?" Kronn asked, looking at his father sharply.

"Yup. It wasn't a small boat, either. Just plucked it from the sea, flew over and past us, and dropped the thing somewhere in the forest. Saw it with my own eyes."

"But you say she's harmless?"

"Oh no, she's harmful," Kronin said. "But like I said, she doesn't seem terribly interested in us."

"Then why's she heading straight this way?" Kronn asked.

"Eh?" With some difficulty, Kronin pushed himself to his feet. He looked north through the gathering gloom. The great, red dragon was indeed coming toward them, moving with dizzying speed. "Well, that's unusual. I wonder what she's up to."

"I don't like dragons," said Kronn.

"Me neither," said Kronin. He shrugged. "But what can you do? Don't worry. Maybe she's chasing something in the water—sharks, sea elves, that sort of thing. If she really meant to attack us, she'd come from above, not straight on like th—"

Before he could finish speaking, Malystryx pulled up sharply, climbing high into the sky. The two kender watched her rise, until at last she disappeared into a cloudbank.

"Hmm," said Kronin.

A deafening screech descended from the clouds, a furious sound that made Kronn clap his hands over his pointed ears. In the town below, the music and laughter came to a sudden stop.

Kronn looked at his father, who was still staring up.

"Definitely unusual." Kronin's face darkened as he

stared. "Go!" he said all of a sudden, through clenched teeth.

"What?" Kronn asked.

"Go! Find your sister, and that fellow of hers," Kronin ordered. "Get the villagers into the woods."

"But," Kronn sputtered.

Kronin shook his head stubbornly, raising his hoopak. "I'll only slow you down. Don't wait for me."

"Father—"

"Quickly, boy!" Kronin snapped. "Move!"

Kronn ran, leaping onto the ladder and sliding down to the ground. He bolted toward the courtyard, glancing over his shoulder. Kronin still stood atop the palisade, gripping his hoopak tightly. Then Kronn rounded a corner, and the village's thatched rooftops blocked his father from view. He sprinted even faster, bursting at last into the center of town.

The courtyard was filled with kender who stood in clusters, watching the dragon's long, sinuous form slip from cloud to cloud. They felt no fear, of course; just rapt fascination. A second shriek rang down upon them, loud enough to rattle windows.

"Catt!" Kronn shouted, pushing through the astonished crowd.

"Kronn!" answered a voice. Catt shoved several kender aside as she hurried to her brother's side. Giffel jogged along behind her. "Where's Papa? What's going on?"

"We've got to get these people out of here," Kronn said tersely. "Giffel, can you round up the other off-duty guards?"

"Sure, Kronn."

"Then do it," Kronn ordered. "Get to the town gates, and wait for us there."

"Right." Giffel dashed off.

Kronn grabbed Catt's arm. "Try to get everyone's attention."

"Oh," she murmured, looking up worriedly. "All right." She took a deep breath, then cupped her hands around her mouth. "Excuse me!" she bellowed in an exceptionally loud voice. All around her, kender jumped, startled by the sound. "Hey! Everyone, listen up!"

Hundreds of eyes turned toward them. Kronn pursed his lips, impressed, then went over to a nearby tree stump and hopped up on it. "Folks," he said, raising his voice so everyone could hear him, "I'm afraid I have to break up the party. Can everyone please start heading for the gates?"

* * * * *

They listened up well and moved in surprisingly orderly fashion. Kronn and Catt jogged along at the rear of the throng, as Giffel and his fellow guards ushered the villagers through the gates and down the path toward the Kenderwood. Once they were free of the town, the kender broke into a run, glancing up and behind as they sought some sign of the dragon. They moved with eerie silence, their puffing breaths and the whisper of their feet through the grass the only sounds of their passage.

Kronin watched them go from atop the palisade. Grunting with satisfaction, he reached into his belt pouch, pulled out a slingstone, and loaded it into his hoopak.

A third screech descended upon Woodsedge. Kronin glanced up and saw the dragon drop through the clouds. Her wings were folded back against her, her fang-lined mouth gaping wide as she came down like a falling star. The sound of her descent was the howl of a hurricane.

"Wow," Kronin said, duly impressed.

He brought his hoopak back, watching, waiting, then slung it forward in a quick, practised motion. The slingstone shot far upward, straight toward Malys, and struck her square between the eyes. It bounced off her scaly hide and fell out of sight without even slowing her flight. She drew a great breath into her cavernous breast.

"Oh, drat," Kronin muttered.

* * * * *

The fleeing kender were almost to the sheltering forest when the roar of flames caught their attention. They turned in their tracks, to see a column of fire streak down from the dragon's gaping jaws and strike Woodsedge like a burning fist. Looking to the palisade, Kronn and Catt saw a figure silhouetted against the bright orange glow, clutching a hoopak in his hands.

"What does he think he's doing?" cried Catt.

"Hero stuff," murmured Kronn.

As they watched in horror, the figure flared and vanished amid the flames.

"No!" Catt cried. She started back toward the village. Kronn caught her arm.

"Catt!" he shouted. "We're not done here! We've got to get these people to safety!"

She looked at him blankly for a moment, then blinked. The thunder of the firestorm was growing steadily louder, and a hot wind blew outward from Woodsedge, carrying ashes and embers. "You're right," she said. "Into the woods, everyone! Quickly, while she isn't looking!"

It took some doing—Catt wasn't the only kender who tried to turn back toward the town—but with the help of Giffel and the other guardsmen they managed to herd the villagers into the forest. Behind them, Malystryx continued to blast Woodsedge with her fiery breath. Houses and shops blew apart. The protective palisade became a curtain of flame. Kronn and Catt crouched at the edge of the Kenderwood, watching the whole town become a raging inferno.

At last, Malys's jaws snapped shut, her breath expended. She wheeled above the town for an hour after that, fanning the flames with her wings. Then she turned, her golden eyes gleaming in the moonlight, and stared straight at the Kenderwood. It seemed to Kronn and Catt that her gaze bored right through them.

She laughed, a cruel, mocking sound. "Run now, little kender!" she taunted. "Much good it will do you! When I am done, there will be nowhere left for you to flee!"

With that, she wheeled majestically and flapped away

over the Blood Sea. It was some time before any of the
hiding kender emerged from the forest.

* * * * *

For the whole day after the attack, and the night after
that, Woodsedge continued to burn. The kender who had
escaped the blaze could do little but watch as their homes
and all their possessions, went up in flames.

Houses and trinkets were not all that were lost, though.
While Kronn and Catt's swift action had gotten many of
the villagers to safety, some had not been saved. Those
who had passed out from food and drink, the few guards
left on duty atop the palisade, and anyone who was otherwise too slow to run—the sick, the crippled, young children, old people—had perished in the conflagration. Of
the thousand or so kender who had dwelt in Woodsedge,
more than two hundred did not survive.

Including the great kender hero, Kronin Thistleknot.

At last, on the second morning after the attack, the
flames died down enough for the kender to start sifting
through the rubble. They waded ankle-deep in ashes,
trying to find something—anything—to salvage.

Late that afternoon, Catt—her yellow dress and pale
face smudged with soot—found her brother on his knees
at what had been the north edge of town. Stubs of charcoal, which once had been the palisade, smoldered before
him. He rocked slowly back and forth, cradling something
in his arms.

"Kronn?" Catt whispered.

He shook his head, moaning angrily. She hesitated, then
stepped forward, leaning in to see what he clutched to his
breast.

It was almost unrecognizable, scorched and blackened
by dragonfire. Part of it, however, had been untouched by
the flames, and her eyes clouded when she realized what
Kronn held.

It was a shoe, purple and faded with age.

Chapter 2

The door of the Inn of the Last Home cracked open, then flew wide as the wind caught it. The tavern's patrons glared, huddling over their drinks. Their expressions softened, though, when they saw the massive form that squeezed through the doorway. Caramon Majere stomped in, carrying a load of firewood that would have stooped a man half his age. Sweating and panting, he lugged the wood to the hearth and dropped it with a clatter into the firebox. Moving stiffly, he lifted the poker and stirred the fire. A storm of glowing cinders rose up the chimney. Satisfied, he shuffled away from the hearth and slumped into an armchair with an old man's aching grunt.

Caramon had a right to that grunt. On the downward slope of sixty, he'd already seen more years than the Inn's previous owner, Otik Sandath, had when he'd retired. He folded his hands over his girth—he'd fought its spread all his life, but was finally losing—and leaned back, letting his eyelids droop closed.

The next thing he knew, old Rhea, the Inn's cook, was shaking him. Snorting, he wiped his eyes and peered blearily up at her. "What's the trouble?" he asked.

Rhea, who was more than seventy years old, was a severe-looking woman at the best of times. The look she gave him now made it seem as if she'd just taken a large bite of a lemon. "Well," she said pointedly, "for one thing, the windows were about to break, you were snoring so loud."

Chuckles filled the tavern. Caramon glowered at her. "I don't snore," he grumbled.

"Of course you don't," Rhea snapped sarcastically. More chuckles. "I also brought your supper. Think you can stay awake long enough to eat?"

"Keep talking like that," Caramon warned. "You'll see how awake I am."

With a mocking laugh, Rhea signaled to one of the serving girls, who brought out a sizzling platter and placed it on the table before him. Rhea set a tankard of tea beside the plate, then bustled away.

Not long ago, it had been rare for Caramon to take his supper at a civilized hour. The Inn had been too busy, with travelers on their way south to Haven and Qualinesti, or north to Crossing and the New Sea. "Blackguards and barmen dine 'neath the moons," the old saying went.

The moons were gone now, though, replaced by a single orb that hung, pale and strange, in the night sky. It seemed the old proverbs no longer applied, either. Since the Summer of Chaos, Caramon had found time to dine with the Inn's patrons three days out of four. That was because there were few patrons to dine with anymore.

For such a big man, Caramon ate little nowadays, and what there was on his plate, he picked at listlessly. He took sips of tea between mouthfuls of marjoram-rubbed rabbit and spiced potatoes, but most of the time, he just stared around the tavern.

There had been a time, just a few years ago, when the Inn had been packed at this hour. The tables and booths had been full, people had lined the bar shoulder-to-shoulder, and the air had rung with talk and laughter and cries for ale. Caramon had wished, on more than one occasion, that business would cool off so he could have some rest. Now he looked back on those days and wondered if, maybe, he hadn't wished too hard.

Tonight, he could count the folk in the tavern without taking off his boots, as Tika was wont to quip. In the back sat two hooded elves, probably refugees from the ongoing troubles in Qualinesti. Clemen, Osler and Borlos—regulars who'd hang in till either the Inn closed for good or someone dragged them out feet-first—were drinking mulled wine and playing a game of cards over by the kitchen door, cursing and laughing loudly. A weary-looking tinker, who had found less work in Solace than he'd hoped and would surely move on soon, hunched over a bottle of dwarf spirits. And that was it.

Things just hadn't been the same since that terrible summer. True, the Knights of Takhisis no longer ruled this part of Ansalon, but their absence was a double-edged sword. They'd been hard masters, and Caramon had hated every moment he'd lived under their sway, but at least they'd kept the bandits and goblins from running rampant. Now the road were more dangerous than they'd been in many years, and no one seemed to travel much anymore. On top of that, the world seemed to have slowed down since the Second Cataclysm. At first, folk had been preoccupied with rebuilding the damage wrought by the Dark Knights and the armies of Chaos. Now, though, with the scars of that summer at last starting to heal, few people wanted to do anything but stay at home. Nobody seemed to hunger for adventure any more. There had been enough excitement of late to last a hundred lifetimes.

When Caramon finished his tea and grew tired of pushing cold food about his plate, he decided he could afford to have another sleep. If anyone tried to cause trouble, Clemen, Osler and Borlos would give them a knock on the head for interrupting their card game. "Yes," Caramon muttered, lacing his fingers behind his head and leaning back, "another nap sounds just fine."

He was just shy of slumber when the door opened and closed again. The chatter of the card game stopped.

"Look sharp, big guy," called Osler. "You're about to get yourself thumped."

Caramon looked up in time to see Tika, who was moving quickly across the tavern, toward him. Her eyes were blazing, and the look on her face could have frozen Crystalmir Lake, though there was still a week left of summer. Caramon rose quickly, nearly knocking over his chair, and stepped between his loving wife and the iron platter on the tabletop. Judging by the way Tika looked,

Caramon didn't much want her within reach of anything that looked good for bashing heads.

"You're home early," he said, trying to sound as if the world were made of sunshine and blooming roses. "How's Usha?"

Pregnant was what Usha was, of course. Over the past few months, Tika had taken to going to Palin and Usha's house, fussing over her daughter-in-law incessantly. Palin, having inherited some of his father's wits, knew enough to let his mother have her way, and to make himself scarce in the meantime. He was at Wayreth now, searching the libraries vainly for some inkling of how to reawaken magic. He'd be coming home soon, though. The child was almost due. Usha was as huge around as a well-fed ogress, and Tika was anxious over the impending arrival of her first grandchild. Caramon was looking forward to the birth too, of course. Life was lonely, even with his daughters to help out around the inn.

"Usha's fine," Tika snapped, drawing up so close that he fell back a pace. "I left Laura and Dezra at her place. The child will come before the moon's full."

"That's good," Caramon said, smiling.

Tika didn't say anything. She glared at him, her silver-shot red hair gleaming in the firelight. She'd had more than fifty years to perfect her accusing look.

"Rhea's got supper on," Caramon offered. "I'll go get you some, and a glass of that Ergothian wine you like—"

"You don't have any idea what's on my mind, do you?"

Caramon met his wife's fiery gaze for a moment, then looked away. "Nope," he said sheepishly.

Clemen, Borlos and Osler continued their card game quietly, being very careful not to draw attention to themselves.

Tika took a long, slow breath. "On my way back here, I stopped at Tanin and Sturm's graves."

Caramon nodded. Though his wife was excited by the prospect of a new baby, no grandchild would ever take the place of her two lost sons. She spent a great deal of time at their graves, often leaving behind wildflowers or toys they'd played with as boys. She always returned from the graves in a grim mood, but today it was different. Grief for her sons wasn't the only thing bothering her.

"What is it, Tika?" Caramon asked.

"You honestly don't know?"

"No. I don't." Worry was beginning to fray his patience. "For the last time, Tika, what's the matter?"

She relaxed a little, the anger in her eyes giving way to sorrow. "Riverwind's come to Solace."

* * * * *

Caramon hurried down the stairs that led from the tavern to the ground. He was confused, and Tika hadn't helped much. Riverwind's arrival in Solace should have been a joyous occasion—he was a friend, after all, and they hadn't seen him in years—but Tika had been on the verge of tears when she'd spoken his name.

His first guess had been that something awful had happened on the Plains. "Has something happened to Goldmoon?" he'd demanded. "To Wanderer? The girls?"

"No," Tika had said. "Riverwind said Goldmoon and Wanderer are well, and the girls came here with him. They . . . wanted to see the graves."

Moonsong and Brightdawn, Riverwind's twin daughters, had been fond of Tanin and Sturm. They had played together as children, and both Caramon and Riverwind had watched with amusement as their children developed their first adolescent crushes on each other. Of course, that had come to nothing—the twins would marry men of the Plains when the time came, and the Majere boys had fallen in love, or something like love, with other women—but they'd remained friends up until the day Tanin and Sturm died. The twins hadn't come to Solace since then, but Caramon had known that one day they would. Their father, evidently, had come with them.

"Why is Riverwind here?" Caramon had asked his wife.

"You know where to find him," was all she would say in reply.

It was to the Last Heroes' Tomb, then, that Caramon hastened. It stood outside the town proper, in the peaceful field where the gods—and Raistlin with them—had bidden the world farewell. Low and square, it might have been mistaken by a careless traveler for just another barrow in a world where tombs had grown all too common. There were few travelers in Ansalon, however, who were so ignorant. The tomb was a sacred place, regarded with awe and reverence by everyone—human and elf, dwarf and kender. Even the goblins dared not disturb it.

The sun was setting in the west, the pale moon rising full in the east, when Caramon arrived at the tomb. He hastened through the sheltering ring of trees the elves had planted—saplings two years ago, they grew quickly, spreading their slender limbs toward the pewter-colored sky—and jogged toward the tomb itself. It was crafted of marble and obsidian, white stone and black woven together by dwarven hands in memory of the alliance between Good and Evil that had brought down Chaos. Its gold and silver doors, one etched with the Solamnic symbol of the rose, the other marked by the lily worn by the Knights of Takhisis, stood open. Torchlight glowed within, and Caramon could hear a faint voice chanting in a language he didn't understand but had heard before. It was the language of the Plainsmen.

Caramon paused at the doors, just for a moment, and glanced at the name carved on the lintel. No one could prove that Tasslehoff Burrfoot was indeed dead, for there was no body to be found, but Palin and Usha both had sworn they'd seen him crushed beneath Chaos's heel. That was enough for Caramon, whose heart ached whenever he saw the kender's name, and the hoopak graven beneath it.

There were, thankfully, no kender here tonight. They had been turning up in greater and greater numbers lately, making pilgrimages to the tomb from every part of Ansalon. The kender were the only people who could be counted on the travel in these dread times; unfortunately, much to the townsfolk's horror, they could also be counted on to continue being kender. The Inn of the Last Home was missing several dozen mugs, half its silverware, and—Caramon had never been able to explain it—a couch. Similar losses had been reported all around Solace, and all fingers pointed at the light-fingered kender. The captain of the town guard was prone these days to uncontrollable facial tics.

Caramon stepped into the tomb, and for a moment was blinded by darkness. When his eyes adjusted, he descended the stairs that led down into its depths, following the ever-brightening light and the soft, familiar voice. He hastened along a long tunnel, passing vaults containing the bodies of knights slain in battle with Chaos, until finally he reached the innermost sepulcher. Swallowing, he ducked through the doorway and beheld the biers.

On his left stood a slab of black marble, graven with skulls and thorns and other fearsome things. Despite the gruesome carvings, though, there was an aura of peace about the bier. The sigils were those of the Knights of Takhisis, but they held a certain beauty, just as the lily the knights venerated smelled sweet when it bloomed.

Upon it, undisturbed by the passage of time, lay the body of Steel Brightblade. He wore black armor, grimly etched, and in his hands he clasped an ancient sword. The blade had been handed down through the Brightblade family from ancient times and had been buried with Steel's father, Sturm, in the Tower of the High Clerist. Caramon had been in Sturm's tomb when the dead knight's ghost had risen and passed the sword on to his son. Steel had fought with the blade in the battle that had killed him.

All around Steel's body, the bier was strewn with black lilies. Caramon raised his eyebrows at this. No one but the Dark Knights would leave such tokens for their slain hero, but there had been no word of members of that brotherhood around Solace for months. Yet the lilies were fresh, as though they had bloomed this very morning.

Shivering, Caramon let his gaze drift from the black bier, over to the white one on the room's other side. The second bier bore no carvings. It was a simple block of white marble, veined with blue. It was heaped with white roses, just as Steel's was covered with lilies. In the midst of the roses lay the body of Tanis Half-Elven.

Caramon looked upon his friend's face, at the odd smile that twisted his gray beard. After a moment, though, he bowed his head, grimacing. The pain of seeing Tanis, quiet and still upon the slab, had not lessened with the passage of years. It still made him feel terribly alone.

He wasn't alone this time, though. At the bier's foot knelt a tall man clad in buckskins and furs. A many-feathered headdress—doffed out of respect for the dead—rested on the floor by his side. Long hair, once black but now mostly white, spilled loose over his shoulders. The firelight came from a torch in the man's left hand. He chanted softly, then stopped suddenly, raising his head.

"My friend," the man said. "I am glad you've come."

"Riverwind?" Caramon asked.

The man nodded, but still he did not turn. He raised a muscular arm, deeply tanned from years spent in the wilderness. "Please, Caramon," he beckoned. "Come see what we have brought, my daughters and I."

Caramon stepped forward. As he did, he glimpsed something on the bier, beside Tanis's body. It was a long, slender staff with a plain shaft and an ornately carved head. The torchlight caught it, and it flashed with bright blue light.

Slowly, stiffly, Riverwind rose. He turned to look at Caramon. His face was as it had always been—more weathered and wrinkled, perhaps, but the strength and kindness were still there. His dark eyes shone.

"Goldmoon felt it would be fitting," he said.

Caramon gazed upon the staff that lay beside his friend's body, and words would not come. It had been more than thirty years since he had seen it, but it was just as he remembered: hewn of blue crystal, a single sapphire shaped with craftsmanship beyond the ken of man. So much had begun with that staff.

"Is it real?" he asked, his voice faint with wonder.

Riverwind nodded. "When the war with Chaos ended, Goldmoon and I went east again, on a pilgrimage to Xak Tsaroth. I had found proof of the old gods there before. We hoped to find it again." He was silent a moment, frowning, then cleared his throat awkwardly. "We did not. When we reached the temple, the statue of Mishakal there had fallen and shattered upon the floor. We found the staff amid the rubble and took it with us. It is not a holy relic any more, Caramon. It has no magic. But when we learned of this tomb, we knew it belonged here. Tanis would understand."

Caramon blinked back tears. "I'm sure he does."

Neither man said anything for a long while. The torch crackled and popped.

"Where are the girls?" Caramon asked.

"I asked them to leave me here," Riverwind replied. "They went, I think, to visit Usha."

"Tika told me they've been to the graves."

The Plainsman nodded solemnly. "They wanted dearly to see them and begged to come with me. I am sorry we couldn't visit sooner, my friend. Things have been difficult for our people, these past two years."

"So I've heard," Caramon said. "Are you still having trouble keeping the alliance between the tribes?"

"From time to time," Riverwind answered. "But that is no great worry. When the Dark Knights left these lands, though, they left their Brutes behind. Several clans have settled in the Eastwall Mountains. My son is seldom home these days, there is so much fighting."

Caramon nodded. "But Wanderer is well?"

"As well as one might expect," Riverwind said grimly.

Caramon hesitated. "And Goldmoon?"

"She fares well," Riverwind assured him. "The loss of the goddess weighs on her, of course, but she has always been strong. She wanted to come, but with Wanderer away she couldn't afford to leave Qué-Shu."

"That's a shame," Caramon said earnestly. "I'm sure she'd want to see—" He stopped abruptly, his hand waving feebly at the green-cloaked body upon the bier. Together they stared down at Tanis's remains.

"Do you know," Riverwind said sadly, "the last time I saw him was ten years ago? He and Laurana came to visit us on the plains. I wanted to return the favor, to go to Solanthus, but—" He spread his hands. "I always thought there would be time for such things later. I was sure he'd outlive us all."

"Well," Caramon said, "he was part elf."

"That's not what I mean." Riverwind pressed his hands together, raising them to his lips. "Tanis always knew what to do. Even when we didn't think he did—even when *he* didn't think he did—in his heart he knew."

"I know," Caramon answered. "And that's what killed him. Just like Sturm—he knew the right thing to do, and he did it, damn the cost." He bowed his head. "Sometimes, I wish he hadn't. I know it's selfish, but even so. Sometimes I wonder if any of us will ever die peacefully in bed, with the people we love all around us."

Riverwind flinched, then looked away. For a moment, the Plainsman said nothing. When he spoke again, his voice was tight and strained. "Be careful what you wish for, Caramon."

Caramon stared at him, his forehead creased with confusion. "What do you mean?"

The Plainsman turned to face him, his eyes shining in the torchlight. "My friend," he said, "I am dying."

Chapter 3

Caramon said nothing. He stood silently, staring at River-wind. He fell back a pace and leaned against Steel's skull-carved bier. The attar of lilies surrounded him, a cloying scent that made him want to retch.

"How?" he asked.

The Plainsman nodded thoughtfully. "A fair question." He bent down, lifting up his headdress, and gestured toward the door. "I will answer it, but not here. I have already broken a taboo of my people, speaking of death in such a place. Go on ahead, Caramon. I will finish saying my farewells, and then I will join you outside."

Thankful to be out of the dark, close crypt, Caramon turned and hurried out of the Last Heroes' Tomb. He didn't stop until he was outside the gold and silver doors. The air outside was cold, heralding the coming autumn, and he drank it down deeply. His breath misted in the air before him.

There was movement off to his left. He glanced at it sharply, but it was just a pair of kender—come, no doubt, to pay honor to Tas. One of them, a male, held what looked like a burnt shoe. The other one was female; her hands were empty. They looked up at him, their eyes wide.

Not wanting to deal with kender just now, Caramon shook his head and marched across the meadow away from the tomb. After a few dozen paces he stopped, looking up at the single, pale moon. He continued to stare at it, even when he heard the scuff of soft boots in the grass.

"It still seems strange to me, as well," said Riverwind, drawing to a halt beside Caramon. He looked up at the ivory disk. "I often dream of the red moon, you know. Sometimes, when we could steal away without anyone noticing, Goldmoon and I would climb the hills east of Qué-Shu and watch it rise. We would hold hands, and one thing would lead to another. . . ." He smiled an old man's smile, remembering. After a moment, it became a sly grin. "That's how the girls came about, if you take my meaning."

Caramon chuckled. "I certainly do. With Tika and me, it was sunsets."

" 'Was?' " Riverwind asked, his eyes sparkling.

"Well-ll," Caramon said.

They laughed together, then Riverwind grew solemn. "Be thankful, Caramon. You still have the sun. In my heart, this pale moon will never take the red one's place."

The wind gusted, icy fingers clawing up Caramon's spine. He hunched his shoulders.

"So," he murmured.

"So," Riverwind agreed. "You asked me how, a moment ago. I'm glad you did—I owe you answers, after setting this burden upon your shoulders. Let us walk."

They set out across the meadow toward the distant lights of Solace. The vallenwoods muttered as the wind played among their boughs.

"This isn't the first time I've been ill, my friend," Riverwind said. "Five years ago, I woke one morning with a terrible pain inside me. It felt as though someone had set a hot stone in my belly. At first I thought it was nothing but food that disagreed with me—my stomach's not as hardy as it once was—so I ignored it, waited for it to go away.

"It got worse, though, and I began to fear I had been poisoned. There were some, then, who might have done so. There still are. A man makes enemies doing what I have done—not everyone believes it is best that the tribes should unite as one. It was then that I first began to fear for my life, though for the wrong reasons.

"I hadn't told Goldmoon about it yet. You may have noticed," he added, with a wry smile, "I can be a bit stubborn at times. By the time I finally confided in her, the pain was such that I could no longer eat—not even plain corn porridge. When I told Goldmoon how sick I was, she was so angry she didn't speak to me for a week.

"She tended me, though, and prayed to Mishakal. There was a foulness inside me, and it had grown so large I could feel it when I touched my belly. It was hard and sore, but the worst part was knowing it didn't belong. I wanted to cut myself open, to pull it out and cast it into the fire. I might even have tried it, too, in my fever madness, but I lacked the strength.

"I lay in bed for nearly a month. Goldmoon acted as chieftain in my absence, keeping the Qué-Teh and Qué-Kiri tribes from slitting each other's throats. My daughters fed me broth—the only thing I could keep down—and Goldmoon gave me medicine and chanted by my bedside. In time, the goddess blessed me. The pain subsided, and the corruption that had been growing inside me went away. I had never known such relief, my friend. My father died of such an illness when I was a child. It is a bad end."

They reached the edge of the meadow, where the grasses gave way to the vallenwoods. Riverwind took a deep breath, then bent down and picked up a brown vallenwood leaf. He twirled it between his fingers, lost in thought. "A month ago, I woke with the pain again," he said quietly. "Only now, Mishakal is not around to hear Goldmoon's prayers. The foulness is growing within me again, and there is no stopping it. Before long, it will kill me."

He released the leaf, and the wind sent it spinning away into the shadows. Caramon watched it go, then looked up at his friend. They regarded each other silently. Then Caramon gripped Riverwind's muscular arm with his own massive hand. The Plainsman regarded him silently.

"Thank you for coming," Caramon said. "It must have been a hard thing, convincing Goldmoon to let you travel."

Riverwind shook his head, the feathers of his headdress rustling. "She does not know."

"What?" Caramon's eyes widened. "What do you mean?"

"I mean I haven't told her I'm sick again," Riverwind answered. "And I'm not going to. Neither do I mean to tell my daughters. I have told Wanderer, Tika, and now you, but no one else must hear of it . . . least of all Goldmoon."

"But," Caramon sputtered, "she's your wife, Riverwind."

The Plainsman nodded sternly. "I know, my friend. She is my wife, and I love her more than anything in this world. I would spare her this pain. You didn't see her face five years ago, when she learned I was ill. It . . . crumpled. She has lived through this before. When I was gone on my Courting Quest, Arrowthorn, her father, was stricken. When I left Qué-Shu, he was a strong man, a hunter and a warrior. By the time I returned, he was wasted and old, babbling and drooling. Goldmoon had to feed him, wash him, see to his every need. She watched him wither like grain after a frost, and there was nothing she could do about it."

"And you don't want to put her through that again," Caramon said.

"I do not." Riverwind sighed wearily. "How could I tell her, Caramon? At least before, she had her faith to draw upon. Mishakal gave her strength. Even if I had died, she would have known it was the goddess's will. Whose will is it now, when the gods have gone?"

Caramon bowed his head, blinking back tears. When the Chaos War ended, the loss of the gods had struck everyone hard, but none had suffered more than those who had devoted their lives to their faith. All across Ansalon, priests had succumbed to madness or taken their lives in despair. In Tarsis, it was said, a monk of Majere had gone to the marketplace one day and killed six people before the guards could stop him. In Neraka, priests of Takhisis had doused themselves in oil and set themselves ablaze.

Goldmoon had always been strong-willed, however, even for a cleric. Caramon had taken comfort in the knowledge that her strength would not falter. It would take something truly awful to break her. Something like her husband slowly dying, of a sickness she no longer had the power to cure.

"Won't she find out?" Caramon asked. "You said yourself—the first illness left you bedridden, unable to eat. How can you hide that from her?"

"I cannot." Riverwind stared fiercely at Caramon. "This time, I will not let it come to that."

Caramon blew a long, slow breath through his lips. "Are you sure it's what you want?" he asked.

Riverwind nodded. "It will be better, for both of us. Goldmoon will not have to bear watching me waste away, like she did Arrowthorn. And as for me—" He broke off, then shook his head, chuckling grimly. "You know I am no coward, Caramon. But I know what lies ahead for me, and I am afraid. I am sixty-five years old. I have led a life I am proud of. I do not want to end it like that, in pain, waiting for the final hour to come."

They stood together in silence, beneath the pale moon, listening as the cold wind ruffled the leaves. Then Caramon clasped his friend's arms, letting the gesture convey what words could not.

"Come on," he said, clapping the Plainsman on the back. "I'll get you some spiced potatoes."

Riverwind smiled. "I was hoping you'd say that."

* * * * *

The tavern at the Inn was almost empty. The elves had gone, presumably upstairs to their room. The tinker was lost to the world, his head on the table beside the empty bottle of dwarf spirits. He mumbled incoherently in his sleep. Caramon shook his head in pity, knowing well enough the signs of a lifelong drunk.

Of course Clemen, Borlos, and Osler were where he'd left them, playing cards by the kitchen. The game had switched to Bounty Hunter, and from the looks of things—the heap of steel coins in front of him, and Borlos and Osler's glum faces—Clemen was laying waste to the other two. They were just ending a hand as Caramon and Riverwind came in, and Clemen grinned as he turned up his last card: the Dragon of Waves. Evidently Waves were trump, because Borlos cursed under his breath as Clemen raked the pot—which included two silver rings and a small opal—over to his side of the table.

"Evenin', big guy," Clemen said jovially as Caramon crossed the tavern. His eyes flicked to Riverwind. "And bigger guy, too. We can deal the two o' ye in next hand if ye're feeling game."

"Save yourself," Osler muttered grimly. "You'd have better luck in a head-butting contest with a minotaur tonight. I swear, this bugger's put a hex on the cards."

Caramon chuckled, glancing at Riverwind, but the Plainsman shook his head. "The only games I know are wrestling and pole sparring," Riverwind said.

"Pole sparring, eh?" drawled Borlos. "Well, maybe we can arrange something. Caramon, get Clem a broom."

"All right," Caramon said. He started toward a nearby closet.

Clemen's face turned white as a cleric's robes. The others held their straight faces for a moment, but it was a losing battle, and soon Osler and Borlos were howling with laughter, pounding the table. Caramon chuckled along with them, and even Riverwind cracked a smile.

"Had ye goin' there, didn't we?" roared Borlos, slapping Clemen on the shoulder. "Thought ye'd be gettin' yer head clonked by a genuine Hero of the Lance, eh?"

Riverwind glanced at Caramon, surprised. "They know who I am?"

"Oh, great gods, yeah," said Osler.

"Don't believe them, Riverwind," said Tika. She emerged from the kitchen, the smell of spices wafting behind her. "They heard me tell Caramon you were in town."

Osler reddened. "Well, aye, but I reckon I'd a known ye the moment I saw ye, Plainsman. Not many o' yer kind taller than Caramon, here. He's told us all about the whole lot o' ye."

"And told us, and told us. . . ." droned Clemen. Suddenly everyone—Tika included—was laughing again, at Caramon's expense.

"Pull up a seat," offered Osler, gesturing at an empty chair. "You can tell us the truth about the War of the Lance. It'd be nice to hear something other than Caramon's tall tales for a change."

Riverwind looked at Caramon, who waved a hand. "Go ahead. It's a good night for war stories. The boys are right—they've heard everything a hundred times—but don't let that stop you. They're easily amused." He ignored the snorts and scowls the three card players tossed his way. "I'll be right back."

He left the others and went to a storeroom in the back of the Inn. There he bent down and opened a trapdoor in the middle of the floor. Taking a lantern from a nearby cresset, he stepped through the open hatch and climbed down a steep flight of stairs. The stairway smelled of sap, for it led into the trunk of the great vallenwood tree whose branches cradled the Inn. Caramon had built the stairway when the Knights of Takhisis took control of Solace. Hewn out of the living wood, its entrance concealed beneath a wine cask even he could barely lift, it led to a room that had been a safe house for refugees who needed hiding from the Dark Knights. Now, with the Chaos War long over, it served as a cellar where he kept his best stock.

He reached the bottom of the stairs and shone the lantern around the cramped room. Bottles of elven wine and Solamnian brandy sparkled in the ruddy light, but he ignored them. Instead, he walked to a worn, oaken keg. The barrel, carefully sealed, held the last of the ale he'd brewed before the Second Cataclysm. He'd been waiting for almost two years for the right occasion to tap it.

"Well," he said, bending down and hoisting it up beneath his massive arm, "looks like this is an occasion."

* * * * *

The ale was fine, some of the best ever he'd ever

brewed. Caramon didn't drink it, of course—he hadn't taken a drink in more than thirty years, and never would again—but Tika, the card-players, and Riverwind all praised its rich, nutty flavor.

So did Riverwind's daughters. They had come in while Caramon was in the cellar, and had pulled up chairs beside their father. Moonsong and Brightdawn were twins, twenty-four years old and beautiful enough that Tika had to smack Clemen and Osler across the backs of their heads for staring. In many ways they resembled their mother, sharing Goldmoon's silver-gold hair and sky-blue eyes, but there was something of their father in them too—a solemnness in Moonsong's face, a strength to Brightdawn's jaw.

Moonsong, who was the older sister by a few minutes, was the more graceful of the two. Destined, according to Qué-Shu custom, to succeed her mother as high priestess of the Plains, she had trained as a healer under Goldmoon's tutelage. Her hands were soft, her skin unblemished, and she wore her hair loose, held in place by a silver circlet hung with feathers. She was clad in a gown of pale blue, embroidered with abstract patterns in threads of red and gold. Gold shone at her ears, wrists and fingers.

While Moonsong had lived a structured life, ordered by her duties as Chieftain's Daughter, Brightdawn's childhood had been at once rougher and more carefree. A tomboy from an early age, the younger twin had learned wrestling and archery, and had accompanied her father on hunts in the grasslands. She had calluses on her hands, a small white scar on her chin, and her hair was shorter than her sister's, gathered in a single plait that hung down her back. Instead of a circlet, she wore a red headband, which marked her as a warrior—as did the flanged mace that hung from her belt. She was clad in plain, buckskin clothes—brown leggings and a beige vest—and her arms were tanned and bare. She was clad in no jewelry anywhere on her body.

Despite the twins' beauty, however, it was Riverwind who held everyone's attention. The Plainsman sat on a high stool by the fire, his back erect and his eyes gleaming beneath his stern brow. His left hand gripped his flagon of ale, his right dancing like a weaver's shuttle at the loom as he recounted the story of his first meeting with Caramon and the Companions.

"We never expected anything more than a meal and a bed for the night, Goldmoon and I," he said. "We were led here by a man who wore the armor of a Knight of Solamnia—Sturm Brightblade. He was polite, but . . ." He searched for the right word. "Diffident. When he decided we were safe, he went to join his friends, whom he told us he had not seen in a very long time. We sat by the fire, much as we are now, although the Inn was very crowded that night. There was an old man there, telling ancient stories to a young boy. He was the one who started it all."

The tale spun on. Riverwind told of the song he and Goldmoon had played, of how the Seeker Hederick had fallen into the hearthfire while trying to arrest them for heresy, and of how the blue crystal staff had shone after Tasslehoff used it to heal the Seeker's burns. He recalled his shock when the old man—who, he would learn much later, was Paladine himself in disguise—had called for the guards, forcing the Plainsfolk to escape through the inn's kitchen. Joining with Tanis and Sturm, Caramon and Raistlin, Flint and Tasslehoff, they had fled to Tika's house while the goblins searched for them.

"There we were," the old Plainsman recalled, his eyes distant with memory, "hiding in the dark like bandits. I didn't know any of the others yet—and, to be honest, I didn't trust them."

"The man's a good judge of character," drawled Borlos, taking a long pull from his tankard.

"Aw, shut up," Caramon said, scowling. Everyone laughed.

Osler cuffed Borlos on the arm. "Let the man tell his story, Bor."

Riverwind took a drink from his own mug, smiling as the fine ale moistened his parched throat. "The goblins were thorough that night, searching house-to-house," he continued, setting down the flagon. "Our plan was to pretend there was no one home, but somehow no one remembered to shut the door. By the time Tanis realized, it was too late—the goblins were almost on top of us.

"Caramon went over by the doorway and waited. When the goblins came in, he grabbed them from behind, and—" he clapped his hands, the sudden sound making the card players jump "—he cracked their heads together. They were dead before they knew what hit them."

The others laughed at this, but Riverwind raised a hand, silencing them. "That's not the best part," he said, smiling. "When Tanis asked what had happened, Caramon just sighed and said 'I think I hit 'em too hard.'"

The card players laughed uproariously. Riverwind's daughters joined in, and even Tika—who had heard this tale more than any of them—chuckled at her husband's expense. Sighing, Caramon shook his head and rose.

"Who's for another?" he asked.

Everyone, Riverwind included, raised their tankards in the air.

Caramon walked to the keg, listening to Riverwind describe how they had deliberately smashed up Tika's house after killing the goblins—and Tika's half-joking declaration that they could have been less thorough about it. As he poured a new round of drinks for his friends, the door swung open. He glanced up, raising his eyebrows in surprise when he saw who walked in.

It was the pair of kender he had seen outside the Last Heroes Tomb. The female looked to be the older of the pair, as she had more wrinkles on her otherwise girlish face, but it was the male who led the way into the tavern. They were both brightly attired—she in a red blouse and white trousers, he in hunting greens and a vivid yellow sash. The woman held a hoopak in her hands, and the man had something that looked like a dubious mixture of axe and slingshot slung across his back. They both wore their hair—hers was lustrous black, his chestnut brown—in the same style: long ponytails hanging down their backs, and short, tight braids dangling at their cheeks.

Caramon had a vague recollection of Tasslehoff saying once that the strange hairstyle was a sign of noble blood among the kender. Flint had had a thing or two to say about using "noble" and "kender" in the same sentence.

The laughter by the fireside faded as Riverwind and his audience watched them walk in, striding straight up to the bar.

"Caramon Majere?" asked the male.

Caramon blinked, taken aback. "Uh," he said, "yes?"

"I'm Kronn-alin Thistleknot, son of Kronin Thistle-knot," the male stated. He nodded sideways, at his companion. "This is my sister Catt. We need you to come with us to Kendermore."

Chapter 4

It grew very quiet in the Inn of the Last Home. Everyone stared at the kender. Kronn and Catt stared back.

"Kendermore?" Riverwind asked.

Kronn nodded earnestly.

"Kendermore?" echoed Caramon, incredulous.

Catt leaned over the bar, her brow furrowing. "I don't mean to intrude," she said, "but is there a reason you're pouring beer all over the floor?"

Caramon started, glancing down at his feet. He'd forgotten, in his distraction, to close the spigot on the keg, and nut-brown ale was gurgling out, forming a pool around his boots. Tika snorted in disgust as he fumbled to close the tap. In the moment he was turned away from the bar, Kronn grabbed one of the full tankards.

"Wait!" Caramon said. "That's for—"

Kronn downed half the tankard's contents in one deep draught. "Good stuff," he remarked, wiping foam from his lips. "Plenty of hops—I like that. Brew it yourself?"

"Thanks. Yes. I—" Caramon shook his head vigorously. "Kendermore?"

Catt turned to her brother. "Why does he keep saying that?"

Tika strolled over, her hands on her hips. "Now see here," she said. "Kendermore's clear on the other side of Ansalon."

A smile lit Kronn's face as he came near. "You must be Tika," he said.

Caramon looked around quickly, making sure there were no heavy, blunt objects his wife could reach.

"And you must be going," Tika snapped back testily,

"unless you have a damned good reason why my husband should cross an entire continent at his age."

"Oh, there's a good reason," Kronn declared. "We need him to help us drive off an army of ogres."

"An army of—" Tika repeated, her eyes widening.

"Plus there's the dragon," Catt added.

"Dragon?" Tika echoed.

"Her name's Malystryx," Kronn said, his face grave. "She's been causing all sorts of problems, but she didn't bother us, so we let her be. Then, last month—" He shut his eyes, his face pinched with pain. "She destroyed a village—Woodsedge was its name. Burned it to the ground. And she . . . she killed our father."

"Kronin?" Caramon asked, his face ashen. "Kronin Thistleknot's dead?"

Kronn nodded, then bowed his head, his cheek braids drooping. Catt stepped forward to continue the story. "Our sister, Paxina—she's been in charge of Kendermore for about ten years now—sent us here," she said. "We brought one of Father's shoes to put in the Tomb of Last Heroes. I hope you don't mind. And since we were going to be in Solace anyway, Pax asked us to bring back someone who knew a thing or two about dragon-slaying." She looked up at Caramon, beaming. "Naturally, we thought of you."

Caramon and Tika exchanged glances.

"I'm sorry," the big man said, turning back to the kender. "I think there's been a mistake. I don't know anything about slaying dragons. I've never even fought one, not really."

Kronn's brows knitted. "But that's not what the legends say."

"Which legend is that?" Tika asked acidly. "The one where Tanis shot the green dragon out of the sky with his bow, and Caramon cut off its head when it hit the ground? Or the one where the two of them killed and skinned a blue and snuck into Neraka wearing its hide?"

Caramon chuckled. Kronn, however, was serious. "Both of them," he said. "I always wondered, how did you think of that thing with the skin? That's pretty smart. How'd you keep the other dragons from smelling you, though?"

"They didn't—that is, we didn't . . . oh, blast." Caramon put a hand to his forehead. "Look, there are all sorts of stories about us. Bards started making them up before the War of the Lance was even over, and they've had another thirty years to practice. If they were all true, Tanis and I would have killed fifty dragons by ourselves."

"Not to mention the story about Sturm and Kitiara sailing to the moon," Tika added. "Or all the tales about them fighting dragons and draconians years before the War started."

"We even had one idiot come in last year claiming Raistlin once had passed as a woman in disguise!" called Clemen. "The big guy showed him the quick way down from this tree."

"Anyway, I'm afraid the stories you've heard are like those," Caramon finished sympathetically. "The truth is, I've never killed a dragon in my life. And I'm no youngster, in case you hadn't noticed."

Kronn's face fell. "You sure look big and strong to me."

Tika stepped up to the kender, glaring. "Get this straight, Mr. Thistlebulb," she snapped.

"Thistleknot."

"Whatever. My husband has done a lot of boneheaded things in his life, but dragon-slaying isn't one of them—to say nothing of thwarting ogre armies. And there's no way I'm going to let him start up again. Listen to him." She waved her hand at Caramon. "He's not the man he used be, you know. He's old, fat, and slow—and he never was very bright. I doubt he could even kill a hobgoblin these days."

"Thanks, Tika," Caramon muttered.

"Oh dear," Kronn said resignedly. He glanced at Catt, who shared his crestfallen expression. "But we've got to bring some hero to help us."

"I will go."

Astonished eyes turned toward the stool beside the fire. Riverwind rose from his seat and came forward, leaving

Clemen, Borlos, and Osler to gape, wide-eyed, at his back. "I will go with you," he said to the kender.

"Father!" Moonsong exclaimed as she and Brightdawn hurried after him.

Caramon stared at the Plainsman, shocked. "You're not serious."

"I will go with them," Riverwind repeated.

"You can't defeat a dragon all by yourself, Father," Brightdawn argued. "It's impossible!"

"Impossible?" Riverwind asked. "Like a poor, heretic shepherd wooing a princess?" He looked at Caramon. "Like the group of us bringing back the gods? Like stopping Chaos from destroying the world?"

Caramon shook his head, scowling. He started to say something, caught Riverwind's fierce look, and bit his tongue. Brightdawn and Moonsong stared at their father, their faces lined with worry.

"For the love of Reorx, man!" called Borlos, rising from his place beside the fire. "They're just kender."

Riverwind glared at Borlos even more fiercely, and Borlos sank back into his chair and looked at the floor. The Plainsman turned back to Kronn and Catt. Solemnly, he offered them his hand.

"I am Riverwind of Qué-Shu," he said. "I don't know much about dragons either, but I have love and admiriation in my heart for the kender. I will go with you and do the best I can."

* * * * *

The trees of Solace blazed red with the rising sun. Birdsong filled the air, and squirrels chased each other across the inn's steep roof. Caramon and Riverwind stood on the balcony outside the tavern, smelling the tempting aroma of cooking fires that drifted on the wind. They cupped mugs of hot tarbean tea in their hands, taking occasional sips to keep the morning's chill at bay.

"A good day for traveling," Riverwind noted.

Caramon grunted, took another sip of his tea, and set it

down on the balcony's dew-dappled railing.

Neither man had slept; neither man had wanted to. Soon after Riverwind declared his desire to help the kender, Clemen, Borlos, and Osler had slipped away and the rest had gone upstairs to bed—first Moonsong and Brightdawn, then Kronn and Catt. Last of all Tika had kissed her husband good night, embraced Riverwind with tears in her eyes, and left them alone. The Plainsman had helped Caramon drag a straw pallet into the tavern and lay the drunken tinker out on it. After that, the two old men, who had been friends for more than thirty years, had sat together the whole night through.

"Kendermore," Caramon muttered.

Riverwind glanced at him, then chuckled, gazing at the vallenwoods' waving branches. "I know what I'm doing, Caramon."

"Do you?" Caramon persisted. "Riverwind, you're sixty-five years old, and you want to pick up and travel across Ansalon to fight a dragon at the behest of two kender you've never even met before tonight." He scowled. "If that makes so much sense to you, could you please explain it to me?"

"They are the children of brave Kronin," said the Plainsman.

Caramon grunted.

"I owe Tasslehoff as much," Riverwind added.

Caramon snorted, throwing up his hands.

"You know why I must do this," Riverwind said.

"You'll be lucky to survive the trip, let alone kill this Malystryx or defeat an entire army of ogres."

"Maybe so. But I believe there's a reason those two arrived the same day I did. A reason known only to the departed gods."

A thrush landed on the railing, not far from where the two men stood. It peered at them curiously, then twittered and was gone in a flutter of wings.

"You're batty," Caramon murmured.

Riverwind winked. "Not yet, old friend," he allowed. He raised his mug to his lips, draining it in one swallow.

"But dying in battle sure beats dying in bed."

* * * * *

Caramon cooked breakfast, frying eggs and sausage and making a hash of last night's uneaten potatoes. Drawn by the smell, Riverwind's daughters came down from their rooms, as did the kender. Tika brewed a fresh pot of tarbean tea, then went into the storeroom to gather provisions for the travelers: cheese, hardtack, smoked venison and dried apples. She gave them fresh wineskins too, filled with what ale remained from Caramon's special keg. When Riverwind reached for his purse to pay for the supplies, Caramon stubbornly waved him off.

No one spoke of dragons.

"I hear you're betrothed, Moonsong," Tika said.

The Chieftain's Daughter blushed, lowering her eyes demurely. "Yes," she said. "At the beginning of the summer, Stagheart of Qué-Teh promised himself to me."

"He didn't have much choice," Brightdawn added, grinning wickedly. "Not after Father caught the two of them together in the paddocks east of town."

"Brightdawn!" Moonsong protested, her face growing darker still.

"Father gave Stagheart a choice," the younger twin continued, undaunted. "Either he could accept his punishment, or he could agree to a Courting Quest."

"What was the punishment?" asked Kronn around a mouthful of sausage.

"In our tribe, a warrior who disgraces himself must dress in women's clothing for a year," Riverwind explained. "It is a mark of shame."

"Actually, Father could have banished him from the village, if he wanted," Brightdawn added. "Lucky for Stagheart, he's Chief Nightshade's son."

Caramon and Tika nodded, understanding. Nightshade was Chieftain of the Qué-Teh, who were more powerful than any tribe on on the Plains, save the Qué-Shu. He and Riverwind had been friends since shortly after the war, and he had been an important ally in uniting the smaller tribes. A marriage between his son and Riverwind's daughter would only strengthen the link between the two tribes.

"I take it he's on his Courting Quest now," Caramon said dryly.

Moonsong, who had been enduring the conversation in embarrassed silence, raised her chin proudly. "Father sent him into the hills. A griffon has been preying on our tribe's horses in the south fields all summer. When Stagheart returns to Qué-Shu with the griffon's head, we will be married. Mother will conduct the ceremony."

"And if he doesn't," Brightdawn added, "I'm sure Mother can spare him one of her gowns."

Moonsong shoved her sister, nearly knocking her off the bench, then turned to their father. "Why don't you ask her about Swiftraven?" she asked.

"There's nothing to ask!" Brightdawn protested, seeing Riverwind's brows lower. "I swear!"

"Who's Swiftraven?" Catt asked.

"Nightshade's younger son," Riverwind said. "A mere boy."

"He's eighteen, Father," Brightdawn grumbled.

"Six years younger than you. You should find someone your age."

"I'm six years younger than Caramon, Riverwind," Tika interrupted.

Riverwind looked at her, then at Brightdawn. Both women looked back at him defiantly.

"Take my advice, Riverwind," Caramon said, grinning. "Run while you still can."

The room rang with laughter, but soon lapsed into an awkward silence. Riverwind cleared his throat. "We should be going," he said. He pushed his chair back from the dining table and rose, his leather armor creaking. "It is a long ride across the Plains. We must leave if we are to reach my village before dark."

They walked to the door. Kronn and Catt went ahead to fetch their ponies and the Plainsfolk's horses. Moonsong and Brightdawn each embraced both Caramon and Tika, then left as well.

Riverwind stood for a moment, framed by the doorway as he faced his friends. Tika hugged him tightly, burying her face against his fur vest. "Riverwind," she sobbed. "You shouldn't be going to Kendermore. Not now, especially. . . ."

Gently, he pushed her away from him, then put a finger to her lips. He reached out and stroked her silver-red hair.

She shook her head stubbornly, sniffling. He bent down and kissed her forehead.

"I will miss you, Tika," the Plainsman said.

She turned and left, heading into the depths of the inn so she could be alone. Caramon watched her go, then turned back to face Riverwind. The two men regarded each other, neither wanting to speak first.

"Father!" Brightdawn's voice drifted up from the street below. "Come on!"

Caramon bowed his head. "You've been a good friend," he said, his voice trembling despite his best efforts to control it.

"And you have been more than a friend," Riverwind replied.

The two men embraced, neither needing to put further words to what he felt. Riverwind drew Caramon closer.

"Goldmoon will come to you, if anything happens to me," Riverwind murmured. He reached into his fur vest and produced a small, silver scroll tube. "When she does, I want you to give her this."

"Of course," Caramon answered, his voice choked with emotion. He took the tube from his friend and slid it into his pocket.

"Goodbye, my friend," Riverwind said, and walked out the door.

Caramon stood alone in the tavern, his head bowed, listening to the sound of the Plainsman's boots upon the stairs.

Chapter 5

Smoke choked the streets of the town of Myrtledew, rising to blot the sun from the clear, blue sky. Burning ashes floated on the wind, which fanned the flames that crackled all across the village. The air reeked of burning—the rich smell of wood, the wet odor of straw, the sickly sweet stench of hair and flesh. The fire had already consumed the town's entire southern half and had started to work its way north.

Kurthak the Black-Gazer stood amid the carnage, his scabrous lips curled into a scowl. The ogre warlord scratched his coarse, green-black beard and glowered at the flames, shifting the weight of his great spiked club on his shoulder. His eyes—the left one nothing but an empty socket—narrowed with disgust as he regarded the remnants of the kender village.

"Sloppy," he growled.

Tragor, his second-in-command, grunted and spat in the soot. He weighed his massive, two-handed sword, watching the blood run down the groove in the middle of its blade. "We did good enough."

"No," Kurthak snapped. He glowered at Tragor, gesturing at the warrior's bloody blade. "We killed too many."

"Live kender, dead kender," Tragor rumbled. "What's the difference?"

Kurthak shook his great, shaggy head, his ox-horned helmet glinting in the ruddy firelight. "I have explained this to you, Tragor," he snarled. "A dead kender is no good to us."

"At least they shut up when they're dead."

A snort that might have been laughter erupted from Kurthak's lips. "Still," Kurthak grunted, "I gave specific orders. Take them alive. Any clan-chief who didn't heed me will bleed this night."

The attack had begun at midday. When Kurthak's war

band—a thousand warriors, only a fraction of the total horde—had descended upon Myrtledew from the shattered wastelands to the east, the surprised kender had been unable to raise any defenses in time. There had been no keeping the ogres from running rampant through town. A few of the kender had fought, but most sought to escape—not out of fear, of course, but because they knew they had no hope of winning and preferred to fight another day.

Escape, however, had not been so easy. The ogres had surrounded the town, cutting it off and slaughtering those who tried to flee west, into the depths of the Kenderwood. Their bloodlust awakened by the fighting, Kurthak's warriors had rampaged through the village, hacking and smashing anything smaller than they were. By the time the fighting was done, nearly half of Myrtledew's population of several hundred kender were dead. Of the survivors, many were indeed useless to Kurthak—children, the old, the sick. The ogres had put most of them to the sword.

The rest, however, were being rounded up, even now, amid the blazing wreckage. Kurthak watched as a squad of heavily armed ogres locked a cluster of thirty kender in irons and marched them, at spearpoint, toward the edge of the village. The fierce-spirited kender shuffled along, the chains that shackled their ankles rattling as they made their way toward the slave wagons that waited on the east side of town. They looked truly miserable, which only increased Kurthak's satisfaction as he watched them pass.

"My lord!" the leader of the warriors called. He turned away from his men and hurried toward Kurthak and Tragor. He was a wart-covered brute with a jagged brown snaggletooth jutting from his mouth. The ritual scars on his cheeks and the horsetail plume on his helmet identified him as a low-ranking officer in Kurthak's band.

"Argaad," the Black-Gazer responded. "What news?"

"We captured these wretches at the riverside," Argaad reported, his chest puffing with pride as he gestured behind him. "They tried to escape on a barge, but we stopped them."

"Good work," Kurthak said. He slapped the warrior on the shoulder. "You have done your clan proud."

"Thank you, my lord." Argaad bobbed his head, beaming with pride. "I give them to you as a gift. It is an honor to serve you. If you should need a bodyguard, or someone to lead the next attack—"

Tragor cleared his throat. "Argaad," he said in a low voice, "your gift is getting away."

Argaad whirled. Somehow, in the middle of his speech, the kender had slipped out of their bonds. Now one of his men lay on the ground, bleeding from a knife wound in his gut, and the rest were watching, stunned, as their captives dispersed.

"Don't stand there, you louts!" Argaad roared. "After them!" He gave Kurthak a quick glance that was half-apologetic, half-horrified, then turned to lope after his men, driving them after the kender.

Tragor started to laugh, but Kurthak cut him off with a baleful glare. "This is no joke," the warlord snapped. "Each of those kender is valuable to me." He motioned toward the fleeing prisoners and the ogres who gave chase. "Come. We will help Argaad catch them again."

"Good," Tragor declared, hefting his great sword. "I've been hoping for some sport."

They both ran, charging after Argaad and his men. The kender were quick, but the ogres took long strides, and easily kept pace. As they ran, the towering brutes readied large nets to catch their fleeing prey. The kender weaved among burning buildings, splitting up and regrouping as they charged through the streets, but the ogres—Kurthak and Tragor running now in the lead—kept after them, snarling and howling.

At last they reached the edge of the blasted village. A thicket of tall, tangled bushes rose ahead of them, carrying on for five hundred yards before giving way to the dark Kenderwood. The kender sprinted for the thicket, but Kurthak only grinned, waving his arm toward the forest. "Get ahead of them!" he called. "Trap them in those brambles!"

Obediently the ogres fanned out, charging around the bushes toward the woods. Kurthak and Tragor kept on the kender's heels. The first ones disappeared into the bushes with a rustle, and the others followed without hesitation—all except the last one, a golden-haired youngster who glanced over her shoulder directly at the warlord and his champion and smiled. Then she, too, was gone.

"Pen them in!" Kurthak bellowed, pulling up at the edge of the brambles. He pointed at the branches, which rustled with the kender's passage. "Watch the bushes! You can see where they are!"

The ogres soon encircled the rustling scrub, then began to close in, thrusting their spears and swords into the thornbushes. The ring tightened like a noose about the fleeing kender.

"Good idea, my lord," Argaad declared. "We have them trapped—they have nowhere to go. They won't get away."

Kurthak nodded impatiently. "Let us hope so."

The rustling in the underbrush continued to move slowly toward the tree line. Kurthak, Tragor and Argaad watched impatiently as the ogres closed in, flattening the brambles and cutting swaths toward their quarry.

Then, all at once, the rustling stopped.

The ogres stopped too, their brows furrowing with confusion. Involuntarily, Argaad sucked in a sharp breath through his jutting, rotten teeth. Tragor glanced at Kurthak, his eyes questioning, but the warlord was lost in thought, plucking at his beard as he tried to understand what was going on.

"My lord," Argaad asked, his face the color of bleached bone, "what should we do?"

Kurthak pondered a moment, then pointed at the spot where the rustling had ended. "Keep going," he bade. "They must still be there."

The ogres moved on, weapons and nets ready. Argaad held his breath as the circle of his warriors narrowed to a mere two dozen yards, then one dozen. The bushes remained motionless.

The ogres stopped when they were close enough for

their spearpoints to reach the middle of the ring. They jabbed their weapons into the bushes, probing the spot where the rustling had stopped so suddenly. Nothing happened.

"What's wrong?" Argaad called anxiously. "They should be right there!"

The ogres prodded the scrub with spears, hacked with swords and axes, and beat the bushes with cudgels. They trampled the brambles flat in some places, pulled their knotted roots from the ground in others. The kender, however, were gone.

"What witchcraft's at work here?" Tragor grumbled, baffled.

"Torches!" ordered the Black-Gazer, his face creased with rage. "Burn them out!"

A pair of ogres pushed past the rest, wading out of the bushes, then ran toward the fiery ruins of Myrtledew. The other brutes edged outward again, toward the edges of the thicket, always watching for some sign of the vanished kender. Before long the runners returned, each bearing a pair of burning firebrands. They looked to Kurthak, ignoring Argaad altogether. Glowering furiously, the warlord waved them on toward the bushes.

The shrubs' dry leaves and branches caught fire quickly, and the flames spread. The ogres waited all around the bushes, waiting and watching for the kender to flee the blaze. Within minutes the whole thicket was aflame, curling and blackening as the fire raged higher. And still there was no sign of the kender. The ogres watched the conflagration, gaping in confusion.

"You lost them!" Kurthak snapped at Argaad, who flinched beneath the lash of his words.

"I don't understand," the snaggletoothed warrior protested. "They couldn't have escaped the fire. How could they enter the bushes without leaving? You saw them go in there, my lord!"

Slowly, Tragor moved to stand behind Argaad.

Kurthak nodded slowly, pondering. "Yes, I did," he agreed.

"My lord," Argaad began. "I didn't—"

With a suddenness that startled even Kurthak, Tragor lifted his heavy, two-handed sword high above his head, then slammed it down on the cowering warrior from behind. The blade hacked through Argaad's helmet, splitting his skull in half. The snaggletoothed warrior stood rigid for a moment; then Tragor jerked his sword free, and Argaad crumpled in a bloody heap.

Kurthak looked down at the corpse, then shrugged. "Come," he bade, and motioned for Tragor to follow. "There is nothing left for us here."

They left the thicket to burn and Argaad's body to draw crows.

* * * * *

Argaad was not the only warrior to lose his prisoners inexplicably. When the ogres regrouped outside the smoldering ruins of Myrtledew, no fewer than six officers came to Kurthak and reported, with trembling voices, that their captives had broken free, opening their shackles with concealed lockpicks, and fled. Some had made their way to the underbrush or the forest itself; others had ducked into the village's larger buildings. In every case, just when the ogres were sure they had them trapped, the kender had vanished mysteriously. Every one of the penitent officers avowed that the disappearances were the result of some unknown magic. Kurthak, who had never heard of a kender sorcerer, scoffed at the notion.

"Fools," he told Tragor as they struck out eastward from Myrtledew, toward their barren, rocky homeland. "The stupid lackwits let them escape."

Tragor grunted noncommittally, his sheathed sword swinging on his back as he trudged through the woods beside Kurthak. "What will you do?" he asked.

Kurthak pondered, glancing back at the columns of ogres who followed him. Of the thousand warriors he had brought with him on this raid, he had lost perhaps a hundred, with a like number wounded. Except for Argaad, the officers who had failed him marched with the survivors. They took great care not to meet his coal-black stare as he glared at them.

"I am not sure yet," he said, his brow beetling.

"They should die," Tragor declared flatly. He smacked a leathery fist against his palm. "Lord Ruog would not look well on you if you let them live."

Kurthak shrugged as if this meant nothing to him. Ruog, hetman of the greatest ogre horde ever to emerge from the wildlands of the Goodlund peninsula, was a lord who valued swift action on the part of his followers. Kurthak would have to report to him immediately, and Ruog would not be pleased to hear that the Black-Gazer's war band had captured fewer than a hundred slaves. He would demand blood for the lost kender.

Still, Kurthak hesitated as he considered the possibilities. "I hear your words, Tragor," he declared, pursing his lips in concentration. "I think, though, that I have a better idea."

* * * * *

Kurthak the Black-Gazer scowled fiercely, his face glowing orange in the firelight. He stood upon a tall, jagged boulder, looking down at the six officers whose prisoners had escaped. All around him the ogres of his war band shifted and leaned closer, muttering to one another. The flames of great bonfires licked upward, as if seeking to ignite the starry sky.

Though they were fewer than three leagues from the Kenderwood, the land could not have been more different. The ground was parched and rocky, unsuitable for farming—or even herding—and great shelves of rock jutted from the barren hillsides. There was not a single tree to be seen, though clumps of razorleaf bushes clung stubbornly to the loose, sandy soil. Scorpions and snakes scuttled and slithered around them.

The officers who knelt before Kurthak were tightly bound, strong thongs of leather securing their arms and legs. Stripped of armor, helm, and shield, they kept their gaze resolutely on the ground before them. None met the warlord's fierce, one-eyed glare, though at times they did twist and crane to look over their shoulders. Tragor paced behind them, moving from one end of the row to the other. His hands twisted eagerly about the hilt of his sword.

"You have failed me," Kurthak stated. "I do not brook failure."

"But," protested one of the officers, a fat ogre named Prakun, "my lord—"

"Silence!" thundered Kurthak. "There can be no excuses!"

Tragor moved quickly. His two-handed blade flashed in the firelight, cleaving flesh and bone. The ogre to Prakun's right fell heavily against the fat officer, dark blood welling from the stump of its neck. Its head rolled in the dust, its eyes staring sightlessly at the pale moon.

Prakun cried out in terror, shoving the corpse away from him. A sharp stench filled the air as the ground beneath his knees grew dark and damp.

"Lord Ruog will ask for your heads," Kurthak continued, gesturing at the prize that lay pop-eyed before him. "I will give him what he wants."

Tragor's sword whistled through the air a second time. The ogre to Prakun's left drew a sharp breath, but before it could cry out its head came free, flying forward to crack against Kurthak's boulder and tumble to the ground. The new corpse stayed stubbornly upright for a moment, then swayed like a drunk and sagged to the ground. Prakun's face was livid with fear, gleaming white in the firelight. The other officers hunched their shoulders, cowering, as Tragor continued to pace behind them. Blood dripped from the champion's sword, making black stains on the stony ground.

"But," Kurthak concluded, "I am not unmerciful."

Again the sword flashed. Sensing what was coming, Prakun threw himself forward, landing face-first in the dirt. Tragor's swing went wide, and the champion struggled to keep the force of the unexpectedly unhindered blow from pulling him off his feet. Prakun rolled back and forth, blubbering pitifully, but could not otherwise move. Snarling, Tragor stepped forward and brought his heel down hard on the small of the weeping ogre's back. Prakun screamed as his spine snapped, but his cries were short-lived. Tragor drove his sword downward. It took two mighty blows to cleave through Prakun's thick neck.

Kurthak glowered down at the three remaining officers, who trembled as they, in turn, regarded Prakun's unmoving corpse. He smiled, his teeth gleaming sickly yellow in the shadows.

"The rest of you can go," he said.

There was a moment of shocked silence as the assembled ogres looked at one another incredulously. When Tragor stepped forward and cut the remaining officers' bonds, however, the onlookers' disbelief quickly gave way to outrage. Fists waved in the air, and angry oaths rang out in the night. Many of the ogres had come to witness their warlord's judgment, simply for the chance to see blood spilled; denied the slaughter they had expected, they quickly became furious.

"Silence!" barked Tragor, brandishing his sword in the air. "Be still, or you'll taste what you crave!"

Reluctantly, the throng settled down. Angry eyes turned toward the boulder where the Black-Gazer stood.

Kurthak smiled, his eyes glinting, and gestured at the stunned officers who still knelt before him. They were staring at each other in amazement and dread, not understanding what was going on.

"You three," Kurthak declared, "shall receive no punishment for your failure. You shall continue to serve me, just as you did before, and none here shall be allowed to harm you. But fail me again, and I will make sure you wish you had died tonight."

"Y-yes, my lord," one of the officers said in a small voice. The other two simply stared, their mouths hanging slightly open.

Kurthak folded his arms across his broad chest. "Go, then," he growled. "Return to your warriors at once."

The officers quickly scrambled to their feet, their faces deathly pale, and hurried away. The onlooking ogres tarried a moment, then began to disperse, shambling away into the gloom. They muttered to one another as they went, pondering their lord's judgment.

Tragor remained, wiping his sword's blood-caked blade with a tattered skin. He did not look at Kurthak as the warlord climbed down from his boulder.

"You have not asked me yet," Kurthak said, "why I do this."

For a long moment, Tragor silently continued to clean his weapon. Then he nodded and looked at Kurthak through narrow eyes. "I know you, my lord," he said. "You'll tell me, if you wish me to know." He returned to polishing the blade.

"I will explain," Kurthak said. He leaned back against the rock face, eyes glittering with reflected starlight. "What do you think those three will be thinking the next time we attack the kender? I have killed their comrades before their eyes, and threatened to do the same to them if they displease me. They will fight harder now that they fear my wrath."

Tragor considered this. "What if they don't?" he asked. "What if this . . . mercy makes them soft?"

"It will not," Kurthak asserted. He lifted his chin confidently.

"Maybe not," Tragor allowed, not fully convinced. "But what if—"

Suddenly he stopped speaking, sniffing the air. A new smell had risen amid the other stenches that hung about them. There was a strange sweetness to it, marking it as different from the sour odor of ogre sweat.

"Kender?" Kurthak asked, scenting it too.

Tragor sniffed again, then shook his head. "Human."

"Human!" Kurthak exclaimed. He glanced at the shadows, even more alert than before. "How close?"

"Close enough," said a voice.

Tragor whirled, his sword coming up reflexively. Kurthak reached for his spiked club. The two of them watched the edges of the firelight, nostrils flared as they tried to pinpoint the voice's source.

"You will not need your weapons," the voice continued. It was soft and sibilant, low but not deep. A woman's voice. "I have not come to do you ill."

"Show yourself, then," Tragor demanded, not lowering his sword.

Soft, mocking laughter filled the air, making the ogres' skin prickle. "Very well," the voice said.

She was closer than Kurthak and Tragor expected, stepping out of the gloom fewer than twenty paces away. She wore a deep, black cloak, its hood pulled up to obscure her face. She strode forward, opening her black-gloved hands to show that they were empty.

"Stop," Tragor said, brandishing his sword and moving to bar the woman's path.

She ignored him, continuing to walk toward the two ogres.

"I said, stop!" Tragor repeated, his voice rising with fury. The broad, gleaming blade wavered in his hands "Come no closer, or—"

"Call off this yapping dog, Black-Gazer," the woman interrupted, her voice laden with frost. "I would speak with you, and will come as close as I like to do it."

"Impudent wretch!" Tragor barked. He leapt forward, swinging his sword in a blow meant to split the robed woman in two, across the shoulders.

She moved with amazing speed, diving and rolling under Tragor's flashing blade. Before the champion could arrest the blow, she leapt at him, her fists swinging.

The blows—first her left hand, then her right—struck Tragor square in the stomach, below his metal breastplate. The ogre doubled over, making a high-pitched, wheezing noise, and the woman's black-booted foot came up suddenly, catching him full in the face. There was a wet crunch as the kick broke Tragor's nose, then the champion fell back, his face blossoming with blood. Tragor staggered, trying to keep his footing, but the woman spun, her foot lashing out again and connecting solidly with his groin. He sank to his knees, sobbing, and she seized his helmet by its plume and yanked it off. Tragor tried one last time to lift his sword, but the heel of the woman's hand cracked against his temple, and he collapsed in a senseless, flaccid heap.

The fight had lasted less than half a minute, from first blow to last. The woman watched Tragor for a moment, making sure he wasn't moving, then turned to face Kurthak. When she spoke, her voice was soft and calm, displaying no sign of exertion whatsoever.

"I have a proposal for you, Black-Gazer," she said.

Reflexively, Kurthak's grip on his club tightened, but then he glanced at Tragor's senseless form and forced himself to relax. There were few warriors in Lord Ruog's vast horde who could match Tragor's physical prowess. Yet this strange, cloaked woman had bested him without even winding herself.

He lowered the club, his eyes fast on her. "Who are you?" he demanded.

"My name is not important."

Kurthak shook his shaggy head. "I must know your face—at least."

The woman considered this, then shrugged. "Very well," she said lightly. "If it is so important to you." She reached up and pulled back her hood.

Kurthak caught his breath in horror.

She might have been lovely once, or she might have been plain. It was impossible to tell now, for the woman no longer had anything resembling a face. Her skin was a mass of red, puckered burn scars. Her hair had been completely scorched away, leaving nothing but bare, charred scalp. Her ears, nose and lips were gone; any other features were little more than soft, indistinct lumps. Only her eyes survived, blue and glittering beneath puffy, blistered lids. They shone with cruel humor when she saw the disgust on Kurthak's face.

"I am called Yovanna," she told him. Her voice had not

been marred by whatever had ruined her face; the contrast only made her visage more gruesome. "I bring you a message. My mistress wishes to speak with you."

"And who is this mistress?" Kurthak asked.

"Her name is Malystryx."

The Black-Gazer stiffened at the mention of the name. He knew stories of the great red dragon who was said to dwell to the north of the Dairly Plains, but he had never seen her. "What does she want with me?" he asked.

"She doesn't want you," Yovanna replied. "She wants your people, Black-Gazer. So she sent me to summon you."

"And why should I go with you?" Kurthak pressed, his anger growing.

Yovanna regarded him carefully, her blue eyes searching. "Malystryx has been watching your people for some time," she said. "For months, you have been raiding little kender towns."

Kurthak thought he heard derision in her voice, but he wasn't sure—there was no telling from her face. He snorted. "For sport," he said. "And for slaves."

Yovanna's face pinched and creased in what might have been a smile, but which looked like a nightmare grimace. "My mistress would like to join forces with you," she hissed.

"If she is so powerful, why does she need our help?"

"She needs allies as her power grows."

"What will she give me in return?" Kurthak asked.

"She will give you Kendermore."

Chapter 6

Swiftraven reined his dappled horse and faced west, into the storm. On the horizon, black clouds were piling into the storm-green sky. They towered high, dwarfing the distant, gray line of the Kharolis Mountains. His people had a word for such clouds. Hianawek, the Gods' Anvils. The lorekeepers had once taught that the smith-god Reorx would pound on them in summer's dying days, forging the coming winter. Thunder was the clashing of his great hammer, and lightning was the sparks it threw.

It was nonsense, of course. Children's stories. Reorx's hammer had fallen still two summers ago, when he and the other gods left the world, but the Hianawek continued to return, pounding the Plains with rain, hail, and worse things still.

The wind howled in Swiftraven's face, rippling the golden grass like waves on the sea. The cicadas, whose droning buzz was the music of the Plains, had fallen ominously silent, and the only sounds were the distant mutter of thunder and the nervous snorting of the young warrior's horse. The scent of rain, tinged with the ozone tang of lightning, grew steadily stronger.

The horse tossed her head, fighting the young Plainsman's grip on her reins. He stroked her neck, then swung down from his saddle and set about hobbling her, to make sure she didn't bolt. It was promising to be a fierce storm. The horse whickered, rolling her eyes with fear.

"Easy," he cooed, clucking his tongue to soothe her. "It's all right. We're safe here."

There was a haze beneath the clouds, promising rains heavy enough to flatten the grass that scratched at his bare knees. A few drops spat down, forerunners of the impending downpour. The Hianawek glowed as lightning danced from cloud to cloud. Counting the seconds between one such flash and the answering roll of thunder, Swiftraven gauged the storm's distance and nodded. It would not be long. A thrill ran through him, for this was the first time he had faced the Hianawek alone. When he returned to his tribe after the storm, there would be no question of his bravery.

Focused as he was on the massive, coruscating clouds, he didn't notice the riders until they were nearly upon him.

They were five, three astride horses and two riding ponies. There was little more he could make out, with the storm's darkness overwhelming the Plains. They did not appear to see him at all, though, so he moved quickly. With one hand he let slip the knotted rope that kept his horse from bolting, while his other pulled his bow from the saddle. With graceful ease he strung the weapon, then climbed back up on horseback. By the time he was settled in his saddle, he had a white-fletched arrow nocked on his bowstring. He used his knees to turn the horse, then stood in his stirrups, pulled back the string, and let fly.

The shaft fell just short of the riders, which was what he'd meant it to do. Swiftraven knew, as any good archer did, that a good warning shot could tell a man much about a foe. Cowards would balk or flee, cunning opponents would seek cover, and the brave or stupid would charge. As he notched a second shaft, he noticed that the riders did none of these; they reined in, stopping where he could make a clear shot. That meant something else entirely.

The tallest of the horsemen leaned forward in his saddle, peering toward where the arrow had fallen. Swiftraven saw one of the pony riders reach for something across his back, but the tall rider raised a hand, stopping him. The young Plainsman held his breath, sighting down his arrow as the wind whipped his long, brown hair behind him.

A sound rose then, above the clamor of the storm. A whistle, loud and piercing, rose and fell in a regular pattern. It was a language, though few, even among the Plainsfolk, knew how to speak it. Swiftraven, who had trained as a scout, was versed in whistlespeak, as were others who sometimes needed to signal long distances across the grasslands, such as hunters and shepherds.

Put down your bow, the whistler spoke. Would you feather your chieftain?

Starting, Swiftraven lowered his bow so swiftly he nearly dropped it. Without pause he wheeled his horse about and dug his heels into her flanks. He galloped east toward Qué-Shu, riding before the storm to herald the return of Riverwind and his daughters.

* * * * *

The drizzle was just turning into rain when Swiftraven drew up to the gates. The guards, who held their spears ready until they saw who the rider was, exchanged a few quick words with him, then parted to let him pass.

"What's the name of this place again?" asked Kronn, looking up at the village walls as they drew near. They were whitewashed and painted with abstract patterns of red and blue, but they were also stout and sturdy, their tops lined with wicked iron spikes.

Riverwind glanced over his shoulder. "Qué-Shu."

"Bless you!" Kronn exclaimed, giggling.

"Kronn!" Catt said.

The Plainsman shook his head. "It's all right," he said. "I've heard that joke many times before. You're not the first kender to visit the Plains."

The guards at the gate lowered their spears, kneeling, as the party drew near. Seeing this, Riverwind quickly crossed his arms in salute. "Get up," he told them kindly. "Your wives have enough to do, I'm sure, without having to wash the mud from your trousers."

Rising, the sentries returned his salute, then stood aside. They eyed the kender warily. Lightning raged in the inky sky as Riverwind came home for the last time.

Word of the chieftain's return had spread swiftly after Swiftraven's arrival. The thunder of drums called the villagers out of their homes, into the worsening rain. They lined the road, shouting and waving their hands as Riverwind's party rode past the rows of painted skin tents and mud-brick huts, toward the arena at the center of town. In spite of Riverwind's protestations, men knelt to him and women threw autumn flowers in his path. Children laughed and ran about, jumping in puddles with shrieks of delight.

"Quite the welcome," Catt noted, impressed.

"It's better when the weather's nice," Brightdawn remarked. "There are pipers and dancers, and everyone sings the Chant of the Ancestors."

They reached the arena, where a row of grim-faced men, resplendent in beaded jackets and feathered headdresses, stood in their way. As one, the men held up their hands, and the riders reined in. Riverwind climbed down from his horse and handed the reins to a young boy; his daughters and the kender followed suit. As the boy led the animals away, Riverwind bowed to the row of men and crossed his arms again. The men returned the gesture as one.

"Who are those people?" Kronn asked, unabashedly staring.

"The Honored Ones," Moonsong replied. "Chieftains of other tribes, and the elders of Qué-Shu."

"See the young one on the end?" Brightdawn said, pointing to a lean, swarthy man of thirty summers, whose bare chest was marked with a tattoo of a coiled serpent. Riverwind walked up to the man and clasped his arms in greeting. "That's Graywinter. He just became chief of the Qué-Kiri this spring, after his father died."

"He means to court Brightdawn," Moonsong added. Brightdawn shot her a scathing look.

"I thought you said you were going to marry Swiftraven," Catt said innocently.

"I'm not going to marry anyone," Brightdawn said, blossoms of red blooming on her cheeks. "Not until I'm ready."

Kronn yawned, finding this talk of marriage boring. "Who's that big one next to him?"

"That's Nightshade," Brightdawn replied, glad for the change of subject. Riverwind was speaking now with a grey-haired warrior with a jagged scar that ran from his nose his jawline. "He's chieftain of the Qué-Teh. Swiftraven and Stagheart are his sons."

"There's Swiftraven!" said Moonsong, pointing.

The young warrior had not had time to change out of his plain hunting skins before taking his place beside his father. He stared at his leather moccasins, still ashamed at having fired an arrow—even a warning shot—at his chieftain. Riverwind paused before him for a moment, then clapped Swiftraven on the shoulder. The young warrior relaxed, beaming, as Riverwind moved on down the line.

Catt looked around, her brow furrowing. "What about Stagheart? Isn't he here?."

"No," Moonsong said, unable to keep the disappointment from her voice. "He must still be on his Courting Quest."

"So we don't get to see any griffon's head?" Kronn asked, crestfallen.

"I saw a griffon once," Catt stated proudly. "Of course I saw its head too. But the elf she belonged to wouldn't let me ride her. Although I asked really nicely and everything."

"Who's that, Brightdawn?" Kronn pressed as Riverwind approached a fat, kind-faced old man. "Brightdawn? Hey, quit mooning at Swiftraven and pay attention!"

Brightdawn, who had indeed been staring longingly at Nightshade's younger son, started guiltily and stammered.

Moonsong laughed at her sister's embarrassment. "The next few are the elders," she said. She nodded toward the fat man. "Hartbow there used to be one of Mother's suitors, for a time. Briar"—she indicated a short, wiry man whose hair was still charcoal-black, though he was plainly Riverwind's age—"watched over our people when they were exiled in Thorbardin during the war. The man to his right, leaning on the crutch, is Hobblestep. He used to be one of the Qué-Shu's best warriors, but he lost his foot to a draconian soldier."

Riverwind went down the line of elders quickly, then stopped at a gaunt, stooped man, who clutched a thick-bound book to his chest. "Good heavens," Catt exclaimed, regarding the man's bald head, wizened face, and sparkling black eyes. "I think that's the oldest human I've ever seen."

"He looks like a dried-apple doll," Kronn chirped, his eyes wide. "All shriveled and brown."

"That's Far-Runner," Moonsong said. "He is old—more than a hundred, though no one knows his exact age."

Many of the Qué-Shu found it strange that their chieftain and lorekeeper should be friends, given the history they shared. Forty years ago, Far-Runner had been a warrior and a member of the council of elders under Goldmoon's father, Arrowthorn. He had been present when Riverwind, a low-born heretic, had petitioned Arrowthorn for his daughter's hand. He had assented to the Courting Quest that Arrowthorn had imposed upon the young shepherd. He had seen that young shepherd return from the impossible quest, bearing a staff of blue crystal. And he had been present when Arrowthorn condemned Riverwind to death by stoning as a blasphemer. By all rights, the chieftain of the Qué-Shu had reason to resent the old man.

But Riverwind had watched the council carefully all those years ago, even in the face of death. Not all the elders had agreed with Arrowthorn, and Far-Runner had spoken out both before and after the Courting Quest, asking the chieftain to show mercy for Riverwind. In the end, though, his words had not been enough, and he'd had no choice but to abide by the council's decision. Still, Far-Runner had protested the sentence: of all the elders in Qué-Shu, he had refused to go to the Grieving Wall to witness the young warrior's execution. For this reason, the Plainsfolk whispered, the gods had seen to it that Far-Runner survived the War of the Lance, while the rest of the elders had perished, either in the battle against the dragonarmies or in the mines at Pax Tharkas. And for this reason, Goldmoon and Riverwind had forgiven him when they returned to Qué-Shu after the war and had named him lorekeeper of the tribe. He had remained at their side for more than thirty years now, and though he was stooped and frail with age, many of the Qué-Shu believed he would still be there, thirty years hence.

Riverwind tarried at Far-Runner's side for some time, resting a gentle hand on the ancient man's arm as they spoke in hushed tones, then at last he stepped onward, to the last man in the row.

That man could have been the chieftain himself, years younger—he was tall and thin like Riverwind, and had the same sharp, hawklike features. His hair was black, though, instead of Riverwind's white, and he was only starting to show signs of the wrinkles that lined the chieftain's face.

"Let me guess," Catt said. "Your brother?"

"Yes," Brightdawn answered. "That's Wanderer."

"He's a stony looking fellow," Kronn observed. Riverwind smiled as he spoke to his son, but Wanderer's expression remained dour.

Moonsong sighed. "He wasn't always that way," she said. "He used to smile a lot, once—before the Chaos War, anyway."

"What happened?" asked Catt and Kronn at once.

"That's the worst part," Brightdawn said. "No one's sure." Seeing the puzzled looks on the kender's faces, she shook her head. "Have you heard tales about the shadow-wights? Of their powers?"

Kronn nodded gravely. "I have. From what I hear, a shadow-wight doesn't just kill you—it destroys you. If you look into its eyes, there's nothing there, but it can catch you with its gaze, and tear out your soul. Bit by bit you cease to exist, until nothing remains. Not even—" He gasped in horror, his hand going to his mouth.

"Not even in the minds of those who loved you," Moonsong said gravely.

"Wanderer has a son," Brightdawn added, her voice heavy with sorrow. "Cloudhawk. He's three years old. And no one, not even Wanderer, can remember the mother."

"A shadow-wight killed her?" Catt asked, her eyes wide.

"Like I said," Brightdawn repeated, "no one knows."

Wanderer stepped forward, unbuckling the bone-lattice plate he wore upon his breast, and held it out to Riverwind. "I return this to you, Father," he said tonelessly.

Riverwind took the breastplate and held it a moment, turning it over in his hands, then gave it back to his son. A murmur rippled through the crowd. Wanderer's eyes widened, but he said nothing.

"I will only be staying in Qué-Shu one night," Riverwind said. He nodded back toward Kronn and Catt. "I have promised our guests my help. We will be leaving on the morrow."

The villagers began to grumble, disbelief in their voices. The curious glances they cast at the kender grew hard, suspicious. The Honored Ones—even old Far-Runner—stared at Riverwind as the rain hammered all around them.

"You mean to help them?" Graywinter asked, his serpent tattoo swelling as he puffed out his chest. There was no mistaking the distaste in his voice.

"No, not just us," Catt answered. She stepped forward and bowed before the elders. "He's coming to Kendermore to help the kender nation fight the ogres and the dragon."

Scattered laughter rose among the crowd. The Honored Ones regarded Catt sourly. "Madness," said Hobblestep, shifting on his crutch. "You can't be serious about such a mission, my chief. Ogres? Dragons?"

"We've been trying to dissuade him," Moonsong said.

"I have sworn to help," Riverwind stated simply. "I leave with them tomorrow."

"But, my chief," Swiftraven blurted. "Why should you help them? They're just kender."

"Hey!" Kronn said peevishly.

"Just kender?" Riverwind demanded. He stalked over to the young warrior, who lowered his eyes self-consciously, and glowered at him. "Perhaps you're right, Swiftraven," he said after a moment. "Not worth the bother. Let the kender die. That's what you mean, isn't it?"

"I—" Swiftraven stammered. "No . . . I don't . . ."

Riverwind turned away from him in disgust, walking back to his son. Of all the Plainsfolk, Wanderer alone seemed untroubled by his father's words. His face was impassive.

"Where is your mother?" Riverwind asked.

"She waits for you in the chieftain's lodge," Wanderer replied, glancing toward a wooden longhouse at the far side of the arena.

Riverwind nodded, taking a deep breath to calm himself. His face stern, he turned to face the nervous crowd. Thunder roared.

"Go home," he told them. "All of you. Get out of the storm."

He walked past the still-amazed Honored Ones, bound for the chieftain's lodge. The villagers dispersed, running for shelter as the rain of the Hianawek overtook Qué-Shu.

* * * * *

She had not changed as much as her husband, but age had not left Goldmoon of Qué-Shu untouched. She was plumper than she had been in her youth. Her long braided hair was more silver now than gold. There were crow's feet around her pale blue eyes and worry lines around her mouth.

"You are still beautiful," Riverwind told her as he stepped into the chieftain's lodge.

Goldmoon looked up from where she sat, smiling. "And you still flatter me too much."

She rose from her sitting-blanket, pushing herself gracefully to her feet, and stepped forward to meet him. They embraced, but when his lips sought hers, she turned, allowing him to kiss her cheek only.

"You weren't at the Ceremony of Greeting," Riverwind chided gently.

"I'm sorry," said Goldmoon. "Did I miss something? I thought it might not be good for my illness to be out in the rain."

"Illness?" Riverwind paled with worry. "What has—"

"Don't fret so," she scolded him gently. "It isn't serious. Merely a cold, but I don't want it to grow worse—nor would I want you to catch it."

He gazed at her a moment, his eyes filled with pain. Then, before she could turn away, he kissed her full on the lips, hard and fierce. When they parted, she looked at him with piercing eyes.

"I can tell by your face," she said. "You aren't staying. Why?"

He shook his head. "When I was in Solace, two kender came to the inn. There is trouble in Kendermore—ogres, and a dragon. I told them I would help them."

"Kender?" she asked.

"Two children of Kronin Thistleknot. All grown now, and kender through and through."

"And you promised to help them?"

Another woman might have wept, might have begged him not to go. Goldmoon only studied his face, nodding. There was sorrow in her gaze, but there was also understanding. "If you must," she murmured. "It will not be the first time I have waited for your return."

Thunder bellowed, and brilliant light blazed outside the lodge's narrow windows. The flash drew Goldmoon's attention, and she did not see the grimace that twisted her husband's face. When she turned back to him, he was composed and stoic once more.

"When do you leave?" she asked.

"Tomorrow," he said. "In the morning."

She nodded, then reached out and took his hand. Her grasp was strong, sure. His breath quickened as she raised his fingers to her lips.

"What fools we would be, then," she murmured, "to let

this night go to waste."

They went to the bedroom then, husband and wife. The storm raged on, but they paid it no heed.

* * * * *

The folk of Qué-Shu rose early the next day. It was a clear morning, with a chill in the air that spoke of summer's end. The villagers set about mending what the storm had broken. The wind had torn tents from their moorings, and debris was scattered through the streets. As the sun rose above the Eastwall Mountains, however, the folk began to set aside their work and gather at the gates to see their chieftain off on his journey.

Kronn and Catt were the first to arrive. The Plainsfolk muttered darkly at their approach, making warding signs and glowering balefully. A few of the younger men spat in the mud as the kender passed.

"They don't seem very pleasant this morning," Kronn remarked, regarding the Plainsfolk in puzzlement. "Must be something they ate, although I thought supper was fine. Breakfast too. And I'm looking forward to lunch."

"It's because we're kender, you ninny," Catt said. She forced a smile at the angry Plainsfolk. The muttering was getting louder. "They're not all as nice as Riverwind."

Kronn frowned thoughtfully. "I hope this doesn't have anything to do with that misunderstanding last night. I thought I explained that it wasn't my fault those sacred talismans ended up in my pouch. If they'd taken them down when the storm started, they wouldn't have been blowing around like crazy, and I wouldn't have had to keep them safe. They should probably thank me, actually."

"No," Catt replied. "I think they've calmed down about that—although I'm a bit miffed they decided to post guards outside our hut. I was hoping to do some more exploring."

"Me too," Kronn agreed with a disappointed sigh. He glanced back toward the arena. "Hey, someone's coming."

The Honored Ones were striding down the street, toward the gates. Wanderer walked in the lead, his face looking as if it was carved of stone. The elders followed, then Greywinter of Qué-Kiri and Nightshade of Qué-Teh. At the last came Moonsong, Brightdawn and Swiftraven.

"No Riverwind," noted Catt in a low voice. "Do you think he maybe changed his mind? People here don't seem to be too keen on him going. Maybe they convinced him to stay."

The Honored Ones stopped at the edge of the crowd, which grew quiet at their approach. The Plainsfolk continued to glare at the kender, and Greywinter and some of the elders did the same.

Kronn nodded to them respectfully. "Say," he said, "what's with Brightdawn?"

Catt looked at the young Plainswoman and frowned. While Moonsong was clad in an embroidered white dress and buckskin slippers, Brightdawn still wore traveling clothes: a brown tunic and leggings, with high boots and a plain, fur cloak. Her mace still swung from her belt. Swiftraven was similarly attired, a quiver of white-fletched arrows on his back and a slender sabre at his hip.

Catt opened her mouth to answer, but at that moment the crowd stirred again, pointing. Looking, the kender saw Riverwind and Goldmoon walking toward them from the center of town. As one, the villagers knelt before their chieftain and priestess.

Riverwind marched up to Brightdawn, scowling. "Where are you going?" he demanded.

"I'm riding along with you," she replied, her chin rising defiantly.

"You'll do no such thing." Riverwind's tone was harsh. "I alone agreed to make this journey."

"Actually," Kronn piped up, "Paxina said it would be fine if we brought more than one person back with us. . . ."

Riverwind ignored him, rounding on Swiftraven. "And you," he growled. The young warrior fell back a pace, paling. "What do you think you're doing?"

"Leave him be, Father," Brightdawn said. "He only

wants to come along so he can protect me."

"No one is 'coming along,'" Riverwind said. "This isn't like a sleigh ride to Solace, Brightdawn. It's dangerous business."

"You weren't much older than me when you went on your Courting Quest," Brightdawn challenged. "You're always telling us how dangerous that was."

"This is different. I was a shepherd boy; I had no choice in the matter. But you're—"

"I'm what?" Brightdawn asked, her eyes flashing. "A girl?"

"My daughter."

Those words, and the plaintive way her father spoke them, gave Brightdawn pause, but only for a moment. "I'm not helpless, Father," she said. She held up her mace. "I know how to use this. I fought against the Brutes when they attacked Qué-Shu."

"That was different," Riverwind reasoned. "We had no choice but to fight. You should know your place is here with your mother."

"My place," Brightdawn repeated. "And what is that, Father? Wanderer has his—he wears the champion's breastplate, for he is Chieftain's Son. Moonsong is Chieftain's Daughter and will become high priestess when Mother is gone. One day, she and Stagheart will lead the tribes. But who am I, Father? Chieftain's Third Child, the extra daughter. I have no place."

Riverwind shook his head stubbornly, then glanced at the Honored Ones. They returned his gaze, saying nothing. Riverwind then looked to his wife.

"It's your decision," Goldmoon said simply. Riverwind raised his eyebrows at that but said nothing.

Moonsong stepped forward. "Let her go, Father."

Riverwind frowned at her, then looked to his son. Wanderer nodded once, silently. At last, the chieftain sighed. "Very well, Brightdawn," he said. "You may come to Kendermore." He turned to Swiftraven. "And you, as well, son of Nightshade. If you have any wish to marry my daughter, then let this be your Courting Quest. If any harm comes to her, then woe to you."

The villagers murmured at this. Swiftraven beamed with pride, then turned to his father.

"Go," Nightshade said simply.

His smile growing even wider, the young warrior dropped to his knees before Riverwind. The arrows in his quiver rattled. "I accept, my lord."

Riverwind nodded, his face troubled, then walked to the Honored Ones. He moved down the line, clasping arms with each man in turn. There was doubt and worry in the elders' eyes, but none spoke against him. No matter how grave their misgivings were, he was their chieftain, and his word was law. When Riverwind reached Far-Runner, though, the ancient man bowed his head and began to cry softly.

"What is this, lorekeeper?" Riverwind asked gently. "Why do you weep?"

"My chief," Far-Runner murmured. "I weep because my heart is heavy. I have wronged you in the past, when I let Chief Arrowthorn use the Courting Quest to keep you from his daughter. I would be doing you wrong again if I did not ask you to reconsider, and stay with us on the Plains."

Riverwind smiled. "You have long been loyal to me, Far-Runner," he said. "If I had not gone on Arrowthorn's impossible quest, the gods might have remained lost. The dragonarmies might have won the war—and Chaos might have won the next. If you hadn't wronged me, so many years ago, we might not be here today. I forgive you—but I cannot stay. I have given my word, and I will not break it."

Far-Runner nodded slowly, looking up at Riverwind. "Farewell, my chief," he murmured.

"Farewell, lorekeeper," Riverwind said, resting a comforting hand on the old man's shoulder.

He walked onward, to Wanderer, and father and son embraced in silence. Riverwind met his eyes. "I will tell my son of you," Wanderer murmured, his face dark.

Moonsong, who had remained stoic thus far, broke

down completely, sobbing as she threw her arms around her father. She clutched him tightly, refusing to let go, and in the end it took both Swiftraven and old Hartbow to pull her away. No sooner did she release Riverwind than she fell upon her sister. Both twins' faces shone with tears when at last they parted.

The stableboy strode through the gates leading three horses and two ponies. Catt and Kronn climbed into their saddles, then Brightdawn and Swiftraven, but Riverwind made no move toward his bay stallion—a gift bestowed upon him by Chief Greywinter when the Qué-Kiri joined the allied tribes. Instead, he turned toward Goldmoon, his heart in his eyes. He dropped to one knee before her. Mud soaked through his pantleg, but he paid it no heed.

"Kan-tokah," he said, choking. "My beloved."

Smiling serenely, she bent down and kissed him on the forehead. Then she cupped his chin with her hand and raised his head so he looked into her bright, blue eyes. "Why so solemn, my hero?" she asked. "We have been separated before."

He nodded, unable to find his voice.

"You have always followed your heart," she said, smiling. "It is an arrow that flies straight and true. I will await your return."

Taking his hand, she pressed something into his palm, then kissed his fingers, turned, and walked away.

He watched her go, his gaze seeking her as she approached the chieftain's lodge. He could feel eyes on him—the villagers, the Honored Ones, his children—but he did not rise. Instead, he opened his hand, and his face lit with wonder at what his wife had given him.

It was a simple chain, shaped of common brass. The charm that hung from it was crafted of shining, silver-blue steel. It was shaped like two teardrops, touching tip-to-tip—the symbol of Mishakal.

He had given her the medallion many years ago, so long it seemed another man's life. It was called a Forever Charm, and it was both a sign of the goddess and a token of his neverending love. She had never given it to him before. He looked up through clouding eyes to ask her, "Why?" But she had already disappeared into the chieftain's lodge.

* * * * *

While the rest of the villagers watched their chieftain ride out through the gates, Goldmoon sat alone in the chieftain's lodge. She did not cry, but rather picked up an old, worn lute, nestled it gently in her arms, and set her fingers to her strings.

She played an old song, laden with memory. She had sung it for the first time many years ago, at the Inn of the Last Home. She sang it today, for what she hoped would not be the last time.

> *O Riverwind, where have you gone?*
> *O Riverwind, autumn comes on.*
> *I sit by the river*
> *And look to the sunrise,*
> *But the sun rises over the mountains alone.*

Chapter 7

The eastern tip of the Goodlund Peninsula had never been what humans and their ilk would call hospitable. Only the most stubborn trees and bushes had clung to the barren, gravelly steppes. Dry, dusty wind had gusted through its narrow canyons. Water had been hard to come by, save for the Heartsblood River, and even that had been tainted, stained rusty red in grotesque mimicry of the sea to the north.

To Kurthak's people, it had long been home. The grasslands to the south had provided livestock and slaves for plundering, as had the Kenderwood to the west. The steppes were shot through with veins of copper, iron, and silver, ripe for mining. Sometimes, when a ship foundered on the rocky outcroppings along the coast—a treacherous stretch of shoreline mariners called Land's End—the ogres had waded out to them through the surf, to slaughter their crews and loot their holds.

Kurthak and Tragor stood at the edge of the Heartsblood, in a place where it had once flowed quick, wide, and deep. Now, though, it was nothing but a meager, muddy trickle, seeping down the middle of what had been its bed. The Black-Gazer stared hard at the feeble rill, his brow furrowing as if he could will the flow to return to its former strength. His champion scratched his pock-marked jawline, confused.

"The land's changed," Tragor said.

Slowly, as if reluctant to do so, the Black-Gazer nodded. "I'd thought I was imagining it. It's been many weeks since Lord Ruog led us west, to the kender lands."

"You imagine nothing," Tragor declared, shaking his

head. "I have forded the Heartsblood here many times. The current was nearly strong enough to drag me off my feet."

Kurthak considered the muddy creek a moment longer, then looked around. "The river's not the only thing that's changed. Speargrass and eaghon trees used to grow here." He glanced around, looking for some sign of the sharp-thorned plants that once had clustered thirstily along the riverbanks. The earth, though, was barren. He looked up, squinting north, and pointed a hairy finger. "Do you know what lies ahead there?"

Tragor followed the gesture, past the Heartsblood toward the far-off, dust-cloaked horizon. Some five leagues away, a mass of jagged, stony crags groped toward the sky. Above them hung a black, hazy pall, as might swathe a burning city.

"Mountains," Tragor said.

"Mmm. But that isn't what should be there." Kurthak regarded his companion, his single eye boring deep. "Think, Tragor. Do you recall what the humans call the lands beyond the Heartsblood?"

"I don't—" Tragor began; then his jutting brows lifted. "The Hollowlands!" he exclaimed, his eyes on the towering peaks. "They called that place the Hollowlands."

Kurthak nodded gravely. "Not so hollow now, are they?"

"Black-Gazer!"

Both ogres looked toward the voice, which came from the far side of the riverbed. The black-cloaked form of Yovanna emerged from a cleft in the rocks there. Her hood was up again, hiding her blasted face from the glaring red sun—and from the ogres' eyes.

Reflexively Tragor scowled, reaching up to probe his face with thick fingers. He touched the great, swollen knot where her knee had smashed his nose, then growled, his hand straying toward the hilt of his sword.

Kurthak saw this, and laid a staying hand on Tragor's arm. His champion hesitated, then relented.

Yovanna had followed Kurthak's band and its captive

kender back from Myrtledew to the valley where Lord Ruog's horde camped. Once they were there, she had come to Kurthak's tent at midnight, night's shadows forming a second cloak about her.

"Malystryx awaits," she had said.

Kurthak had wasted no time. Gathering his traveling gear, he summoned Tragor and followed Yovanna into the night. He had told Lord Ruog nothing, and the hetman was doubtless ready to gut him by now for abandoning his post.

They had walked for nearly a week through the wasteland. Yovanna would disappear ahead of them, moving swiftly and surely among the crags and boulders, then would reappear a short time later, beckoning the ogres urgently on. Now she called them forward, over the river's drying bones, toward the towering mountains of the Hollowlands.

"Quickly," she urged. "The place for meeting my mistress is not far. Come!"

Kurthak gave the river and the peaks beyond it one last suspicious glance, then turned to Tragor and nodded ahead. They slogged on, over the dying Heartsblood, red mud sucking at their boots as they went.

* * * * *

They walked for hours, not even slowing their pace when the sky began to darken with dusk. Yovanna had not so much as paused before leading them into the towering crags. Both ogres, who knew much about highlands, had noticed how new these mountains appeared. They showed no sign of weathering or erosion. Instead, they were all sharp angles and deep cracks, as though someone had pulled them up from the earth's bones.

The crags were all around them now, stretching leagues in all directions. In the distance, one peak loomed above the rest. Its tip was burning.

"Is that Blood Watch?" Kurthak asked.

Yovanna did not look at him, nor did she break stride.

"It is," she answered, her voice cool and toneless as ever. "Though the ruins that gave it its name are long since gone. Now it is my mistress's lair. She has chosen to keep the name."

They clambered up a razorback ridge, Yovanna moving nimbly from rock to rock. The ogres climbed with greater care, sending rocks the size of their massive fists clattering down the steep slope behind them. When they crested the top, they saw that the ridge was the edge of a great, bowl-like crater. The bowl's sides were streaked with yellow dust, and the stench of brimstone hung heavy in the air. A black cleft in the crater's center hissed unclean-looking, brownish steam that rose in a column hundreds of feet high. The ground rumbled faintly beneath their feet.

Wrinkling his nose, Tragor shrugged and started to pick his way down into the crater. Before he could take two steps, though, Yovanna's black-gloved hand shot out and clamped tight on his wrist. Though her arm was like a reed next to his own, oaklike limbs, he still winced at the tightness of her grasp. He stopped.

"Go no farther," Yovanna said, releasing him. "We wait for her here."

"Here?" Kurthak repeated, surprised. "I thought we were bound for Blood Watch."

She shook her hooded head. "You thought wrong, then, Black-Gazer," she told him. "Do not worry. My mistress will not be long."

The ogres looked around. Kurthak squinted at the burning spire to the north. He could see the red glow of lava oozing down its sides.

"Impressive, isn't it?" Yovanna asked. "Malystryx is proud of her work here. Soon these peaks will dwarf the Lords of Doom themselves. After that—"

She stopped, her body stiffening suddenly. For a moment she was silent, then she swept her arm forward and up, her sleeve fluttering in the hot, fetid wind.

"She comes," she hissed.

Kurthak didn't see the dragon until she was almost

upon them, so heavy was the pall of smoke and ash that hung over the Hollowlands. When she emerged from the haze at last, he could do little but hold his breath and stare, while dragonfear clamped around his innards like a vise.

Malystryx the Red was larger than any dragon either ogre had seen before. She stretched more than three hundred feet long, nearly half of that a sinuous, snaking tail; her wingspan was similarly huge, blocking out half the sky as she dipped through the smoke toward the crater. The air howled with the rush of her passing. She banked sharply as she passed overhead, then began to circle the caldera, scanning the ground with eyes like forge-fired steel. If she saw the three tiny figures atop the ridge, she gave no sign.

Beside Kurthak, Tragor moaned and began to tremble. Kurthak glanced at him harshly, but said nothing, afraid of revealing his own terror.

At that moment, the dragon threw back her head and roared. The ogres clamped their hands over their ears, wincing at the sound. The rock beneath their feet shivered. The shriek carried on for nearly a minute, and when it ended Kurthak wiped tears from his eyes, wondering if the ringing sound that lingered after it would ever go away.

"Mistress!" Yovanna cried, exulting.

The great scaly head whipped around, and Malystryx stared straight at them, her eyes smoldering. Smoke curled from her nostrils, and her lips curled into a vicious leer. She circled once more, then set down on the floor of the caldera. The beating of her wings as she landed whipped stinging chips of stone in the ogres' faces; when they could see again, the dragon had curled around the sulfur-steaming cleft in the crater's midst. She studied them, her head angling from side to side.

"Good," hissed the dragon. "Very good, Yovanna. You may leave us now. Go to Blood Watch and await me there."

The black-cloaked figure bowed. "Yes, mistress,"

Yovanna said. Without even a sidelong glance at the ogres, she turned and walked away, disappearing down the lip of the crater. Kurthak and Tragor watched her go.

Malys stretched lazily, writhing around the warm steam vent. Her claws flexed, cracking stones. A sigh of contentment escaped her lips, accompanied by a puff of flame that could have reduced both ogres to ashes. When she was done, she looked at Kurthak. He stared back, wide-eyed.

"Black-Gazer," she purred. "Yovanna has watched you for some time now. She has told me great things about you."

Kurthak goggled for a moment, then bowed abruptly. "I've heard far greater things about you," he responded. Despite his efforts to control it, his voice shook as he spoke.

The dragon chuckled. "Indeed." Her gaze flicked to Tragor, and her scaly brows knitted. "This one I do not recognize."

Tragor swallowed, shuddering.

"This is Tragor," Kurthak stated. "He is my champion."

"A warrior?" Malys asked, her voice mocking. Her great forked tongue flicked in and out of her mouth. "You wouldn't use that mighty blade against me, would you, Tragor?"

The champion fell to his knees, weeping. "No," he whimpered. "Please . . ."

With a snort of amusement and disgust, Malys turned back to Kurthak. "I hope Yovanna did not . . . disturb you too greatly," she said.

He shook his head. In truth, though, he had seen the woman's disfigured face in his nightmares.

"You want to know what she is," Malystryx declared. "Don't you?"

Kurthak nodded wordlessly.

The dragon grinned, flames crackling between her tree-trunk fangs. "Call her an experiment," she said. "When I first came to these lands, I laid waste to a village. Ran-Khal, I believe, was its name. Most of the barbarians living there died, but when the flames abated I found Yovanna still alive, though badly scarred . . . as I'm sure she has shown you. I took her back to Blood Watch and remade her as my servant. The spells I cast upon her destroyed the peasant girl she once was. Now she is strong and cunning, and she would leap from the top of one of these peaks if I wished it."

"Spells?" Kurthak asked. "But magic is gone. The moons—"

Malystryx laughed. Her breath smelled like burning metal, making the ogres' nostrils sting.

"Perhaps to you mortals there is no magic," she said. "Dragons need no moons for their power." She raised a long-taloned claw, pointed it at Tragor, and spoke several guttural words. Tragor gaped in horror, and Kurthak took a quick step away, expecting him to explode or rot before his eyes. Instead, though, Tragor rose from the ground and floated through the air toward the dragon. His terrified cries ended abruptly as he fainted dead away.

Sneering, Malys lowered her claw and turned back to Kurthak. Tragor continued to hang in midair, his feet dangling a hundred feet or more above the stony ground.

"Now," Malystryx said, "enough idle talk. I have chosen you for a reason, Black-Gazer."

With effort, Kurthak tore his gaze away from the hovering, limp form of his champion and focused on Malys. "Very well," he said, trying to sound as though he were somehow on even footing with the gigantic wyrm. "Your servant sought me out. She said you had a bargain to make—my people's allegiance in exchange for Kendermore."

Malystryx's head bobbed. "That is indeed what I intend to offer you," she said. "I have watched your people for some time, Black-Gazer, and I see great promise in you— promise I did not see in the puny humans who dwelt in this land."

Kurthak didn't miss the carefully chosen word—dwelt. There had been thousands of humans in the Dairly Plains to the south of the ogres' lands.

"They are mostly gone now," Malys hissed, guessing his thoughts. "Many are dead, though some of them fled.

I could have destroyed your people with no more effort than I crushed the humans, but I have chosen not to. Do you know why, Black-Gazer?"

"Because you wish to ally with us instead?"

"Precisely. I mean to turn my attention to the kender next."

He swallowed. "To destroy them?"

"If I must," she said. "But the kender are not very filling and I find simple slaughter somewhat boring. I like to . . . play with and savor my food. That is where I need your help."

"I don't understand."

"You have been attacking the kender," she explained, her tone that of a patient parent speaking to a dull-witted child. "Your chief—Ruog—has sent you and others to destroy villages along their eastern border. But you aren't content with simple slaughter either, are you? No, instead you take them prisoner. Why?"

"We want them as slaves," Kurthak said.

"Slaves!" Malystryx laughed. "Of course. But who would buy one? I am still somewhat new to this land, but I've learned enough about the kender to know they are not well-respected. Most of the other races consider them nuisances, I understand."

"We don't mean to sell them," Kurthak said. "We mean to keep them."

"To what end?"

He pursed his lips, hesitating.

"Oh, come now, Black-Gazer," Malys purred. "Don't be so reluctant. I can always use my magic to pluck the answer from your mind—something you'd find quite uncomfortable."

She twitched another claw, and instantly Kurthak's brain flooded with agony. He staggered, gagging, but the pain ebbed as quickly as it had risen. For a moment he stood silently, fighting to keep his gorge from rising. Then he wiped cold sweat from his forehead. "Th-the mines," he stammered. "Our people have found many new lodes of ore. Narrow, cramped, dangerous work. Lord Ruog wants to use the small kender to dig them out."

"Ah," the dragon declared, smiling. "I see. And when the ore is gone . . . you will kill them then?"

"Yes."

"Very clever. Put them to use before they die. But you're having trouble, aren't you?"

Kurthak scowled, his face darkening. "They're trickier than Lord Ruog expected," he admitted. "They elude us constantly. We've captured more than a thousand of them, but—"

"But you want more," Malys interrupted. Her smile widened. "I think I can help you with that, Black-Gazer."

"In exchange for my people's allegiance?" Kurthak asked.

The dragon's head bobbed, her smile never wavering.

"What could we possibly do for you that you can't do yourself?"

"A good question," Malys hissed. "For an ogre, you're terribly bright, Black-Gazer. I like that. It is true, I am mighty, but I am only one being. Shaping the land into this Desolation requires great concentration, and it draws attention. I need your people to patrol and police my conquered lands. In return, I will let them have plenty of slaves."

"What about me?" Kurthak asked. "We've spoken of what you want and what my people have to gain. You must have something to offer me, too, or you'd have approached Lord Ruog directly."

She barked a harsh laugh. "So daring, too. You're right, of course, Black-Gazer. I did not approach Lord Ruog because he is a fool. He could conquer the kender with ease, but instead he picks meaninglessly at their borders. You, however, are everything I had hoped you would be."

She made a swift gesture, and Tragor floated back to Kurthak's side. The champion's feet touched the stone of the ridge; then he collapsed in a heap.

"So, my new friend," purred Malystryx, "let us speak of what you shall gain."

* * * * *

The black stain of the ogre horde grew darker still as night settled over the land. In a series of shallow, barren valleys to the east of the kender lands, thousands of ogres gathered around flickering campfires. Gray, greasy smoke drifted up toward the clear, violet sky, where the pale moon waned and the first evening stars flickered. Sounds, too, rose above the camp: a ghastly din of snarls, shouts and guttural laughter, mixed with the thundering roll of war drums and the fierce blare of horns. The ogres roasted fresh meat over their fires—venison, boar, and other things best left unmentioned—and devoured it when it was still pink and sizzling. They washed it down with copious amounts of beer, both their own sour brew and kegs of kender lager plundered from Myrtledew and several other towns. Drunken skirmishes soon followed, rival war bands attacking each other with fists and blades. Blood was spilled, skulls were cracked, and a few of the brutish creatures were crippled or killed before their clan chiefs could break up the brawling. Once the fighting was done, the ogres turned to other sport. A few captive kender, deemed too weak or sickly to be useful as slaves, were brought forth from their cages, and led to where the drunken ogres waited with axes, knives, and iron stakes heated in the fires until they glowed golden-hot. The kender's screams soon joined the ogres' wild howls in a chorus of despair.

It was a night like any other in the war camp of Lord Ruog, hetman of the ogres of Goodlund.

In a narrow dale in the camp's midst, the hetman and his warlords had gathered about a huge, roaring bonfire for some sport of their own. They roared with approving laughter at the sound of bones breaking, and Ruog leaned forward on his makeshift stone throne, pounding his great fist against his knee.

Between the hetman and the raging fire, two of the ogre horde's finest warriors were wrestling. It was not wrestling as humans knew it, since there were no rules of propriety: vicious bites and gouged eyes were commonplace, and fights were not called because of injury. Such was the case now, for one of the wrestlers, a shaggy brute named Grul, had just finished crushing his opponent's wrist. The wounded ogre, a wiry, hairless creature named Baloth, howled with pain, madly trying to pry his opponent's fingers from around his arm, but Grul only smirked and tightened his grip. Popping, snapping sounds filled the air, and Baloth's cries grew louder.

"More!" Ruog howled. "Finish him!" To either side, his warlords echoed his words, their eyes gleaming feverishly in the firelight.

Suddenly the tenor of Baloth's cries changed, shifting from pain to fury in an eyeblink. His foot lashed out at Grul's knee. The blow might have crippled the shaggy ogre, but he saw it coming and leapt aside, rolling in the dust before twisting back to his feet. Freed at last from Grul's vicious grip, Baloth clutched his injured wrist and staggered back. The wrestlers glared at each other, battered and bleeding. Their sweat-soaked bodies gleamed in the firelight as they circled, seeking an opening.

"Come on, you cowards!" shouted one of the warlords. "This is no dance!"

Grul snarled and lunged, his hands grasping. He found a hold about Baloth's leg, and the bald ogre struggled to stay upright as the shaggy brute pushed him back toward the flames. Baloth, in turn, tore at Grul's long beard with his good hand, ripping out hanks of black, wiry hair. Grul spat and cursed, then let go when a vicious tug at his bristly moustache nearly tore off his upper lip. Baloth didn't miss a step, his horny fist cracking against Grul's jaw. Grul stumbled, tripped over a sharp rock, and fell backward, nearly landing in the fire. The assembled warlords shrieked with lusty approval. Lord Ruog's grin vanished, however, as Baloth stalked forward to stand over his supine foe. Ruog had bet twenty kender slaves that Grul would win the fight.

Baloth stood above Grul, leering cruelly. Grul stared hatefully back, his eyes turning to ice, then reached back into the flames. The stink of searing flesh quickly filled the air, and the shaggy ogre's face contracted with pain, but when he pulled his scorched hand out of the fire, it gripped a long, burning log. Baloth only had time to blink in surprise before the burning branch swung, striking him in the groin. He doubled over with a grunt, and Grul brought his new weapon up sharply, smashing it against the underside of Baloth's chin.

Ruog leapt up from his throne, cheering exultantly. Grul, his arm red and blistered from fingertips to elbow, sprang to his feet, wailing with battle rage, and struck Baloth on his bald head. Baloth crumpled, moaning. Blood trickled from his mouth and nose. Triumphant, Grul raised the firebrand and held it poised for the kill.

The onlookers, half of them elated and the other half furious, looked to Lord Ruog. The hulking hetman stared down from the earth mound that served as his dais. It was his decision, according to tradition. Grul could either spare Baloth's life or smash it from his body.

The hetman paused—not to make up his mind, but to draw out the moment, reminding one and all of his power within the horde. He shrugged off his bearskin cloak and threw it aside, then folded his massive, corded arms. Brown, rotten teeth revealed themselves as an evil smile split his face.

"You have both fought well," he said. "But there can be only one victor, and so I say—"

"It seems an awful waste," said a mocking voice from beyond the fire. "To kill one of our best for sport, when he could be fighting the kender instead."

At once the crowd's attention left Lord Ruog, shifting to the one who had spoken. Ruog glowered as an ogre wearing a horned helm stepped around the fire, striding forward to stand beside Grul.

"Kurthak," Ruog spat. "So you've returned to us, have you, coward?"

The circle of warlords tightened around the fire, muttering darkly.

"I am no coward, my lord," Kurthak said confidently. "But you are a considerable fool."

The hetman's scarred face grew very dark. His hand went to the haft of the great axe he wore on his belt, but he did not draw it yet. The warlords hung back, watching this surprising new confrontation as intently as they had watched the wrestlers.

"I don't think I heard you," Ruog growled. "It sounded as if you just insulted me—and without your dog of a champion beside you, even."

Kurthak smiled unpleasantly. "Tragor," he said.

Holding his great sword ready, Tragor strode into the circle of firelight. Seeing the cruel glint in his eyes, the warlords parted to let him through. Kurthak's champion strode forward to stand beside his master. His blade flashed red in the firelight.

"Good dog," Kurthak said. Tragor grinned.

Ruog grew even more livid than before. "I should have the both of you drawn and quartered. First you show mercy to your officers, then you abandon your war band to flee back into our homeland."

"We didn't flee," Tragor snarled. His sword quivered in his hands, but Kurthak, who held no weapon, laid a steadying hand on his arm.

"My champion speaks truly," Kurthak said, his good eye still on the hetman. "We went east, yes, but at the behest of one who would be our ally. I have made a pact with Malystryx the Red."

The warlords all started shouting at once—some in rage, others in excitement.

"Silence!" Ruog bellowed, spittle flying from his lips. Reluctantly, the warlords fell still. "You cannot make pacts for this horde, Black-Gazer! Only the hetman may do so!" He thumped his chest soundly.

"Yes," Kurthak agreed. "That is so. And that is why I intend to replace you as hetman."

The stillness that settled over the crowd was almost eerie, disturbed only by the crackling of the fire. Kurthak looked up at Ruog, his face maddeningly calm. The warlords glanced at each other, not knowing what to do.

Ruog seethed for a moment, then looked toward Grul

and nodded once. With a howl, the wrestler spun and swung his firebrand at Kurthak's head.

Kurthak moved so swiftly that to many of the watching warlords it seemed his spiked club appeared in his hand by magic. He brought the weapon up to block Grul's attack. Wood cracked against wood, loud as a thunderclap, and the firebrand shattered in a burst of flaming splinters.

Baloth stirred as Grul stared stupidly at the stump of charred, broken wood in his injured hand. Still dazed from his beating, he lurched up and struck Grul from behind. Before Grul knew what hit him, Baloth seized his shaggy head and twisted, breaking his neck.

Most of the warlords hung back, unwilling to enter the fray. Still, half a dozen of Ruog's staunchest followers surged toward the melee by the fire, screaming of treason. Tragor fell upon these attackers, his sword flashing. Blood washed the dusty ground as he cut the first two down with a single stroke, then charged the others with berserk fury.

Ruog bellowed for his guards. No one answered his call.

"You great idiot," Kurthak sneered, striding toward the dais. "Do you think I would challenge you without dealing with your guards first? Most were easy to bribe. Tragor took care of the rest."

His temper finally snapping, Ruog yanked the war axe from his belt. He leapt down from the dais, swinging a mighty, two-handed blow. Kurthak blocked it, the head of the axe notching the thick wood of his club. He shoved Ruog back, then lashed out himself. Ruog batted the attack aside with his own weapon.

Behind them, Tragor cut down a third warlord, then drove his sword through the belly of a fourth. He dodged a spear thrust, then yanked his blade free and stood ready, facing his last two opponents.

"I'll tear out your heart!" Ruog bellowed at Kurthak as axe met club again and again. "I'll rip it from your chest and eat it while it still beats in my hand!"

One of Tragor's foes swung a wicked, sickle-bladed

sword, scoring a cut across the champion's chest. Dark blood welled from the gash as Tragor returned the blow, slicing off the top of his assailant's head. The warlord stubbornly remained on his feet for a moments, blinking stupidly, before he toppled over sideways into the fire. A blossom of cinders erupted from the blaze.

By the dais, Kurthak ducked a clumsy swing, then lashed out at Ruog's legs. The hetman's iron greaves turned the blow aside, however, and Ruog's next attack nicked Kurthak's shoulder.

Tragor's last opponent swung a knobbed mace in both hands. Wounded, Tragor backed away from the whistling weapon, parrying only the blows he couldn't dodge. Laughing, the warlord drove him away from Kurthak and Ruog, so when Kurthak stumbled at last beneath the hetman's whirling axe, Tragor was too far away to help.

At that moment, Kurthak did something very strange. Reaching to his belt, he drew out a dagger as long as his arm and threw it behind him. It landed next to Grul's limp body.

As Kurthak tossed the knife, Ruog kicked him solidly in the belly. A great whoosh of air escaped the Black-Gazer's lungs, and he dropped his club as he fell. Roaring with triumphant laughter, Ruog loomed above his writhing, winded foe, and brought up his axe.

A shriek tore the air. Baloth, who had been watching the fight from beside Grul's corpse, scooped up the dagger Kurthak had thrown. Then he hurled himself at Ruog, who had been a heartbeat away from ordering his death only a minute before.

Ruog could only gape in bewilderment as the hairless ogre leapt upon him and drove the knife into his throat. They fell in a tangle, the axe forgotten, and Baloth stabbed Ruog again and again, until his arms were black with blood.

The warlords watched in mute shock. On the other side of the fire, Tragor's opponent glanced at the dais in astonishment. Tragor put five feet of steel through his chest.

By the time Kurthak and Tragor dragged Baloth off him,

Lord Ruog was unrecognizable. Baloth stared at Kurthak a moment, his eyes wild, then came to himself, dropping to one knee. He extended the gore-caked dagger, hilt-first, toward the Black-Gazer.

"My lord," he said.

Kurthak took the knife, grinned quickly at Tragor, then strode to the dais and sat upon the crude throne that had, until now, belonged to Lord Ruog.

"Hail the new hetman!" Tragor bellowed, kneeling beside Baloth.

One by one, the gathered warlords followed his example, until every ogre around the great, roaring fire knelt before Lord Kurthak the Black-Gazer.

Chapter 8

Brightdawn stumbled sideways, grabbing the railing before her to keep from losing her footing on the ship's pitching deck. Salt spray, surprisingly cold, splashed her as *Brinestrider* descended into a trough between waves. By the time it started to climb the next swell, Swiftraven was at her side, touching her arm with a steadying hand. With an embarrassed smile, she let him help her regain her balance.

"Lean on me, if you will," he offered.

She did, clutching his arm as the ship rolled under their feet.

Brinestrider hadn't been the largest or finest vessel in New Ports—it was a simple, square-sailed double-master—but her captain, a swarthy Ergothman named Kael Ar-Tam, had been the only man bound for the port of Ak-Thain who hadn't refused outright to take kender aboard.

"As long as the little squeakers stay out o' the way," he'd declared sourly, "I'll try to keep my boot out o' their backsides."

His misgivings, it turned out, had been misplaced—at least where Catt was concerned. The older kender had pitched in with the sailors from the start, proving particularly adept when it came to knot work. Catt knew more about ropes than even Captain Ar-Tam himself, and had taught the sailors several new, maddeningly complicated hitches that were strong as iron but could come apart at the slightest touch in the right place. That, and the vast number of sea chanteys she knew, had quickly endeared her to *Brinestrider*'s crew.

Which was the main reason they hadn't yet killed Kronn. If Catt was a boon to the sailors, her brother was the bane of their existence. They had scarcely cleared the harbor before he'd been caught poking around the hold, trying to see what was inside the great crates and barrels the ship was hauling. Only Riverwind and Catt's pleas, and a few extra steel coins, had kept Captain Ar-Tam from heaving Kronn overboard. Since then, in the four days they had sailed the waves of the New Sea, Kronn had brought down two sails, taken the wheel when the helmsman wasn't looking, and pulled countless ropes he shouldn't have. Once, he'd uncleated a single halyard, and the ship had nearly capsized. Each time his excuse was the same. "I only wanted to see how it works."

Brightdawn glanced up and down the deck, looking for the kender, but couldn't see him anywhere. She wasn't sure if that was a good thing.

Brinestrider crested the wave and started to descend its other side. Brightdawn clutched Swiftraven, but the young warrior's footing was no more sure than hers; he staggered as the deck shifted, and both of them nearly fell. A nearby sailor laughed as the Plainsfolk lurched about, and Swiftraven flushed with anger, glaring at the dusky-skinned mariner.

"Be easy," Brightdawn murmured. "Mind your temper."

Shaking his head, Swiftraven jerked free of Brightdawn's grasp. He continued to stare at the sailor, though the man had turned his back and blithely returned to his work. "I'd like to see him try to shoot a bow while riding at full gallop," the young Plainsman growled.

"The horses are in the hold," Brightdawn countered. "Shall I bring yours up so you can show off?"

He looked at her, then saw the sparkle in her eyes and laughed in spite of himself. He slid his arm about her waist. "I'm sorry," he said, and kissed the nape of her neck. "I just miss having solid ground beneath my feet."

"So do I," Brightdawn agreed. "At least we're not seasick, though, like Father is." She nodded toward the stern of the ship, where Riverwind and Kael were talking together. The Plainsman was stooped and ashen-faced. He had been feeling ill since the second day of their voyage but had refused when the captain advised him to go below and lie down. Instead, though each sway of the deck brought a spasm of nausea to his face, Riverwind bore it out.

The deck shifted again, and again Brightdawn stumbled, knocking Swiftraven against the railing.

"Damn it," the young warrior grunted irritably.

"Watch yourself there," said a voice at their elbows.

The Plainsfolk looked down. Catt had come up, and was watching them seriously. She stood still, apparently unaffected by the pitching of the boat. Swiftraven scowled as he fought to regain his footing.

"Keep that up," the kender observed, "and you'll see the water much closer than you'd like." She grinned, not unkindly. "I can tell you what you're doing wrong, if you want."

"We don't need—" Swiftraven started to say.

Brightdawn dug her elbow into his stomach. "We'd like that very much," she interrupted. She shot Swiftraven a look, and the young warrior rolled his eyes.

For a moment, Catt regarded Swiftraven, then she shrugged. "Well," she said, "your big problem is you're locking your knees. You'll never get your sea legs that way. Watch Captain Ar-Tam." She gestured down the deck. Kael was striding forward now, barking orders to his men. The sailors scrambled to obey. "See how he walks, like he's bowlegged? That's not just because the food on this tub's so bad, you know. A sailor's got to roll with the waves, not fight them like you're doing, or he'll spend as much time on his back as on his feet. Here—like this." She demonstrated, shifting her weight as the deck rocked. "There. Now you try."

Brightdawn followed Catt's example, bending her knees and planting her feet apart. "How do you know so much about ships?" she asked.

"Oh, I served aboard a merchant ship for a few years when I was younger," the kender answered. "Watch, now. Here it comes."

When the ship pitched again Brightdawn still stumbled, but not as badly, and on the next sway she didn't lose her balance at all. She grinned at the kender.

"That's it!" Catt said, immensely pleased. "You're getting it."

Suddenly *Brinestrider* skipped over a series of low, choppy waves. Following the kender's lead, Brightdawn rode them out. Swiftraven, however, finally lost his balance and fell on his rear. His face turned bright red as sailors all over the ship laughed and pointed.

Catt offered her hand. "Get up," she said. "Try again—"

"Get away from me!" he snapped, his face twisting into a snarl. Catt pulled her hand back as if he'd stung her. With some difficulty, he pushed himself to his feet. "The only way you can help, kender, is to stay away from me."

"Swiftraven!" Brightdawn exclaimed, reaching for his arm. He jerked away from her grasp and stomped down the deck, toward the stern.

Catt watched him go. "Grumpy sort of fellow."

"He's just proud," Brightdawn replied.

Catt continued to frown at Swiftraven's back as the young Plainsman stumbled toward Riverwind and Kael. "I don't think he shares your father's approval of kender."

Brightdawn chewed her lip. "He doesn't think we should be helping you. He wouldn't say that in front of Father, of course," she added quickly, "but he thinks it's foolish to go to Kendermore."

"What about you?"

"Me?" Brightdawn asked, startled. "I-I don't—"

"That's okay," Catt cut in. "Many of our people thought it was foolish of Paxina to ask the help of humans. 'Humans make a mess of everything,' they said. Lucky thing we found someone like your father."

Suddenly curses sounded above them—oaths so vile, only a sailor could utter them. Brightdawn followed Catt's glance up the mainmast. Kronn had climbed high into the rigging and somehow gotten himself and the ship's dwarven first mate snarled among the ropes. The dwarf was swearing at the top of his scratchy voice as he tried to untangle himself.

"Not again!" snapped Captain Ar-Tam, storming up the

deck. "Get down from there, you little squeaker, or I swear I'll cut your—"

"It's all right, Captain," Catt said. "I'll get my brother down." She scrambled nimbly up the rigging and quickly worked both her brother and the mate loose. The dwarf made a wild grab for Kronn, who jumped out of the way, leaping from one rope to another with glee, apparently unconcerned that he was thirty feet above the deck of a rocking boat. "Kronn!" Catt snapped. "Stop with this game!"

"Oh, we've got games he can play," the red-faced dwarf growled as Kronn and Catt descended the ropes. "There's keelhaul-the-kender, for one. And catch-the-anchor—and guess who gets to go first."

"Who?" Kronn asked.

The dwarf made a rude gesture.

At length, the two kender made their way back to the deck. As soon as they were both down, Catt cuffed Kronn on the back of his head.

"Ow!" he exclaimed. "What did you do that for?"

"Listen to me, Kronn," Catt said. "You've got to stay out of trouble. Captain Ar-Tam is tempted to throw you to the sharks."

Kronn's eyebrows shot up excitedly. "Sharks? In these waters?"

Catt nodded gravely. "Bull sharks, to be exact. Big enough to swallow you whole—if you're lucky."

"I'd love to catch a glimpse of one," Kronn said, his brow furrowed with thought. "Father told me once that Uncle Trapspringer got attacked by sharks, you know. Or maybe it was a giant squid. Anyway, it happened when he was on his way back home after winning the minotaurs' arena tourney on Kothas."

Catt raised a skeptical eyebrow. "Attacked by sharks?"

"Or a giant squid, I said," Kronn noted. "Anyway, he couldn't use his hoopak underwater, but fortunately he had a brainstorm. . . ."

"Let's go talk to Father," Brightdawn interjected. "He'll be wanting to plan our route after we reach Ak-Thain."

Kronn gave his sister a look.

She nodded. "Let's."

"Great!" Kronn exclaimed. "Come on. I've been looking for a chance to show off my maps."

He ran off toward the stern, where Riverwind stood with Kael and Swiftraven. Catt watched him go, then looked up at Brightdawn, her mouth crooking into a wry half-grin. "Boys," she said.

Laughing, Brightdawn started aft with the kender to join the others. The boat rolled under their feet as they walked, but no longer did she notice.

* * * * *

"Oh, no," Swiftraven groaned softly.

Riverwind had been looking back over the rail, at *Brinestrider*'s foam-speckled wake, which stretched out behind them toward the sea-gray horizon. Abruptly he straightened and turned, following the young warrior's gaze. He frowned when his eyes fell upon Kronn, who was walking cheerily toward them. Glancing at Swiftraven, he saw the young man's lip curl. Riverwind's brow furrowed. "Is something wrong, boy?" he asked.

Swiftraven started, then quickly shook his head, his cheeks burning red. "No, my chief."

It was a lie, and Riverwind knew it, but he let it pass. Swiftraven was uncomfortable around the kender, but now wasn't the time to confront him about it. He watched Kronn approach, Catt and Brightdawn coming up behind him.

"Kronn's come back here to help you, Riverwind. Haven't you, Kronn?" said Catt.

Kronn beamed at the old Plainsman. "That's right," he declared. "I've come to show you my maps. It's a long way to Kendermore, even after we reach Ak-Thain."

"Kendermore?" Captain Ar-Tam asked, incredulous. "You're going there? What in Habbakuk's name for?"

"We're having some problems with a dragon back home," Kronn replied.

Kael barked a harsh laugh, then checked himself, glancing at the old Plainsman. "Don't tell me he's serious," he said.

"He is," Riverwind stated, drawing himself up proudly so he towered over the captain. His face, though still pale from nausea, grew stern and severe. "We're going east to help the kender."

"You're mad, then," Kael said firmly. "No sane man would leave his home and kin and travel across Ansalon, just to help a bunch of bloody kender."

"No offense intended, I'm sure," Catt interjected, bristling.

Kael said nothing, smiling unpleasantly.

"What I choose to do is of no concern to you, Captain," Riverwind said. He turned away, striding purposefully toward the hatch that led down into *Brinestrider*'s hold. "Come on, Kronn. We have the rest of our journey to plan."

* * * * *

The hold was dim, lit by a single lantern that swung from the ceiling, in time with the creaking of the hull. A strange smell hung in the air, mixing salt and stale sweat with the scents of spices and wine, remnants of cargoes the ship had carried before.

Riverwind paused at the lamp, twisting its key until its light was bright enough to read by, then led the way to a broad table near the fore of the ship. He shoved aside the dirty bowls and playing cards the sailors had left on it.

The kender unslung a large, overstuffed pack from his shoulder. As Catt, Brightdawn, and Swiftraven gathered around the table, Kronn plopped the pouch down and began to root through it. It was stuffed almost to bursting with maps of all shapes and sizes, from vellum charts illuminated in gold leaf and precious inks to tattered scraps of rag paper whose markings were almost unreadable.

"These aren't all mine, in case you're interested," Kronn declared. "That is, they're mine now, but a lot of them used to belong to my father. This isn't even his whole collection, either. You see, the strangest thing happened in Kendermore at the reading of the will. A bunch of his maps just sort of disappeared. So did a lot of his other possessions. It was most peculiar."

Swiftraven snorted derisively, but Brightdawn cut in before Kronn could respond. "I've heard stories about Kronin," she said. "Your father sounded like quite a fighter."

"He was," Kronn agreed proudly.

"There's something I always wanted to know, though," Brightdawn continued. "There's all sorts of stories about how he killed Lord Toede, back during the War of the Lance. Which one of them is true?"

Kronn exchanged glances with Catt, then shrugged and returned to rustling through his pouch. "Beats me."

"But certainly you must know the truth," Brightdawn ventured. "You're his son, after all."

"You know, that would make sense, especially to a human," Kronn agreed. "Unfortunately, I happened to be away from home when it all happened. I—we . . . Catt was with me—had gone to the slave markets at Trigol—"

"It was Ak-Krol," Catt interrupted. "Trigol was earlier in the war."

Kronn hesitated in mid-rustle, frowning. "Was it? I thought we went to Ak-Krol first, then Trigol. Remember, at Ak-Krol we had that little problem when the lighthouse mirror fell into my pouch, and that dragonarmy galleon crashed and sank? All because the lighthouse-keeper couldn't keep better track of his things . . ."

"That was Trigol," Catt said. "Ak-Krol was toward the end of the war."

Kronn's frown deepened. "I don't think so."

"Anyway," Swiftraven cut in impatiently, "wherever it was, you were there for some reason."

"Eh? Oh. Right," Kronn said. "Well, I suppose the 'reason' was to organize a revolt. Although it all just kind of happened. That was quite a bit of fun, wasn't it, Catt?"

Catt nodded. "We couldn't wait to hear what that lump

Toede would say about us freeing all those slaves."

"When we got home, though, Toede was already dead," Kronn said. "Which was a bit of a disappointment. My father told us all about it. Of course we had our own heroic story to tell. So maybe we didn't pay as much attention as we should have. I forget the details."

"He told it various ways," Catt offered.

"So did other folk, not only kender. Bards and such."

"After a while, all the versions just melted together in my mind," said Kronn. "I sure remember Trigol, though."

"Ak-Krol," insisted Catt.

The Plainsfolk nodded patiently. After a moment Kronn pulled out a map scrawled on what looked like lizard skin and turned it this way and that, trying to make it out in the lamplight. Then he tucked it away again, flipped past a few more maps, and stopped.

"Ah! Here we go."

With a flourish, he produced a sheaf of brittle, yellowed parchment from his pouch. He unfolded it with great care and spread it out across the table. Scrawled on it in smudged charcoal was a crude map of the eastern half of Ansalon.

"Is this accurate?" Riverwind asked, leaning forward.

Kronn shrugged. "More or less."

"It looks kind of old," Brightdawn noted. "I can't even find Ak-Thain on it."

"Oh, that's because it wasn't called Ak-Thain when the map was made," Kronn said. "It used to be an ogre town called Thulkorr. Here it is." He stabbed a finger down on a river mouth on the eastern coast of the New Sea. "The ogres there were all wiped out during the Chaos War—daemon warriors got them, from what I gather. Men from Khur took it over afterward and changed the name. Darned nuisance from a map-lover's point of view."

Riverwind squinted at the map, then shook his head. "This is old. It says the area we're heading toward is rife with the Green Dragonarmy. It's been years since anywhere's been rife with the dragonarmies."

"Hmmm." Kronn stroked his chin thoughtfully. "I suppose you're right."

"So where do we go from Ak-Thain?" Brightdawn asked, peering at the map.

"Oh, we just follow the Spice Road," Kronn said.

"I don't see that here," Riverwind said.

"That's because it's not on the map. It's new. The Khurmen set it up as a trade route to the west when they took over Thulkorr." Kronn peered at the Plainsman, his brow furrowing. "Don't worry, all the new roads are in my head."

Swiftraven groaned and began to rub his forehead.

"Where does this, uh, Spice Road lead?" Riverwind asked.

"Here," Kronn replied. He traced a snaking path east from Ak-Thain across the desert land of Khur. "If I remember right, and I very nearly always do, it should come out right here at Ak-Khurman. Strange, how so many Khurrish towns are Ak-Something, isn't it? I wonder what Ak- means?"

Riverwind examined Ak-Khurman, which was perched on the tip of a peninsula on the western coast of the Bay of Balifor. "Then our direction is clear enough," he said. "We'll cross the desert, then take another boat from Ak-Khurman across the bay to Port Balifor. From there, we can ride straight on to Kendermore. We should arrive in less than a month, well before winter."

"I hope that's in time," Catt said ruefully.

Kronn folded the map and clamped it in his teeth as he leafed through his map pouch, looking for its place. "Solamnia," he muttered around the parchment, "Estwilde, Qualinesti, Icewall, Thorbardin, Nordmaar, Balifor, Tarsis . . . ah, here it is. Ansalon, East." Smiling in satisfaction, he slid the map back into the case.

Brightdawn, having watched him sort through the maps, frowned in confusion. "Is there some sort of system to that?" she asked, nodding toward the pouch.

Kronn looked at her. "Of course there's a system," he said, a bit put out. "You don't think I'd keep my maps all willy-nilly, do you? I'd never find anything. I've sorted them alphabetically, I'll have you know."

"But," Brightdawn protested, "you've got Solamnia before Estwilde, and Nordmaar before Balifor. It's all out of order."

"I organized them by the last letter," Kronn said. "That way, I know where everything is, but someone who rifles through my bag when I'm not looking won't find what they're looking for very easily. You can't be too careful, with all the pickpockets out there, you know."

Swiftraven's mouth opened and closed, but no sound came out. Beside him, Riverwind chuckled, but his laughter quickly turned into a hacking cough, and soon the Plainsman was doubled over, fighting for breath.

"Father?" Brightdawn asked, concerned. She rested a hand on his heaving back. "Are you all right?"

Riverwind nodded. "Seasickness," he wheezed when he could find his voice. "That's all." He straightened up and swept his gaze across the others, all of whom were staring at him.

"Sure, seasickness," Catt said, smiling. "I have a little cough too." She coughed to demonstrate. Then, suddenly, she cocked an ear. "What's that?"

The others froze.

They heard it then. The sound of feet pounding on the deck had grown frantic. There was shouting, too, though it was impossible to make out what was being said.

Reflexively Swiftraven reached for his sabre and loosened it in its scabbard. The shouts were getting louder now. The ship began to lean, timbers groaning as it tacked sharply. A few copper coins, forgotten stakes from the sailors' card game, rolled off the table and clattered across the floor.

Riverwind moved first, dashing toward the ladder that led up to the ship's deck. The hatch above him flew open before he could step on the first rung, though, and a spear of daylight stabbed down into the hold. "Out of the way!" shouted a voice. Riverwind leapt aside, and a sailor slid down the ladder, landing beside him with a thump.

"What's going on?" Brightdawn asked.

The sailor didn't stop to answer; pale with fear, he fumbled with a ring of keys as he ran toward a locked chest near the door to the officers' cabins.

"What is it?" Catt demanded. "Why are we turning?"

"Pirates! It's *Red Reaver*," the man answered. He had the chest open now, and the others could see it was a weapons locker. He started pulling out cutlasses and cudgels. "Just sighted her dead ahead, making straight for us. Cap'n Ar-Tam wants the lot o' ye and your swords up on deck."

Chapter 9

Above decks, it was as if Chaos himself had returned. *Brinestrider*'s crew ran everywhere, securing everything that wasn't already firmly tied down. Captain Ar-Tam and the helmsman, a young Solamnian lad, were both hauling on the wheel with all their might, muscles standing out on their necks as they fought to bring the broad, ungainly ship about. *Brinestrider* leaned over farther and farther as she came about.

"Mind your heads!" Kael roared.

Riverwind ducked as he emerged from the hold, and the beam swung wildly overhead, barely a hand's-breadth above him. The ship's blue sails fluttered for a moment, then snapped suddenly as the wind filled them. With a groan of straining timbers, *Brinestrider* lurched forward, running back the way it had come. Slowly, as if weary from the effort, it began to right itself.

As soon as the ship finished tacking, Captain Ar-Tam let go of the wheel and started forward from the helm. He glanced at the sails, swore viciously, then pointed at Swiftraven, who had come up the ladder with Brightdawn. "You, boy! Go help my men let out the mainsail! We need all the wind we can catch!"

Swiftraven took a step toward the sailors, then stopped and looked at Riverwind, his eyes questioning.

"Go," Riverwind commanded, waving his hand. As Swiftraven ran to help the crew haul on the halyards, Riverwind turned to Kael. "What are you carrying that would interest a pirate ship?" he asked.

The captain shoved past him, snarling a curse, but

Riverwind followed him toward the ship's prow. Spray washed over the bow as *Brinestrider* leapt across the choppy waves.

"What's your cargo?" Riverwind repeated.

Kael glared at him. "What business is that of your'n?"

"If there are pirates after us, I want to know why." The old Plainsman caught Kael's arm as the captain tried to walk away. "You need my people's swords. Tell me what we're defending."

"Grain!" Kael snapped. "I'm not carrying silver or spices, Plainsman—just crates of grain and a few tuns of wine. The *Reaver*'s dogs might take the drink, but if they open those crates below and see nothing but bloody barley, they won't be pleased. They'll want something for their trouble, and they ain't above taking a few prisoners to sell at the slave markets in Sanction. They'll get a good price for my crew and the boy—but the real prize will be your daughter there." He nodded toward Brightdawn, who had joined Swiftraven at his rope. "A lass as fair as her will fetch a pretty price on the block . . . provided the pirates don't use her up first themselves, of course."

Riverwind glowered at the captain, then turned away and hurried aftward. The man who had gone below to fetch weapons came up through the hatch and began to pass out blades and clubs to his mates; many of the sailors also seized belaying pins and gaff hooks from racks on the masts and gunwales, looping them into their belts and muttering angry oaths.

From the stern Riverwind saw *Red Reaver* not far off. She was a tall, fast warship with deep crimson sails. Atop her mainmast, he could make out a black flag emblazoned with a white scythe. Though *Brinestrider* was running hard, moving faster with every heartbeat, the *Reaver* was gaining on them steadily, cutting through the water like an arrow. Dark shapes swarmed over her decks and crowded against the rails, waving wicked swords in the air. The pirates' war cries were faint, but they grew louder every moment.

"She's gaining on us," Brightdawn noted, joining her father at the rail. She rubbed her hands, which were red with rope burn. "I doubt we can outrun them."

"Bloody right we can't," snapped the helmsman, glancing nervously at the *Reaver*. "*Brinestrider*'s a stout one, but we ain't meant to move so quick. She'll be on us right soon—Cap'n only brought us about to buy us time." He spat vehemently on the deck. "You'd better be good with that sword there, old man."

With all the cutlasses handed out, the sailor who'd brought them up from the hold ran to the hatch and slid down the ladder again, disappearing from sight. Less than a minute later, he scrambled back up, carrying crossbows and quivers of bolts. He handed the weapons to four sailors, who ran to the stern and began to cock the heavy weapons. As they fitted quarrels in place, Captain Ar-Tam hauled on Swiftraven's arm, dragging him toward the stern.

"String up your bow, lad," Kael ordered, shoving the young warrior into line with the crossbowmen. He turned to Riverwind. "You, too, old man. Let's put a few of the bastards down before they get too close."

As Swiftraven and Riverwind bent their bows and nocked arrows onto the strings, Brightdawn continued to peer at their pursuers. "How many of them are there?" she asked.

Kael squinted at the *Reaver*, then shook his head. "Dunno. Two, maybe three dozen."

"Three dozen!" Swiftraven exclaimed, shocked.

"Against how many?" Brightdawn asked

"We got twenty crew, countin' meself," the captain answered. "Plus the three o' ye, an' the two kender."

"The kender!" Brightdawn yelped. She cast about, looking up the deck toward the ship's leaping prow. "Where did Kronn and Catt go?"

"I didn't see them come up with us," Swiftraven said, his eyes fast on the onrushing *Reaver*. He gauged the distance and the wind, waiting for the ship to get into range. "I think they stayed below."

"Bloody cowards, is what they are!" snapped Kael.

"Mind your tongue," Riverwind warned. "Kender can

be many things, but they're not cowards. They don't know fear."

"Well, if they're so fearless then why in the Abyss aren't they up here?" the captain shot back.

Riverwind glanced at the hatch, his brow furrowing, but said nothing.

Just then, one of the crossbowmen, overeager to draw first blood, raised his weapon and fired. His quarrel soared high, its steel head shining in the sunlight, but it fell quickly, splashing down into the water a hundred yards in front of the *Reaver*. Mocking laughter rang out from the pirate ship.

"Hold your fire, lackwit!" Kael snarled. "If ye put another bolt in the water, ye're goin' in after it! Watch the Plainsmen, if you ain't got the sense to figure out when the *Reaver*'s in range. They know what they're doing."

"Swiftraven's the best archer in Qué-Teh," Brightdawn declared proudly.

"Hush, Brightdawn," the young warrior muttered.

"What for?" She turned to Kael. "He can shoot a sparrow out of the air at two hundred paces."

"The wind's against us here," Swiftraven returned, "and sparrows don't shoot back." He nodded toward the *Reaver*. Several crossbowmen stood ready at her bow.

"Get some men back here with shields, Captain," Riverwind said. "We'll need the cover, and so will your helmsman."

Kael hesitated, regarding the *Reaver* with a worried eye, then stomped up the deck, shouting to his crew. Within a minute, half a dozen sailors crowded the stern, holding up crude, wooden shields.

The *Reaver* glided closer. "Wait," Swiftraven muttered, his forehead creased with concentration. "Wait. . . ."

"Come on," Kael grumbled, paling at how close the pirate ship was.

"Be still!" Riverwind snapped, his grip tightening on his bowstring.

"Wait," Swiftraven repeated. "Wait . . . now." He raised his bow, pulled the string back to his cheek, and loosed his arrow. Riverwind fired a heartbeat later.

The two arrows dropped into the midst of the pirates, and a grunt of pain sounded across the water as a man fell. The crew of *Brinestrider* cheered, and Swiftraven grinned as he fired his second shot. Riverwind followed suit; then the crossbowmen joined in, peppering the *Reaver*'s deck with quarrels. Three more pirates went down, their bodies feathered.

Then the pirates returned fire.

"Shields!" Riverwind yelled as the snap of crossbow strings sounded from *Red Reaver*. A volley of bolts soared from the pirate ship, and the sailors raised their shields to block them. Even so, one of *Brinestrider*'s crossbowmen cried out as a bolt pierced him, punching into his chest below his collarbone. He dropped his crossbow and slumped to his knees, staring dumbly at the shaft that quivered in his body. A moment later, he fell face forward and lay still, blood pooling around him.

A second bolt struck the deck next to Brightdawn, burying itself an inch deep in the wooden planks. She cried out in alarm, and Riverwind's next shot flew wide of the *Reaver* as he twisted to look at his daughter. "Move forward!" he shouted. "You'll only draw their fire back here. You too, Captain!"

"This is my ship!" Kael yelled back, furious. "I'm the one who gives the orders here—"

He gasped suddenly, seeing a glint of metal above him. He jumped aside as a bolt came down; it grazed his shoulder, drawing blood, then struck the deck where he had been standing.

"Move forward," he muttered, then glanced irritably at Brightdawn, who hadn't budged from where she stood. "You too!" he snapped, grabbing her arm and hauling her away from the stern.

The pirates scattered on *Red Reaver*'s deck, shouting curses as Riverwind, Swiftraven, and the crossbowmen continued to rain shafts down on them, but the ship did not veer from its course. She continued to slice through the waves, now a hundred yards off *Brinestrider*'s stern, now eighty, now fifty. Swiftraven and Riverwind fired shot after shot, but the pirates had shield men, too. Even so, by the time the Plainsmen were on their last arrows—and the *Reaver* was only twenty yards away—nine pirates lay dead, and an equal number were wounded. Riverwind loosed his final shaft, but it missed its mark, sticking in the *Reaver*'s railing. Swiftraven's last arrow flew true, though, and hit one of the injured pirates in the eye. The man stumbled like a drunk for a moment, then pitched overboard and vanished into the churning sea.

Another one of *Brinestrider*'s crossbowmen fell, a quarrel lodged in his throat. Elsewhere on the ship, two of the shield men and three other sailors lay dead; another bolt knocked a man out of the rigging. He fell into the water and disappeared.

Red Reaver was only ten yards away. The sailors and pirates exchanged one more pair of volleys—one man on either side fell—then dropped their crossbows.

"Well shot," Riverwind told Swiftraven.

Swiftraven tossed his bow aside and jerked his sabre from its scabbard. "Not well enough," he grumbled in disgust.

Riverwind drew his own sword as he watched the distance between the ships dwindle to nothing. *Red Reaver* missed ramming *Brinestrider* by an arm's length, slipping up alongside her.

"Everyone to starboard!" Captain Ar-Tam yelled, running to the rail. "Prepare to be boarded! Get down from the rigging, you fools, and grab a blade!"

Her face pale, Brightdawn watched as the sailors rallied to Kael's call. She reached for her mace, but Riverwind caught her arm.

"I want you to go below," he said.

Stubbornly, she shook her head. "No. I'm staying up here."

Riverwind looked at her, his eyes pleading, but she refused to relent.

"Let her fight," Kael growled. "We need every arm we've got."

Riverwind slumped, defeated. He glared sourly at the captain, then grabbed Swiftraven and shoved him toward Brightdawn. "Watch her," he said. "Remember your Courting Quest."

Captain Ar-Tam waved toward the helmsman, who was still standing at the wheel, gripping it firmly with his right hand. The man's left arm hung limply, a crossbow bolt stuck in the shoulder. "Move away from there, you idiot!" Kael shouted. "Lash the damned wheel and get over here!"

The helmsman obeyed, looping a leather thong over one of the wheel's handles and fixing it in place. He pulled a belaying pin from his belt with his good hand and rushed forward, joining the mob of sailors who stood ready, glaring at the pirates scarcely five yards away.

"Too far to jump," Swiftraven noted. "How will they come across?"

"Boarding planks," Riverwind answered, pointing with the blade of his sabre. Several pirates stood at *Red Reaver*'s railing, holding broad wooden planks with iron spikes driven into either end.

The Plainsmen watched as the pirates raised the planks high into the air, then brought them down with a shout, slamming them into *Brinestrider*'s gunwale. The spikes drove deep into the ship's hull, bridging the gap between the ships. Several sailors hewed at the planks with their cutlasses, but the wood was tough, and they didn't have time to do more than carve off a few splinters before the pirates began to charge across.

The dwarf first mate was the first to die, his skull crushed by a boarder's cudgel. As he fell, he drove his blade through his attacker's thigh. The pirate staggered with a shout, and another sailor cut his throat. Two more men fell on either side as the pirates pressed forward, weapons glinting in the sunlight. Captain Ar-Tam slashed open a pirate's belly with his cutlass, dancing aside as the dying man made a last, feeble attempt to run him through.

Riverwind waded into the fray, sabre flashing. He traded blows with a pirate, their blades clashing against each other. Brightdawn followed him, but Swiftraven leapt in front of her, trying to keep her out of danger. His whirling sabre kept the pirates at bay.

For a minute or more, it seemed the sailors might hold the pirates off. Riverwind stabbed one raider through the heart. Swiftraven raked his blade across the stomach of a second. Kael cut off yet another pirate's sword hand, then cracked his cutlass's basket-hilt across his face. For every pirate who fell, however, another stepped forward to take his place, and *Brinestrider*'s crew began to falter. The wounded helmsman died, a bloody hole in his chest. Another sailor took a belaying pin across the side of his head and slumped senseless to the deck. A third crashed back, clutching at a deep wound in the base of his neck.

Captain Ar-Tam and Riverwind fought on, even as men fell all around them. Again and again, Brightdawn swung her mace, trying to join the battle, but every time Swiftraven interposed, shoving aside the pirate she had meant to attack.

"Let me fight!" she snarled.

Swiftraven shook his head stubbornly. Sweat poured down his face, mixing with blood from a gash a pirate's sword had opened on his cheek. He fought like a madman, facing two or more pirates at a time, always keeping himself between his love and those who would hurt her.

Then, at last, the sailors' flank collapsed, and the pirates surged over the ship's deck. In moments, the Plainsfolk and the surviving sailors found themselves encircled by their attackers, trapped in a ring of steel.

"Where in the Abyss are Kronn and Catt when all this is going on?" Swiftraven growled, batting aside a pirate's blade with his sabre.

"Bastards," Captain Ar-Tam snarled at the pirates. He had lost his cutlass, but held a dagger in each hand, poised and ready. "I swear, I'll die rather than—"

"That will be your choice."

The voice, low and coarse, belonged to a man who could be no one but the pirates' leader. He was enormous, standing taller even than Riverwind, with a chest as broad as two men standing side by side. His skin had a yellow-ish cast, and his face's flat, ugly features spoke of ogrish blood in his ancestry. He was clad in leather armor, and a heavy war hammer hung at his hip. He stood between the two ships, atop the boarding planks, his feet planted wide apart and his muscular arms folded across his chest. To either side of him stood a pirate with a loaded crossbow.

"You've put up a good fight, all of you," he said. "But the time for fighting has ended. I'd rather not have to kill the lot of you here and now. Surrender."

"And what?" Kael challenged. "Let you put us on the block in Sanction?"

"Perhaps." The half-ogre smiled, revealing a mouthful of brown, rotten teeth. "You're beaten, Captain. Half your crew are dead. Even with those barbarians' help, you can't win this fight. I'm offering you a chance."

"How merciful," Swiftraven snarled.

The half-ogre fixed the young warrior with a cold stare. "That one," he said. "The young barbarian. Shoot him."

Before anyone could move, one of the crossbowmen beside the half-ogre raised his weapon and fired. The bolt struck Swiftraven's shoulder, spun him around, and knocked him to the deck.

"No!" Brightdawn cried. Dropping her mace, she threw herself on top of Swiftraven. He moaned in pain, writhing on the deck and clutching at the shaft lodged in his arm. Acting quickly, she tore a strip off his tunic and pressed it to the bloody wound. Riverwind looked on, helpless.

"There, you see?" the half-ogre declared. "I am merciful. Now, if I have to command my other man to shoot anyone"—he gestured at the second crossbowman, who still stood with his weapon ready—"he will shoot to kill. Then my men will slaughter the rest of you—except the woman, of course. We'll keep her alive . . . for a while, at least. Now, I will say it one last time." The half-ogre's voice was thick with menace. "Throw down your weapons and surrender."

Stricken, Riverwind looked at his daughter and Swiftraven, then at the pirates who encircled them. He dropped his sword. It clattered loudly on the deck.

One by one, the surviving sailors—there were only six of them still standing, though some of the fallen were unconscious rather than dead—laid down their arms. Last of all, Kael Ar-Tam tossed his daggers aside.

The half-ogre smiled mirthlessly. "Good," he hissed.

At that, the pirates stepped forward, grabbing the sailors and binding their hands. As they wrenched his arms behind his back and wound strong jute cord around his wrists, Riverwind glanced at his daughter. Still kneeling over Swiftraven, she glanced back at him, her eyes filled with fear.

Desperately the old Plainsman looked about the deck. Where indeed were the kender to whom he had given his trust?

* * * * *

"Sounds like the fighting's stopped up there," Kronn said. He fingered his chapak's axe-blade, his eyes fixed on the ladder leading above decks.

"You don't suppose things worked out all right, do you?" Catt asked. She crouched beside him, in the shadows cast by a large stack of crates. "That they killed all the pirates, and don't need our help after all? That would be disappointing."

Kronn listened, then shook his head. "Too quiet up there."

Catt nodded. "So what's our plan?"

"Plan?" said Kronn. "The plan is to rescue them."

Catt made a face. "And how do you think we're going to manage that?"

"I'm working on that part."

Chapter 10

The pirates were busy gathering the dead — both friend and foe — and throwing them overboard. A handful stood guard over their prisoners, cutlasses ready. The survivors of the attack — the Plainsfolk, Captain Ar-Tam, and eight sailors — sat at the foot of the mizzenmast, hands bound behind their backs.

"These waters are infested with sharks. Did you know that?" the pirate captain asked them. He nodded toward his men, just as they heaved the dead helmsman over the rail. "All those bodies. All that blood in the water. It's bound to draw attention."

Brightdawn looked up from Swiftraven, who lay unconscious beside her. The quarrel was still embedded in his shoulder, and blood continued to seep slowly from the wound. "What are you going to do with us?" she asked.

"Ah, lass," the half-ogre replied, "what I do with the rest of these fools and what I do with you will be two quite different things."

"I thought you were slavers," Riverwind muttered.

"Oh, we're slavers, all right," the half-ogre said. "But I'm afraid our hold's a bit full right now. You're not the only ship we've waylaid since we last saw port, and we don't have room for any more slaves aboard the *Reaver*. So that doesn't leave us with much choice, does it?"

"Are you going to kill us?" Kael asked.

The half-ogre's smile broadened, revealing even more rotten teeth, "Let's just say we're going fishing," he rasped.

* * * * *

"What's happening now?" Kronn demanded, standing on tiptoe at the bottom of the ladder.

"Shhh," Catt hissed. "Keep your voice down." She stood above him, near the ladder's top, and peered out through the hatch. "Captain Ugly just said they were going to go fishing." She glanced down at Kronn and shrugged. "Don't ask me. The pirates are gathering them up and taking them over to where they've been dumping the bodies—except Brightdawn. They're bringing her over to him." She craned her neck, then winced. The pirates' coarse, brutish laughter rang out loudly. "He just kissed her. I don't think she liked it very much."

"I imagine not," Kronn agreed.

"Look out below," Catt whispered. Kronn stepped aside, and she slid down the ladder, landing with a thump beside him. "Come on. They're up at the bow. There's portholes up there. We can get a better view."

The two kender scrambled forward through the hold, dodging between barrels and crates, until they reached the crew's sleeping quarters. They threaded their way among the bunks, coming to a halt at a pair of portholes. Catt tried to peer through one, standing on her toes and craning her neck, then stopped and shook her head. "Too high," she said. "You'll have to give me a boost."

Kronn knelt down, and she climbed nimbly onto his shoulders. Grunting with the effort, he straightened back up again. "Branchala bite me, you're heavy," he groaned.

"Keep still," Catt returned. She leaned forward, peering out through the porthole. "That's better. I can see pretty good now."

"What's going on?"

"Shhh. It looks like they're setting up some kind of block-and-tackle," Catt noted. She shifted on Kronn's shoulders, looking down toward the water, and caught her breath. "Reorx's beard," she swore.

"What?"

"Sharks. The dead bodies must have drawn them, like

Captain Ugly said."

She shifted again, looking up. "They're looping a rope over the block-and-tackle, and—oh—oh, no!"

Kronn glared up at her. "Oh, no—what?"

Catt didn't answer. She simply stared out through the porthole, her eyes wide. Listening, Kronn could hear a voice, taut with panic, from the deck above. "No!" the voice called. "You bastards! You can't do this!"

"Who's that?" Kronn asked.

"One of the sailors," Catt replied. "He's on the end of the rope."

"Stop!" cried the voice from above. "No!"

Suddenly, something fell past the porthole. There was a splash, then laughter from above and screaming from below. Catt looked down toward the water. "Great Fizban's ghost," she swore. "They're dragging him through the water, like—like bait. Dipping him in and out. I think he's—"

A cry of agony tore through the air. Startled, Catt stiffened, pushing away from the porthole. Kronn stumbled back, then the two kender fell in a heap.

"What happened?" Kronn asked, straightening himself up.

It was a moment before Catt found her voice. When she did, it was quiet and small. "Shark got him," she replied, leaning against a bunk and breathing heavily.

"We've got to do something quick!"

"Like what?"

"Let me think," Kronn answered. He tugged on his cheek braids, pondering, then snapped his fingers. "All the pirates are over here on *Brinestrider*?"

"Yup."

"All right, then," Kronn said. "If they're going to board our ship, we'll just board theirs." He stood up and hurried to the starboard portholes. When he got there, he shrugged off his pouches, then turned to motion to Catt. "Come on. My turn for a boost."

* * * * *

The sailor's screaming carried on until the other prisoners were on the verge of tears. The rope threaded through the block-and-tackle went taut, and it took six pirates, hauling with all their might, to resist the pull on the other end. The rest of the raiders lined up along the gunwale, peering over the edge. They laughed and cheered as the sharks tore the sailor apart below.

"What do you want from us?" Riverwind demanded, a strain in his voice.

"Want?" the half-ogre asked. "I think you're taking this the wrong way, old man. We just want to kill you. Is it wrong that we have fun doing it?"

Brightdawn began to sob.

Below, the screams changed to a guttural, choking sound, then quickly faded away. Suddenly the rope went slack; the six pirates hauling on it stumbled back, then reeled it in. It ended in a frayed stub, soaked red with blood.

"Good," the half-ogre declared. "Next!"

The pirates picked a second victim—a boy of perhaps sixteen summers, whose beard was still patchy and soft— and dragged him to the block and tackle. He kicked as they tied the frayed end of the rope to the cord binding his hands. Laughing, the pirates shoved him overboard. After a few moments, the rope went taut again.

Swiftraven groaned softly. He had regained consciousness, though his wound had left him weak and faint. "My chief," he moaned.

Riverwind glanced around, to see if any of the pirates had heard, then bent over the young warrior. "What is it?" he asked.

"I'm sorry," Swiftraven moaned. "I failed you—my Courting Quest. I didn't . . . I didn't protect Brightdawn."

Riverwind shook his head. "You did all you could."

Swiftraven shook his head bitterly. "But it wasn't enough," he said. Below, the young sailor began to scream.

* * * * *

Catt had her hands locked around Kronn's ankles, and her brother was hanging outside the side of the ship upside down by his knees. Beneath him, below his dangling ponytail, the water churned into foam between *Brinestrider* and *Red Reaver*. He paused a moment to catch his breath, then unslung his chapak from his back. "All right," he muttered. "Now for the hard part."

Being a kender weapon, the chapak was much more than a simple axe. It had more uses than a dog has fleas, and one of those was as a grappling hook. Its hollow iron-wood haft held a length of thin but strong silk rope. Carefully, Kronn unscrewed the cap from the butt of the weapon's haft and let the rope spool out. He grabbed one end of the line and tied the other to the axe. Then he swung the chapak a few times, and hurled it at *Red Reaver*.

The throw was good. The axe clattered onto the pirate ship's deck and caught firmly on the gunwale when he tried to reel it back in. Smiling in satisfaction, Kronn pulled the rope taut. "All right, Catt," he said. "Let me go."

She did, and he fell out of the porthole. He swung out and down, hitting the *Reaver*'s hull like a sack of potatoes. His grip on the rope slipped, and by the time he grabbed it tight again, he'd slid down until his legs were trailing through the water.

"Well," he wheezed, wondering if he'd bruised any ribs, "that was fun. Now, up we go." Hand over hand, he began to pull himself up the rope. He was nearly out of the water when he saw the fin.

It appeared near the sterns of the two ships, cutting between them with breathtaking speed. For a heartbeat, Kronn could only stare at it, amazed; then he started to climb again, faster then before.

The fin vanished under the water, disappearing in an eye blink. Kronn groped upward, his feet splashing through the waves. His hands burned as he pulled himself up the rope. His arms felt ready to pop out of their sockets.

His clutching fingers had just brushed the gunwale

when the water below him turned into an explosion of foam. Glancing down, he saw the shark's head burst from the water with just as many sharp teeth as he'd imagined. He looked into its empty, black eyes, then—with a surge of energy he didn't even know he had—he hurled himself up and over the gunwale, onto the deck of *Red Reaver*.

"Teeth . . ." he mumbled, lying on his back and gasping for breath. For a moment, all he could see was the wide, gaping maw, rushing up at his dangling legs. Then he shook his head. Even from here, he could hear the poor sailor screaming on *Brinestrider*'s far side.

He sat up, looking around as he stuffed the rope back into the chapak's haft and stuck the cap back on the end. Yes, he was alone over here. He glanced at *Brinestrider* and nodded in satisfaction. None of the pirates had seen him. They were all too busy watching the gruesome show.

The sailor's screaming was beginning to falter.

"Not much time," he grunted, rising to his feet. He looked wildly up and down *Red Reaver*'s deck, spotted the hatch leading belowdecks, and ran for it. When he reached it, he leapt onto the ladder and slid down into the pirate ship's hold.

What he saw there stole his breath away. Belowdecks, the *Reaver* was crammed with riches of all kinds—silver and pearls, bolts of silk and urns of rare spices. He stared at it all, his mouth hanging open, then shook his head again.

"Get a hold of yourself, Thistleknot," he muttered.

He pushed his way past the treasure—pocketing a few loose strings of pearls as he passed—and started to search the hold. Catt had heard Captain Ugly talking about how many slaves the pirates had in their ship.

"Hello!" he called, moving toward the ship's stern. "Anyone here?" He passed the pirates' bunks, then heard a sound, coming from ahead of him.

Voices.

"Help us!" they cried. "In here!"

There was a door at the back of the bunkroom. He ran to it and pushed it open, revealing a large cabin at the very back of the hold. It was a supply room, littered with food, rum, rope, sailcloth, and small barrels of pitch for sealing the hull. There was also a weapons chest, like the one aboard *Brinestrider*. It still held a dozen or so cutlasses.

He ignored all of these, however, moving quickly to a locked iron grate in the floor. The voices came from it.

"Help!" they cried. "Get us out of here!"

Kronn knelt by the grate and peered inside. Below him were people—dozens of them, gaunt and pale from hunger. They stared up at him silently, their eyes pleading. Hands reached toward the grate, fingers groping between the bars.

Kronn examined the lock, reached into a small purse he wore at his belt, and pulled out a long, slender lockpick. "Don't worry," he told the slaves. "I'm going to let you out. But once you're free, I'm going to need you to give me a little help. All right?"

* * * * *

Down in the crimson surf, the young sailor's screaming was cut off by a terrible, rending sound. For a second time the rope became taut, then went limp. The pirates reeled it in. Something still hung from its end, and they cut it loose and threw it overboard again. Brightdawn caught a glimpse of fingers before it disappeared from sight, and she choked with nausea, trying to look away.

The half-ogre, however, grabbed her by the hair and shook her. "No, you don't," he told her. "You're watching this, girl." With his free hand, he waved to his men. "Tie the spirited youngster up."

"You want me to open him up?" asked a pirate with a gaff. His eyes glinted unpleasantly as his fellows fastened Swiftraven to the rope.

The half-ogre laughed. "Be patient, Hurth. Wait till he's hung up first. We want the blood in the water, not all over the deck."

"Let him go!" Riverwind roared as the pirates shoved Swiftraven toward the gunwale. He started toward them, but stopped when a blade pressed against his throat.

"I'm sorry, my chief," Swiftraven moaned from beside the railing. "The Courting Quest—"

The pirates gave a great pull at the rope, and his words cut off in a cry of pain as he jerked up off the deck. He rose four feet into the air, the rope lifting him by his arms. The quarrel in his shoulder gouged deeper into his flesh as he swung slowly above the water. The dark shapes of the sharks circled beneath him, waiting with predatory patience.

"Brightdawn," he moaned.

She looked at him, her eyes gleaming. "Please put him down," she murmured. Her voice broke, and she coughed raggedly. "I'll do whatever you want."

"Yes," the half-ogre hissed. "You will." He bent forward, his tongue brushing her ear, then nodded toward Swiftraven. "Go ahead, Hurth."

The glint in the gaff-wielder's eyes became a horrible blaze. He stepped toward Swiftraven, raising the hook, and pressed the point against the young warrior's belly, just below his breastbone. "This is going to hurt," he breathed. "Now hold st—"

Suddenly, seemingly out of nowhere, a fist-sized stone shot through the air. It struck Hurth in the side of the head with a wet smack. The gaff fell from the pirate's suddenly nerveless hand, hit the deck, and bounced overboard. Hurth's knees buckled and he crumpled in a lifeless heap.

A stunned silence fell over *Brinestrider*. Everyone— pirates, sailors and Plainsfolk—turned to look down the length of the ship, toward the stern. A female kender stood at the hatch, hoopak in hand. There was already a second stone in its pouch.

"Reel him back in," Catt said, gesturing toward Swiftraven with her hoopak. "And hurry up."

A strange sound rose, then—a dull roar of vengeful hate, coming from *Red Reaver*. They came out of the pirate ship's hold, pale and ragged, scrawny and battered, a tide of near-naked men bearing blades and clubs. Shrieking with bestial rage, they rushed toward the boarding planks, then surged aboard *Brinestrider*.

Kronn was in the front of the mob, chapak in hand, gemstones and steel coins falling from his overstuffed pockets. Behind him, several slaves were pouring pitch over the *Reaver*'s deck and setting it alight. Black, oily smoke started to rise from the ship.

It had all happened so fast, so suddenly, that the pirates' captain could only watch the charging slaves with open, dumbfounded shock. Finally he shoved Brightdawn away from him—she tripped over a coil of rope and stumbled to her knees—and jerked the massive hammer from his belt. "Attack!" he shouted.

His call galvanized the stunned pirates. They turned toward the boarding planks, then charged toward the slaves, cutlasses held high. The men who held the rope from which Swiftraven hung simply let go; the young warrior dropped over the edge with a shout, followed by a loud splash.

The pirate who held the cutlass to Riverwind's throat had lowered his blade without thinking, gawking as his fellows ran to intercept the attacking slaves. It was all the opportunity the old Plainsman needed. His foot lashed out, slamming against the side of the pirate's knee. Bone cracked, and the man fell, sobbing in pain and clutching his ruined leg. Riverwind kicked him a second time, in the head, and the man fell still.

His muscled arms bulging, Riverwind strained against his bonds with all his strength. The jute cord around his wrists snapped, and he dashed to Swiftraven's rope, grabbing it before it could spool away. He hauled on the rope, slowly reeling it in; moments later, Kael Ar-Tam and two of the sailors burst their bonds and joined him.

The escaped slaves smashed into the pirates, hacking viciously with cutlasses and cudgels. Driven by rage, they drove back their former captors, cutting them down without mercy. Kronn buried his chapak's axe head in a pirate's side, then jerked it free as the man staggered into the railing and fell overboard. Catt jabbed the metal-shod tip of her hoopak at a pirate's throat, then leaped aside as he swung back at her with his sword. A slave buried his cutlass in the pirate's ribs.

The half-ogre captain shoved his way past his faltering men, his warhammer singing through the air. A slave fell beneath the weapon, then another, and then a third. The half-ogre roared with fury.

Then, directly behind him, a scream cut through the din of battle. The half-ogre glanced over his shoulder, and his eyes widened in surprise as he saw the steel head of a mace swinging toward his face. He opened his mouth to cry out, but the mace struck before he could make a sound, and his world vanished in an explosion of red mist. He fell, groping at what had once been his face.

Brightdawn stared at his twitching body, seething with fury, then hit him again. He jerked one last time, then stopped moving for good. Brightdawn stumbled back, her mace dripping blood.

Riverwind and the sailors were trying to reel in Swiftraven. At last, the young warrior surfaced, unconscious and bleeding afresh from a short gash on his leg. The sailors grabbed him and laid him down on the deck, and Riverwind tore a strip from his own tunic, using it to bandage his wounds. When the fighting was all but over, only a handful of pirates remained, pinned against *Brinestrider*'s gunwale by the escaped slaves. One by one they fell, until only one man was left. He stood silhouetted against the leaping flames that raged across *Red Reaver*'s deck, flailing wildly with his cutlass to keep his attackers at bay. In the end it was Kronn who evaded his blade and leapt in, chapak swinging. The pirate leaned back from the kender's axe, overbalanced, and toppled over the railing into the churning sea.

The kender watched him fall, then looked around with satisfaction. His eyes met Riverwind's, and he grinned.

The Plainsman stared back, still half amazed, then slumped wearily to the deck.

*   *   *   *   *

Red Reaver was still smoldering at sunset, creaking and crackling. The cinders of her hull glowed red in the deepening dark. She listed sideways as seawater seeped in through her fire-weakened hull, and her bow was considerably closer to the waterline than her stern, but stubbornly she refused to sink. The black, charred fingers of her masts clutched upward, toward the pale, rising moon.

Amid the fire's dim light, the survivors of the battle wrapped their dead in blankets and lined them along the bloodstained deck. It had been a heavy toll. Nine of the escaped slaves, and all of Captain Ar-Tam's crew save three young seamen, had been slain. The pirates were all dead, too, but the slaves and sailors had given them to the sharks without a funeral.

The slaves' black-bearded leader, a Khurrish mariner named Alaruq ur-Phadh, bent over each of his dead fellows and placed a steel coin—given to him by Kronn, who had salvaged some small part of the *Reaver*'s spoils—in each man's mouth. It was an old rite of the Mikku, the clan to which Alaruq and his fellows belonged; the coins were payment for the guardians of the underworld, so the dead could pass by the Abyss and find peace among the stars.

Kael Ar-Tam gave his men no coins, nor did he speak as he looked over the corpses of his men. The creases on his scar-lined face deepened as his eyes flicked from body to body.

Swiftraven lay on a bundle of sailcloth, moaning as Brightdawn tended his wounds. Catt knelt at his side, holding his hand. He managed to smile at the kender.

"I doubted you," he murmured. "I thought you were hiding, that you were afraid to help us." He drew a deep breath, summoning words he found hard to speak. "I'm sorry."

Red Reaver's mizzenmast, made brittle by burning, groaned loudly against the gusting wind, then snapped and fell with a crash. Everyone on *Brinestrider* jumped at the sound. Then Alaruq spoke a word to the other escaped slaves. The men were dressed now, having taken clothes from the dead sailors' lockers, but there was no hiding the hollow pallor of their faces or the difficult shadows deep within their eyes. One by one, the slaves lifted the shrouded bodies and dropped them into the sea. The corpses bobbed briefly on the waves before the waterlogged blankets dragged them down.

When the last of the dead had been cast overboard, Riverwind stood at *Brinestrider's* rail and stared silently out across the sea. After a time, he reached into his fur vest and pulled out the Forever Charm. He looked at it accusingly, his fingers tracing its endless loop. Then he heard footsteps on the deck behind him. Recognizing the rhythm of his daughter's light but confident stride, he curled his fingers around the charm, hiding it from view.

"You're mad at them, aren't you?" Brightdawn asked. She drew up beside him, leaning against the rail and following his gaze across the water. "The gods."

"I braved death on black wings for Mishakal." Riverwind said, frowning. "I brought her staff out of Xak Tsaroth, and your mother and I restored mankind's faith in her."

Brightdawn looked at him. "And, in return, she abandoned you." She reached out, rested a gentle hand on his arm. "She owes you more than this, Father."

The Plainsman sighed, a deep, woeful sound.

Her grasp on his arm tightened. "It's all right to be angry, Father," she murmured. "Do you remember Snaketooth?"

Riverwind nodded. Snaketooth had been the war priest of the Qué-Kiri. Two years ago, when he'd learned that Kiri-Jolith had left the world, he had stopped eating out of despair. Young and strong at the start of his self-imposed fast, he had withered to a skeleton within two months, refusing even simple gruel or broth. Then, still grieving, he had died.

"Chief Graywinter told me, not long after the funeral, that when the women were washing Snaketooth's body, they found something in his hand," Brightdawn pressed. "Do you know what it was?"

Her father shook his head.

"It was a bison's horn," she said. "Kiri-Jolith's holy symbol. They had to pry it from his fingers."

A shudder wracked Riverwind's body. He opened his fist and stared at the Forever Charm. Then he shook his head and draped it around his neck once more. He turned to Brightdawn as he tucked the medallion back into his vest. "I must ask you to do something when we reach Ak-Thain," he said.

"I know."

"Return to the Plains," he pleaded. "Take Swiftraven with you."

She shook her head. "No. There is more at stake now," Brightdawn answered. "I owe my life to Kronn and Catt, after today—so does Swiftraven. Neither of us is going to turn our backs on a debt to the kender."

"You would go against your own father's wishes, then?"

Brightdawn closed her eyes. "Father," she said, "have you heard the story of the princess who loved the shepherd boy? She went against her father's wishes, too."

"Don't play games with me, child," Riverwind snapped.

"I am not a child!" Brightdawn shot back. "I am a grown woman, and I know this isn't a game. But what would have happened if Mother had heeded her father instead of following what was in her heart? I wouldn't be standing here, for one thing." Her strong, sky-blue eyes, so much like her mother's, fixed on his. "I will go on to Kendermore, Father, because I must. Please don't ask me to do otherwise."

With that, she turned and walked away. Riverwind closed his eyes, but tears spilled forth anyway, leaving trails on his cheeks that glistened in the moonlight.

Out across the water, *Red Reaver* tipped up, slowly sinking beneath the waves.

Chapter 11

Hekhorath sighed with pleasure as he glided on the warm updrafts that rose from the blasted ruins of the Dairly Plains. He stretched his claws and hissed with pleasure. He circled slowly over the riven, rocky barrens that once had been fertile grasslands, tendrils of smoke curling from his nostrils and vanishing on the warm, rushing wind. The air held the faint aroma of brimstone and soot. It was a heady scent, and Hekhorath savored it as a man might enjoy the bouquet of a fine wine.

He was still young, as dragons measure time, though he had lived longer than even the oldest elves on Krynn. He had dwelt in the caves to the south of the Dairlies for more than three decades, having been left behind by the retreating dragonarmies at the end of the War of the Lance. He had found plentiful prey there, both animal and human, and though he had to compete with a few other wyrms, he'd carved out his own territory with plenty of livestock and human barbarians to keep him fed. He had even escaped the worst of the fighting during the Chaos War; the All-Father's legions had attacked the Dairlies, but not in force. The devastation that had ravaged other parts of Ansalon simply hadn't come to Hekhorath's comfortable corner of the world. Life had been pleasant, easy.

Then Malystryx had come.

Hekhorath had first heard rumors of the great female red more than a year ago but had paid them little heed. Among the dragons of the Dairlies, a newcomer was always cause for interest, perhaps caution . . . but never alarm. When he'd heard Malys had taken up in Blood

Watch, he had briefly considered flying north to investigate but had set the idea aside and hadn't thought about her for months.

Then one morning last autumn as he was soaring over the Maw, the narrow bay that divided the Dairlies from the rest of Goodlund, he had been approached by a young green dragon. The green, who had been named Sthinissh, had a lair not far from Hekhorath's in a small forest near the place called Madding Springs. Sthinissh, like most greens, was fond of talking. He had been the first one to tell Hekhorath about Malystryx's arrival.

"Hekhorath!" Sthinissh had called to him, arrowing down through a cloud bank. "I must speak with you!"

At first, Hekhorath had considered ignoring him—the green's prattling often wore on his nerves—but something in Sthinissh's voice had given him pause: fear.

That caught his interest. Sthinissh had been barely more than a hatchling, still filled with the hubris of the very young. Hekhorath had never known him to be afraid of anything. He had slowed his flight, allowed the smaller wyrm to catch up. "What's the matter?" he'd asked.

"It's Malystryx," Sthinissh had replied. "She's killed Andorung."

That had given Hekhorath pause. Andorung had been a red, the oldest, largest dragon in the Dairlies and one of the few left in all of Ansalon who'd been present at the great battle between Takhisis and the vile Huma Dragonbane. If the evil dragons of eastern Goodlund revered anything now that Takhisis was gone, Andorung had been it.

"Dead?" Hekhorath had asked. "Are you certain?"

Sthinissh had nodded. "I saw his corpse myself. She'd . . . done things to it."

"Things?"

"Yes." Sthinissh had been silent a moment, an odd look in his glinting red eyes. "He'd withered. It was like he'd lain in the sun for a year."

"Are you sure that is true?" Hekhorath had pressed. "He was very old . . . he could have died on the wing, away from his lair. . . ."

"I'm sure," Sthinissh had retorted. "There was blood on the ground around his body—it was still fresh. And . . ." His voice had trailed off.

Hekhorath had glanced at him sharply. "And what?"

"His head was missing." Sthinissh had swallowed hard. "I think she took it."

"What?" Hekhorath had exclaimed. "Why would she take his head?"

"I don't know. As a trophy, perhaps. But that doesn't explain why the rest of him was a . . . a husk. And this isn't the first time this has happened, either. From what I hear, she did the same thing to a pair of coppers near the Mistlestraits. And others are missing, too."

"How many others?"

Sthinissh had swallowed again. "Ten, maybe more."

"Ten?" Hekhorath had echoed, disbelievingly. "That's almost every dragon north of the Maw!"

"No," Sthinissh had replied gravely. "That *is* every dragon north of the Maw. She's killing them, one by one, and I don't think it's just for territory. Strange things are happening at Blood Watch, Hekhorath. The land's changing. It's grown barren, and I could swear I saw the beginnings of mountains in the Hollowlands."

"Blood of Takhisis." Suddenly, Hekhorath had understood Sthinissh's fear. "You don't think she's responsible for that, do you?"

The green had looked at him. "Can you think of another explanation?"

Hekhorath had considered this, then shaken his head. "If she's shaping the land, she's a more powerful magic user than Andorung ever was . . . or any dragon since the Age of Dreams."

"And if she's slaughtered every dragon in the north," Sthinissh had said, "then maybe we're next."

Hekhorath had thought a great deal about Malystryx over the following weeks. By the time word reached him that she had destroyed the village of Ran-Khal and slain Aester, a bronze dragon who laired nearby, he'd had an idea of what to do about her. When he'd sought out

Sthinissh soon after and found the green's withered, headless body sprawled amid the ashes that once had been his forest, he'd made up his mind. With every dragon who died on the Dairlies, the chances had grown that she would come for him.

And so at the beginning of the winter he had left his lair and flown north, hoping to find her first.

He'd soon discovered that Sthinissh had been right. The land was changing. What had been only a hint of barrenness months before, however, had turned into a full-fledged blight. There'd been more than just the beginnings of mountains in the Hollowlands, and a volcano had risen at Blood Watch. No tree, no shrub, no plant disturbed the parched, stony landscape. The heat was intense, blistering.

In short, for a red dragon it was glorious. A thrill had surged through Hekhorath's veins as he soared above the blasted terrain, streaking toward the smoldering volcano that was Malystryx's lair.

Then he'd seen her, and the thrill had given way to awe. She had been gigantic even then, larger than any dragon he'd ever seen—and he had seen the largest wyrms in the dragonarmies. She had emerged from a shaft in the side of the volcano, her beating wings whipping up great clouds of ash and dust, and had spotted him almost instantly. Hekhorath had forced himself to swallow sudden terror as she'd streaked toward him, moving as swift as a hurricane. He'd known she could kill him as easily as he might slaughter a herdsman's goat. Then she would defile his body, and take his head . . . unless he gave her another option.

When he'd decided she was close enough, he'd pulled up sharply, soaring high, his wings straining against the pull of gravity. The blasted earth had shot away beneath him, the air around him growing cold and thin. When he'd finally judged he was high enough, he'd drawn a deep breath, raised his head skyward, and exhaled a tremendous jet of flame.

The fiery torrent had shot upward hundreds of yards,

hot enough to melt steel. He'd belched it forth until he'd had no more flames in him to breathe. Then, weak and dizzy, he'd tucked his wings in tight against his scarred sides and dived back toward the ground, toward Malys.

She'd looked at him as he approached, her lips curling with amusement. "I take it," she'd said wryly, "that that's your way of saying you wish to be my consort."

"Yes," he'd answered, unable to summon enough breath to say anything more.

"Interesting." She had banked, circling lazily around him, forcing him to keep turning in order to face her. "What makes you so sure I have any desire for such a thing?"

Sensing she was testing him, he'd frowned in concentration, choosing each word of his response with meticulous care. "I'm not sure," he'd said. "But I am drawn to your power nevertheless. If I cannot have this honor, then I beg you to slay me now, for I refuse to live unless I can bask in your glory."

She had circled him silently for quite some time. Then, suddenly, she had stopped, hovering in the air before him. "I cannot decide," she'd told him. "Either you are exceedingly clever, or you are the greatest idiot I have ever met. Whichever it may be, you have intrigued me. Very well, then. Let us be mates."

With that, she had wheeled in midair and soared back toward Blood Watch. Hekhorath had watched her depart, amazed, for a heartbeat. Then, laughing, he had winged after her.

She had shown him many things, both wondrous and horrible, in the months they had shared her lair. Both together and separately, they had scorched the Dairlies, blasting one barbarian village after another. He had watched as she broke the mind of Yovanna, the human woman she had taken as her servant, and remade it to suit her will. He had helped her hunt down and destroy other dragons, though she refused to let him witness what she did to their bodies after they were dead—or what became of the severed heads she brought back to their lair. It was, in every way, a one-sided pairing. Malystryx had power over him, and he had none over her. Even when they lay in her nest, deep within the heart of the volcano, their sinuous bodies coiled about each other, he was always aware that she was his master, and he her thrall.

None of that mattered, though. Of the score of dragons who had once dwelt in the Dairlies, only he remained alive, because only he had been smart enough to make himself useful to Malys, rather than a hindrance.

Baring his fangs in a smile, he banked, gliding north, toward the smoldering peak of Blood Watch.

* * * * *

"Mistress."

Malys stirred, stretching her vast bulk across the enormous cavern of her nest. The room was dark, but that mattered little; the dragon could see as well in shadow as in light. Her golden eyes burning, she arched her neck to look up the wall of the vault.

A hundred feet above the cavern floor, a smooth, narrow tunnel gaped in the wall. It was one of two entrances to Malystryx's nest, and the only one usable by beings incapable of flight; the second, a broad shaft that led from the cavern's ceiling to a fissure in the side of the volcano, was accessible only to Malys and Hekhorath. The mouth of the narrow tunnel led onto a broad ledge that resembled a balcony, and upon that balcony stood a figure swathed in black cloth. Unlike the handful of other mortals who had stood on the ledge, this figure did not shrink back from the dragon's glare, nor did it tremble when Malys snorted, flames flickering briefly from her nostrils.

"Yovanna," the dragon purred, her tone vaguely menacing. "You bring news?"

The robed figure bowed in deference. "Yes, Mistress," she declared. "You asked me to tell you when *he* returned."

Malys couldn't quite hide her smile at the distaste with which Yovanna spoke the word. *He.* There was very little love lost between her servant and her consort. "Where is he?" she asked.

"Over the Hollowlands. He will be here soon, My Queen."

"Will you not say his name?"

"I would rather not."

The dragon growled a chuckle. "It would seem when I reshaped your mind I did not crush your capacity for jealousy, Yovanna."

"Jealousy, My Queen?"

"Of Hekhorath."

The hooded head angled slightly. "I had not considered it that way," she said thoughtfully. "With your pardon, however, I think you misread me."

"Do I?"

"Yes, Mistress," Yovanna replied, nodding. "When you. . . reshaped me, you made me your protector as well as your servant. What you see as jealousy—and I understand how it might seem that way—is, in truth, mistrust. He is disloyal, Mistress. Not now, perhaps, but someday."

Malys laughed aloud, the sound of her mirth ringing from the vault's smooth walls. "Do you think I am blind to this, Yovanna?" she asked.

The robed figure bowed again. "I apologize."

"You need not. I have fooled him, for my own ends, into thinking I value him somehow. In order to do that, it was necessary to deceive you as well."

"I understand."

Malys was silent a moment. "Yovanna," she said, "I wish you to remain here when Hekhorath arrives."

At once Yovanna was alert, her body tensed. "Are you expecting trouble?"

"In a way."

Dragon and servant looked at each other for a long moment, neither speaking.

"Why now?" Yovanna asked.

"Because I have what I need."

Malys stared at her servant, her eyes shining. Yovanna looked back a moment, not comprehending, then gasped.

"Oh, Mistress," she breathed, then shook her head, as if clearing it of cobwebs. "When did it happen?"

"Several months ago."

"Does he know?"

The dragon shook her head, her eyes like stones.

Just then, there came a scratching from the shaft in the ceiling. A shower of dust and rock shards sifted down out of the hole, pattering down the cavern's wall onto the floor. Malys and Yovanna peered up at the shaft, the dragon utterly calm, the human quivering with anticipation. Another small avalanche followed the first; then a crimson claw reached out of the shaft, its talons firmly gripping the stone. A second claw followed, then a horned, reptilian head. Golden eyes gleamed, both below and above, as Malys and Hekhorath beheld each other.

"So," Malystryx said, her voice flat and toneless, "you have returned."

Hekhorath hesitated, halfway out of the shaft, a puzzled look on his face. "You are not pleased to see me?"

"On the contrary. I am overjoyed."

Eyes narrowing, Hekhorath crawled out of the hole. Spreading his wings, he glided down to the bottom of the cavern. His talons clacked against the floor as he landed, then he slithered toward his mate. He held himself tensed, unsure of what to expect. Malystryx, however, raised her wing and folded it about him as he approached, then twisted her tail around his and nuzzled his neck with her muzzle. Gradually, he relaxed, and they coiled about each other.

"How fares my domain?" Malys asked. Her forked tongue flicked between her teeth, dancing tantalizingly along the underside of Hekhorath's chin.

"Well enough," he answered, shivering with pleasure. "The ogres have left their war camp and are finally marching on Kendermore." He bent his head back, letting Malys's tongue work its way from his chin down his throat, then back up again. He squeezed his eyes shut, sighing, then opened them again. His gaze focused on the balcony, high above.

"What is *she* doing here?" he demanded.

Malys nuzzled him again. "She brought me word of your return. I asked her to stay."

"You did?" Hekhorath asked. "What for?"

"This."

Hekhorath shrieked in sudden agony as Malys dug her claws into his belly and breast. Her talons drove through his tough, scaly hide, and blood pooled on the floor, running into cracks in the stone. He thrashed, kicking against her, but she clutched him close, keeping him from finding any hold. Slowly, painfully, she ripped open his flesh, tearing into his guts, disemboweling him. His cries grew more frantic, and his wings flapped furiously, buffeting Malys's body. The blows bounced uselessly off her tough hide.

High above, Yovanna smiled.

Growing more desperate with each fading moment, Hekhorath opened his mouth and breathed fire all over her. She only laughed, though, as the flames enveloped her. "Do you really think that will be of any use?" she asked. He began to weaken in her grasp.

"Why?" he moaned, his voice wracked with agony. Blood bubbled in his throat. "What did I do?"

"Everything I wanted," she answered.

Then her fangs clamped around his throat, crushing his windpipe, and his voice choked off with a wet gurgle. He bucked wildly, so violently he nearly slipped out of her iron grasp. Then she rolled him over on the blood-slick floor, clenched her jaw even tighter, and viciously twisted his neck.

Bones snapped. Hekhorath twitched once, then died.

Malys released him, her claws and face dripping red. "When you first asked to be my consort," she snarled, "I said you were either clever or an idiot." She sneered at his tattered corpse, her teeth glistening. "Now I know which."

A moment passed, then something began to happen to Hekhorath's body. A lambent, scarlet mist rose from his shredded flesh like bloody steam. She shuddered as it enveloped her, seeping between her thick, crimson scales. As Hekhorath's life essence flowed from his corpse into her body, Malystryx's body grew—and his shriveled.

Finally, the last of the mist faded away. Malys looked down upon Hekhorath's body, which lay withered on the cavern floor, as if he'd lain in the sun for a year. She clamped her jaws around his neck once more and began to saw with her teeth, grinding and crunching. At length, she tore his head from his body.

"Will we add that to the rest, My Queen?" Yovanna asked from high above.

Malys grasped Hekhorath's head in her claws and examined it, an odd wistfulness in her eyes. "Yes," she said at last. "But this one, I think, will have a special place."

She bent over the head, tenderly, running her tongue under his chin one last time. Then, using her teeth, she began to strip the shriveled flesh from Hekhorath's skull.

Chapter 12

"You never mentioned you played the flute," Kronn said as the five travelers walked down the dock, leaving behind the ship that had borne them across the Bay of Balifor. The inns and rowhouses of Port Balifor stretched before them, hearth glow and candlelight shining from their windows as twilight stole across the city. Down the wharf, roaming fishmongers were calling, trying to sell the last of their wares before darkness fell.

Riverwind glanced at the kender, who trotted beside him, ponytail and cheek braids bouncing with each step. Brightdawn and Swiftraven came behind, whispering to each other and laughing softly. The young warrior still favored his healthy leg, but the wounds he'd suffered during the pirate attack had almost completely healed during their long trek across the sands of Khur. Catt came last, whistling a jaunty sea chantey as her hoopak rapped against the wooden planks of the dock.

Kronn looked up at the old Plainsman, his eyebrows raised.

"Yes," Riverwind answered, his voice thick with memory. "Wanderer, my grandfather, taught me to play many years ago. Many years . . ." His voice trailed off, his gaze sliding away into the past. " 'Tending his flock under the stars, a man needs music,' he said. I was to be a shepherd, you see. He carved my first flute from the branch of a bonewood tree, and showed me how to play. It was . . . one of many things he taught me." He paused again, a complicated mix of emotions playing across his face. "Sometimes, when I was older, I would play with Goldmoon. We seldom make music together any more, I'm afraid, except on festival days. But sometimes . . ."

He stopped suddenly, his brow furrowing. "Wait a moment," he said slowly. "How did you find out I can play the flute?"

Kronn frowned, thinking it over. "I'm not sure," he said. "I might have guessed. I'm a good guesser."

Riverwind, however, had already shrugged off his pack, and was rooting through its contents. After a while, he looked up from the pouch, leveling a hard stare at the kender.

"Or-rrr," Kronn amended slowly, "maybe it was because you dropped your flute this morning, back in Ak-Khurman."

He reached into his pouch, his arm disappearing up to his elbow into the bag, then pulled a simple flute, hand-carved from white wood and worn from years of use. Riverwind snatched it from his hands and examined it closely for cracks. It seemed intact. Making sure, he blew softly into the mouth hole. It answered with a sweet, warm note. A look of relief smoothed the lines of his face—then he looked at Kronn, his brow darkening once more.

"All my life, through darkness and light," he said, "I have kept this flute. I took it with me on my Courting Quest and carried it to war. I played it that night in Solace, when I met Tanis and Caramon and the others. And—it is the only thing I have left to remind me of my grandfather. Even his face is no longer clear in my memory, but I can still see his hands as he guided my fingers over its holes."

The kender nodded solemnly. "I'm surprised you're so careless with it, if it's so important. You're lucky I'm around to pick up after you. I play too, you know." He twisted sideways, displaying the chapak slung across his back. "Have a look at the handle."

Riverwind looked. The axe's ironwood haft was dotted with dark finger holes.

"Neat, huh?" the kender asked. "I had it specially made. It's a pain unscrewing the axe head and taking out all the rope, but, 'It's not a proper weapon unless it can play a tune,' as my father used to say. Of course," he added sadly, "poor Father couldn't carry a tune in a wheelbarrow. He was a great hero, but unlike myself, completely tone deaf. So's Catt, you know."

"I am not," Catt snapped.

Kronn glanced back at her, a mischievious grin on his face. "Give us a song, then."

Catt glowered at him, her lips pursing. "I don't feel like it."

"Mmm-hmm," Kronn said. He leaned toward Riverwind, whispering conspiratorially. "Good thing, too. Her voice can curdle milk."

Behind them, his sister harrumphed loudly.

"Hey," he went on, "we're both so musical, we should play a duet together sometime."

They stopped at the boardwalk, facing the row of inns and taverns that overlooked the docks. Riverwind looked up and down the wharf, then his eyes fixed on a low building with walls of mortared flagstones and a slate-shingled roof. Gaily colored awnings hung above its stained-glass windows, and a pair of brass lanterns flickered on either side of its open front door. A smile of recognition curled his lips.

"Yes," he said. "I would like to play with you, Kronn. How about tonight?" With that, he started toward the inn.

Blinking in surprise, the kender hurried to catch up.

* * * * *

The wind picked up as nighttime settled over Port Balifor, and the front windows of the Pig and Whistle tavern began to moan. Slowly, the noise grew louder, rising to a shrill keening that rattled the glasses above the bar.

William Sweetwater glanced at the windows, his fat face puckering with disgust. "I really ought to fix them damn things," he grumbled.

"Bah," scoffed old Erewan the Shaggy, who sat on his usual stool at the bar, nursing a tankard of foaming black ale. His long, yellow-gray beard quivered as he scowled.

"Ye've said the same bleedin' thing every night for the past forty years, Pig Face."

"I mean it this time," William shot back sourly. "Put an end to that bloody racket, once and for all."

"Talk, talk," crowed Nine-Finger Pete, hunching over a mug of foul-smelling grog.

William Sweetwater grunted, a porcine sound that matched his countenance perfectly. He had been born with the mark of a pig on his face: small, squinting eyes, full cheeks, and a sharply upturned nose. Now that he was well over eighty years of age, his sagging jowls, bristling gray whiskers and enormous girth—the Pig and Whistle's regulars often expressed their amazement that he could even fit behind the bar—gave him the appearance of a stout and grizzled old boar.

The lamplight that streamed in through the tavern's open doors flickered as a group of travelers came in. The regulars looked up, squinting, then stared with red and rheumy eyes as the five strangers made their way to a booth near the back. Strange visitors were far from rare at the Pig and Whistle—Port Balifor was a wayfarer's town, after all—but this party held their attention.

"Barbarians and kender," Nine-Finger Pete muttered, and took a swig from his mug. "Bloody bones. Good thing this dump's got nothin' worth stealin', eh Pig Face?"

William Sweetwater wasn't paying attention, though. His low brow furrowed as he watched the travelers— three Plainsfolk from Abanasinia and two kender—settle into their seats. His gaze fixed on the oldest of the barbarians in particular—a tall, stern man with white hair. "I know that one," he muttered, thinking fiercely. "I've seen him before somewhere. . . ."

One of the kender—a male with an axe on his back and odd chestnut braids hanging over his cheeks, looked William's way and snapped his fingers, breaking the old innkeeper's concentration. "Ale here!" he called. "In clean cups, if you please. And some of whatever's on the spit."

Erewan grinned, his eyes narrowing to crinkly slits.

"You heard the little squeaker," he snickered. "Step lively, Pig Face."

With a withering look at the bristle-bearded old salt, William grabbed a handful of mugs and waddled to the keg of Arnsley Black he'd tapped earlier that day. He bellowed into the kitchen as he poured the newcomers' drinks, and by the time he was on the fourth beer, a wench brought a tray of bread, cheese, and roast mutton to the table. William filled the last mug, blew nut-brown foam onto his well-stained floor, and waved the wench away when she came to collect the mugs. "Get back to yer work," he grumbled. "I'll take these to them myself."

With some effort, he squeezed out from behind the bar, grabbed up the tray of drinks, and puffed over to the table. His gaze was fixed on the old Plainsman the whole way, and when he drew near to the table, his eyes widened and he started so violently that he nearly dropped the tray. "Great holy Habbakuk," he cursed, amazed. "It *is* you, at that."

Riverwind of Qué-Shu looked at up him and smiled. "Hello, William," he said. "It's been a long time."

The other travelers looked at the old barbarian, confused. "Father?" asked one of the other Plainsfolk, a young, golden-haired lass. "Do you know this man?"

Riverwind nodded. "We met a long time ago, Brightdawn, during the war. William was good enough to give us a place to rest, even though we didn't have the steel to pay him."

"Bah," William snorted as he passed out the drinks. He clapped Riverwind on the back. "It were the least I could do. Your father, lass, was part o' the finest travelin' circus ever to pass through these parts."

Riverwind's companions looked at him in surprise. "Circus?" Brightdawn asked. "You, Father?"

The Plainsman cleared his throat, his cheeks slowly turning red. "Well, I would hardly call it a circus. . . ."

William interrupted him with a laugh. "You mean yer da here never told ye, lass?" he asked. "He and his mates were the Red Wizard and His Wonderful Illusions."

"The Red Wizard and His—" the male kender gasped, his mouth dropping open. "That was you, Riverwind?"

"Sure it was!" William declared, beaming proudly. "They got their start right here, in this very room."

"So," he said warmly, "what brings you away from the Plains this time? Where ye bound?"

"Kendermore," the male kender answered.

The Pig and Whistle's patrons stared at them, dumbfounded, then began to laugh. William slapped his broad belly, snorting with mirth. Riverwind and his companions looked back, the Plainsfolk frowning and the kender wide-eyed with confusion.

"What's so funny?" the female kender asked.

Suddenly, William stopped laughing. "Zeboim's twenty teats," he blurted, staring at Riverwind. "Ye're serious?"

The old Plainsman nodded slowly, his lips pressed firmly together.

"Kendermore?" asked Nine-Finger Pete, his voice rising with disbelief. "Why in the Abyss would you want to go there?"

Riverwind leveled a piercing glare at the ancient seaman. "Because," he said simply, "they need our help."

The old sailor snorted derisively, turning back to his grog. "Bloody idiot," he muttered softly—but not soft enough.

"Shut yer hole, you mangy cur!" William barked toward the bar. "Talk that way about my friends again, and ye're barred from my place. I mean it." He turned to Riverwind and smiled. "I'm sorry. Pete's been pickling in that slop he drinks for so long, he ain't got half a brain left. Eat. Drink. There's more were that came from, too. It's on the house! Ye're my guests, all o' ye."

That said, William bowed—a valiant feat, given his girth—and waddled back to the bar. Neither the Plainsman nor his companions missed the look in his eyes, however, as he turned away from the table. Though he would never say so, William clearly thought little more of Riverwind's quest than did Nine-Finger Pete.

* * * * *

The candles on the Pig and Whistle's bar had melted to misshapen stumps when Riverwind rose from his chair. He wobbled slightly as he did so—Arnsley Black was a potent brew, and the companions had put away a healthy dose of it—but he quickly steadied himself and waved to William.

The innkeeper leaned on the bar, which creaked ominously beneath his weight. "What can I get for ye?" he asked.

"Nothing, thanks," the Plainsman answered. He reached into his pouch, producing an old, worn flute. "For old time's sake?"

William grinned. "I'd be a damn fool to say no." He raised his voice to a bellow that made Erewan and Pete wince and cover their ears. "Quiet, the lot o' ye!"

The tavern's patrons swiftly fell still. Riverwind walked to a corner by the hearth—the same corner where, more than thirty years before, he and Goldmoon had once played. With quiet dignity, he sat cross-legged upon the sawdust-covered floor, then looked back at the table where his companions sat. "Will you join me, Kronn?" he asked.

The kender jumped up from his chair and hurried over to join the old Plainsman. He busily dismantled his chapak, setting its various pieces in a pile at his feet, then set his mouth to the end of the haft. "Ready," he said.

Nodding, Riverwind looked out over his audience. "I played this song for the first time in this very tavern," he said, his sonorous voice filling the room. "It tells of the ancient gods . . . and how they wait to return to the world."

A murmur rippled through the room. No one was sure what to make of this. Didn't the doddering Plainsman know the gods had left again, this time for good? What was the meaning of playing such a song now, when the pale moon shone above Balifor Bay?

Riverwind didn't bother to answer those muttered questions. Instead, he raised his flute to his lips, and its plaintive sound filled the room. He played alone for a moment, then Kronn picked up the simple tune, weaving his own melody in harmony with Riverwind's.

As the Plainsman and the kender played, the patrons of the Pig and Whistle discovered something remarkable. Even now, after so much change had visited the world, the song still spoke to them of hope.

* * * * *

Three days later, as the companions rode past the farmlands and windmills of Balifor, the low, green line of the Kenderwood at last appeared upon the horizon. It was still a long way off—three leagues, maybe four—but Kronn and Catt leaned forward in their saddles, eagerness on their faces. Seeing this, Brightdawn couldn't help but smile.

"It must be exciting," she remarked. "Coming home, I mean, after being so long away."

"Sure is," Catt agreed enthusiastically.

"I thought you people were born wanderers," Swiftraven said. "I've seen enough of you on the Plains, anyway, always on your way somewhere."

Kronn shook his head at the young warrior. "Just because I love the road, that doesn't mean I'm not happy to see my homeland," he replied. "Besides, my wanderlust ended years ago."

"It's not just that," Catt said. "We're worried about the ogres. . . and the dragon. Sometimes, when we were far from home, I worried that when we finally got back, there'd be nothing left. Kendermore would be gone, and Paxina . . ."

"Not to mention Giff," Kronn added, grinning slyly. Catt glared at him, flushing with embarrassment.

"Who's Giff?" Brightdawn asked.

"Giffel Birdwhistle," Kronn answered before Catt could intervene. "A friend of ours, from when we were children. He's a warrior now—he came to Kendermore after Woodsedge burned, and Pax put him in charge of part of the town guard. He and Catt are sweet on each other."

"Kronn!" Catt objected, but he only laughed.

"Father, have you ever been to Kendermore?" Brightdawn asked. "Is there anyone you're returning to?"

The old Plainsman sat astride his horse, a faraway look in his eyes. His face was drawn, his skin sallow. To the others, he seemed to have aged ten years or more since they'd broken camp. They all looked at him worriedly now as he continued to stare down the road, not even glancing at Brightdawn in reply.

"My chief . . . ?" Swiftraven asked.

"Father?" Brightdawn said at the same time, her voice low with concern. "Are you well?"

He started, blinking, then looked at the others as if seeing them for the first time. "I-I'm sorry," he said, spots of color blossoming in his cheeks. "I wasn't listening."

"You've been quiet all day," Kronn noted solemnly.

Riverwind looked away, momentarily unable to meet the others' questioning looks. "It's nothing," he said. "Only a feeling I haven't had . . . since I set out on my Courting Quest, I suppose. I'm leaving everything behind—every place I've ever seen, everyone I've ever met—except the four of you, of course. Back then, though, it was exciting. Now . . ." He pursed his lips, shrugging. "I guess I'm older now."

"Well," Catt said, "what about Brightdawn's question? You've never been to Kendermore, Riverwind?"

The old Plainsman shook his head, his gaze still abstracted.

"You're in for a treat, then," Catt promised. "Just wait till we're in the Kenderwood. The bloodberries should be ripe about now, for one thing . . . or maybe not. It's a bit warm for this time of year, to be sure."

"I was thinking that myself," Kronn agreed. "We're well into fall. Last year we'd had our first frost by this time, but now it feels like summer just plain forgot to leave." He pondered this thought grimly. "You don't think it has anything to do with Malys, do you?"

An uncomfortable silence fell over the party. Brightdawn and Swiftraven exchanged troubled glances, then looked away, toward the still-distant Kenderwood. Catt and Kronn swallowed, their brows furrowed. Only River-wind dared to speak, and only softly, as if he feared being overheard. "No," he told the kender. "I'm sure it's just a warm spell."

The others could tell, from the tone of his voice, that he didn't fully believe the words either.

* * * * *

Unlike the sylvan homes of the elves, the Kenderwood was not an ancient forest. In fact, as the lives of woodlands are measured, it was quite young. Before the Cataclysm, the lands surrounding what was now Kendermore had been part of the empire of Istar, a place of fertile farmlands, isolated abbeys, and a few human towns. They had even been home to one of the fabled Towers of High Sorcery, although the wizards themselves had destroyed that august edifice during the Lost Battles rather than let it fall into the Kingpriest's hands.

When the fiery mountain sundered Istar, however, the humans had fled, leaving their monasteries and cities to ruin. Some had gone west to found such cities as Flotsam and Port Balifor; others traveled east to the Dairly Plains and became barbarians. By the time the kender arrived, traveling north from the ruins of their ancient land of Balifor, central Goodlund was abandoned—a place of ghosts, if the rumors were to be believed.

The kender, however, didn't let anything as paltry as ghosts stop them from making the land their new home. Indeed, they explored the supposedly haunted ruins with glee, "borrowing" anything the humans had left behind to help them erect their own villages and towns. Kendermore, built only a few leagues from a fallen city the kender pragmatically called "The Ruins," had quickly risen as the hub of the new kender nation.

Shortly after the kender's arrival, the land had begun to change. The farmlands the humans had tended grew wild, and trees began to appear. According to legend, the new forest was the work of a kender lass named Oletta Maplekeys, who had traveled from one end of the land to the other, spreading seeds in the fallow fields the humans had left behind. Of course, this was a kender legend, so Krynn's other races didn't believe it for a moment—but regardless of the reason, the forest continued to grow, slowly spreading to engulf the kender's new homeland.

Being a new forest, the Kenderwood was not as dark and dense as Ansalon's older woodlands. Instead of the huge, looming trees of Silvanesti, it was a place of papery birches and golden willows, maples and poplars, apple orchards and berry bushes. Unlike Darken Wood, which came by its name honestly, the Kenderwood was bright and airy, the canopy of its leaves sparse enough to let plenty of sunlight through. Ferns and wildflowers grew among the tree trunks, a lush carpet that provided homes for badgers, skunks and other small animals. Larger beasts dwelt within the Kenderwood, too—deer, boars, wildcats, and even a few black bears. Birds of all kinds flitted from branch to branch, filling the air with music, and bees hummed contentedly from blossom to blossom. When all was said, the Kenderwood was one of the most idyllic places in Krynn: a tranquil woodland stretching nearly fifty leagues from east to west, and another twenty north to south, unbroken except for the occasional clearing where a kender farm, vinyard, or town stood.

Now, however, there was something wrong.

* * * * *

The day wore on, and the weather grew warmer with each passing mile. The sun hung fat and red behind Riverwind and his companions when they finally reached the edge of the forest. It curved ahead of them, its slender trees hissing as the summery breeze brushed through their leaves. None of the companions missed the fact that those leaves were still green; by all rights, they should have been ablaze with color at this time of year—or even already fallen brown and dead upon the ground. Somehow, the beauty of the foliage seemed more sinister than soothing.

They could do little but ride on, though; spurring their mounts, they continued, their long shadows sliding into the dappled shade of the woods.

"The bloodberries aren't ripe yet after all," Catt noted as they passed a tall, leafy bush. Bright red blossoms still bloomed upon its branches, instead of the fruit the kender had hoped to find. She nodded toward a thorny thicket, where bees hummed lazily around fat blackberries.

"It's like it's still midsummer," Kronn murmured. He pointed at a nearby tree, where an azure-breasted songbird perched, whistling a tune to welcome the oncoming dusk. "Branchala bite me, Catt—is that a bluetwitter?"

"Kronn," Brightdawn said suddenly, her voice very soft.

"I've never seen one this far south past Summer's End, and that was more than a month ago!" Kronn went on, his eyes fast on the bird.

"Kronn." The Plainswoman's voice was stronger this time, and louder.

He looked at her sharply. "What is it?"

Brightdawn hesitated, then raised her hand, pointing down the trail before them. "That light," she said. "Do you recognize it?"

Kronn followed her outstretched finger. In the distance, dimly visible through the trees, a dull, red glow was rising into the twilight sky. His eyes widened when he saw it. Beside him Catt gasped in amazement.

"It's a fire," Riverwind said, a sudden tension in his voice. "A great fire."

"Trapspringer save me," Kronn murmured. "The Kenderwood's burning."

Chapter 13

They slept fitfully that night, at the very edge of the forest. Each took a turn at watch, looking to the north and east where the ruddy glow continued to light the sky. By morning the wind had shifted, and smoke drifted into their eyes as they packed their bedrolls, quickly broke their fast with cold biscuits and sausage from the Pig and Whistle, and took to the road once more.

As they rode, their horses grew more and more nervous. The smell of burning was everywhere, though the fire was yet miles away. There was another scent too, still faint but unmistakably foul, which made their mounts even more skittish. Around midday they gave up riding, finding it faster to dismount and lead their steeds along Kendermore's winding main road.

Kronn and Catt took the lead, marching swiftly and wiping stinging soot from their eyes as they crested one low hill after another. Every league, Swiftraven sought out a suitably tall tree and climbed it, nimbly ascending until he was above the blanket of boughs that spread above the path. Each time he jumped back down with the same report. The fire was still far ahead and did not look to be getting any closer. They passed the whole day that way, never stopping for more than a few minutes. They kept moving on through the deepening dark, always toward the glow. All five knew it would be fruitless to make camp. None of them would be able to sleep with that terrible light before them.

Then, sometime in the morning's smallest hours, the glow began to waver and fade. The smell of smoke still clung to the woodland like a shroud, maddeningly strong, but there was no doubting what they saw. The fire was going out. Long before the sky began to bruise with the promise of dawn, the light had vanished entirely. If anything, it only strengthened their resolve to go on.

The sun still had not risen halfway to its full height when the forest ended. It was as if the party had struck a wall. The underbrush stopped suddenly, giving way to blackened earth. For a hundred yards or more, there were no trees at all, only stumps. Beyond the strange, razed clearing—which stretched out of sight to either side—the poplars and maples resumed, clawing upward with leafless, ash-caked branches. Smoke hovered around their sooty trunks like mist, swirling as the wind clawed past. Here and there, orange light flickered where small, stubborn fires still smoldered.

Riverwind bent beside a blackened stump, his hand running over the charred wood.

"Too even," he pronounced. "This tree did not fall. It was cut with a saw. So were the others."

Swiftraven crouched down, running his hand through the ashes. "This was burned on purpose."

"Someone cleared the trees away, then scorched the earth," Riverwind agreed. "A firebreak, to keep the flames contained."

"My people did this," Kronn said. He unslung his chapak from his back and compared its blade to the axe marks on a smoking stump. "They trapped the fire and let it burn out."

Catt whistled, impressed. "It must have taken hundreds of them, cutting the whole day long."

"Where is everyone, then?" Brightdawn wondered, looking around the clearing. "If there were so many of them here, where did they go now that the fire's out?"

"The same place we're going," Kronn answered. "Kendermore. Paxina said she'd order people back from the outlying villages . . . if there was trouble. . . . Make no mistake," he added solemnly, "those woods ahead of us were burned just as deliberately as the firebreak."

* * * * *

Morning wore on to midday as they picked their way through the burnt forest, holding Kronn's handkerchiefs over their noses and mouths to keep from choking on the lingering smoke. All around them the bare trees moaned, blackened branches clawing upward like the hands of a thousand charred skeletons. It was almost noon when they reached the remains of a tiny cottage, reduced to nothing but a chimney and stone foundation. For a while they searched for bodies but found none. "Whoever lived here got out in time," Riverwind said.

"There aren't any axes here," Swiftraven added, rooting through the ruins of a tool shed. The metal heads of shovels and hammers glinted dully amid the ashes. "They must have gone to help make the firebreak."

"And the children?" Brightdawn asked, holding up another bit of metal. It was a toy knight, made out of tin.

Catt shrugged. "Fled to Kendermore, I guess."

"Come on," Kronn said, his voice firm with determination. He had already begun to walk onward, leaving the cottage behind. "It's not much farther to the nearest hamlet—Weavewillow."

* * * * *

Weavewillow was no more. The town, which had once been home to some eight hundred kender, had been blasted from the face of Krynn. Like the cottage, wood and plaster and thatch were gone, leaving nothing but empty, stone husks where homes and shops had stood. Chimneys had blown apart, and cobblestone streets had cracked from the heat. The town well was nothing more than a pool of glassy rock around a steaming hole.

"What could have done this?" Brightdawn wondered, staring at Weavewillow's five-towered town hall. The spires had melted, then hardened again, so they looked like candles that had burned down to stubs. "I've never seen a fire that could do this to solid rock."

"I have," Riverwind said, his face dark. "In old Qué-Shu, after Verminaard's troops laid waste to it. The stones were melted there. The only thing I've ever seen that could make flames this hot is a red dragon."

"It's just like Woodsedge after Malys attacked," Catt agreed.

"Then—are we too late?" Swiftraven asked. He held his sabre naked in his hand and was watching the woods, his body tensed.

"No," Catt answered. "I saw tracks, leading away from town. They went to Kendermore, I'm sure." She scratched in the soot with the butt of her hoopak. "Kronn, we'd better get moving. Pax will be waiting for us."

A moment passed, and no one answered. Catt looked around. "Kronn?"

Her brother was gone.

Instantly alert, Riverwind and Swiftraven fanned out, combing through the rubble with their swords ready. Catt followed, calling Kronn's name. It was Brightdawn, though, who found him, at the far edge of Weavewillow. Her horrified cry brought the others running.

Beneath the blackened arch of the ruined gatehouse, Brightdawn stood over Kronn, who was on his knees, face buried in his hands. He had found the bodies.

They were everywhere around him, dozens of them, burnt black by the conflagration. The Plainsfolk felt bile rise in their throats as they beheld the tiny corpses, frail as birds, strewn upon the earth like a child's discarded toys.

"There was a fierce battle here," Swiftraven noted, moving from one body to the next. Many still clutched weapons in their charred hands. "A fighting withdrawal, I'd say."

"A withdrawal from what?" Brightdawn wondered, putting her arm around Kronn. She was close to choking on the sickly sweet smell that hung in the air. "Not the dragon, surely."

"Here!" Riverwind called suddenly. He had wandered away from the others and was staring at something on the ground. Brightdawn remained with Kronn, but Catt and Swiftraven hurried to see what the old Plainsman had found.

There were more bodies where Riverwind stood, but they were not kender. They were too big—larger than humans, many more than eight feet tall. Swiftraven nudged one with his foot, and winced as its burnt flesh crackled. Its had fallen forward, and so its face had escaped the worst of the fire. The blistered skin was brown, mottled with dark, hairy warts, and its features were ugly and brutish. Low, heavy brows surmounted a blunt, broad nose. Teeth that were almost tusks jutted from its mouth above a strong, square chin. The creature wore a leather breastplate and bracers, and near its blackened fist lay the iron head of a massive battle axe.

"Ogre," Swiftraven said, and spat in the ashes.

Catt nodded slowly. "They must be in league with Malys now. These died fighting my people before the dragon burned the town."

"Could there still be more around here?" Swiftraven asked, his sharp eyes flicking from shadow to shadow.

"No," Riverwind said. "They would have left before the dragon attacked. They probably chased the kender north, toward Kendermore."

Swiftraven's eyes widened with sudden understanding. "They're driving them," he murmured. Riverwind nodded.

"Driving them?" Catt asked. "But—what does that mean? What are we going to find at Kendermore?"

The others looked at Riverwind. He thought on this, then shook his head. "I don't know."

*　*　*　*　*

Kronn trudged along like a wounded man, his head bowed in grief. Catt walked beside him, her hand on his shoulder, but she was too stricken herself to give her brother much comfort. In her other hand she held the reins of their horses, who followed nervously, eyes rolling and nostrils flaring at the strange sights and smells that surrounded them.

Swiftraven stalked ahead of the party, an arrow nocked

on his bowstring, alertly watching for signs of movement among the blasted trees. Riverwind brought up the rear, also ready to loose a shaft, should anything choose to loom at them from behind. It was Brightdawn, though, who first heard the sound.

It was soft, almost too quiet to discern, and for a moment she hesitated, wondering if she had heard it at all. Then it rose again and she held up a hand, hissing through clenched teeth.

The others stopped immediately, Swiftraven pulling back his bowstring as he hurried to Brightdawn's side. "What is it?" Catt asked.

With a sharp gesture, Brightdawn waved her silent. She cocked an ear, concentrating. The sound grew momentarily louder, so everyone could hear it—a low, tired whimper.

"What is it?" Swiftraven whispered. "A wounded animal?"

"No," Brightdawn replied. "It's a child crying."

"A child?" Catt asked. "Out here?"

The Plainswoman didn't bother to answer; she started walking. Swiftraven jogged to catch up with her.

"Brightdawn!" Riverwind hissed. "Wait! It could be a trap!"

Ignoring her father's call, Brightdawn continued to move, pausing only to listen a moment and make sure she was still headed toward the sound. They were nearly a league north of Weavewillow, and the ground here was rocky. Great boulders dotted with charred moss loomed among the blasted trees. Swiftly, Brightdawn made her way toward a cleft between two such rocks.

Swiftraven eyed the gap, which was dark, wide and deep. He trained his arrow on it. "I think maybe we should wait for your father, Brightdawn," he whispered. "There could be anything in there."

Stubbornly, Brightdawn shook her head. "No," she answered, and started toward the cleft. Swiftraven quickly relaxed his pull on his bowstring and caught her arm.

"At least let me go first," he said.

Seeing the pleading look in his eyes, Brightdawn nodded. "Watch what you shoot at," she told him.

Moving slowly, arrow ready, Swiftraven stepped into the gap. For a moment he couldn't see anything, but then his eyes adjusted to the shadows, and he discerned the walls of the cleft. He continued to creep forward, Brightdawn right behind him. The whimpering was much louder here, ringing weirdly off the stones.

Then, suddenly, he stopped, staring at something on the ground. Slowly, he relaxed his pull on his bow. "Merciful goddess," he swore.

"What?" Brightdawn asked. "What is it? Let me through." She pushed past him, following his gaze, and stopped.

There, huddled in the bottom of the cleft, weeping uncontrollably as she hugged her knees to her chest, was a little kender girl. She looked up, her eyes wide, and drew back from the Plainsfolk.

"It's all right," Brightdawn said. She crouched low, moving forward slowly to keep from startling the child. "Hush, now. I'm going to help you."

The girl was tiny. She couldn't have been more than eight years old. Brightdawn crept toward her, making soothing sounds. At last, the child stopped sobbing and stared up at the Plainsfolk, her bottom lip quivering.

"That's better," Brightdawn said, smiling. "What's your name, little one?"

The girl hiccuped a few times, trying to find her voice. "B-Billee," she stammered. "Billee Juniper."

"Hello, Billee," Brightdawn said, stopping in front of the child. She crouched down and held out her hand. "I'm Brightdawn. That man there is Swiftraven. Don't worry, he's here to protect you, not to hurt you. Where are your parents?"

For a moment, Billee didn't answer. Then she started to cry again.

"All right, shhh," Brightdawn said, fighting back sudden tears herself. "We're going to take you out of here to someplace safe. Would you like that?"

The little kender stared up at her, eyes gleaming. Then she clasped her own tiny hand around one of Brightdawn's fingers. Gently, the Plainswoman gathered the child to her chest. Billee wrapped her twig-thin arms around Brightdawn's neck and held tight, trembling, as the Plainsfolk turned and moved back out of the cleft.

Kronn and Catt were waiting where they'd left them; Riverwind was with them, his expression sick with worry. A look of immense relief settled over his face when his daughter returned.

"You should have waited," he told her.

At the sound of his stern voice, Billee started to cry again. Shooting her father a reproachful look, Brightdawn stroked the child's long, black hair, clucking her tongue soothingly. "It's all right," she cooed. "It's going to be all right, Billee. Don't be afraid."

Kronn looked up at her, startled. "What did you say?"

"I'm just trying to calm her down," Brightdawn answered tersely.

Catt, however, had the same strange look on her face as her brother.

"Let me see her," Catt said. "Please."

Her skin growing cold, the Plainswoman knelt down. Catt reached out, hesitantly, and touched Billee's shoulder.

"Trapspringer's ghost," she gasped. "She's shaking. She *is* afraid."

"I don't understand," Swiftraven said. "I thought you people weren't supposed to be able to feel fear."

Catt looked up at the Plainsfolk, her eyes wide and confused. "That's what I thought, too."

* * * * *

The light of the waning moon streamed through the window of Moonsong's bedchamber, falling across her body as she writhed among the blankets. She moaned in anguish, fighting against the throes of a terrible nightmare.

"No," she mumbled. "Bodies . . . fire . . ."

The sound of her despairing voice woke Stagheart from his own slumber. Blearily, he wiped his eyes and rolled over to look at her. "Moonsong," he whispered. His strong hand reached for her, brushed the smooth curve of her shoulder. "You're dreaming, love."

She cried out, her voice slashing the stillness like a razor. "No!"

"Moonsong!" Stagheart sat up quickly, then bent over her and shook her gently. "Wake up!"

For a moment she resisted, beating at him with her fists, but he held her fast until her eyes fluttered open. She looked at him blankly, seeming to stare through him. "Where . . ." she began, her voice trailing away.

"It's all right," Stagheart said. "You're in Qué-Shu. I'm here."

"Stagheart?" She blinked. "You came back."

He nodded, folding his arms about her. His face, however, was troubled. He had returned to Qué-Shu more than a week ago, bearing the head of the griffon that had been troubling the herdsmen to the south. He had brought the grisly trophy into the Lodge of Brothers at the center of the village and laid it at the feet of Moonsong's mother. Goldmoon, in return, had declared that, with his Courting Quest completed, he was free to marry her daughter.

Moonsong, however, appeared to remember none of this, even though they had spoken of the wedding earlier in the night as they lay flushed and breathless in each other's arms. They had agreed the day would come as soon as possible. "But not until Brightdawn returns," Moonsong had said, kissing him. "Your brother, too."

Now, she barely seemed to recognize him at all. Stagheart held her, running his fingers through her long, golden hair. She trembled like a newborn foal, her skin rising in gooseflesh, and clutched at him in return.

"Oh, Stagheart," she moaned.

"What's the matter?" he asked. "Was it Brightdawn?"

She nodded, sucking a shuddering breath through her teeth. In the moonlight, her tanned skin looked pale and wan, and she glistened with cold sweat.

"Moonsong, you have to tell me. Was she in danger?"

She shook her head. "No. Not yet . . . but—"

Suddenly, the door swung open. Orange light spilled through the entrance, falling across the bed. Standing in the doorway was Goldmoon, clad in a sky-blue robe and cupping a tallow candle in her hands. The dim light flickered as she stepped into her daughter's bedchamber.

"Mother!" Moonsong gasped, her mouth dropping open.

Goldmoon said nothing, only stared at the two of them as they clung to each other. There was an odd look in her eyes, an incongruous mixture of disapproval and grudging empathy.

"My chief," Stagheart said, letting Moonsong go. He scrambled out of the bed to kneel before her, grabbing a blanket as he did so to conceal his nakedness.

"You know the custom, both of you," Goldmoon said sharply. "You should not share a bedchamber until you are married. This is an ancient tradition, not to be taken lightly, Stagheart of Qué-Teh."

Stagheart dropped even lower, prostrating himself before her. The rushes on the floor pressed against his face. "Forgive me, my chief," he pleaded.

She paid him little attention, however; her concentration focused on her daughter. "Child," she murmured. "Have you dreamt of your sister again?"

Moonsong looked up at her mother, her eyes dark, and nodded wordlessly.

Goldmoon's stern expression softened. She and Stagheart exchanged a knowing look. Moonsong and Brightdawn had shared dreams since they'd been babies.

"Moonsong," Goldmoon said. "Tell me. Where is she? What has happened?"

"Near Kendermore," Moonsong answered, her voice faint and wavering. "She is well—and so are Father and Swiftraven. Their journey shall end tomorrow. But—the Kenderwood has burned, and ogres lurk among the ashes. And the kender are—" She stopped abruptly, her gaze drifting. "The kender are in terrible danger," she said.

Goldmoon, lost in thought, regarded her daughter.

"You want to go to her, don't you?" she said.

"Yes."

Goldmoon sighed heavily. Her shoulders slumped, and a weary look settled over her. "There's little to say, then," she said. "Go. Take Stagheart with you."

Stagheart looked from mother to daughter, saw the conviction in both women's eyes, and knew it would be little use to argue.

Moonsong, however, regarded Goldmoon with an expression of worry and guilt. "I'm sorry, Mother," she said. "We're all leaving you. I can wait until Wanderer returns to Qué-Shu—"

"No." Goldmoon shook her head firmly. "I will not hold you here. Go to Kendermore, child. Find your sister." Her eyes shining, she started to turn away—then stopped, her hand on the door. "Take my blessing with you."

Then she was gone. Moonsong stared at the door as it eased shut, then slumped back among the blankets with a quiet sob. Stagheart climbed back into bed beside her, gathered her in his arms again, and held her close, whispering softly as, outside, the moon slid slowly among the clouds.

Chapter 14

The day dawned gray, the sun reluctantly shedding its dim glow through the haze of drifting smoke. The companions rose slowly, their bodies and hearts heavy. None of them had found much solace in sleep, their dreams haunted by memories of what they had seen yesterday and thoughts of what might yet lie ahead. Little Billee Juniper whimpered softly, cradled in Brightdawn's arms as the others broke camp.

"How far is it to Kendermore?" Riverwind asked, taking a long pull from his water skin. When he'd finished drinking, he poured another measure over his face and tried to scrub away the soot that darkened his skin. He was haggard underneath the black smudges, hollow-eyed and ague-cheeked.

Kronn glanced around, studying the blasted forest. The Plainsfolk marveled that the kender could pick out any landmarks at all amid the ruined woodland. "A few leagues, I think," he judged. "It's only about three hours' walk from the Wendle River to town." They had crossed the river last night, shortly before darkness cloaked the Kenderwood. It had been like the rest of the woods: black and foul, choked with ash.

"We'll be there by midday, then," Riverwind judged. He shouldered his pack and went to unhobble the horses. "Come on," he said. "Let's put an end to this at last."

* * * * *

An hour up the road to Kendermore, they reached another firebreak. The companions stopped, staring back and forth along its charred breadth. On the far side the forest was whole, untouched by the flames that had ravaged the land around Weavewillow. The sight of green leaves came as a shock. They had been walking through ashes for nearly a day and had seen little color in all that time. Even Kronn and Catt's bright clothing was smudged with black and gray. The vibrancy of nature before them seemed alien.

"This one's even wider than the one we saw yesterday," Riverwind remarked, studying the firebreak.

"They must have made this to protect Kendermore," Kronn surmised. "They didn't have time to save Weavewillow, but here they managed to stop it. I recognize those trees on the far side there." He pointed across the blackened clearing with his chapak, which he'd had in his hand since they'd set out that morning. Slender-limbed trees grew in even rows. "Erryl Locklift's orchard—well, half of it, anyway. Looks like they made the firebreak right through the middle of it."

They crossed the firebreak. The welcoming embrace of the forest folded around them when they reached the other side. For the first time since they'd entered the Kenderwood, the air did not reek of burning, though the smell of smoke still clung to their skin and clothes. The rustling of the leaves soothed their beleaguered spirits. Even little Billee Juniper, who rode upon Swiftraven's shoulders, stopped trembling as they left the devastation behind.

As they made their way between the orchard's orderly rows, Catt reached up and plucked a green apple from an overhanging branch. She eyed it critically, then took a crunching bite. An instant later, she spat it out again. "Phooey!" she blurted, her mouth puckering. "Branchala's boots, that's awful!"

"They're probably not ripe yet," Kronn told her. "It's like the bloodberries—the apples still think it's midsummer. This crazy weather's messed all the crops up."

"That isn't it," his sister replied, her lip curling with

disgust as she regarded the rest of the apple. "I mean, yes, it's sour, but there's something else."

"What is it, Catt?"

She opened her mouth to reply, then shut it again, shaking her head in frustration. "I don't know. Here." She tossed the apple to her brother. Kronn caught it easily, looked at it, then bit into the fruit's hard flesh. Immediately, his face contorted into an astringent grimace, and he also spat out his mouthful.

"Ack," he declared, wincing as he smacked his lips. "It tastes like . . . I don't know. Rotten eggs." He sniffed the half-eaten apple, wrinkled his nose, and threw it away. It disappeared into the bushes with a rattle of branches.

"Could all that smoke have poisoned the apples somehow?" Brightdawn asked, glancing warily at the fruit-laden boughs that spread above their heads.

Riverwind shook his head. "Even if it could, the wind's blowing south. The smoke would have gone the other way. Something else is at work here."

It wasn't just the apples. When the party left the orchard, returning to the wilder expanses of the Kenderwood, Riverwind stepped from the path and examined an old, moss-dappled elm tree. Its bark was brittle, and flaked away at his touch like old parchment. Beneath, the living wood was gray and riddled with cracks. Drawing his knife, he carefully carved a piece out of the tree and held it to his nose. It, too, smelled of brimstone.

"This whole forest is dying," the old Plainsman declared, crouching to look at a hawthorn bush. The plant's leaves were curled and brown at the edges.

"I don't believe it!" Catt exclaimed. "What could be causing this?"

"I don't know," Riverwind answered helplessly. "The signs point to drought, but that doesn't explain the smell."

"It's magic," Brightdawn interrupted.

Everyone stopped what they were doing and looked at her, astonished. "Brightdawn," Swiftraven said, "there's no such thing as magic any more—not since the moons disappeared. You know that."

"Even so," she answered, "there's some kind of magic at work here. It's in the air, all around us. It's what's making the weather so warm. Something's cast a spell over this whole land. Can't any of you feel it?"

They stood still, concentrating, and each of them sensed it too. It was faint, but there was no mistaking the feeling that hung about them: pain, as if the earth itself were in torment. They shuddered.

"It's horrible," said Kronn. "I've never felt anything like it before."

"I have," Riverwind said. He shut his eyes against a sudden rush of memory. "Once, many years ago, in Silvanesti. It was stronger there than it is here, but . . ."

"Silvanesti," Brightdawn echoed dully. "Oh, no."

"What happened in Silvanesti?" Swiftraven asked.

The old Plainsman heaved a sigh that seemed to come from the depths of his soul. He opened his eyes again. They were like open wounds. "I died," he answered. "In Lorac's nightmare."

No one spoke. There was no need—all of them had heard the tales. During the War of the Lance, Lorac, the elven Speaker of the Stars, had tried to use a dragon orb to drive the dragonarmies from his realm. Instead, it had ensnared him, trapping him in an unbreakable dream. Drawn by the orb's power, the green dragon Cyan Bloodbane had come and whispered nightmares into Lorac's ear. The elven king's dark dreams, given form by the orb's magic, had broken the land and driven his people into exile. Riverwind and his companions had entered the nightmare, winning their way to the Speaker's throne room so that Lorac's daughter Alhana could end his torment, but the wounds inflicted upon the land had remained. It had taken the elves more than three decades to heal those wounds and reclaim the forest.

"Malystryx is doing this, isn't she?" Kronn asked. "It's her magic that's killing the trees. That's why everything smells of brimstone."

"Yes," Riverwind answered grimly. "And from what you've told me of her, I don't know if we can stop her. If she keeps doing this to the land here, soon there won't be anything left to save."

* * * * *

The forest's pain stayed with them as they walked, a dull, aching throb that stubbornly refused to go away. Billee Juniper began to cry again, and nothing Brightdawn or any of the others said or did would calm her. The horses, too, grew agitated. Every few hundred yards, one of the animals would freeze where it stood, refusing to move on. Each time, Riverwind and Swiftraven managed to coax it back into motion, but the interruptions slowed their progress. The sun passed its apex and was sliding down into afternoon before they made it a league from the orchard.

Then, at last, the woods ended in a vast clearing, a meadow several miles across. In the middle of the clearing stood Kendermore.

It was much larger than the Plainsfolk had imagined. Looking upon it, Riverwind realized that only a few of Ansalon's grandest cities—Palanthas, Tarsis, Sanction, Qualinost, Silvanost, and the dwarves' underground city of Thorbardin—could be said to be larger. He was heartened to see the town was surrounded by a tall wall of pale stone, surmounted by crenelated battlements and punctuated by stout, circular towers. Scores of gaily colored pennants—red and gold, sky blue and sea green, orange and purple, and many other hues—stood atop the wall, waving listlessly in the meager breeze.

The battlements hid much of the city from view, but the buildings that rose above the wall were more than enough to give the Plainsfolk some idea of what lay within. There didn't seem to be any plan or order to anything, and there certainly didn't seem to be a single "style" particular to the kender. True to their nature, they borrowed whatever ideas they wanted from Krynn's other cities. Here a strong, square tower in the old Ergothic style loomed at least four storeys above the city walls. There a domed minaret that resembled the temples they had seen in Khur stood beside a crude wooden structure that would have seemed quite at home in a hobgoblin village. Elsewhere the kender had erected several slender, silvery spires that might have been plucked from the elfhome in Qualinesti, and Riverwind even saw what looked like a miniature version of the fortress of Pax Tharkas. The old Plainsman covered a sudden smile with his hand, wondering what visiting dwarves thought of that—especially since it seemed to be slightly askew, leaning a little to one side like a drunken man.

Kendermore was alive with activity, too: guards lined the battlements, peering out across the grassy meadow and gripping bows and hoopaks in their hands. Shouting, laughter, and music rose from within the walls, mingling with the sounds of hammering, digging, and other work. Somewhere, a large bell was tolling the hour—glancing across the city's mismatched skyline, Riverwind picked out the source of the sound: a building resembling an old Istarian church but painted a garish mix of violet and turquoise. It stood near the gatehouse, where the road the companions stood upon wound toward a pair of stout oaken doors. Smoke rose lazily from a multitude of chimneys, curling on the warm, dry wind. It carried the tempting scents of cooking food, making the companions' mouths water.

Kronn's face, which had set into a tense scowl as they walked, relaxed into a glad smile. He reached for his sister and grasped her arm. "We made it," he said. "We're home."

Catt returned her brother's smile, and both Brightdawn and Swiftraven breathed sighs of relief. Riverwind, however, looked upon Kendermore and frowned.

The old Plainsman's brows knitted as he studied the town. "Something isn't right," he said quietly.

Everyone looked at him.

"Father?" Brightdawn inquired. "What is it?"

At first, Riverwind didn't seem to have heard. He continued to stare at Kendermore, lost in thought. At length, he shook his head in frustration. "I don't know," he said, "but I don't think we should go on."

"What are you talking about?" Catt asked. She laughed, spreading her hands. "We've only got another mile to go."

"She's right, my chief," Swiftraven agreed. "We've come so far. We can't stop now, with our goal in sight." As he spoke, however, he pulled his bow from his saddle and slid an arrow out of his quiver.

They stood at the edge of the dying forest for several long minutes. The companions stared at Riverwind, who stared at the city. The horses whickered, stamping the ground nervously.

"Father," Brightdawn said finally, "we can't stay here forever. Do we turn back or go on?"

Riverwind swore under his breath, cursing his inability to find a source for his misgivings. "We go on."

They set out across the meadow, moving briskly but warily toward Kendermore. The golden grass whispered about their boots as they walked. Then, suddenly, when they had gone five hundred paces, Riverwind stopped again, his brow furrowing fiercely. After a moment, the others realized he wasn't with them and glanced over their shoulders.

"Father?" Brightdawn asked. Seeing the disquiet on his face, her eyes were filled with worry.

"Come on, Riverwind," Kronn urged.

Suddenly, the old Plainsman stiffened, sucking in a sharp breath. "By the gods," he swore. "The gates . . ."

"What?" Brightdawn asked.

"Closed!" Riverwind shouted. "The gates are closed!"

Everyone looked down the trail. Sure enough, Kendermore's tall, wooden gates were tightly shut. No guardsmen stood outside. No one rode out to meet them. When the figures atop the battlements saw them at last, they began to wave their arms and shout.

Brightdawn glanced at Kronn and Catt. "What's going on?" she demanded, her voice brittle with tension. "What are they saying?"

"Shhh!" Kronn interrupted, holding up a warning

hand. His eyes pinched shut, his face creasing with concentration. The kender's eyes flew open. "They're telling us to go back," he hissed, the words coming out in a rush.

"Father?" Brightdawn cried, looking back toward Riverwind. "What do we—" Then her breath caught in her throat, and she could only gape in shock.

"Brightdawn?" Swiftraven asked as the others turned to follow her horrified gaze. "What's the—merciful goddess!"

They came out of the woods behind Riverwind, boiling across the meadow toward the companions—hundreds of ogres, running at full speed and howling with battle rage. Swords and axes, spears and clubs waved in the air as the war band charged toward the companions, a great wave of iron, muscle, and hate.

The sight of the onrushing horde paralyzed the companions, momentarily stunning them into inaction. All they could do was stand still, mouths agape, as their doom bore down upon them.

Then Riverwind was moving, running to his horse's side. "Go!" he roared, planting a foot in the stirrup and hoisting himself up. The horse was already galloping toward Kendermore as he swung onto its back. "Ride, damn it! Ride!"

The sound of his frantic voice woke the others from their trance. They dashed for their mounts, vaulting into their saddles and spurring the beasts on, away from the thundering mass of ogres. Swiftraven twisted about, firing an arrow back at the monsters. It dropped uselessly into their midst, a raindrop in an angry sea. He turned back around, not even bothering to mark where it fell. "Head for the gates!" he cried. "We can beat them there yet!"

"No!" Riverwind bellowed in return. "The kender would never get the gates open fast enough to let us in— and they'd never get them closed again in time."

"Well, we can't go back!" Brightdawn shouted. "What do we do?"

"Go right!" Riverwind shouted at last. "Around the city! We'll try and escape to the north!"

They turned away from the unyielding gates, the ogres running behind, cutting narrow swaths through the grass of the meadow. The tall curtain wall streaked by on their left, little more than a gray blur. Atop the battlements, the town's guards continued to yell, but the rushing of the wind in the riders' ears made it impossible to hear what they were saying. As the ogres approached, the kender on the wall stopped yelling and started to rain arrows and stones down upon them. The war band's front ranks fell, pierced and crushed by the bombardment; the next rank, however, was not so blinded by bloodlust. They made a wider circuit around Kendermore, outside the range of the kender's weapons. This bought time for the riders, letting them put more ground between them and their pursuers.

After long minutes of hard riding, the companions cleared the far side of Kendermore and broke out across the open meadow toward the welcoming green line of the northern Kenderwood.

Then more ogres swarmed out of that green line, lumbering straight toward the riders. "No!" Brightdawn cried, her voice raw with despair. She leaned over, little Billee Juniper clinging to her neck, and called out to her father. "What now?"

Riverwind, who had been asking himself that very question, glanced back at the horde some distance behind them, then forward at the onrushing numbers that barred their way. "We go through!" he answered, his sabre ringing in challenge as he drew it from its scabbard.

"Through?" Swiftraven repeated, astonished. "Are you sure, my chief?"

"Do you see a choice?" Riverwind shot back angrily. He flipped his reins, digging his heels into his horse's flanks. The animal tossed its head, galloping even faster toward the oncoming horde. "Would you rather go back?"

There was no further argument. As one, the riders guided their mounts straight toward their onrushing foes. Swiftraven drew his sword, and together he and Riverwind brandished their blades in the air. Kronn raised his chapak, and Brightdawn her mace. Unable to wield her hoopak from astride her pony, Catt drew a long dagger from her belt and held it ready.

The distance to the ogres dwindled with astonishing speed as the horses' pounding hooves devoured the land. Seeing that their quarry didn't mean to turn aside, the ogres raised their weapons. The companions gritted their teeth and spurred their mounts. The terrified horses ran on, flecks of lather flying from their bodies. As the last yards of open ground disappeared between the companions and their foes, Swiftraven raised his voice in a loud, ululating Qué-Teh war cry. Riverwind echoed the young warrior's shout, and Brightdawn and the kender hollered as the riders struck the horde.

If it wasn't for their momentum, the wall of sinew and steel would have stopped them dead. As it was, the front line of ogres scattered to avoid being trampled. Horses' hooves and flashing weapons felled nearly a dozen of the monsters, darkening the grass with blood. Riverwind moved at the fore, guiding his horse on little more than instinct. He sought the weak points in the ogres' ranks, striking all around him with his sabre, his blade flashing in the sunlight.

Swiftraven's blade also ran red as he laid about, and to his right Brightdawn fought ferociously, her mace waving wildly as Billee clung to her. Kronn swung his chapak high, cleaving an ogre's snarling head from its shoulders; swiftly he reversed the blow, and the axe struck a second beast in the gut. The ogre slumped to the ground, clutching at its riven belly.

"Yippee!" Kronn cried.

The ogres tried to fight back, lashing out with their pole-cleavers and massive war hammers, but they were slow, and the Plainsfolk and the kender evaded their blows.

The old Plainsman was the first to make it to the edge of the forest, the others close behind, when one ogre got a clear shot at Catt, thrusting his spear at her. The kender ducked nimbly aside, but the point impaled her pony through the neck. The animal fell with a scream of agony. Catt clutched the horn of her saddle and went down. She regained her wits an instant before the horse crashed to the ground, however, and leapt off its back, throwing herself clear. She fell some twenty feet away and heard a snap as her right arm struck the ground. Then her head struck a tree and her world crashed into darkness.

When Kronn saw his sister fall, he hauled on his reins with all his might. His mount stopped so suddenly, he nearly pitched out of the saddle himself.

"Catt!" he shouted, then wheeled about and rode back toward her senseless, crumpled form.

The ogres stumbled about him in confusion, caught flat-footed by his reversal. He slammed his blade into one monster's chest, cleaving through its ribs. The ogre stumbled back, blood welling from the deep wound. In an eyeblink Kronn was at his sister's side. Without hesitation, he leaned sideways in the saddle, gripping his pony with his knees, and snagged the collar of Catt's shirt. Her head lolled limply against his shoulder as, muscles straining, he hoisted them both astride the pony's back. Then he started to turn back toward the forest.

Ogres blocked his way, driving back his fear-maddened steed with great, sweeping swings of their weapons. One came too close, and he hacked off its arm with his chapak, but Kronn quickly realized that he was trapped. Glaring at the ogres as they closed in around him, he did what any self-respecting kender would do. He began to taunt them.

"Look out!" he shouted at one. "There's a great, big leech sucking on your face . . . oh, wait. That's your nose."

"What's the matter?" he asked another. "Did someone spill a jug of ugly on you when you were a baby?"

"Is that how your breath normally smells, or did a gully dwarf crawl down your throat and die?"

His taunts were too much for the ogres to bear. Howling with rage, they charged. He spun his chapak, laughing as he cut down one after another. They were many, though, and at last one of their reaching hands latched around his elbow. The fingers' viselike grip numbed his arm, and his chapak fell from nerveless fingers to dangle from a leather thong looped around his wrist. He fumbled at his belt for his knife.

Then the sound of galloping hooves filled the air. The ogres turned to look behind them, then let out a cry of alarm, raising their weapons. They were too late. Swiftraven fell upon them from behind, sabre rising and falling, slashing and stabbing. In moments, the Plainsman cut a path through the mob; the ogre who had grabbed Kronn's arm died with Swiftraven's blade in its throat.

Even as Swiftraven urged him to hurry, the kender spurred his horse once more, charging along the path the young warrior had carved through the ogres' midst. Swiftraven followed, his sword still dancing.

Then they were on the other side of the ogres, riding north through the sparse, light forest. The enemy gave chase, but the kender and Plainsman quickly outpaced them, and by the time they were two leagues north of Kendermore, there was no longer any sign of pursuit. Kronn and Swiftraven reined in.

Immediately, the kender examined his sister. He pressed his fingers against her throat, holding his breath as he felt for a life beat, then closed his eyes and sighed with clear relief.

"How is she?" Swiftraven asked. He wiped streaming sweat from his face. "Is she badly hurt?"

"Judge for yourself," Kronn returned, gesturing at Catt's broken arm. Her hair was also sticky with blood from a gash where she'd struck her head. "What happened to Riverwind and Brightdawn?"

Swiftraven glanced around. "I don't know," he admitted. "They were ahead of me when I turned around and went back for you. They must be around here somewhere." He hooked his fingers in his mouth and shrilled a call in whistle-speak.

The woods were silent a moment; then another whistle trilled in reply, echoing among the trees. Swiftraven and Kronn craned their necks, looking around for its source.

"There they are," Swiftraven said, pointing to the east. Riverwind and Brightdawn were trotting toward them, still on horseback. Bringing their own mounts about, Kronn and Swiftraven rode to meet them.

"Thanks, by the way," Kronn said, "for coming back for us." He glanced down at Catt, whose face tightened with pain as the pony jounced up and down.

Swiftraven smiled warmly. "You already did the same for me. I honor my debts."

* * * * *

The companions rode onward without any clear destination. They continued north, watching behind for signs of pursuit, until they reached a small creek whose clear water carried only the faintest whiff of brimstone. They drank thirstily, washed the blood and grime from their bodies, then set about tending their wounds. Riverwind, who had been struck a glancing blow on his shoulder by an ogre's axe, winced as Brightdawn rinsed and bound the cut. When she was done, he rose and hobbled over to where Kronn and Swiftraven were splinting Catt's arm.

"How is she?" he asked.

Swiftraven shrugged. "It's hard to say. We've set her arm, but she took quite a bump on her head, and there isn't much we can do about it now."

"She needs a healer," Kronn declared. "We've got to get her to Kendermore."

"We could take her west, back to Balifor," Riverwind mused, stroking his chin. "Maybe we can find help for her there."

Kronn said. "I'm telling you, Kendermore's her best chance."

"Kronn," said Swiftraven sympathetically, "we could

never get through the gates."

The kender's eyes narrowed. "I wasn't saying we should go that way."

"What are you talking about?" Riverwind asked.

"Just because the gate's blocked, that doesn't mean we're stuck out here. There are other ways."

"Other ways?" Brightdawn echoed.

"Of course," Kronn said. "Kender always leave a back way in."

Chapter 15

"It should be around here somewhere," Kronn said, poking at a thornbush with the head of his chapak.

Swiftraven glanced at Riverwind, who shook his head and shrugged. "It might help if we knew what you were looking for," the young warrior observed.

"Oh, I agree," Kronn agreed sincerely, "but every one of these is different."

"What are you talking about?" Brightdawn asked. "Every one of what is different?"

Kronn's mind was elsewhere, however; he squinted up at the sun, then glanced to his left. "I'm sure I'm remembering this right. That's the lightning-forked tree over there"—he pointed at a dead ashwood that had a scorched crack down its middle. "It should be right here—so where is the blasted thing?"

"What are we looking for?" Swiftraven asked skeptically. "A secret . . . bush?"

"It doesn't have to be a bush," Kronn answered. "It could be a tree stump, or a mushroom ring, or a rock. . . ." He stopped, bent down beside a flat stone, and lifted it up, muscles straining. When he had it high enough, he peered beneath it, frowned, and let it drop back to the ground with a thud. "Yuck. Nothing but bugs."

"Is there a key of some sort?" Brightdawn asked, looking around dubiously.

Kronn tugged his cheek braids as his eyes scanned the undergrowth. "No, not a key," he muttered. "Not a key . . . aha!" With a snap of his fingers, he trotted over to an old, fallen tree. It was old, its bark covered with fungi and thick, green moss. "This is it, I'm sure of it." He spat in his hands and gave the log a push. It didn't budge. "Humpf. It's stuck. Can someone help me over here?"

Riverwind and Swiftraven exchanged confused glances, then walked over to join Kronn. Brightdawn and little Billee stayed with Catt.

"That thing must have been lying there for a hundred years," Swiftraven said, shaking his head as he looked at the tree. "Look, it's sunk halfway into the ground. I don't think an ogre could lift it—and I know we can't."

"We can try," said Riverwind.

As Swiftraven looked on incredulously, the old Plainsman and Kronn braced themselves against the tree and shoved. It resisted a moment longer, then moved so suddenly that Riverwind fell to his knees. The log wasn't embedded in the earth at all; it had been sawn in half, then carefully laid upon the ground to give the illusion that it was nothing but an old, fallen tree.

It wasn't just a tree, though. It was a door.

"Mishakal's mercy," Riverwind gasped. The log swung aside, revealing a dark, yawning hole in the ground.

The others gathered around the opening. It was deep, sloping out of sight beneath the earth. Worn steps, made from packed earth, led down into the gloom.

"The entrance might be a bit cramped," said Kronn, "but things should open up a bit down below. Here we go." Smiling with satisfaction, he produced a small, brass lamp from his pouch.

Riverwind frowned as he looked at the lamp. "Isn't that from the Inn of the Last Home?"

"Is it?" Kronn asked, surprised. "You know, now that you mention it, it does look familiar. Caramon must have given it to me as a going-away gift, I suppose." He examined it carefully. "Good, there's still oil in it. Can anyone give me a light?"

* * * * *

There was no room in the tunnel for the horses, and though they were loath to do so in such dangerous lands, the companions had no choice but to set them free. They stripped off their mounts' saddles and bridles, gave each of them a handful of oats from their feed bags, then slapped them on their rumps, sending the startled animals trotting away through the forest. When the animals were gone from sight, Riverwind and Swiftraven fashioned a stretcher from a pair of stout branches and an old blanket, and laid Catt on top of it. The wounded kender grimaced, groaning dully, as the Plainsmen lifted her off the ground.

Kronn lit his lamp and gave it to Brightdawn. "Go on ahead," he told the others. "Wait for me at the bottom of the stairs."

They moved slowly down the crumbling steps, the little lamp dimly lighting their way. When the Plainsfolk had vanished into the darkness, Kronn descended the first few stairs, then reached to the wall. His grasping hand closed around a rope that hung down from the log door above. He pulled at it with all his strength, bracing himself against the wall of the tunnel. Slowly, the log slid back into place across the opening. Daylight narrowed to a sliver of dancing dust, then disappeared completely, replaced by utter blackness. Carefully, Kronn headed down the stairs, moving by touch as he followed the Plainsfolk.

The stairs wound down for what seemed forever, though Kronn knew from experience it was less than a hundred feet. Tree roots hung down from the ceiling, slapping at the kender's face in the darkness. The steps were treacherous and uneven, some of them slick with moisture. The air was dank and close and smelled of wet earth. It took Kronn many long minutes to grope his way to the bottom.

At last, he saw the ruddy glow of lamplight below. Recklessly quickening his pace, he bounded down the last dozen steps. The Plainsfolk were waiting for him, staring about in amazement.

They stood in a dark tunnel, which stretched out of sight in either direction. It was much broader than the stairway, and higher as well. Even Riverwind, who towered a head above the rest, could stand in its midst without stooping. The walls were made of packed earth, shored up with broad timbers every dozen paces or so. Next to each timber, a wall sconce held an unlit torch. Kronn pulled down two such torches, lit them with the lamp, and handed one to Brightdawn. The crackling flames seemed almost blindingly bright after their dim descent, but they still only carved small pockets of light out of the gloom.

"Almighty goddess," Swiftraven breathed. "Did your people build these, Kronn?"

"Us?" the kender asked, and chuckled. "No. We just keep them from falling apart. Come on, it's this way." Holding his smoldering brand aloft, he led the company down the passage to the left.

"Who did build them, then?" Brightdawn asked. Her voice echoed weirdly off the walls of the tunnel.

"Goblins, mostly," Kronn answered. "At least, they were the first—that was about five hundred years ago."

"Before the Cataclysm," Riverwind murmured, regarding the earthen walls with renewed awe.

Kronn nodded. "Before both Cataclysms, actually. It started when the Kingpriest of Istar issued some edict or other, saying the goblins were a pox upon the land and had to be exterminated. Now don't get me wrong, I don't much care for goblins, but that seems a bit extreme, you know?

"Anyway, suddenly there were warriors everywhere, hoping to collect the bounty the clergy put on goblin ears. I guess things got pretty bad, because the goblins decided to go underground, literally. They dug warrens and hid down here, only going up to raid for food and such.

"Of course, it doesn't end there. As time went on, the Kingpriests had started to get a little . . . funny. Not calling-down-fiery-mountains funny, but not at all right in the head, either. With the goblins gone, they needed a new enemy. They started going after heretics—and their definition of 'heretic' kept getting broader all the time. The heretics, in response, came up with the same idea the goblins had. They started to dig catacombs.

"It didn't take long, of course before the heretics and the goblins met. There was fighting at first, of course, but after a few battles the two groups decided they'd be better off working together. Kind of like how everyone fought together against Chaos, actually. So they called a truce, and the warrens and catacombs became one great, big underground city. And it just kept on growing, every time the Kingpriest declared holy war on some other group—priests of the neutral and evil gods, wizards of all kinds . . . even a lot of my people, toward the end. Can you imagine? The Kingpriest thought we were a blight upon the land!"

Swiftraven made a soft, snorting noise. Brightdawn glared at him. "I don't understand," she said. "Istar was hundreds of miles to the north of here. What are these tunnels doing here?"

"Istar was more than just a city, Brightdawn," Riverwind answered. "It was a great empire, stretching all the way from Nordmaar to Balifor, and from Neraka east to the sea."

"Right," Kronn agreed. "The Kenderwood didn't always belong to the kender, you know. Before the Cataclysm, this was actually the southernmost province of Istar—the part that didn't fall into the sea when the fiery mountain fell. After the Cataclysm, when my people came north out of the ruins of Balifor they found the tunnels here, abandoned. The people who'd lived in them had all died or moved above ground. The tunnels were in rough shape then, from what I gather, but we fixed up what we could, sealed off what we couldn't, and hid the entrances with secret doors like that log back there. These passages run almost the whole length of Goodlund and connect every town from Flotsam to Blood Watch—including Kendermore, of course. We've got tunnel entrances all over the place there."

"Hold on," Swiftraven interrupted. "If you knew these tunnels were here, why didn't we take them in the first place? We could have avoided almost getting killed, earlier today."

Kronn thought it over. "Two reasons. First, these tunnels are a sacred kender secret. No one knows about them but us—and now the three of you. Can you imagine what would happen if people in Flotsam found out there was an underground road that led all the way from their wharf to Kendermore? We'd never be able to use that tunnel again.

"Second, I didn't expect us to have any problem going in through the front gates. I certainly didn't think the place would be lousy with ogres. So it didn't even occur to me to use the tunnels until after that little showdown earlier today. It would be like entering a house by crawling through the window—it doesn't make much sense unless the door is locked."

Riverwind, who had been mostly silent during the kender's lecture, cleared his throat. "Kronn," he began thoughtfully, "If I'm going to help your people fight Malystryx and the ogres, I'll want to know where everything is—down here as well as up there. Do you have any maps of these tunnels, including all the entrances?"

A sudden grin split Kronn's face. He patted his bulging leather map case. "Come on, Riverwind," he said. "Look who you're talking to."

* * * * *

The tunnel went on, twisting and turning for miles. In some places, such as where the companions had entered, the passage was pristine, but elsewhere it was in disrepair. Piles of loose dirt covered the floor where sections of walls had crumbled, and buckled shoring timbers creaked ominously. The Plainsfolk quickly became acutely aware of the weight of earth that hung above them. Swiftraven in particular, who had spent much of his life on the open Plains and had slept more nights beneath the stars than under a roof, grew downright edgy whenever he heard the timbers' weary groans.

After an hour of walking, they reached a fork in the passage. A sign stood between the two branches, marked with runes the Plainsfolk didn't recognize. "It's Kenderspeak,"

Kronn explained. "It says Kendermore's to the left."

"What about the right?" Brightdawn asked.

"That way leads east," the kender said, pointing. "There should be a few villages that way—Sprucebark, Myrtledew, Deerfield—but everything else belongs to Malys and the ogres now. Actually, now that I think about it, if the ogres are at Kendermore, just about everything must belong to them by now. They're probably stomping around above our heads right now."

Impelled by that grim thought, they quickened their pace as they followed the left branch. Another hour passed.

"We must be getting close by now," Swiftraven grumbled, squinting ahead as though he could somehow bring his eyes to penetrate the darkness beyond the torchlight.

Not long after, the passage narrowed, then branched off in several directions at once. Kronn read the runes on the signs, twisting his cheek braids between his fingers, then nodded and chose a passage. He cocked an ear as they pressed onward. "There," he said. "Do you hear that?"

For a moment, the others couldn't hear anything other than the sounds that had followed them during their walk through the tunnel—the scuff of their soft boots on the dirt floor, the crackle and pop of the torches, Catt's pained mutterings as she tossed and turned upon her stretcher. In time, though, the humans detected what Kronn had heard. The faint sound of voices murmured from somewhere ahead of them. They frowned, straining to make out what was being said, but the distance and the eerie echoes of the tunnels made it impossible.

There was, however, no mistaking who was talking. The shrill, lilting voices belonged to kender.

The voices slowly grew louder as they walked. Soon, there was something else. Torchlight gleamed dead ahead. "Hey!" Kronn shouted. "Over here! We need some help!"

The voices suddenly fell silent, and the light snuffed out. Kronn, however, refused to douse his torch. Instead he held it high, raising his other hand to show that it was empty.

"Hold," a voice answered from the darkness. "I have an arrow aimed at you right now."

A delighted grin spread across Kronn's face. "That would impress me more if you could hit an ogre's bare backside at twenty paces, Giff," he said sarcastically.

There was a short silence, then the voice ahead of them called out again. "Kronn Thistleknot?"

"No," Kronn quipped, "it's the ghost of Fewmaster Toede."

With a suddenness that nearly made Riverwind and Swiftraven drop the stretcher, a tall, burly kender with short-cropped yellow hair loped out of the darkness. Kronn had just enough time to toss away his torch before the big kender tackled him. They flung their arms around each other, then fell laughing in a brightly colored heap.

They wrestled on the ground for a few seconds before the tall kender pinned Kronn to the ground. "All right, I give," Kronn said.

With a hearty laugh, the big kender rolled off him and stood up, brushing the dust from his leather armor. Then he saw the Plainsfolk and blinked in astonishment. "Great Trapspringer's ghost!" he swore. "You brought humans with you!"

"Of course I did," Kronn answered. "That's what Pax sent us to do."

"But I never thought you'd actually find someone who was willing to come or find your way back through the army of ogres."

"Thanks for your confidence in us," Kronn said. "Riverwind, Swiftraven and Brightdawn, this is Giffel Birdwhistle."

But the tall kender wasn't listening. His eyes fell upon the stretcher and the figure who lay upon it. "Oh, no!" he cried, lunging forward. "Catt!" He stopped beside her, took her uninjured hand in his, and looked back toward Kronn. "What happened to her?"

"She had a bad fall," Kronn answered. "Broke her arm, and took a nasty crack on the head. We need to get her to a healer."

"Of course," agreed Giffel. "Come on. Follow me," he said, already walking off down the passage.

As they hurried after him, Kronn turned to the Plains-folk and grinned. "*Now* we're home," he said.

* * * * *

Paxina Thistleknot stood upon the east wall of Kendermore, the setting sun stretching her shadow across the field below. The wind blew in her face, whipping her silver ponytail and ceremonial purple robes behind her. Her gaze settled on the edge of the forest, where large shadows moved among the dying trees.

"Why don't they attack?" she wondered aloud, talking to no one in particular.

"They don't have to," answered Brimble Redfeather, a grizzled, old kender who was the closest thing Kendermore had to a warlord. He chewed hard on a licorice root, spitting the juice on the flagstones beside him. "Time's on their side. Makes more sense for them to wait, anyway. The scouts say there's more ogres coming out of the east all the time. And then there's the dragon to consider. . . ."

"Thorns and nettles, the dragon," Paxina groaned. "What in Reorx's name can we hope to do about her?"

Brimble shrugged and spat again. He reached to his back and patted his chapak reassuringly, as if yearning for the chance to bury the weapon in Malys's scaly hide. "I can send another man to Blood Watch, if you want."

Paxina shook her head firmly at the suggestion. The kender had already dispatched three different volunteers to scout the dragon's lair. None had returned. The rosters listed them as Missing, Presumed Eaten.

"Save your men, Brimble," she told him. "If the entire ogre army is on its way, and it sure looks like it is, we're going to need everyone we can spare." She heaved a sigh that came all the way from the soles of her bright green shoes. "What about those riders your men saw cross the field this afternoon? Has there been any word of them?"

"Nothing new," Brimble answered. "I've had some

people ask around. Near as I can tell, there were three humans and two kender. They came from the south, made for the gates, then realized we weren't going to open them and rode north like their hair was on fire. The ogres chased them, of course. Some of the men say one of the kender didn't make it."

Paxina bowed her head, pressing her lips together to keep from cursing. "Did anyone—did they get a good look at them?" she asked.

Brimble nodded, a wry smile on his lips. "They were tall, they were short. They had light hair, they had dark hair. They rode brown horses, they rode black horses. You know how it goes—if I could gather together everyone folk think they saw, we'd have an army big enough to rout the ogres from the field right now."

"Your Honor!" called a voice from the courtyard below. "Paxina! Come quickly!"

Turning, Paxina and Brimble looked down, toward the base of the wall. Someone was sprinting toward them, waving his arms in the air: a tall, stout kender with yellow hair. They both recognized him immediately. "Giffel!" Paxina shouted.

"What are you doing up here, Birdwhistle?" Brimble demanded. "You're supposed to be down in the tunnels, keeping an eye on things."

"I *was* down in the tunnels," Giffel returned, breathless from running. He bent over, fighting to regain his wind. "We found someone—or they found us. Anyway, it doesn't matter—we found each other."

"Who, Giff?" Paxina asked. "Who did you find?"

Giffel looked around him. Paxina and Brimble weren't the only ones listening. Just about every kender within earshot had turned to look at him curiously. A modest span of the wall was, in effect, unguarded because the sentries manning it were all staring his way.

Paxina started toward a flight of steps that led down from the wall. She waved Brimble off as he started to follow. "Stay there," she told him. "You've got work to do. If there's trouble, Giffel will take care of it."

Brimble looked doubtful but bowed obediently and turned back to his men. "Quit gawking, you bloody mooncalves!" he snapped, stabbing a finger out across the meadow. "You're supposed to be looking that way! Branchala bite me, how are you going to keep the ogres out if you can't even guard the wall properly?"

Paxina trotted down to the courtyard below, her grin fading as she noted Giffel's solemn expression.

"Pax," Giffel said, "Kronn and Catt are back."

"So," Paxina said quietly, "they were the riders. Did they bring anyone with them? Humans?"

"Yes. Three humans, and a little girl—a kender girl."

Paxina blinked, not sure what to make of that.

"That's not all. Catt's hurt, Pax. I don't know how bad," Giffel added, heading off her next question. "I took the lot of them over to Arlie Longfinger's house and left them there while I came to look for you."

"Thanks, Giff," Paxina replied. She glanced around anxiously. "Is Arlie's place still on Henstooth Street?"

He nodded. "Over by Sneezing Goblin Fountain."

"All right, then," she declared, already heading briskly up the street. "Let's go."

Chapter 16

Giffel pointed at a small, gingerbread-festooned bungalow, half a block up on the right. It sat back from the road, fronted by a large, orderly garden. Giffel held open the house's whitewashed gate as Paxina passed through, then followed her up the winding path through the midst of the blighted garden. As they passed, they saw that the plants were brown and dying, giving off the same faint, sulfurous stink that shrouded the Kenderwood.

A sign hung above the bungalow's door. It read "Arlie Longfinger: Herbalist, Chirurgeon and Healer of Ills. Reasonable Rates." Underneath, stenciled in red, were the words "No Livestock."

The cottage's front door swung open. An ancient, wizened kender tottered on the stoop, peering out at them through bottle-thick spectacles. "Yes, what is it?" he snapped. "Someone's cow giving sour milk? Or does one of your chickens have the mumps? Honestly, I—"

He broke off abruptly, squinting, then took off his glasses and wiped them with his sleeve. When he slid them back on his face, his eyebrows shot up like two white feathers. "By my boots! Lord Mayor! I'm sorry, I didn't recognize you at first."

"Pax!"

A green blur came charging out of the depths of the cottage, pouches bouncing. Paxina had enough time to brace herself and open her arms before Kronn leapt on her, smothering her with a hug. "Kronn!" she gasped, returning the embrace. "Kronn, you're crushing my ribs."

"Sorry," he said, letting her go. "It's just so good to be back home—especially after what happened to us today." He grinned broadly. "You heard about our little ride past town around lunchtime, I'm sure."

His smile was so infectious she couldn't help but return it. "I didn't know it was you," she said. "I had my suspicions, though."

"Catt got hurt, Pax," Kronn said, suddenly serious.

"I know. How bad is it?"

"She'll be fine," Arlie Longfinger said. "She's sleeping now. Kronn did a good job setting her arm—it should heal well. She took a bump on her head, and it knocked her out for a while, but there's no permanent damage. I've given her a poultice and some tea, and I think she'll be all right to move in a few days, once the dizziness and nausea pass. She can rest here until then."

"I always said it was a good thing you Thistleknots had such thick skulls," Giffel joked.

Kronn smacked him on the shoulder. "Incidentally, Pax," he said, "I found someone who will help us. And best of all, he's a genuine Hero of the Lance."

Paxina caught her breath. "Not Caramon Majere."

"Well, uh, no—but we did try for Caramon."

"Oh. Oh, well," Paxina said. "But—I thought the rest of them were dead."

"Not yet," said a booming voice.

The four kender started and turned toward the voice. Riverwind stood at the end of the hall—or, rather, he stooped there, beneath the low, kender-sized ceiling.

"Whoa," said Paxina. "You got him. The Plainsman—uh . . ."

"Riverwind," said Riverwind.

Paxina snapped her fingers. "Riverwind, right! Well, who needs Caramon? You're just as good. Better, in fact."

The Plainsman smiled kindly, inclining his head. "Thank you. You must be Paxina."

"Come in, all of you, before you let every fly in

existence into my home," Arlie said, ushering Giffel and the Thistleknots through the open door. "You can go talk in the dining room. The big fellow's friends are there. I was just fixing a light supper. You're welcome to join us, Your Honor." His face crinkled into a grin. "There's plenty of bacon sandwiches for everyone."

* * * * *

"All things considered, I was fairly sure I was dead," Kronn said, speaking around a mouthful of bacon and bread. "The ogres had me penned in. I doubt Balif himself could have fought his way out of it. But then Swiftraven came riding out of nowhere and pulled Catt and me out of the fire, so to speak." He grinned, clapping the young warrior on the shoulder. "Which makes us even for that bit with the pirates, as far as I'm concerned. Anyway, since the front gate was obviously a bad idea, I figured we'd take the tunnels. We ran into Giff down there, and he brought us here."

Paxina leaned forward, still taking in her brother's story. Kronn had told the whole tale, from his departure from Kendermore to his return, without even pausing to take a breath. Paxina took a sip of cider from the goblet Arlie had poured for her and looked at the Plainsfolk.

"Your turn, Pax," Kronn said. "What happened while we were gone? When Catt and I left, the ogres were still far away, raiding border towns, and that was only a season ago. Now it looks like they're camped on your doorstep."

"A lot can happen in a season, Kronn," Paxina replied. She set down her goblet and sat back, her expression glum. "After you left, the ogres kept raiding, here and there—Deerfield, Myrtledew, a few other places. Some of our people got captured for slaves, but many got away through the tunnels. Pretty much the way things have been since last spring. Malys stuck to the north coast, burning villages whenever she had the hankering."

"Anyway," Paxina continued, "that's the way it was until about a month ago. Then, as best as we can figure, two things happened. First, someone killed the hetman of the ogres and took his place."

"The new one's named Kurthak, but they also call him the Black-Gazer," Giffel said. "He's smart, for an ogre."

"Worse, he's ambitious," Paxina added. "Ruog, the old hetman, was content with sending small war bands on border raids. Not Kurthak, though. Since he took over, it's become pretty clear he's more interested in out-and-out expansion and conquest. Instead of war bands, he sent in the whole army."

"Nettles and thorns," Kronn swore. "None of the villages could stand against that."

"They didn't," Giffel said grimly.

"We lost battle after battle, more and more ground, Kronn," Paxina said. "Their ultimate target is Kendermore." She ran a hand over her face, looking tired.

She fell silent, bowing her head. Kronn blew a long, slow sigh out through his lips. For a moment, no one spoke.

"I'm sorry, Your Honor," Riverwind murmured. "You said two things happened a month ago. What was the other?"

Paxina looked up. Riverwind couldn't help but shudder at her expression. There was a hopelessness there that he'd never seen before on a kender's face.

"Malys," the Lord Mayor said. "She's the other thing. She and Kurthak must have joined forces. After the ogres were through with a town, she'd fly in and burn it, to make sure nothing survived. We had to make firebreaks to keep the whole Kenderwood from going up."

"We saw that," Brightdawn said solemnly. She looked down at Billee Juniper, who was asleep in her arms. Tears shone in the Plainswoman's eyes. "We passed through a town on the way here."

"Weavewillow," Kronn added, in reply to Paxina's inquisitive look. "The whole place was blasted."

"That was one of the last to go," Giffel stated.

"Actually, Weavewillow wasn't quite as bad as some of the others," Paxina said. "By the time the ogres attacked there, most of our people were already gone. You see, a couple of weeks ago I sent messengers to every village that was still standing, telling them to evacuate and come here. Just about everyone did, although there were stragglers who didn't make it out."

"Only two days ago," Giffel continued, "the ogres started showing up outside Kendermore. They've been arriving steadily ever since. You're lucky you got here when you did—by this time tomorrow, their numbers will have doubled. You'd never have escaped if you'd tried to ride for the gates then."

"So we're just in time," Kronn said cheerfully. "Wouldn't want to miss this battle."

Paxina nodded grimly. "There's nowhere left to run."

"A last stand," Riverwind said.

"Yes."

"They won't take us easily," Giffel declared. "Kendermore isn't like the other villages. Our walls are strong, and we've got eighty thousand kender to defend them, if need be."

"Who's leading the defense?" Kronn asked.

"Well, right now it's Brimble Redfeather," Paxina answered, "but I was hoping you'd come back in time."

"There will be a siege," Riverwind said. "If this Black-Gazer's as smart as you say, he won't attack right away. He'll set up his army outside your walls, and he'll wait, and try to starve and worry you out. I assume you don't have any supply lines?"

Paxina shook her head. "Even if we did, where would we get supplies from? Flotsam? I don't know if you've noticed, Riverwind, but most humans would be quite happy if our people disappeared from Krynn tomorrow. As of right now, we have enough foodstuffs for a few months, maybe longer. After that, to be frank, I expect we'll starve."

* * * * *

It was dark out when they finished their supper. Wiping his mouth with a napkin, Giffel pushed back his chair and rose. "I'm afraid I have to go," he said, bowing to Paxina, and left.

"You'll pardon me, too," Arlie said. He stood and began to collect crumb-dusted plates from the table. "I've still got lots of work to do. You can go look in on Catt if you like, but don't wake her. For now, sleep's the best thing for her."

The Plainsfolk and kender sat in silence for a time, sipping their drinks.

"They're going to need a place to stay," Kronn told Paxina. "Preferably somewhere Riverwind doesn't have to worry about bonking his head on the ceiling all the time. She eyed the old Plainsman carefully. "I think there's a house down on Cherrystone Boulevard that might do. Used to belong to a kender wizard, a few years back. He had a tall hat." She winked. "Kronn and I will take the three of you there tonight, after we're done here. Now," she added, nodding at the little kender girl in Brightdawn's arms, "as for our other visitor . . ."

"Billee can stay with me, if you like," Brightdawn offered. "Until we find her family, that is."

"Brightdawn," Kronn said, "I'm pretty sure we aren't going to find her family." He peered at the child, making sure she was asleep before he went on. "Her mother and father are probably dead—I think we can be sure of that."

"There are orphanages," Paxina said. "Billee's not the only child to lose her parents to Malys and the ogres. And some parents have lost their children, too—I'm sure we can find a foster family for her."

Brightdawn looked at the kender gravely. "If it's all the same to you," she said, "I'd rather keep her."

Paxina and her brother exchanged troubled looks, but Riverwind spoke before they could say anything. "Maybe the two of you should go see your sister now," he told them.

Kronn rose from his seat, understanding. He gulped down the last of his cider, then casually tucked the goblet in one of his pouches.

"Come on, Pax," he said. "Catt was asking for you earlier, before she dozed off." The two kender left the room arm-in-arm. Kronn pushed the door shut behind him.

When it clicked closed, Riverwind turned to his daughter. She returned his gaze, a challenge in her eyes, but the old Plainsman did not relent. He leaned forward, his face grave. "You know you can't keep her," he said.

"Why not?" she asked. She raised her chin haughtily. "I'm the one who rescued her. If I hadn't heard her crying, you would have ridden on by . . . and then who would have taken care of her? The ogres?"

"I've seen how attached you've grown to her, child. But Billee's no human girl. She's a kender."

Brightdawn opened her mouth to reply, then closed it again. She turned to Swiftraven. "I don't see you helping me."

The young warrior shifted uneasily. "I'm sorry, Brightdawn," he said. "I agree with your father. I don't think you can handle a kender child. I know I couldn't."

Brightdawn's lips tightened bitterly. "You're both so sure you know what I'm capable of."

"Not just us." Riverwind's voice was gentle. "Paxina thinks the same way. I could see it in her eyes when you asked to take care of Billee. She belongs with her people. Paxina was just too polite to say anything at the time."

For a moment, Brightdawn met her father's steady gaze. Then her shoulders slumped, and she bowed her head. "You're right. I'm just being selfish."

"Not just, Brightdawn," Riverwind said, shaking his head. "I want you to leave. Go back to Qué-Shu."

"We've already discussed this. I can't leave these people here, any more than you can, Father." Before he could respond, she stood, propping little Billee on her shoulder, and walked to the door. "I'm tired now. It's been a very long day. I'm going to ask Paxina to show us to that house she was telling us about."

With that, she strode from the room. Swiftraven glanced apologetically at Riverwind, then rose and followed her out.

When they were gone and Riverwind was alone, he let out a groan of pain, his hand pressing against his belly. Tears spilled down his old, weathered face.

Chapter 17

The next day, Catt Thistleknot woke with a headache the likes of which she had never felt before. Though the little bedroom where Arlie had put her was mostly dark, what little light there was stabbed at her eyes like spears. She moaned, wincing, and tried to roll over. A flash of pain stopped her, however, and she lay back, the room spinning wildly about her. "I wish I were dead," she moaned thickly.

"Good morning to you, too," said Kronn. He leaned over her, a cheery smile on his face. "Of course, any morning you wake up alive's a good one, after what you've been through."

She squinted, her bleary eyes fighting to focus. "Kronn?" she asked. "Why are there two of you?"

Kronn's eyebrows shot up—all four of them, in Catt's eyes—and he glanced across the room, at Arlie Longfinger. The old herbalist nodded. "Double-vision's normal for someone who's taken that kind of knock," he said.

"Quit complaining, Catt," said another voice, from the other side of the bed. Painfully, Catt looked that way, and saw a silver-haired kender clad in the purple robes of a Lord Mayor. She frowned, trying to focus on the woman's face. "You could at least be grateful to Kronn. You'd be dead if it weren't for him."

"Pax?"

Paxina looked at Arlie, who shrugged. "Short-term memory loss," he said. "That isn't unusual, either."

Catt looked at them blankly. " So what happened to me?"

"You fell off your horse," Kronn answered. He squeezed

her good hand; the other arm lay across her chest, bound in fresh, linen bandages. "You conked your head pretty good too."

"Kronn went back for you, Catt," Paxina said. "He picked you up and put you on his pony. If he hadn't, the ogres would have gotten you."

"Ogres . . ." Catt slurred. "I thought I'd dreamed that. I remember Swiftraven too."

Gently, Kronn touched her cheek. His fingers felt cool against her livid skin. "We all made it. The Plainsfolk are out in the hall, Catt. Arlie didn't want you to have too many visitors in here at once. Do you want to see them?"

"No," she mumbled. "Not right now. I'm tired, Kronn. Let me sleep."

He laid her hand across her breast as her eyes drooped closed. A moment later, she began to snore.

The Plainsfolk looked up as Kronn and Paxina emerged from the darkened room. "How is she?" Brightdawn asked, her brow knitting with concern.

"Fine," Paxina said. "A bit delirious, but that'll pass. She's sleeping now."

"In that case," Riverwind said, "I think it's time for you to give me a tour of the town's defenses." His knees creaked and popped as he pushed himself up from where he'd been sitting on the floor.

"Sounds like a good idea to me," Paxina said, shrugging. "Arlie, when Giffel comes by, tell him we're on the wall." The herbalist nodded, then shuffled off down the hall.

Paxina headed the other way, toward the front door. "Come on, then," she said. "And keep your eyes on your pockets. Try not to let anything fall out of them."

* * * * *

Riverwind had heard about Kendermore from Tasslehoff Burrfoot. Of course, Tas had also told him stories about woolly mammoths, hovering plants and goatsucker birds, so he'd always been somewhat skeptical of his friend's tales.

According to Tas, Kendermore was a place unlike any other in all of Krynn, a full-fledged city designed and built by and for kender. As such, it was somewhat like a human town, only a hundred times more confusing. Roads changed direction, switched names, widened and narrowed, all seemingly at random. Intersections were chaotic affairs, with streets seldom meeting in groups of less than five and never at anything resembling a right angle. Buildings mimicked, and frequently mixed, architectural styles from every nation and era in Krynn's history, and with a few exceptions—such the house Paxina had given to the Plainsfolk—they were all scaled down to accommodate occupants who seldom grew taller than four feet. Towers leaned at improbable angles because no one had thought to put in foundations. Great stone walls came to sudden stops where their builders had lost interest. The city's library, an excellent demonstration of why Palanthian and Nerakan building styles shouldn't mix, was slowly sinking into the ground because its designers hadn't considered how much more it would weigh with all the books inside. Riverwind had never been completely comfortable in cities, but Kendermore made him especially uneasy. It was a town in complete disarray.

Then there were the kender themselves. None of the Plainsfolk had ever seen more than a handful in one place at any one time. Here, though, there were thousands, more than the city was meant to hold, thanks to the refugees who had flooded into town over the past few weeks. They jammed the streets, a pushing, shoving, yammering sea of topknotted heads. The humans, Riverwind and particular, felt like giants as Paxina and Kronn led them through the crowds. Many of the kender stopped and stared at them, their jaws hanging open in awe as they looked up. The mob around them grew steadily thicker as people crowded around, trying to get a look at the rare Plainsfolk.

That wasn't the worst of it, though. Kender being kender, for every one who was content simply to stand and gawk at Riverwind, Brightdawn and Swiftraven, there were three who just had to find out what was inside the Plainsfolk's purses. The humans quickly discovered they had to carry their pouches—along with swordbelts, quivers, and anything else they wanted to hold on to—above their heads, where the kender's reaching, grasping hands couldn't get near them. Even so, the Plainsfolk lost the buckles off their boots and most of the beads from the fringes of their buckskin tunics.

The noise, too, was incredible. The air was filled with the clamor of voices, screeching hoopaks and other strange weapons, and occasional musical instruments or exploding firecrackers.

They actually became lost for a short time, pulling up short when the road they were walking along—a narrow lane named Broad Street—rounded a sharp corner and suddenly stopped, blocked by a tall, iron fence. There didn't appear to be any reason for the fence to be there—the road continued on its far side—but it was there nonetheless, and there was no way around it.

Kronn stopped, scratching his head. "Now, where did that come from?" he wondered aloud, staring at the fence as if he wasn't quite sure it was there.

"Don't look at me," Paxina told him. "This was your short cut."

"Hmph." Kronn looked around. "Well, this thing wasn't here last time I came this way. But, I think—where in the Abyss is it—" He muttered aimlessly for a moment, then pointed excitedly, back the way they had come. "Yeah, there it is. Straight Street. That'll get us to Tornado Alley, then we can follow that to the gates."

"Are you sure?" Swiftraven asked, dubiously regarding the road Kronn had been pointing at.

Kronn shrugged. "Pretty much."

As it turned out, he was right. They followed Straight Street—which, of course, curved and wended about worse than a drunken sailor at low tide—until they reached Tornado Alley, a wide road that shot straight through the south side of town.

"This really was made by an honest-to-goodness tornado, you know," Paxina announced as they pushed their way down through the street, through the milling throng. "Happened about forty years ago—the thing just tore through town. Sucked poor Uncle Trapspringer up and spat him out its top." She shook her head. "Luckily, he came down again."

As Kronn had promised, the road led almost directly to the gates, ending suddenly only a hundred paces from the city wall. The company snaked its way around several narrower, twisting streets—including one that doubled back on itself unexpectedly—until finally they arrived at a cobblestone-paved courtyard.

"Almighty goddess," Riverwind swore, staring.

The tall, stout gates stood at the plaza's far side, closed, barred, and blocked by a strong but somewhat rusty portcullis. That wasn't what held the Plainsfolk's attention, however. In front of the gates was a heap of refuse. Lumber, paving stones, and old, broken furniture had been piled two-thirds of the way to the tops of the great doors. Even as they watched, kender carried random bits of junk—one brought an old, cast-iron weather vane, and two others hauled a broken wheelbarrow—and threw them on the mound.

"As you figured out," Paxina proclaimed, gesturing at the barricade, "we weren't going to open the gates in any hurry yesterday."

"It certainly doesn't look like anyone's going to get through there now," Brightdawn declared, staring.

"Paxina!" shouted a voice from the barbican above the gates.

The company looked up and saw a grizzled kender waving down at them. Unlike most of the other kender they had seen, he was clad in a chain mail hauberk and metal greaves. A bright red headband held back his long, gray hair, keeping it out of his eyes as the hot wind whipped it about his head.

"That's Brimble Redfeather," Kronn told the others. "He's a bit—something of a war dog, you could say."

"That's one way of putting it," Paxina agreed, grinning.

"Blood and thunder, Paxina!" Brimble shouted down at them, glowering fiercely. "Where in the Abyss have you been? I've got half my runners out looking for you!"

"I was looking in on my injured sister, if you must know!" Paxina shouted back. "What's so important?"

Brimble scowled down from the gatehouse. "Better if you just come up here," he answered. "Bring the barbarians if you want." He turned away, looking out over the battlements at the field below.

There were stairs near the edge of the barricade. Riverwind and Swiftraven helped Kronn clear the refuse away from them; then the party climbed up to the catwalk that ran along the top of the wall. The battlements were lined with kender—archers and slingers, mostly. Some of them stared curiously at the Plainsfolk as they climbed the stairs, but most didn't even turn, their attention directed south across the meadow.

"All right," Paxina said, striding to the battlements. "What's so all-fired important—"

Her voice broke off suddenly, and she could only stare, speechless, at what the other kender were looking at. Riverwind and the others paused, taken aback by the amazement on the Lord Mayor's face, then gasped in astonishment when they beheld what Brimble had wanted them to see.

There were ogres everywhere—thousands upon thousands of them, camped at the edge of the Kenderwood. For every monster who had chased Kronn and the Plainsfolk yesterday, there were five or ten now. Plumes of smoke drifted skyward from hundreds of campfires, and the sounds of shouting, cursing and bestial laughter rang out across the meadow.

"It's a real, no-fooling siege now, Your Honor," Brimble declared as he stumped over to join them. He spat licorice juice down into the courtyard below. "They showed up last night, most of them—and they've been arriving all morning long, too."

"There's so many," Brightdawn breathed.

Riverwind frowned at the camps, which stretched to the left and right as far as they could see. "Is it like this all around the city?" he asked.

"More or less," Brimble affirmed. He peered up at the old Plainsman, then grinned. "Branchala bite me, you're a big one."

"This is Riverwind of Qué-Shu, Brimble," Kronn said, swiftly stepping in. "He's a Hero of the Lance."

"No kidding," Brimble said. He extended his hand, and Riverwind saw he was missing his little finger. "Glad to meet you. I fought in the war myself, way back when. Always good to meet another veteran—we're getting scarcer and scarcer these days."

Riverwind took Brimble's hand and shook it firmly. The old kender's grip was surprisingly strong.

"Know a thing or two about siege craft, then, do you?"

Riverwind nodded, the corners of his mouth rising into the ghost of a smile. "I do," he declared. "I was at Kalaman, at the end of the war."

"Really?" Brimble's eyebrows shot up. "Well, I am impressed."

"What happened at Kalaman?" Kronn asked.

Brimble glared at him. "What happened at—Fizban's britches, Thistleknot, didn't your old dad teach you anything? Kalaman was only one of the biggest sieges since Balif's day!"

"The dragonarmies tried to take the city back from the Golden General's armies in the last days of the war," Brightdawn proudly explained to Kronn. "Father led the defense."

"I wasn't alone," Riverwind added modestly. "I had help from Gilthanas of Qualinesti, and Lord Michael Jeofrey, of the Knights of Solamnia."

"For two weeks solid, the draconians threw themselves at the walls," Brimble said. His tone was almost reverent as he regarded the old Plainsman. "And for two weeks the knights and elves and the rest threw them back. Reorx's beard, I'd have given my other nine fingers to be there." He reached up and slapped Riverwind on the shoulder.

"You're welcome to lend a hand, friend. We could use more like you."

Riverwind returned the old kender's smile, then turned back to the battlements and gazed out across the meadow again toward the enemy camp.

* * * * *

Kurthak stood at the edge of the camp, his good eye fixed on Kendermore's walls. After a while, he snorted and shook his head. "The fools," he growled.

"My lord?" Tragor asked. As always, the Black-Gazer's champion stood nearby. He leaned against his great sword, which was planted point-down in the parched, dusty earth.

"They fortify their walls," the hetman answered. "They post archers and slingers. They arm themselves for battle. Don't they realize what they face? We could topple their walls today if I gave the order to march. Kendermore would be ashes by nightfall. They'll draw breath tomorrow only because I wish it—I and Malystryx. Surely they must know this, and yet they carry on as if they had a hope of surviving."

"They're kender," Tragor grunted. "What did you expect—surrender? They don't know fear."

"They don't, do they?" Kurthak snarled. He folded his arms, tilting his head back arrogantly. "There's a first time for everything, Tragor. By the time this siege is done, I will have their Lord Mayor on her knees before me." He patted his massive, spiked club, which hung from his belt. Beside it dangled the severed heads of three kender, bound in place by their topknots. Flies buzzed around the grisly trophies, moving in and out of their wide-gaping mouths. He gazed down at the heads fondly for a moment, then reached down and cupped one in his hand. It lolled sideways as he stared at it, its rolled-back eyes showing little but whites. The stump of its neck smeared his palm with sticky, half-dried blood.

"She'll beg me for mercy," the Black-Gazer continued.

He closed his hand around the head and squeezed until he felt the kender's skull crack. "I will show her none, though—not even that of a quick end. First, I think, I'll cut out her tongue." He tore the shattered head from his belt and tossed it away into the bushes like a piece of rotten fruit.

"Why do we wait, then?" Tragor asked hungrily. His black eyes flashed as he looked toward the city. "Why not attack now, as you say, instead of waiting here, watching them watch us?"

"Because," Kurthak replied evenly, "the time is not yet right. Malys wants us to let them be while she works her magic."

At the mention of the dragon, Tragor shuddered. "Relying on magic," he said, his voice thick with disgust. He glanced around him, scowling furiously. "Skulking in the forest. Such things might be proper for elves, but not our people."

"What would you do, champion?" Kurthak sneered. "Throw yourself at the walls? Charge across that meadow this instant and impulsively batter down the gates?"

"Better than wait here."

The Black-Gazer laughed roughly. "And the kender within? What would you do with them, when they faced you without fear?"

Tragor's scowl deepened, and his eyes vanished into the shadows of his massive, lowering brows. "Kill them," he snapped. "Cut them down, one and all."

"And probably get cut down yourself, too. You were there at Weavewillow, champion. You saw how they fought to hold us off while many of their fellows escaped. Kender are many things, but cautious isn't one of them."

Tragor shook his head darkly. Kurthak was right. At Weavewillow, and at every village before, the kender had fought like badgers. Many ogres had fallen to their sling-stones and arrows, hoopaks and chapaks. The kender had refused to relent. It was all part of their nature, their maddening refusal to fear their foes. Now the badgers were in their den—thousands of them—and completely surrounded by the camps of the Black-Gazer's horde. They would fight even harder, for they had nowhere else to run.

A slow smile lit Kurthak's face as he regarded his champion. "We have the upper hand, Tragor," he said. "If we ended this now, it would be too soon. Our advantage over them can only grow. They're trapped, and that city holds more kender than it can support. In time their supply of food will run low. The dragon's magic will cause their wells to run dry. They will grow weak, while we remain strong. How much of a fight will they be able to put up if they're too feeble from hunger to lift their weapons and draw their bows?

"Besides, if we attacked now, we'd have no choice but to kill them all, as you said," he continued. "What good would that do us? You forget, we aren't here to slaughter them—not only, anyway. We began this conquest because we desire slaves. We'll capture more of them when they're weak—and they'll kill fewer of our people as well. That is why we wait."

"Patience," Tragor said, and grimaced. "It isn't an easy thing. My blood runs hot for war." He pulled his sword out of the ground and began to jab the earth repeatedly with its blade. As he did so, he fixed his eyes on the distant walls.

"But why are there humans among them now?"

Kurthak's head snapped up. He squinted across the meadow. "Humans? Where?"

"There. Above the gates," Tragor replied, pointing.

For a moment, Kurthak didn't see anything. Then his good eye widened with surprise. There were humans— three of them, two men and a woman. There was little more either ogre could tell from so far away.

"Blood of my ancestors," the Black-Gazer swore in astonishment. "Baloth! Come here!"

The hairless ogre loped to Kurthak's side, carrying a massive war axe. He was clad in leather armor covered with metal studs, and about his neck he wore an elaborate necklace of bone, claws, and teeth. The necklace was an unmistakable sign of his new place the horde. Since killing Lord Ruag, Baloth had risen to the rank of warlord, answering only to Kurthak himself.

"My lord?" he rasped. "What is your wish? Should we signal the attack?"

"No," Kurthak said. "Send a scouting party. There are humans on the city wall. I want them described to me."

Baloth's expression grew doubtful. "They'll have to get within range of the archers. Are you sure, my lord?"

"Yes! I'm sure!" Kurthak snapped. His face was dark with anger. "Go."

Bowing, the hairless ogre sprinted away. Before long, a party of six ogres split off from the camp and started toward Kendermore. Kurthak and Tragor watched as they crossed the meadow. Shouts rang out from the town's walls, and the kender scrambled into position behind the merlons, readying their weapons. The camps at the edges of the forest stirred, too, as the ogres watched the scouts cross the meadow

Soon, the thrum of bowstrings carried across the field. Arrows soared high, arcing across the clear, blue sky, then dove at the scouts like angry wasps. One of the ogres fell immediately, his body pierced by the deadly shafts, but the rest raised great wooden shields, deflecting the shots as they pressed closer. The kender loosed a second flight, then a third. Another scout caught an arrow in his shoulder, spun with the force of the blow, and swiftly died, another shaft lodged in the back of his skull.

The remaining four scouts stopped barely a hundred yards from the wall. Arrows and stones fell upon them like hail, but they did not falter. They peered out from behind their shields, up at the top of the wall.

Two of the humans—the men—stood at the battlements, firing longbows along with the kender. The woman had disappeared from view. The scouts stared at the two men for a few heartbeats,then turned and started to run, back toward the woods.

One died, his back riddled with arrows, before he could

take two steps. Another fell before he took ten. A victorious whoop rose from the walls. A third nearly made it to safety, then caught an arrow in his leg and collapsed. He tried to crawl and was pierced six more times before he finally lay still. The last scout won clear, however, and continued to run, even when he was out of bowshot. His eyes flared with wild desperation, as if the legions of Chaos pursued him.

Baloth loped from the tree line to meet the scout and had to catch his arm and drag him to a halt. The scout rested a moment, catching his breath, then, made his way to Kurthak. Baloth walked behind, axe in hand.

"What news?" the Black-Gazer demanded as they approached.

"My lord," the scout said, and bowed. "They are two men, dressed in leather and furs. One wears a feathered headdress."

Tragor spat. "Barbarians," he sneered. He looked at Kurthak. "From the Dairlies."

The Black-Gazer pursed his lips. "I don't know," he said, scratching the back of his neck. "I've never seen a Dairly barbarian in a feathered headdress." He glowered at the scout. "What else can you say about them?" he demanded. "Their faces! Their hair!"

"They looked . . . like humans," the scout said lamely, quivering before the hetman's wrath. "The feathered one was old . . . white hair. Many wrinkles. He wore a fur vest, and his arms were bare except for bracers. And—he was very tall . . . for a human. The younger one spoke to him."

"Yes?" Kurthak thundered, his eyes widening. "Did you hear what he said?"

The scout hesitated, his eyes flicking about as if he sought to flee the Black-Gazer's sight. Baloth raised his axe, but Kurthak stayed his hand with a glare.

"What did he say?" Kurthak boomed again. "Tell me!"

"I—didn't hear all of it, my lord," the scout said hesitantly. "We couldn't get close enough. But he called the older one his chief, and spoke his name."

Kurthak's eye shone. "His name," he said. "What was it?"

"R-Riverwind, my lord. . . ."

The Black-Gazer caught his breath suddenly, and the scout squeezed his eyes shut, whimpering and hunching his shoulders in expectation of Baloth's axe's descent. After a moment, however, Kurthak exhaled slowly. He stroked his chin, wondering, and then his face hardened as he reached a decision. Muttering an oath, he turned away from the meadow and headed into the Kenderwood.

Tragor hurried to catch up, caught off-guard by his master's sudden movement. "My lord!" he shouted. He reached out and caught the hetman's elbow.

The Black-Gazer's single eye was ablaze as he whirled to face his champion. Tragor didn't balk, however; he stood his ground and returned his master's smoldering stare. "My lord, what is it?"

"A danger," Kurthak replied. He glanced behind him, deeper into the woods. "I must go to Blood Watch."

"Blood Watch!" Tragor blurted, astounded. "What for?"

"To tell Malystryx."

Kurthak turned to go again, but once more his champion caught him. "My lord," Tragor said. "Must you leave now? The army . . ."

"Is yours to command while I am gone," Kurthak replied. "Keep them here, away from the walls. Let no one enter or leave Kendermore."

Tragor bowed. "Yes, my lord."

"I will be swift. Don't try to take the town while I am gone. If I find that you have disobeyed me . . ." He let his voice trail off, the threat in his single eye enough to make his mind clear. Then he looked past Tragor, back toward the edge of the meadow. "Baloth!" he shouted. "See to that coward, then come with me."

The hairless ogre grinned, understanding the tone of the Black-Gazer's voice. He brought down his great axe, cleaving the scout's head from behind. As the slain scout crumpled to the ground, Kurthak turned and stormed urgently away through the forest. Baloth hurried to follow.

Chapter 18

Malystryx slumbered in her nest deep within Blood Watch, her serpentine form shuddering and twisting as she dreamt of carnage. Her breath came in great snorting rushes, a massive bellows that fed the forge-fires in her belly. Smoke hung around her, swirling and eddying with the twitching of her wings. Her claws scratched the floor, scoring the stone with long, jagged furrows.

"Mistress."

Even in the depths of sleep, she heard Yovanna's voice. Angrily, she hauled herself back to wakefulness, her bloody dreams forgotten. She cracked open a golden eye, glaring at the black-cloaked form on the balcony above her. Yovanna met her baleful gaze calmly from within the dark depths of her hood.

"I have told you about waking me," Malys hissed.

Yovanna nodded. "I would not do so, Mistress, if it did not seem urgent to me. The Black-Gazer has come."

A jet of flame erupted from Malystryx's maw, scorching the stone. She raised her head to look straight at the black-cloaked figure. "Kurthak?" she demanded. "Why has he left Kendermore?"

"He would not tell me, Mistress. He insisted that he speak with you."

With an impatient snort, Malystryx slowly uncoiled and stretched her sinuous form. "You shouldn't have disturbed me, Yovanna. The fool could have waited until I woke."

"That was my thinking, Mistress," Yovanna replied carefully. "But he came here three days ago, and you have been asleep the whole time. I thought you would prefer to see him now, so he can go back where he belongs."

The dragon unfolded her wings, fanning them slowly to work out the stiffness of slumber. "Very well," she rasped. "Where is he? Not within this mountain, I hope."

Yovanna shook her head. "I left him and his companion on a ridge, a league west of here."

Malystryx said nothing more to her servant. She tensed, then leaped almost straight upward, her legs launching her like coiled springs. Her wings beat slowly as she streaked up past Yovanna and caught the stony edge of the shaft with her clutching claws. With practised ease she pulled herself up into the cleft, then squirmed up through the rock, away from her nest. It was a tight fit, the shaft's rough walls scraping her hide as she slithered along. It had not been so when she'd first claimed Blood Watch as her lair, but that had been quite some time ago. Malys had grown a great deal since then. There had been many other dragons to feed upon.

Daylight shone above her, a spot of blue amid the blackness of the stone. She heaved herself toward that light, her tail thrashing behind her. Then she was free, emerging from a vent in the side of the volcano like some terrible butterfly leaving its chrysalis. She sprang from the hole, away from the mountain, and her membranous wings caught the hot wind that gusted among the jagged hills that surrounded Blood Watch.

As she flew, she surveyed the Desolation she had shaped. It continued to grow more barren with the passage of time—even now, after only a few days of sleep, she could see how the land had changed. Flats of hot mud had dried and cracked. The last stubbornly hardy grasses had finally withered and fallen to dust. To the east, a thick plume of smoke and ash marked the birth of a new volcano. She regarded the Desolation proudly, soaring high above it. Then with an exultant screech she angled downward again, toward a narrow ridge of brown rock that stretched between two looming, fanglike peaks. She swooped in, the hot wind buffeting her body, and saw two tall figures standing atop the balk. Her lips curling back from her massive fangs, she dove.

The two ogres watched her descend, shock registering in their faces as she streaked straight toward them. She screamed, and the towering brutes covered their ears. They ducked as she swept over their heads, skimming barely ten feet above the stone of the ridge. Malys laughed mockingly and banked, watching them struggle to their feet again. She came around, spotted a large outcropping of rock on the nearest peak, and winged mightily toward it. She settled onto the perch gingerly, testing it first to see if it would bear her enormous weight. It held, and she folded her wings, glaring down at the ogres.

They were nearly half a mile away. She could have flown across the distance in little more than a heartbeat, but she let them come to her instead. A few minutes later, Kurthak and Baloth knelt before her.

"Wretch," she snarled at the hetman. "Have you forgotten your place? I should burn you where you stand." She sucked in a long, slow breath, flames crackling in her throat.

Baloth quailed, his face stiff with terror, but Kurthak the Black-Gazer mastered the almost overwhelming force of her dragonfear and returned her gaze. "You'd be wise not to do that," he told her. "I bear news you must hear."

Malys angled her head, her forked tongue flicking between her teeth. "Do you, now?" she asked. "What news could be so important that you would abandon your own army to bring it to me? Who did you leave in charge? That lackwit of a champion? I see you brought a new dog to skulk at your side," she added, her gaze falling heavily upon the hairless ogre.

Baloth fell back a pace, unsteadily, but Kurthak grabbed his arm, stopping him from running away. "Tragor leads the horde, yes," the Black-Gazer answered evenly. "He only needs to hold them where they are until I return. As to the word I bring, it is this. Riverwind of Qué-Shu is among the kender."

A silence descended over the ridge, broken only by the moan of the hot wind among the crags, and the rumblings of the restless earth beneath their feet. Ogre and dragon faced each other, neither speaking a word. Then Malys arrogantly tilted up her chin, her lip curling once more.

"Who?" she asked.

Kurthak blinked, surprised. "Riverwind of Qué-Shu," he repeated.

Malys thumped the mountainside with her tail. The impact knocked stones loose from the peak, sending them bounding down its slopes. "I do not know this man," she said evenly. "Who is he that his presence in Kendermore would make you leave your place?"

"He's a Hero of the Lance," Kurthak said.

"A what?"

The Black-Gazer stared, dumbfounded; then his eyes narrowed as he tried to understand the dragon's joke. He soon realized, however, that Malys was serious. "You haven't heard of the Heroes of the Lance?" he asked. "But they're known everywhere in Ansalon!"

"I am not from Ansalon," Malystryx replied. "And I care little for the legends of mortals. This Riverwind is one man. He is of no concern to me. You should not have left your army, Black-Gazer. You will not leave it again, even if more of your precious 'Heroes' arrive in Kendermore."

Stunned by her intransigence, Kurthak could do nothing but bow his head obediently. "Yes, Malystryx."

"Very good," she said to him. "Now come here, Black-Gazer. I have a gift for you."

Kurthak walked forward, his legs moving against his will. He tried to stop himself, but he kept on moving until he was less than ten yards from Malystryx. He winced at the heat that emanated from her immense body.

"Kneel," she breathed.

The word lodged in his mind, driving out all thoughts of resistance. He knelt. Gracefully, she extended a long, taloned finger and touched its tip to the middle of his forehead. Back along the ridge, Baloth winced and turned away, waiting for the dragon's claw to plunge through Kurthak's skull.

Malys's touch, however, was gentle, almost a caress. She

held her talon against him, and whispered words in a strange language the ogre didn't understand. The air seethed with unseen energies. The Black-Gazer tensed as magic coursed both around and within him.

He sucked in a long slow breath, shivering. His good eye glazed, becoming as vacant as the empty socket that had once held its twin. His lips formed words, but it was the dragon's sibilant voice that issued from his mouth.

"My mind to yours," Malystryx said, her voice coming from two tongues at once. "I am in your thoughts, Black-Gazer. I can see inside your mind. And you are in mine. If you come to Blood Watch again, I shall destroy you. But"—her voice became acerbic with irony—"if you should choose to warn me of anything more, you need only call to me with your mind. Our thoughts are linked. I can speak to you, and you to me, though we are a hundred miles apart.

"Listen for my call, Black-Gazer," she continued. "The time will come when I am done working my magic upon the Kenderwood. I will tell you when to attack. The kender will be yours to do with as you please, and their forest will be mine to shape to my whim. I will raise a new lair, a peak to dwarf even Blood Watch, where Kendermore stands." The dragon and ogre both smiled at this.

Kurthak took a deep breath, then answered with his own voice. "I don't understand," he mumbled. "Why don't you attack them yourself?"

"I could do that, yes," said the dragon. "But I choose not to—yet. I must conserve my strength, Black-Gazer."

"Why?" Kurthak asked.

"To shape the land, as I've told you," she answered. "To corrupt the Kenderwood—and the kender. But there is also another reason—one that only Yovanna and I know. Shall I tell it to you, Black-Gazer?"

"Yes. Tell me."

Malys' crimson lips curled into a cruel, mocking smile. So did Kurthak's.

Standing away from them, forgotten for now, Baloth shut his eyes tight, whimpering wretchedly as Malystryx spoke.

* * * * *

The attackers rushed the base of the wall, howling for blood. Atop the battlements, kender scrambled to repel the assault. Shouted orders rang through the air as Kendermore's defenders ran this way and that, flinging debris down upon the invaders. Below, the attackers toppled beneath the pelting bombardment and lay still upon the ground. The kender atop the wall raised a hearty cheer for every foe who fell and did not rise again.

"The cauldrons!" Brimble Redfeather barked hoarsely. His wrinkled face was red from shouting. "Don't just throw things at them! Use the cauldrons!"

At his order, dozens of kender scurried to several huge cast-iron pots that stood atop the wall. The cauldrons, which had been brought from Kendermore's many feast-halls and hauled up to the walls, could each hold enough riverbean stew to feed a hundred kender. Today, though, they brimmed with something other than stew.

"Don't touch them!" Brimble shouted as several kender reached for the cauldrons with bare, curious hands. "You'll burn your fingers off, you lamebrains! They're scalding hot, remember?"

The kender snatched their hands back, grinning sheepishly at what they had almost done. "Sorry," one of them said.

"Don't be sorry, doorknob!" Brimble roared back. He jerked his thumb down at the ground below, where the attackers continued to surge against the base of the wall. "Pour the stuff on them! Now!"

"Right!" the kender replied. Grabbing pry bars from the catwalks, and working in teams of twenty, they levered the cauldrons up. Muscles bulged and teeth gritted as, groaning with the effort, they tilted the enormous kettles toward the edge of the wall. The contents of the cauldrons lapped against their rims.

"Heave!" the kender shouted, more or less at once.

Leaning on the pry bars, they tipped the cauldrons still farther. Streams of liquid spilled from the pots, first in thin drizzles, then building into deluges that drenched the attackers below. Shrieking and clutching at themselves, the wall's assailants fell to the ground. They writhed a while in the mud, then were still.

But it wasn't enough. The attackers kept on coming. More debris hammered down on them from the walls. "That's it!" Brimble bellowed. "Keep at 'em! Don't stop to watch them fall! Grab something else to throw!"

Suddenly, a new chorus of shouting sounded from below. Another wave of attackers surged forward, these ones carrying long ladders. They charged the wall, yelling wildly, and though the kender on the battlements felled many of them as they ran, more than half of them evaded the defenders' bombardment. A dozen ladders slammed down into the dirt, then swung up toward the top of the wall. Hollering attackers lunged up the ladders before they were even in place, brandishing weapons and taking the rungs two at a time.

"Stop them!" Brimble shouted. "They'll take the wall! Move!"

The defenders grabbed up pitchforks, billhooks, and other pole arms, and used them to push the tops of the ladders away from the wall. One by one, the ladders tipped over, swinging back away from the wall and crashing down to the ground.

It wasn't enough, though. Two ladders stayed up long enough for the attackers to reach the top. Quickly the attackers cleared away the wall's defenders, more of them coming up every second. The defenders backed away, forced to give up more and more ground.

"Come on, you mangy, lazy halfwits!" Brimble was roaring. "Keep them back! Contain them, or they'll take the whole bloody wall! Move, or I'll—"

Suddenly, one of the attackers broke past the wall's defenders and charged across the battlements. Before anyone could stop him, or even knew what he was doing, he grabbed Brimble and threw him off the wall. The old kender howled furiously, cursing the air blue, as he fell.

The kender atop the wall watched him drop. The

attackers did not. All at once, the faltering defenses crumbled. Attackers boiled across the battlements, knocking down Kendermore's defenders or shoving them off the catwalk. Soon there was no one left on the wall but attackers.

"Stop!" shouted Riverwind from atop the battlements.

At once, the attack ceased.

"All right, everyone get up," the Plainsman commanded. "Including the ones who are dead. Come on."

Kender who had lain unmoving on the catwalk, or on courtyard below the wall, pushed themselves sorely to their feet and started to clean up the mess left by the attack. They scraped up the red pulp of the kurpa melons the kender atop the wall had thrown, and mopped up the water that had poured down from the cauldrons. Those who had caught the brunt of the cauldrons' deluge wrung out their topknots and wiped mud from their faces and clothes.

They all started to talk at once. The predominant topics were how much fun Riverwind's war games were, how interesting it was to pretend to be under siege, and how weird it was to pretend to be under siege on the inside of the wall when, technically, they really were under siege on the outside.

Riverwind and Brimble had been conducting drills for three weeks. One brigade of kender would assail the inside of the wall, while another would attempt to fend them off. It was not going well.

Scowling sourly, Brimble Redfeather fought his way out of the haystack he'd landed in when he'd fallen. He muttered to himself, picking straw out of his hair as he made his way up the stairs to the battlements. He went to meet Riverwind, who stood solemnly, his strong arms folded across his chest.

"All right!" Brimble snarled. "Listen up!"

A few of the kender became quiet, but most kept jabbering, bragging about how well they'd fought and teasing those who had "died."

Brimble rooted in his belt pouch, pulled out a tin whistle,

and blew as hard as he could. The whistle's shrill note split the air like a hatchet. Even so, Brimble had to sound two more blasts before things finally settled down to something like silence.

"That was better," Riverwind announced with a sigh.

The kender cheered for themselves.

"Shut up, all of you!" Brimble barked back.

"However, you lost the wall," the Plainsman continued. "Think about what that would mean if it had been ogres instead of other kender attacking. You'd be dead, and Kurthak's horde would run rampant through Kendermore, killing your families and burning your homes.

"This may seem like a game," Riverwind added, "but it's not. You've got to do things right, or you'll end up dead when the ogres attack."

The kender stared at their shoes. Beside Riverwind, Brimble groaned in exasperation. The Plainsman rested a silencing hand on the old veteran's shoulder.

He waved his arm behind him, out across the meadow. "All of Kendermore is depending on you to stop that horde out there. There's no room for mistakes or sloppiness. Now, everyone can rest for an hour, and then we'll do this again."

Exhausted groans rose all around him as Riverwind turned and strode away along the battlements, following the catwalk to where Kronn and Paxina stood. He was pale and haggard, his white hair pasted to his forehead with sweat. Involuntarily, he pressed his hand against his stomach.

"Are you all right, Riverwind?" Paxina asked.

The Plainsman looked at her sharply, moving his hand away from his belly as he drew up to them.

"I'm fine," he murmured.

Concern flashed in their eyes, and he looked away irritably, staring out toward the Kenderwood. Across the meadow, the towering figures of the ogres moved restlessly about their camps. Their snarling, bestial voices carried across the field.

"They're certainly taking their time," Kronn observed. "Are all sieges this blasted boring?"

"Most of them," Riverwind replied, smiling. "The battle was over quickly at Kalaman, but I've heard of sieges that lasted for months—even years."

"Years," Paxina echoed, wondering. "We can't hold out that long. We've barely enough food stocked to last us the winter, even if we ration."

"I wouldn't worry about that too much," Riverwind replied. "I doubt the ogres have that kind of patience. They'll come soon enough. I just hope there's enough time to get ready." He turned, glancing back along the wall. Brimble Redfeather was berating the other kender, trying to get them to set up for the next drill. Riverwind heaved a leaden sigh.

"They'll be ready," Kronn told the Plainsman. "I've been watching them, especially the past few days. They really are improving—just not very quickly, is all."

"Plus those drills you're doing aren't completely fair," Paxina chimed in. "The melons make good rocks, and the water in the cauldrons is all right, but we'll have them, too." She nodded down toward the base of the wall, where a makeshift archery range was set up. Kender took turns firing arrows at straw dummies. More often than not, the shafts struck them in places that would kill a man—or an ogre. Watching them shoot, Riverwind marveled at the archers' skill.

Down a few blocks, a second group of kender stood in line, facing a row of catapults. Riverwind watched as they loaded slingstones into the pouches of their hoopaks, then held them poised. A moment passed, then the catapults' arms sprang forward, launching a volley of clay discs into the air. One by one they swung their hoopaks forward, flinging their stones at the discs. The targets shattered, raining down on the ground in pieces.

The old Plainsman nodded pensively, watching the slingers whoop in exultation as the catapult operators prepared their engines for another volley. "True," he said. "The archers and slingers will kill many ogres before they even get near the wall. But even so . . ." He shrugged, looking away toward the Kenderwood once more.

"You don't think we can hold them back?" Kronn asked.

Riverwind didn't reply. He gazed out across the meadow. "The forest will be dead soon," he observed.

Over the weeks since his arrival, the weather had continued to worsen. The heat had become even more intense and dry as an oven. The winds that swept over the town were much closer to the siroccos that scoured the sands of Khur than the damp, rainy gusts Paxina said were normal for autumn in Goodlund. Last year, she had said, it had rained for two-thirds of the month of Bleakcold, including a stretch of nine days without sunshine. Now, though, Bleakcold was nearly done, and not a drop had fallen.

Gradually, as the drought continued, the grassy meadow beyond the wall had turned from golden to the gray-brown hue of ashes. Then the grass had withered, leaving behind nothing but bald, barren earth. Stones pushed up through the soil where none had been before. Once the grass was gone, the trees had begun to change. Silver and green leaves had changed color—turning not red and gold, as was normal for autumn in the Kenderwood, but rather becoming brown and shriveled, many of them crumbling to dust before they had a chance to fall. Now many trees stood bald and gray, dead or nearly so.

And the stench of brimstone was stronger than ever.

"The dragon's magic," Paxina murmured, her face dark with emotion as she regarded the wasted husk of the Kenderwood. "I've heard the Dairly Plains became like this, when Malystryx started attacking the humans there. Now, from what I hear, there *are* no Dairly Plains any more—just mountains and badlands."

"Desolation," Riverwind murmured.

Kronn nodded, his eyes grim. "Even if we do beat the ogres when we attack, how can we stop this?"

"Defeat the dragon," the Plainsman said.

"But how?" Paxina said. "You told Kronn that you never slew a dragon in your life!"

"And Malys is more than 'just another dragon,' you know," Kronn put in. "I saw her when she burned

Woodsedge—and killed our father. She's incredibly huge."

"From the stories told by Weavewillow survivors," Paxina added, "she's almost four hundred feet long. How can we hope to slay any creature that big?"

"I didn't say 'slay,'" Riverwind answered, his brow furrowed with thought. "I said 'defeat.' There must be some way to beat her even if we can't kill her. We just need to discover her weakness."

"Oh," Kronn said. "But how are we going to figure out what—"

Before he could finish his question, though, a commotion rose in the courtyard below. Someone was running toward them, waving his arms. Looking down, the Plainsman and the Thistleknots saw it was Giffel Birdwhistle.

"Riverwind!" the tall kender shouted, his pouches flapping with every loping stride. "Kronn! Pax!" He sprinted toward the wall and bounded up the stairs, taking them two and three at a time.

"Giff?" Kronn asked. "What's the matter? Has something happened in the tunnels?"

"No," the tall kender replied, puffing with exertion as he finally reached the top of the stairs. He leaned heavily against a merlon. "I mean, yes. Something's happened." He looked at Riverwind, with a pitying expression that made the white hairs on the Plainsman's arms stand on end. "You've got to come to Arlie's place," he said.

* * * * *

Riverwind walked so swiftly through Kendermore's twisty streets that the kender had to jog to keep pace. For every step he took, they took three. The crowds of kender, who usually made it so hard to move quickly through the city, hurried out of his way to keep from getting trampled. Somehow, though he was still unfamiliar with the tangled layout of the city, Riverwind made his way without having to stop or double back even once. Mere minutes after leaving Brimble to oversee the next wall-defense drill, the Plainsman strode up the path to Arlie Longfinger's house, past the parched earth that was all that remained of the herbalist's garden. He stepped up onto the porch, pushed past several kender who waited outside the shop, and pounded on the door with his fist.

For a moment, no one answered. Then, as Riverwind tensed to knock again, the door swung open. Catt stood inside. Her injured arm was still in its sling, but the bandages that had covered her head were gone. She looked up at the Plainsman, then quickly stepped aside.

"That was quick," she said as Riverwind and the others hurried in.

"What's going on, Catt?" Kronn asked.

"Is it Brightdawn?" Riverwind demanded impatiently, giving voice to the terrible fear that had been welling inside him since they had left the battlements. "Has something happened to her?"

"No," said another voice.

They all looked down the dimly lit hallway that led into the depths of Arlie Longfinger's home. Swiftraven stood in the passage.

"It isn't Brightdawn," he said. "It's—"

"There you are!" snapped Arlie Longfinger. The old herbalist shoved past Swiftraven and marched straight up to Riverwind. "He's been asking for you. He has a message."

"Message?" Kronn echoed, confused. "Who has a message?"

At last, Riverwind's frayed patience snapped. "Would someone tell me what in the Abyss is going on?" he shouted.

Arlie blinked at him, startled, then turned and headed down the hallway, beckoning with his hand for the others to follow. They did, Riverwind at the fore. The herbalist reached a door—it led to the same room where Catt had lain, while she'd recovered from her head wound—and gently pushed it open.

The room was dark, but it was not empty. From the bed, the sound of ragged breathing mixed with moans of pain.

The tang of fresh blood hung in the air.

"What is this?" Riverwind demanded as he entered.

Arlie pushed past him and went to an oil lamp that sat, flickering faintly, upon a small table by the bed. He turned its key, and the lamp's light rose to a lambent, ruddy glow.

When Riverwind saw the man who lay upon the bed, he blew out his breath and staggered as though he'd been punched in the stomach. Swiftraven was at his side in an eyeblink, taking the old Plainsman's arm and leading him to a low stool beside the bed. Riverwind sat down heavily and stared in mute horror.

The man on the bed was badly injured. He had been stabbed in the gut, and even though the bandages Arlie had used to bind the wound were fresh, they were nonetheless dark with blood. Despite the seriousness of his wound, however, the man stirred when he saw Riverwind and even tried to sit up. Swiftraven rushed to his side and eased him back again, whispering soothing words and mopping the man's sweat-soaked brow.

"I don't understand," Paxina said, staring at the injured man. "He looks like one of your people, Riverwind—but what is he doing here? Who is he?"

Riverwind opened his mouth, but could say nothing. He bowed his head, overcome. Swiftraven turned toward the Lord Mayor, his face contorting into a grimace of pain.

"It's Stagheart," he said. "My brother . . . and Moonsong's beloved."

Chapter 19

"My chief," Stagheart of Qué-Teh moaned, through teeth clenched with pain. He clawed for Riverwind with a strong, sweat-soaked hand. The old Plainsman gripped it tightly, tears spilling down his cheeks. "Oh, my chief."

Riverwind forced himself to speak calmly. "Be easy, Stagheart," he said. "Still yourself, then speak."

Stagheart relaxed, slumping back in the bed and breathing heavily. It was a long while before he could summon the will to speak again. When he did, his terse words sent a chill through the old Plainsman.

"They took her," Stagheart gasped. "I tried to stop them, but—" He stiffened, grimacing as the wound in his belly wracked him with pain. "They took her . . . Moonsong . . ."

Riverwind jerked away from Stagheart's touch as though the younger man had stung him. Shakily, he rose to his feet and backed away from the bed until he bumped into the wall. His face was as pale as a corpse, his eyes wide with horror.

The old Plainsman said nothing. He only stared at Stagheart, scarcely even breathing, his lips moving soundlessly.

Paxina nodded to Catt, who slipped out of the room. Paxina followed her, casting a troubled glance at the old Plainsman before she stepped out the door.

Riverwind raised a shaking hand to his head. "What happened?" he asked. "How did he get here?"

"I was leading a scouting patrol out beyond the ogres' camp," Giffel answered. "Down by Chesli's Creek. We found him, unconscious and covered in blood. We bound his wound as well as we could, and brought him to Kendermore through the tunnels. It took eight of us to carry him here."

"They took her," Stagheart wept as Swiftraven smoothed back his damp, brown hair.

Drawing a long, slow breath to calm himself, Riverwind knelt by the bedside. "Stagheart," he said, at once gentle and insistent. "What happened?"

Stagheart's eyes rolled, showing nothing but white, then his gaze settled on Riverwind. "My chief," he breathed. "I have failed you."

"Tell me," Riverwind said.

The two men held each other's gaze for an excruciating moment, then Stagheart grew calm. Drawing upon some deep well of strength within himself, he began to speak.

"We left Qué-Shu a month ago," he said. "Moonsong had a . . . a nightmare. She dreamt that Brightdawn was in danger, that she needed her, so she pleaded with Goldmoon to let us go after you. We rode south to New Ports, found a ship to bear us across the New Sea—"

"Then crossed the desert in Khur, crossed the Bay of Balifor, and headed inland, toward the Kenderwood," Kronn finished proudly. "The same route we took."

"Kronn," Riverwind snapped.

"No, he's right," Stagheart said. A smile flickered across his face, then vanished. "When we reached the Kenderwood, though, it had been burned. Whole towns destroyed."

"You should have turned back," Riverwind said.

"I told Moonsong just that," Stagheart agreed. "But she would hear nothing of it. She wouldn't leave. . . ."

His voice broke, and he squeezed his eyes shut. Riverwind laid a hand on his arm, and after a time Stagheart grew calm again. He went on. "We'd bought a map in Port Balifor. It showed the way to Kendermore. We followed a trail, and as we neared Kendermore we reached a firebreak. Beyond, the forest was untouched by fire—but it was ailing, brown, and foul. Still we went on. We were so close—even I didn't think of turning back. . . .

"By the time I saw the ogres, it was too late to run. They

came out of the forest on all sides. I tried to protect her, my chief. I swear. I must have slain half a dozen of them. I did everything I could to keep them away from her—but it wasn't enough. Then one of them stabbed me." He gestured feebly at the bloody bandages girding his stomach. "It is . . . hard to remember everything that happened after that. I fell, and they left me for dead on the ground. Then they took her. She tried to run, but they were all around her. I tried to rise, but my wound . . . I no longer had the strength. I lay on the ground, calling her name. I don't know how long. Then I gave in to despair and blacked out."

He paused, drawing a deep, shaking breath. "When I woke again, I was here, in this room, and Swiftraven was with me. I asked for you so I could tell you of my failure before I died."

"You're not going to die," Swiftraven said firmly. He looked to Arlie, silently beseeching.

"He's right, actually," the old herbalist agreed. "I've looked at the wound. It's grievous but not fatal. You must rest and heal, but you'll live, Plainsman."

"No!" Stagheart shouted. His body jerked with the force of his rage. When he calmed down, he looked directly at Riverwind. "I have failed, my chief. Your daughter is lost, and I am to blame. Bring me a dagger, and let me end my shame."

Riverwind, however, was staring into the distance, thinking. His grip tightened on Stagheart's arm, his knuckles whitening. He looked at Arlie Longfinger. "How old is his wound?" he asked.

"Only a few hours."

A fire kindled in Riverwind's gaze. He rose and started toward the door. "There's still a slim chance," he said. "Giffel, where did you say you found Stagheart?"

"Chesli's Creek," the tall kender answered. "Why?"

Kronn gasped suddenly, his eyes wide. "You're not going after her—"

"You're damned right, I am!" Riverwind snapped. "She might still be alive. Giffel, I need you to take me to Chesli's

Creek. If I can locate the ogres' trail . . ."

"Okay, then I'm going too," Kronn declared. He rose.

"Very well," Riverwind agreed. "Come. There's no time to lose."

Kronn, Giffel and Riverwind started toward the door. Before they could leave the room, however, Swiftraven rose from his brother's side. "No, my chief!" he called.

The old Plainsman stopped, his hand on the latch of the door. He turned to glower at Swiftraven.

The young warrior did not quail. He stood firm, his head upraised. "Do not go, my chief," he said. "The kender need you here to help prepare for the siege. You cannot risk your life this way."

"Boy, you presume too much," Riverwind growled. His eyes blazed. "Moonsong is my daughter. Would you have me do nothing, knowing those beasts out there have her?"

"No, my chief," Swiftraven replied gravely. "But you do not need to go. I can follow the ogres' trail as well as you. Better, perhaps. Let me go in your place."

Riverwind and Swiftraven looked at each other. With a great effort of will, the old Plainsman nodded. "Very well, Swiftraven. Go. Find my daughter."

"Brightdawn should know about this," Kronn said as Swiftraven strode toward the door. "She's at your house, Riverwind. Pax and Catt can go get her, bring her here before we leave."

Swiftraven, however, shook his head. "No, Kronn. We've lost enough time—we can't afford to lose any more." He paused, though, then reached over his shoulder and slid an arrow out of his quiver. He offered the shaft to Riverwind. "It is the way of the Qué-Teh to leave a token for those we love when we go to war," he said. "My chief, will you give this to Brightdawn after I have gone?"

Nodding, Riverwind accepted the arrow. "I will."

Beaming with pride, Swiftraven turned back to the sickbed. "Farewell, my brother," he said. "I will bring Moonsong back to you."

Moving with swift purpose, he marched out of the room, Kronn and Giffel on his heels.

* * * * *

Chesli's Creek had been a clear, babbling rill five miles west of Kendermore. It had been a popular picnicking place among the kender, and its bed had been covered with smooth, round stones, perfect for hurling from hoopaks.

The blight Malystryx had brought upon the land had changed the clear waters to a narrow, brown drizzle that trickled from one stagnant pool to another. The greenberry bushes that grew along its grassy banks were leafless skeletons that rattled in the hot wind. A fawn, scrawny and shivering with sickness, dipped its head to lap at the fetid water. Warped by the dragon's curse upon the Kenderwood, it was blind in one eye and barely had the strength to stand.

On a low rise that once had been an islet in the middle of the stream, a large, lichen-crusted rock split down the middle. With a soft click it swung open, revealing a shaft and earthen staircase that led down into the ground.

Swiftraven emerged stealthily from the rock, an arrow nocked on his bow, and quickly looked around. As Kronn and Giffel climbed out of the shaft behind him, the young warrior's gaze focused on the fawn. It looked at him, quaking, but did not flee. Instead, it kept its head low, bleating softly.

Without hesitating, he pulled back his bowstring and shot the fawn through the heart. It groaned thankfully for the end to its pain, slumped to the ground, and died.

Kronn looked at Swiftraven and nodded silently. Behind them, Giffel bent down by the false rock and pushed it shut. It clicked closed, once more nothing more than another boulder in the increasingly barren, rock-strewn landscape. He hurried over to the others, pulling his battak—a studded club with a short blade at its tip—from his belt. "All right," he whispered. "In case . . . well, just in case, there's a small stone next to the boulder there. Twist it to open the shaft."

Swiftraven had another arrow ready. His eyes flicked

from tree to tree, constantly searching for movement. "Where did you find my brother?"

"This way," Giffel answered. "It's not far." He crossed the ruins of the creek, and the others followed, tense and alert. They moved through the dead forest like ghosts, making no more sound than the wind. Giffel threaded through the barren undergrowth for five hundred paces, then stopped and pointed.

A small clearing lay before them, with a worn, exposed rock in its midst. Beside the stone, the dark stain of Stagheart's blood lingered on the ground.

Slowly, Swiftraven crept toward the stain. He crouched down beside it, examining it, then looked back at the two kender and jerked his head for them to come forward.

Moonsong's abductors had been ogres, and they had not been concerned about hiding their passage, so it only took him a minute to find their spoor. Branches had snapped off trees, and bushes were uprooted. There was blood, too. At least one of them had been wounded, most likely by Stagheart before he fell.

The track led back toward Kendermore. Toward the camps of the ogre horde.

Swiftraven looked at Kronn and Giffel. Both kender nodded silently. The young warrior pointed forward with his readied arrow; then the threesome started forward. They stayed off the ogres' trail, keeping a dozen paces to the side. They walked a league, neither stopping nor talking. Then suddenly Swiftraven stopped, hunkering low. Behind him, the two kender also drew to a halt.

"What?" Giffel hissed.

"Ogres," Swiftraven said. He pointed.

Peering ahead, the kender saw dark shapes among the trees, barely fifty yards in front of them.

"Guards," Kronn said. "Two of them. We must be very close." Moving quickly, he started taking apart his chapak.

"What are you doing?" the Plainsman asked.

Kronn didn't answer. He unscrewed his weapon's axe head, removed the plug from the butt of its handle, and dumped out the coiled rope inside. Then he gave the haft a twist, and a metal plate covered the insides of the flute's fingerholes, locking in place. "Let me take care of them," he said, setting aside the haft and fishing in one of his many pouches. "I can do it neatly and quietly."

After a moment's digging, he pulled out a long, thin wooden box and opened its hinged lid. Inside were a dozen slender darts. He removed two and clamped them between his teeth as he returned the box to his pouch. Then, carefully, he pulled out a small, dark vial. Smiling grimly, he unstopped it and dipped one of the darts into it. The dart's needle-sharp point came away coated with glistening, black fluid. Then he did the same with the second dart.

Clutching the blowgun, he crept forward on his haunches, through the undergrowth. Giffel and Swiftraven watched him go. Kronn crossed half the distance to the ogres, moving from cover to cover in quick, silent bursts. At last he stopped behind a low, brown-needled shrub. He set down one of his darts, slid the other into the blowgun, and raised the weapon to his lips. Lining up his sights with the farther of the two ogres, he drew in a deep breath, puffed out his cheeks, and blew.

The dart hissed through the air, striking the ogre in the neck. The creature swatted at it irritably, as if it were a mosquito. Then it blinked twice, fell to its knees, and slumped limply to the ground.

Its fellow stared at it in shock. By the time it realized what had happened, Kronn had fired his second dart, hitting it in the leg. It took a moment longer for the venom to work its way through the second ogre's veins, but it was still dead before it could do more than grunt in surprise.

Kronn crept back to the others and swiftly reassembled his chapak. "I doubt they posted more guards than that," he murmured. "They won't be expecting anything to come from this direction, really. Our way should be clear from here."

* * * * *

Moonsong drifted along the shores of consciousness. Her head lolled from side to side, and she moaned in pain. Her right cheek was badly bruised, and blood was drying on her bottom lip. Her ribs ached fiercely, too. She had dim memories of an ogre's booted foot slamming into her side. Worst of all, though, was the burning in her wrists.

The ogres had bound her hands tightly with coarse rope, then had hung that rope from a stake in the middle of their camp. She had tried to fight them, but one had punched her, and her world had fallen into blackness. Now, as she fought her way back toward lucidity, she could no longer feel her fingers, and her wrists blazed with agony where the ropes had chafed them raw.

At long last she opened her left eye; the right was swollen shut. For a moment, she could see nothing, and the afternoon sunlight filled her aching head with fire.

She counted eight ogres before her and heard what sounded like two more behind. Some of the brutish creatures stood at the edges of their simple camp, watching the dying forest around them. Another tended a fire, carving strips of flesh off what looked like a scrawny, dead boar, and setting them on hot stones beside the flames. The meat's rancid stink made Moonsong's gorge rise.

The two largest ogres were also the ones closest to her. They were arguing, barking viciously at each other in their harsh, guttural language. She didn't understand the words, but she didn't have to. Shuddering, she realized they were arguing over her.

The argument grew more fierce, becoming a shoving match. At last, one of the ogres backhanded the other across the face. The second ogre stumbled back, then wiped blood from its mouth and balled its hands into fists. The first one—a tan-skinned, fur-clad monster with a pockmarked face—snarled, and the second stayed where it was.

The pockmarked ogre turned to face Moonsong, leering cruelly, then walked toward her.

"No," Moonsong pleaded. Loathing choked her.

She tried to struggle. Fresh blood ran down her arms as

the rope rubbed against her wrists. The pockmarked ogre only chuckled, though, reaching for her with a filth-smeared hand. Its sour breath watered her eyes, and she gasped in disgust as its greasy fingers touched her face.

"Pretty," it growled.

Moonsong tried to scream, but the only sound that escaped her fear-tightened throat was a thin, shrill wail. The pockmarked ogre threw back its head and laughed.

Then, abruptly, it fell silent. Eyes widening with shock, it fell forward against her, then toppled sideways onto the ground. A white-fletched arrow quivered in the back of its neck.

The other ogres gawked at his body, stunned. A second arrow struck one of them in the chest, punching through its leather breastplate and burying itself in its heart. The monster clutched feebly at the feathered shaft, then fell. A third shot grazed the arm of the one tending the fire, drawing a line of blood.

The ogres started shouting, grabbing up clubs and axes. They cast about madly, trying to find the archer among the trees. Another arrow hit one in the eye, killing it—but the shot gave away the archer's position. Growling with rage, they started toward the arrows' source.

As they charged, however, slingstones started to rain down on them from behind. Two more ogres fell beneath this new bombardment. The others looked around in amazement, unsure of what to do, then scattered as more stones fell among them. Two charged into the woods after the archer. Another pair went the other way, trying to find the slinger. The last one stayed in the camp, moving to stand by Moonsong's side. Its face was livid with fear and rage.

The thrum of the bowstring and whistle of the sling-stones stopped, then the sounds of fighting rang out on either side of the camp, steel clashing against steel as the ogres fell upon their attackers. Voices grunted in pain, and metal sliced through flesh. The ogre beside Moonsong stared around the camp in indecision, its spear quivering in its grasp.

It jerked suddenly, its body going rigid as something hit it from behind. It swayed unsteadily for a moment, then crashed headlong to the ground.

Behind it stood a tall, stout kender with short-cropped, yellow hair. In his hand he held a metal-studded club, tipped with a long knife blade. The blade gleamed with the dead ogre's blood.

"Who—" Moonsong began to ask.

The kender shook his head and started toward her. "Later," he said. He swung his club at the stake, and the knife-blade cut through the rope. Moonsong dropped to her knees with a groan, then struggled to rise.

"Giffel!" shouted another voice. A second kender dashed into the clearing, a bloody axe in his hand.

Seeing his chestnut cheek braids and green clothes, Moonsong gasped in recognition. "Kronn?" she breathed.

"Hi, Moonsong!" the kender said. He waved to her as he hurried over. "Can you walk? No, on second thought, can you run?"

The Plainswoman regarded him blearily, then nodded.

"Good." Kronn looked across the camp, toward the direction the arrows had come from. "Swiftraven should be about done with the others."

"Swift-Swiftraven?" Moonsong gasped confusedly.

"Right here," said a voice as the young warrior strode into the clearing. He held his sabre in one hand, a knife in the other. Both dripped crimson. He smiled when he saw her. "Stagheart told us what happened," he explained. "We came after you."

"Stagheart . . ." she murmured. "He's still alive?"

"And safe in Kendermore," Kronn averred, "which is where we're taking you."

New sounds rose around the camp. More ogres were crashing through the trees, shouting in their guttural tongue. Swiftraven glanced around sharply. "Damn," he swore. "They were faster than I'd thought. We've got to get out of here."

"Back west!" Giffel shouted, waving his bladed club. "To the creek!"

He dashed off into the forest. Kronn grabbed Moonsong's hand and dragged her after them. Her legs burned as she ran, but fear kept her on her feet. Swiftraven came last, watching their backs as they fled.

The sounds of pursuit dogged them as they dashed through the woods. Glancing back, they saw the dark shapes of their pursuers. A dozen more ogres had picked up their trail, howling with battle lust as they crashed through the forest.

They gasped and wheezed, leaping over rocks and fallen trees as they ran. Their pursuers paused when they found the guards Kronn had shot with his blowgun, but soon they were running again, weapons held high.

"How much farther?" Swiftraven panted. The ogres were less than two hundred yards behind them. He could see the fury in their eyes.

"Two miles," Giffel answered breathlessly.

Kronn and Swiftraven exchanged looks, sharing the same dire thought. The ogres would catch them before they made it another two miles. They ran faster, Kronn pulling Moonsong along with him. She sobbed incoherently, tears streaming down her face, as she stumbled after the kender.

They ran another mile, then Moonsong stumbled over an exposed root and fell. Kronn jerked to a halt, and he and Swiftraven tried to drag her to her feet. The pounding of the ogres' footsteps grew closer with every exhausted heartbeat.

Swiftraven didn't hear the faint hum of the javelin flying through the air. It struck him in the back of his knee, impaling his leg. He fell to the ground with a cry.

"No!" Kronn cried.

Swiftraven reached back and pulled the spear from his leg. Bright blood coursed from the wound, and he ground his teeth together and struggled to his feet. When he tried to take a step, though, his knee buckled and he nearly fell again. He groaned with pain. The charging ogres heaved more javelins, which fell all around them.

Swiftraven looked at Kronn, then, his eyes like stones. "Go," he said.

Kronn's face was also hard. "Swiftraven . . ."

A spear hit the ground at Moonsong's feet. She stared at it dully, uncomprehending.

"Go!" Swiftraven bellowed. "Get back to Kendermore! I'll try and slow them. Now, Kronn!"

Obediently, Kronn grabbed Moonsong's hand and ran to catch up with Giffel.

Swiftraven watched them go, then turned, dragging his injured leg, to face the onrushing ogres. He raised his arms, drawing their attention. "Here!" he shouted.

The monsters threw the last of their javelins, but their shots went wild. Then they stopped, all twelve of them, and stared at the wounded Plainsman. They circled around him warily, starting to laugh.

"Damn the lot of you," Swiftraven snarled, brandishing his sabre. "Who's first?"

A hulking brute strode forward, chuckling darkly. In his meaty paw he held a sword that a human would have needed both hands to wield. His face twisted into a sneer, revealing a mouthful of black teeth.

"Come on," Swiftraven growled.

Crossing the distance from his fellows to the young Plainsman in two long strides, the ogre raised his sword and slashed downward in a vicious arc. Swiftraven lifted his sabre to block the blow, and the crash of blade against blade numbed his whole arm. He stumbled back, nearly falling as his bleeding leg faltered under him, then regained his footing and lunged. He thrust upward with his sabre, seeking to pierce his opponent's scale armor. The ogre swatted the blow aside with his blade, then struck Swiftraven across the face with his free hand.

A bright sun exploded in the Plainsman's head, but stubbornly he spat blood and teeth on the ground.

"You'll have to do better than that, you bastard," he growled.

The ogre raised its massive sword above its head a second time. Again, Swiftraven raised his sabre to parry. Steel met steel.

Then the Plainsman's blade was spinning through the air, shorn off by the might of the ogre's attack. Swiftraven felt the monster's weapon bite into his right shoulder, cleaving through his collarbone. He heard something heavy—some distant part of his mind told him it was his sword arm—drop to the ground.

He fell, Brightdawn's name on his lips.

* * * * *

In his sickbed, Stagheart was weeping. Catt and Paxina's faces also shone with misery. Riverwind stood very still, his face ashen, hands clenched into fists at his sides. Kronn bowed his head, sucked in a deep breath, and blew it out again through tight lips.

"We waited at the entrance to the tunnels," he said quietly. "I don't know—I thought maybe, somehow, he might make it. But when we saw the ogres coming through the woods, Giff had to close up the rock, and we headed back to Kendermore." He raised his gaze from the floor, turning his head to look at a chair by the window. "Brightdawn . . . I'm sorry."

She sat rigidly, her blue eyes vacant. The only parts of her that moved were her hands, which twisted around the arrow Swiftraven had left for her.

She did not cry.

When Riverwind had come to her and told her where Swiftraven had gone, and why, she had been furious—at her father, at Swiftraven, at Moonsong, at herself. In her anger, she had nearly gone down into the tunnels after him, but Riverwind had held her until some semblance of calm returned to her.

"He sacrificed himself for us," Kronn stated. "If he hadn't distracted them, the ogres would have caught us before we made it to Chesli's Creek."

"It should have been me," Riverwind said dully. "Oh,

Mishakal—he took my place. . . ."

"It's my fault," Kronn disputed. "I'm the one who left him there."

"No." Brightdawn's voice was as brittle as old parchment. She stood, numb with anguish. "He chose to go. Don't blame yourselves—either of you."

The old Plainsman looked at his daughter and saw the void in her gaze. His eyes gleaming in the lamplight, he reached out to her. With an inarticulate sound, Brightdawn shook off his gentle touch. She turned and walked out the door, which slammed shut behind her.

* * * * *

It was almost sunrise when Riverwind found her, standing atop Kendermore's western wall. She stared intently at the dark line of the forest as the sky behind her turned gold with the promise of dawn. She still held the arrow in her hands.

"Brightdawn," the old Plainsman said softly, walking toward her along the battlements.

She didn't answer. He opened his mouth to say her name again, but before he could speak, she bowed her head, and her knees gave way beneath her. Riverwind was at her side before she could fall, though. He caught her up in his arms and held her close. She sobbed in agony as the tears she'd been holding back all night came all at once.

"Brightdawn," the old Plainsman murmured, stroking her golden hair. "My child. My sunrise."

"He didn't say goodbye," she moaned. "That's the worst part. That and knowing Moonsong would be dead now if he hadn't done what he did. Now I'll never see him again."

"You will," Riverwind said solemnly. "Someday."

She raised her head, her eyes accusing. "How do you know?" she demanded. "The gods are gone, Father! How can you be sure we'll be together, after we die? How can you be sure there's anything waiting for us?"

A spasm of anguish crossed his face. "I know, child," he told her, "because I have faith. The gods would not have left us without making sure our spirits were cared for after we died. In my heart, I prefer to believe that I'll see them all again—my grandfather, Sturm, Flint, Tanis, Tas . . . and Swiftraven will be waiting for us, too."

She shook her head. "I wish I had your faith, Father."

"You will, when your pain subsides," he answered. He pointed up at the sky. "Do you see that star?"

Reluctantly, she looked. Most of the new stars had faded into the violet, pre-dawn glow, but one light lingered longer than the others. It shone red, like a glowing ember, above the northern horizon.

"Paxina tells me the Silvanesti elves have a name for it," Riverwind said. "They call it Elequas Sori—the Watcher in the Dark. They say that to look upon it is to know peace, that we are not alone."

Brightdawn looked at the red star a long time, and finally she relaxed in her father's grasp. He let her go, smiling kindly. "You should go to your sister, child," he said. "Moonsong will want to see you when she wakes. But first . . . I have brought you something."

He reached over his shoulder and unslung his bow from his back. Wordlessly, he offered it to Brightdawn.

She looked at it a moment, then her gaze dropped to Swiftraven's arrow. Its steel head gleamed in the morning light. She took the bow from her father, fitted the shaft on it, and pulled back the string, aiming out across the meadow. Then she fired.

The arrow carried a long way, soaring high against the brightening sky.

Chapter 20

Two weeks passed.

When Moonsong recovered from her injuries, she offered her skills as a healer to Arlie Longfinger, who consented gladly. Then she visited Stagheart and lay with him in his sickbed, holding him while he wept.

"Forgive me," he pleaded, sobbing quietly.

She kissed him gently, tasting the salt of his tears. "Oh, my love," she told him. "There is nothing to forgive."

Meanwhile, the kender continued to prepare for war. Riverwind, Kronn, and Brimble Redfeather held more drills atop the walls. Brightdawn helped Catt and Paxina oversee the daily struggle to keep the people fed as the town's foodstocks dwindled.

Then, one warm evening early in the month the kender called Blessings, the ogres launched their attack.

They came at twilight, when the shadows of the Kenderwood were long upon the land. They were only a fraction of the whole horde, marching across the field toward the city's east wall, but their numbers were still vast: two thousand ogres—two full war bands—all howling for blood.

Thousands of kender, packed shoulder to shoulder atop the wall, peered between the merlons, watching the ogres advance. Some were resolute, their mouths drawn into tight, lipless lines as their hands twisted around their weapons. Others grinned and laughed, shouting at the onrushing attackers with mocking, singsong voices. Still others, who had come off watch only a short time before and had been called back when the alarm sounded, leaned sleepily against the battlements, their shoulders stooped and eyes drooping. A few took quick swigs from jugs of kender lager or flasks of lukewarm tarbean tea. Archers fitted arrows onto bowstrings; slingers tucked stones into the pouches of their hoopaks and chapaks. In the courtyard below, kender grabbed flagstones and hauled them up to the catwalk; the wall's defenders would not be throwing kurpa melons at their assailants today. Others carried up buckets of steaming pitch, which they poured into the waiting cauldrons instead of the water they had used in the drills. They wrinkled their noses against the pungent smell, taking care not to touch the searing-hot kettles, then tossed the buckets back down into the courtyard when they were empty. Then they grabbed up weapons and squeezed into place at the battlements with the rest of their fellows. The tension on the wall was like the tingling of the air before a thunderstorm.

The ogres were already halfway across the meadow when Riverwind dashed up the steps, joining Brimble and Kronn on the battlements. He stared over the merlons, down at the city's attackers, and said nothing.

"Why aren't they sending more?" Kronn wondered aloud. "Can they take the city with so few?"

Brimble shook his head. "I doubt it," he said. "But that's not what they're aiming to do."

"They're going to test our defenses," Riverwind agreed. He bent his bow around his leg, strung it quickly, and readied an arrow. "They'll engage us, try to find our weaknesses, then withdraw. Brimble, you should get your men in position."

The grizzled kender had already turned to bark at his troops. Archers and slingers ran to their posts, then stood ready, waiting expectantly as their foes moved toward the town. Then, when the ogres were in range, they raised their weapons and began to fire.

The first volley of shafts and stones slammed into the front ranks of the horde, a rain of death that felled a hundred ogres in an instant. The second flight streaked into their midst, but the attackers were ready for it. They stopped, raising their shields over their heads to block the barrage. Even so, three score of their number dropped, dead or dying.

When the ogres lowered their shields and began to move again, they did so at a run, charging toward the walls. Kendermore's defenders slew another hundred and fifty attackers before they reached it. Riverwind picked off three ogres with his bow, and Kronn and Brimble pelted the attackers with stones hurled from their chapaks.

Then the wall shuddered, dust rising from its flagstones, as the ogres slammed against it with all their might.

Brimble blew on his whistle. "Rocks!" he roared, his shout carrying above the din of the attacking ogres.

As the archers and slingers continued to pepper the town's assailants, other kender picked up stones from the battlements and heaved them off the wall. The rocks ranged from stones the size of a kender's fist to great slabs so heavy it took two kender to lift them. They crashed down upon the horde, smashing the ogres' upraised shields and crushing whatever they struck. The ground beneath the wall quickly grew littered with rubble and broken bodies.

Below, ogres heaved javelins with all their might; many of the spears clattered uselessly against the wall, but here and there they flew true, arcing over and between the merlons to impale the kender atop the battlements. Some of the dead collapsed on the catwalk. Others fell from the wall, their arms and legs windmilling as they plummeted to the hard ground. One javelin flashed by Riverwind, lodging in the stomach of the archer to his right. The skewered kender, a woman with a bright red topknot, staggered and fell back, screaming, into the courtyard below. Her cries ended with a crunching of bone as she struck the cobblestones.

"Cauldrons!" Brimble roared. He lifted a stone the size of his head and hurled it down, smashing an ogre's skull. "Move it, you laggards!" he bellowed, and blew on his whistle. "Douse them now, before you get stuck with one of those spears!"

Obediently, the kender nearest the steaming kettles grabbed up their pry bars and began to heave, tilting the cauldrons. The thick, black pitch was more stubborn than water to pour, but the kender heaved with all their might, and soon steaming tar splashed down upon the ogres. Cries of agony rose from the ground below. The pitch clung to whatever it hit, and black-drenched ogres howled, clawing at their faces and bodies as it scalded their flesh. Several archers nocked arrows wrapped in oil-soaked rags and touched them to nearby braziers. The arrows burst into flame, and at another shouted order from Brimble they loosed their shafts toward the pools of pitch below. Fires leapt into life where the arrows struck, killing many more ogres. The stench of burning rose from below, mixing with the brimstone reek of the wind. Black smoke filled the air.

"That's it!" Riverwind shouted. He loosed another arrow, which flashed through the air, hitting an ogre in the neck. "You're doing it! Keep at them!"

The assault continued in this way for an hour, though to Kendermore's defenders it felt more like an eternity. In time, half the attacking ogres lay unmoving at the base of the wall, pierced and smashed and burnt. But half still remained, and the supplies of arrows and slingstones on the battlements ran perilously low. One by one, the archers and slingers cast their weapons aside and joined their fellows at rock-heaving.

"There!" Kronn cried, pointing out across the meadow. "Ladders coming! They're going to try and scale the wall!"

Riverwind squinted, leaning dangerously out over the merlons. He ducked a soaring javelin, then peered toward the distant Kenderwood. Night had fallen, but in the glow of the fires and the pale moon, he could make out several hundred more of the ogres, charging forward to join their fellows. They carried at least two dozen long, sturdy ladders.

"Get ready!" Brimble shouted. With practiced ease, he slung his chapak across his back with one hand, picking up a long military fork with the other. "They'll all come at once. Be prepared to repel them!"

Hurriedly the kender set down or cast aside their weapons and pry bars, discarding them in favor of pole arms. The few remaining archers and slingers concentrated their last shots on the ladder bearers. They succeeded in stopping a third of them before they could get near the wall, but the rest came on, driving their ladders into the ground and swinging them up toward the walls. Then the ogres began to climb.

Wherever a ladder rose, kender ran to intercept it. They pushed with their bill hooks and pitchforks, trying to shove the ladders away before the ogres could reach the top. Several ladders fell, crashing back to the ground and crushing those who had tried to climb them.

But the ladders were sturdier than the ones Riverwind and Brimble had used in their drills, and the ogres who held their bases steady were strong. Of the seventeen ladders that went up, nine refused to fall.

Brimble Redfeather swore like a sailor, shoving his fork against a ladder with all his might. "Damn it!" he snarled. "They're going to make it up here! They're going to take the wall!" He blew hard on his whistle, sounding a signal he'd hoped he wouldn't have to use. "Arm yourselves! Be ready when they come! Kill them as soon as you can see their ugly faces!"

The kender dropped their pole arms, which were ill-suited for close-quarters fighting, and took up their own weapons again. Hoopaks, chapaks, clublike battaks, hammer-headed hachaks, and many other strange weapons rose in anticipation of the first ogres to crest the wall.

The kender didn't have to wait long. The ogres climbed quickly, and soon they began to appear at the top of every ladder. The kender laid into them, shouting as they chopped and slashed and thrust with their weapons. Surprised by the defenders' fury, the first few ogres fell from their perches, bloody and battered. In several places, the ogres steadying the bottoms of the ladders had to leap aside to keep from being struck by the plummeting corpses. The kender promptly responded by toppling those ladders to the ground.

Not all of the attackers were so easily thwarted, however. In three different places along the wall, the ogres forced the kender to give ground, vaulting over the merlons to land on the catwalk. The kender rallied quickly, sprinting along the battlements to hold the intruders at bay. In one place, they forced the attackers back quickly, toppling their ladder when they were done, but the ogres held the other two breaches. Kronn and Riverwind ran to one of those battlefronts, and Brimble dashed to the other.

More and more kender died, in ever-increasing numbers. Ogres continued to climb up the ladders onto the wall, and for each attacker who fell, three of Kendermore's defenders died, smashed by cudgels or hacked to pieces by axes and swords.

Riverwind shoved his way to the front of the battle, his sabre flashing in the moonlight. He stabbed one ogre in the face, then swept the blade low and disemboweled another. The stones under his feet were slick with ogre and kender blood. To his left, Kronn hewed away with his chapak. To his right, a golden-haired kender woman swung a hoopak. She killed three ogres with the weapon, but a fourth seized her by the arm and lifted her up into the air. She slashed at the creature with her hoopak, but it only laughed, raising her high and flinging her out over the merlons. She dropped out of sight, plunging to the ground far below.

For a moment, Riverwind and Kronn held the line alone, using all their strength to stave off the surging tide of the ogres. Then someone stepped in on the old Plainsman's right, shouting with berserk fury. Two ogres fell, in rapid succession, to her whirling, flanged mace.

"Brightdawn!" Riverwind shouted. He thrust his sabre through an ogre's ribs, and it fell face-forward on the stones. "I was wondering where you were! We need your help!"

His daughter laid into the ogres with two weeks' worth of seething rage, wreaking bloody vengeance for

Swiftraven's death. Bones cracked and blood spattered beneath her pounding mace. With the added force of her attack, Riverwind and Kronn began to push the ogres back toward the ladder.

The kender at the other battlefront did not fare so well. The catwalk was littered with their broken bodies, and the survivors faltered beneath the onslaught of the ogres. The wall's defenders fell like grain at harvest time.

"Come on, you lamebrains!" roared Brimble Redfeather as he chopped at the attackers with his chapak. "Tighten up those lines! We've got to stop these bastards!"

But the ogres continued to press, and the kender continued to give ground. Brimble glanced up and down the wall and cursed. Then he looked toward the ladder, where more and more ogres continued to pour up onto the battlements, and his eyes narrowed with sudden determination.

Shouting at the top of his lungs, the old veteran leapt up onto the merlons and began to run toward the ladder. "You won't take this city while I live, you goblin-spawned, lackwitted dogs!" he roared.

The old kender dashed recklessly across the merlons, leaping across the crenellations, his chapak held high. Attackers and defenders alike stared in amazement as he sprinted to the ladder, knocked away the topmost ogre with his axe, and hurled himself off the wall, onto the rungs. Pushing with all his strength, he used his own weight to tilt the ladder away from the wall. It swung back from the battlements, stood straight upright for a heartbeat, then fell away. Brimble shouted triumphantly as he rode the ladder all the way down, then disappeared amid the throngs of ogres at the bottom of the wall.

Galvanized by the old veteran's last, crazed act, the kender who had been fighting at Brimble's side began to make headway against their attackers. The ogres, suddenly stranded and bereft of reinforcements, cast about in panic, seeking to escape. The hesitation cost them dearly. The kender closed in, slaughtering them without mercy.

At the other battlefront, Kronn, Riverwind and Brightdawn continued to force their opponents back. Soon they were at the ladder. Riverwind raked his sabre across the chest of one last ogre, who screamed and fell from the ladder. Without pausing, the old Plainsman dropped the blade and picked up a discarded bill hook from the catwalk. He lunged at the ladder, using all his strength to shove it away.

The ogre at the very top of that ladder happened to be Baloth, Kurthak's lieutenant, whose job it was to command this first charge. For just a moment, the hairless ogre locked eyes with the fierce old Plainsman.

Feeling his footing give way beneath him, Baloth dropped his war axe and made a wild leap for the wall. He landed on top of a merlon, fought momentarily for balance as the ladder fell away, then sprang forward, toward Riverwind. The old Plainsmen jumped aside, swinging the bill hook. The butt of the weapon's long handle cracked against the underside of Baloth's chin, and the ogre reeled back.

Riverwind didn't hesitate for an instant. He jabbed with the pole arm again, striking the hairless ogre between the eyes. Blood erupted from Baloth's face as he dropped senseless to the catwalk.

At once, several kender surged forward, raising their weapons to finish the hairless ogre, but Riverwind held out his hand. "Stop!" he shouted. "Don't kill him." He pointed at Baloth's intricate bone and tooth necklace, draped in a tangle across his comatose form. "That must mean he's a leader of some sort. This one is of more use to us alive than dead."

Nodding their understanding, the kender ran, shouting for strong ropes to bind the unconscious ogre leader. Riverwind, meanwhile, whirled back toward the battle, relieved to see that it was all but over.

"They're retreating!" Brightdawn announced, looking out over the battlements. "They're running away! We beat them!"

The surviving kender atop the wall cheered heartily at this, lifting their weapons high above their heads. Riverwind and Kronn did not share their joy, however. They looked gravely at each other, sharing the same thought. Brave Brimble Redfeather and hundreds of kender were dead, they had nearly lost the battle, and they had only faced two thousand of Kurthak's troops.

There were some ten thousand ogres still out there, waiting for the real assault to begin.

* * * * *

When the sun's light touched Kendermore's rooftops once more, it found the courtyards beneath the town's east wall littered with the wounded and the dead.

The surviving kender had found no rest after the ogres' retreat. Some had spent the night heaving dead ogres off the battlements onto the bloody field outside the city, while the rest lifted those of their fellows who had fallen to the onslaught and laid them out in rows upon the ground. Now, as the sky paled with morning light, there was scarcely room to walk for bodies. Healers—including Arlie Longfinger and Moonsong of Qué-Shu—moved among the fallen, helping those who could be saved and comforting those who could not. Many other kender picked their way through the aftermath too, searching for parents, siblings, children, and friends. The usual tumult of noise that hung over Kendermore had changed. Rather than shouts and laughter, the air rang with weeping and groans of pain.

Riverwind stood wearily above it all, looking down upon the casualties from atop the wall. Brightdawn and all three of the Thistleknots stood with of him.

"We can't do it," the old Plainsman said at length, putting a hand to his head. He was shaking with fatigue, and cramps wracked his old muscles.

The others looked at him sharply. "Father?" Brightdawn gasped.

"What do you mean, 'can't?' " Paxina asked.

Helplessly, Riverwind gestured at the carnage below. "I mean that," he snapped. "One-fifth of Kurthak's army did that—and we were fortunate. When the rest of the army attacks, we will certainly lose. I can't lie to you, or to myself. There's no way we can hold the walls against that horde. It's simply a matter of numbers—we'd still be hard-pressed if our forces were doubled.

"And," he added, seeing Paxina open her mouth to object, "even though we drove them back, the ogres won the battle last night. They accomplished what they set out to do—they have learned our weaknesses. Now they know how to beat us."

Riverwind hesitated a moment, frowning. "There's something else working against us. We nearly lost the wall last night because, I hate to say it, our warriors are acting afraid."

"What?" Kronn asked, offended. "Riverwind, you know kender aren't capable of fear."

"Aren't you?" the old Plainsman shot back, turning his hard gaze on Kronn. "You saw little Billee Juniper when we found her, Kronn—and you were there with me last night. Didn't you see how the kender behaved when the ogres started to take the wall? They hung back—and Brimble died because of their hesitation. Why would they do that?"

Scowling angrily, Kronn opened his mouth to answer. Before he could speak, however, Paxina interrupted.

"It began a few months ago," she said, "when the Kenderwood began to wither."

"Nettles and thorns," Kronn gasped. "Pax, you can't be serious."

She looked up at him, her eyes flashing. "Look at me, Kronn. I'm telling the truth. Malystryx's magic isn't just corrupting the Kenderwood; it's corrupting us. Fear, hopelessness, despair—some of us are feeling all of these emotions for the first time. You don't notice it, Kronn, because you've been away. And you, Catt. But the first time you wake up in the middle of the night, scared half to death by your first nightmare, you'll believe me."

"Nightmares!" Catt scoffed.

"All the kender?" asked Kronn solemnly.

"No, thankfully," said Paxina. "But many . . . too many." She turned to the old Plainsman. "Riverwind, I should have told you, but I was too ashamed."

It was a long time before anyone spoke. Then Catt sighed softly and looked up at the old Plainsman.

"You should leave, Riverwind," she said solemnly. "You still have a chance to get away before the final attack—all of you." She glanced at Brightdawn. "We shouldn't have dragged you into this in the first place."

"I'm not leaving," Brightdawn said.

Smiling, Riverwind reached out to his daughter and took her hand. "Neither am I," he stated. "I, too, am afraid. But there must be a way to defeat the ogres—and the dragon. In this situation, fear or no fear, my friend Tasslehoff wouldn't have given up and neither will I. There must be a way."

"How?" Paxina asked.

"I don't know yet," the old Plainsman said. "Kronn, let's talk. . . ."

Chapter 21

It had been a long, woeful day but now it was evening at last. Kronn and an exhausted Riverwind walked together through the maze of Kendermore's streets, bound for the Plainsman's house.

"Well, the answer seems pretty obvious to me," Kronn was saying. "My father used to say, 'The best solution to a problem's usually the one right under your nose.' Only this one's a bit farther down. It's under our feet."

Riverwind bowed his head, pinching the bridge of his nose as his head throbbed. "The tunnels?" he asked, skeptically.

"Of course!" Kronn declared proudly. He stopped for a moment and stomped his foot on the cobblestone street. "Right down there! We've got a ready-made escape—and the tunnels lead all the way to Flotsam, if we want to go that far."

The old Plainsman shuffled wearily to a halt, his face clouding with thought. "True," he mused. "But there are thousands of your people in Kendermore, Kronn. It would take days, maybe weeks. Don't you think the ogres would notice?"

"So we don't do it all at once," the kender answered. "We can send a bunch at a time. With all the entrances to the tunnels there are in town, I figure we can get about two hundred people out every hour. Which means maybe five thousand a day, give or take."

"If we keep it up all day and night," Riverwind argued. "And it means abandoning Kendermore."

"Yes," said Kronn. "I hate to do that, just handing it over to the ogres. But you were right earlier: we can't keep the ogres from taking the city. That doesn't leave us much choice but to evacuate. Let's say three thousand people a day. Sound better to you?"

Riverwind shrugged. "I suppose it's possible—"

"So at three thousand a day, and with roughly eighty thousand people in Kendermore, counting the refugees from the other towns and everything, we're looking at"— he counted on his fingers, muttering to himself—"somewhere around twenty-six days. Less than a month. We'll be done a few days after Year-Turning."

"If you can convince everyone to go along with it," said Riverwind. "And if you can make things work as smoothly as you say."

"You're missing the point," Kronn said. "You're thinking about it from too high up. All you see is the problem of organizing the whole thing. Look at it from the perspective of a kender. It's a big adventure, Riverwind—maybe the biggest in Kendermore's history. And there's nothing my people love more than adventure."

"All right," Riverwind relented. "I'll think about it tomorrow. But I really need to go home and sleep, Kronn."

The kender nodded happily. "That's good enough for me. Now," he added, looking up and down the narrow, twisting street, "if I can just figure out which way your home is. . . ."

Riverwind groaned.

* * * * *

Before noon the next day, Riverwind had convinced himself Kronn's plan might work. "We just have to spread the word," he told Paxina when the Thistleknots and the Plainsfolk gathered at his house that afternoon. "And we have to make sure everyone doesn't try to leave at once."

"Well, the first part's easy," Paxina said. "Word spreads quickly around here, in case you haven't noticed. I'll call an emergency meeting of the Kender Council for tomorrow morning. With their help, every kender in town will know about it by sunset. As for the second, we'll draw lots and make lists. Make a game of it. It could be quite an adventure."

Kronn winked at Riverwind.

Brightdawn, who had listened to Kronn's plan dubiously, narrowed her eyes. "Do we really have enough time?"

"Not if we sit around talking," Catt said. "If you ask me, it's worth a shot."

"Good," Paxina said, "because I'm putting you in charge."

"Great," Catt said. "I'm up for the challenge."

"There it is." Kronn said. He started toward the door. "Come on, Riverwind. Let's go see if Giffel's done with that ogre leader yet."

* * * * *

One of the problems with Kendermore—although its people never really considered it a problem—was that it had nothing whatsoever that resembled a jail. There wasn't much point, according to kender thinking. After all, a city only needed a jail if it had criminals, and Kendermore was happily short of crime. Murder was unheard of. The worst fights that broke out among the city's denizens were vicious taunting contests that never resulted in physical violence—well, rarely. And theft . . . well, as everyone knew, the kender never stole anything.

The lack of a suitable place to keep prisoners had seldom bothered anyone in Kendermore before. When it had come to deciding what to do with Baloth, the ogre officer Riverwind had captured during the attack on the walls, however, the kender had been at a loss. They'd needed somewhere to put him immediately, and there was nowhere suitable for something as large and dangerous as an ogre. Baloth, who was relatively short for one of his kind, still towered two heads above even Riverwind. The ogre was more than twice as tall as the largest kender in the city.

It had been Giffel Birdwhistle who'd come up with the

solution to the problem. "If there's nowhere to put him up here in the city," he'd told Riverwind and Kronn the day after the attack, "maybe we can stash him down in the tunnels. They were built by humans, so I think we can squeeze him in, and there's a few locked vaults down there. We can put Old Hairless in one of those."

So, with Riverwind's agreement, the kender had dragged Baloth down into the catacombs beneath the city. It hadn't been easy—the ogre barely fit down the narrow stairs and had struggled all the way—but at last they'd hauled him into a large, high-ceilinged chamber, shut the door, and used their picks to lock it.

"I'll tear off your arms and legs!" Baloth's muffled voice had shouted from within the vault. "I'll crush your skulls like walnuts!"

Giffel had only smiled again. "Don't worry. He may not feel like talking now, but give me a day alone with him. I'll wear him down."

"What?" Riverwind had asked, horrified. "You're not going to torture him, are you?"

"Torture?" Giffel had asked. His face had contracted into an offended frown. "What kind of fiend do you take me for? I'm not a goblin, you know. When I said I needed a day alone with him, that's just what I meant."

"Look, Riverwind," Kronn had explained. "The dwarves have a saying about us—well, actually they have a lot of sayings about us, and frankly I find most of them pretty offensive. But this one's true. 'There's nothing worse than a bored kender.' "

Riverwind had nodded, recognizing the sentiment. He'd heard Flint Fireforge say it, years ago, on more than one occasion.

Giffel had puffed out his chest at this. "So I'm going to go in there"—he'd jerked his thumb at the vault, where Baloth was still shouting—"and I'm not bringing anything with me. No weapons, no pouches, nothing. I figure it'll take a few minutes before I start getting bored. Then, to pass the time, I'll talk to Baloth. Ask him questions, tell him stories, maybe even sing some songs. Come back tomorrow—he'll be ready to tell you anything you want by then."

Kronn and Catt had grinned, and Riverwind had raised his eyebrows. "It could work," he'd said.

"It *will* work," Giffel had answered. "Uncle Trapspringer did the same thing with a hobgoblin once. That was just before he almost blew himself up trying to use that gnomish flying machine."

With that, Giffel Birdwhistle had taken off his chapak and armor, removed his pouches and purses, emptied his pockets, and even kicked off his bright blue shoes. Unarmed, empty-handed, and completely bereft of any object of even the slightest interest, he'd walked to the door and waited while one of the guards picked the lock open. Catt had stepped forward, her eyes gleaming with pride at Giffel's bravery, and kissed him on the cheek. Then the door had swung open, and Giffel had turned, waved cheerily to the furious, hairless ogre, and walked into the vault.

"Hi!" he'd begun brightly. "You must be Baloth. Pleased to meet you. My name's Giffel Birdwhistle. I've had a very interesting life. Would you like to hear about it?"

With a loud thud the door had shut, and a kender guard, armed for any circumstance, had locked it again.

At around midnight, a strange sound had risen from behind the vault door—a low, strained whimpering that nearly drowned out the constant sound of Giffel's prattling voice. The guards outside the cell had listened to it with rapt interest. They had never heard an ogre weep before.

* * * * *

That was yesterday. Today Giffel was tired and hungry as he emerged from the vault, but he was smiling nonetheless. "He's ready for you," he said to Kronn and Riverwind. "I'll be waiting out here if you need me."

Kronn clapped the tall kender on the back. Then he and Riverwind walked through the door. The old Plainsman stopped a few steps into the room, his eyes widening as the door swung shut behind them. "Mishakal have mercy," he breathed. "What did he do to him?"

Baloth lay in a corner of the room, hugging his knees to his chest and rocking back and forth. His face was wet with tears and drool, and there was an unpleasant vacancy in his eyes. At the sound of the Plainsman's voice, his head snapped up and he looked around wildly. When his eyes fell upon Kronn, he shrank away, whining feebly. "No," he moaned. "No more kender. Please! Go away!"

"Only," Kronn said firmly, "after you've answered a few questions for us. Does that sound fair to you?"

"Yes!" Baloth cried. "I'll do whatever you want—just don't bring him back."

"All right, then," Kronn said happily. "Let's get started. Riverwind?"

Riverwind stepped forward, his face grave. "What is your position in the army outside our walls?"

Baloth's eyes flared with recognition when he saw the old Plainsman. "I am one of the Black-Gazer's warlords, and his favorite," he said proudly. "I slew Lord Ruog and in return he made me his third-in-command. I answer only to the Black-Gazer."

"The Black-Gazer?" Riverwind asked.

"Kurthak." The ogre's lip curled derisively. "The one who will destroy this city and take its survivors back to our homeland as slaves."

Riverwind leaned forward. "Slaves? Why do you need so many slaves all of a sudden, and why pick on the kender?"

Baloth sneered. "We stick 'em in the mines. Ogres are too big. Besides, it's hard work that doesn't befit warriors."

Kronn let that pass.

"What is this Black-Gazer's plan?" Riverwind continued.

"Batter your walls and burn your homes. Drag the kender away in chains—and you, Hero of the Lance . . . yes, he knows of you. He'll take your head—and those of the other humans you have brought with you."

The old Plainsman paled, his scalp prickling. It was not an empty threat, he knew. The thought of the ogres bearing his daughters' heads back to their homeland as trophies made him furious—and worried.

Kronn glanced at Riverwind. "And when is all this supposed to happen?" the kender demanded.

"Soon," Baloth answered with a snarl. "The day after Year-Turning."

Kronn fell back a pace, his mouth dropping open. He looked back at Riverwind, whose grave expression showed that they shared the same thought. Year-Turning was three weeks away. It was a gift of time, even if they didn't have time to evacuate Kendermore completely.

"But you have us trapped," Riverwind reasoned. "A smart leader would wait and starve us out. Why attack at all?"

"Because Malystryx wills it."

Riverwind swallowed. "The dragon commands your leader?"

Baloth nodded. "She has given us Kendermore . . . as a gift. When we have destroyed it, she will fly to the Kenderwood and burn it to ashes. Then this land will belong to her. She will raise a new lair here, and the Desolation will continue to spread west into the human lands."

"You seem to know a great deal about her," Kronn observed.

"I have seen her," Baloth declared proudly. "I was there when she told the Black-Gazer how and when to attack."

Riverwind stepped forward. "You attacked today. I realize you were merely testing us. Why wait so long before attacking again?"

The hairless ogre opened his mouth to answer, then stopped and shut it again. His eyes, which had been dull and dim until now, flared like torches of hate. "No," he said. "I will not tell you."

Kronn hesitated, then glanced over at Riverwind.

The old Plainsman nodded. "Go get Giffel," he said.

"No!" Baloth yelped. He cringed, the hate in his eyes giving way to dread. "Not him!"

"Then tell us why Malys is delaying the final attack," Kronn said. "If you don't . . . well, I'm sure Giff's got a lot of stories he hasn't told you yet. Maybe a whole week's worth."

The hairless ogre broke down and began to sob. He shook his head stubbornly. "No."

"Tell us!" Riverwind snapped.

Baloth slumped, defeated. "Kurthak asked her why," he blubbered. "Why we must wait to destroy you. She said she couldn't leave her lair, not yet."

Riverwind tensed. "Why?" he pressed.

"Because," Baloth moaned, "she needs to save her strength . . . until she lays her egg."

* * * * *

Riverwind climbed the stairs out of the tunnels, his face gray. Once he was out in Kendermore's streets, he bent over, hands on his knees, and gasped for air.

After a while, he heard Kronn approach from behind. "Riverwind," the kender asked quietly, "are you all right?"

The old Plainsman took a deep breath, wiped his mouth with the back of his hand, and forced himself to stand up straight. He swayed on his feet as he turned toward Kronn. "Just getting old," he breathed. "That . . . and the egg."

"Yup," Kronn agreed. "But that's not what's troubling me most. You heard what Baloth said about the attack, when it's happening. We've only got three weeks."

"I know," Riverwind said. "We can't get everyone out of Kendermore before then."

"We might get about three-quarters of the population out," Kronn said. "Maybe more, if Catt can hurry things up. I'll talk to her about that. But there'll still be ten, maybe fifteen thousand of us left when the ogres attack."

For an instant, Riverwind's shoulders slumped with

defeat, but then he recovered, forcing stoicism back onto his face. "Do you know where Malystryx lives?"

Kronn frowned. "Yes," he said. "Father told me her lair was at Blood Watch. Why do you ask?"

Riverwind didn't answer; he pursed his lips and stroked his chin, deep in thought. He knew of Blood Watch: Elistan had told him the story, many years ago. The old cleric, who had been a leader of the Seeker order before Goldmoon turned him to the true gods, had known many such tales from his studies, and had related them to Riverwind and his companions. Now, Riverwind strove to remember his words.

* * * * *

"Blood Watch," Elistan had said, "was once a monastery devoted to an ancient god of thought—Majere, the Disks of Mishakal call him. Of course, it wasn't called Blood Watch then. That would come after."

"After what?" Tasslehoff had asked. It was rare that Elistan would get through an entire story without Tas interrupting at least once.

"Hush, Tas," Tanis had said.

Elistan, however, had smiled patiently. "I will tell you," he said. "When the Kingpriest grew corrupt in his own goodness, and the persecutions grew worse all over Istar—inquisitions, burnings, stonings—the people went to the monastery and begged the monks for help. But the monks turned them away. 'Our duty to our god,' they told the people, 'is to watch the world unfold, and to think on it. It is not our place to act.'

"In truth, however, the monks could have acted . . . and should have," the old cleric had said. "Who knows what might have been different if they had?"

"Nothing," Raistlin had hissed. "Nothing would have been different. Larger rocks have been thrown into the river of time before, without changing its course. No group of monks could have changed the Kingpriest's mind—the Cataclysm would have happened, whatever they did."

Riverwind had glared at the cynical mage, but Raistlin had only sneered, his disturbing, hourglass eyes glittering as his lip curled in derision.

"The monks thought as you do, Raistlin Majere," Elistan had continued, his rich voice breaking the brittle silence. There had been no sign of reproach in his kind face. "They believed it was better to contemplate life than to live it, so they ignored the people's pleas, no matter how loud they became. Instead they remained in their cloisters, meditating. Whether they saw what lay ahead I cannot say, but if they did, they did nothing to stop it, even when the gods sent their Thirteen Signs to thwart the Kingpriest. Perhaps they thought they were being humble, but too much humility can be just as bad as too much pride—as they learned one day, not long after Yule, when the sky began to rain fire.

"The monks gathered in the courtyard of their abbey and watched as destruction fell upon the land. Even then, with the end at hand, they ignored the cries of the people, who pounded upon the doors of the monastery, begging for succor. Then, with a roar, the Cataclysm struck. The burning mountain streaked down from the sky, far to the north, and the ground erupted. The earth dropped away, and the sea poured in, drowning the empire of Istar—but not all of it. The destruction stopped at the edge of the monastery, cleaving the hill on which it stood in two. The northern slope dropped away into the newborn Blood Sea, but the rest remained, leaving the abbey perched upon a clifftop above the surf, on the north shore of what is now the Goodlund peninsula.

"How the monks perished is uncertain,," Elistan had concluded. "In some tellings of this tale, they choked to death on the smoke and ash of Istar's doom. In others, the desperate peasants broke in at last, murdered the monks, and looted the monastery. And in still others, they took their own lives when they saw the despair their inaction had wrought. In any case, however, they died soon after the Cataclysm, and the ruins of the abbey became known as Blood Watch—both because it overlooks the Blood Sea, and also because of the monks' belief that it was better to contemplate the suffering of the people than to do anything about it. Some legends even say the monks' spirits still haunt Blood Watch, doomed forever to look upon the red waters below and never know if they could have done anything to stop the devastation of the world."

* * * * *

Riverwind became aware that someone was tugging on his arm. He looked down, his gaze still slightly abstracted, and saw Kronn holding his wrist, gazing up at him with concern.

"Riverwind?" the kender asked. "Are you all right?"

The old Plainsman blinked, caught for a moment between memory and reality, then nodded. "I'm sorry," he said. "I was thinking."

"I figured that was it," Kronn said. "Either that or you were having some kind of fit. What's the matter?"

Riverwind put a hand to his forehead, feeling tired. "Kronn," he asked, "do you know the way to Blood Watch?"

The kender nodded, understanding. "I had a feeling you might ask that," he said. He patted his map pouch. "The tunnels go out that way. I've been there once, a while back, to look for the monks' ghosts. Didn't find any, which was a pity—and Paxina tells me the ruins are gone now, thanks to Malys. She's changed the land out there, kind of like she's doing to the Kenderwood. Built herself a volcano for a lair, from what I hear . . . hey, where are you going?"

While Kronn was expounding, Riverwind had started to walk, moving down the street with purpose. The kender had to run to catch up.

"Come on," Riverwind said. "We need to talk to Paxina."

* * * * *

Riverwind and Kronn were hurrying down Milkweed Avenue, a crooked, tree-lined road that periodically grew so narrow that the Plainsman had to turn sideways to keep from getting stuck between the buildings on either side. All of a sudden it bent sharply to the right, and Kronn and Riverwind came to a sudden stop. Ahead of them, right in the middle of the road, stood a house. It filled the whole street. There wasn't even enough room between it and the adjacent buildings for Kronn to squeeze through. The kender and the Plainsman stared at it in astonishment.

"Whoa," Kronn remarked. "That wasn't here last time I went this way. . . ."

"Kronn," Riverwind rumbled, his voice straining with frustration.

Kronn waved at the house. "This was a perfectly good route until someone put that thing in the way!"

"Damn it!" the old Plainsman exploded. "Kronn, this is important! We can't be wasting time on this idiocy!"

"I know that!" Kronn snapped back angrily. "But it's not my fault. Just when I'm starting to know my way around, someone moves a fountain or builds a fence or puts up a whole blessed house. I wouldn't be surprised if one day I got so lost I never found my way out." He put a hand on his head. "All right, look. It's only about six blocks back to Shrubbery Road. We can follow that to Straight Street, and that'll take us to City Hall. All right?" He turned and started back the way they had gone.

"Wait," Riverwind said.

Kronn stopped, looking back. The Plainsman's brow was furrowing as he tried to capture an elusive thought.

"Shhh!" Riverwind hissed. "Say that again."

"It's only about six blocks back to Shrubbery Road," the kender repeated. "We can follow—"

"Not that," Riverwind interrupted. "Before."

Kronn frowned. "I was just saying I wouldn't be surprised if one day I got so lost I never found my way out."

The old Plainsman nodded, thinking hard. Then suddenly he began to laugh.

Kronn looked at him nervously. "Uh," he said, "are you feeling all right, Riverwind?"

"By the gods! That's it!" Riverwind whooped joyfully. "Kronn! I know how to beat the ogres."

* * * * *

Not long after Riverwind and Kronn left, the door to Baloth's cell opened again and Giffel Birdwhistle strode in. Seeing him, the hairless ogre cried out. "No!" he shouted. "I told you everything, I swear! No more!"

Giffel looked the ogre up and down, then nodded to someone outside the door. "All right, let's get him out of here."

"Out?" Baloth blurted. "You're letting me go?"

Giffel nodded. "Kronn's orders. We're not going to feed you and take care of you, and my people don't execute their prisoners. You told us what we needed to know, so we're setting you free."

Baloth gawked in amazement as the guards came in. There were more than a dozen of them, armed with pol-paks—saw-bladed pole arms that they held at his throat as two of their number untied the strong ropes that bound his ankles. Then they used the weapons to prod and herd the ogre out of his cell. With Giffel in the lead, they led him down the tunnel, away from the vault. Baloth stumbled along in a haze, too tired and bewildered to resist.

They followed the passage for what seemed miles and miles, finally stopping at a flight of stairs. Giffel dashed up the steps and opened the secret door at their top. A low, grassy hummock swung aside to let in a shaft of ruddy, evening light.

"Bring him up," he called.

It took some doing, but the kender guards managed to shove the hulking ogre up the narrow staircase. The earthen walls shuddered and crumbled as he wormed his way out of the tunnel. Then he was out, gazing around in bafflement. He was far from Kendermore. The dead trees of the Kenderwood surrounded him.

The guards encircled him, polpaks ready, as Giffel drew a knife from his belt and came forward. The tall kender went behind Baloth and began to saw at the cords around the ogre's wrists. "Just so you know," he said, "your army's about a league north of here. You can go back to them if you want . . . but I don't think you'd better."

The ropes fell away, and Baloth groaned as blood flowed back into his numb hands. "Why not?" he asked.

"Because," Giffel said, "you told us when they plan to march—and that bit about Malys, too. I'm no expert on ogres, of course, but from what I gather, if Kurthak figures we let you go, he'll also figure out you betrayed him. So he'll kill you—and painfully, too. I can't even imagine what'll happen if Malys finds out.

"Anyway, it's your choice. You can go north and hope they don't kill you, or you can head south and try to get away." The tall kender sheathed his dagger and stepped back toward the concealed staircase. The guards fell back with him, polpaks still pointed at the ogre.

"Goodbye, Baloth," Giffel said as he stepped onto the stairs. He grinned. "It was nice talking to you."

He headed down the steps, the guards with him. Baloth watched dumbly as the grassy hummock swung back into place, covering the entrance to the tunnels. The ogre glanced around furtively, making sure he was alone. He went over to the hummock and tried to find the button or lever that made it work. After a while, he gave up.

Then he turned and began to lope away through the forest to the south.

Chapter 22

Once more, Riverwind found precious little time for rest. He spent much of the night with Kronn, Catt, and Paxina. He told Kronn's sisters what Baloth had told them, then revealed his idea for defending against the ogres' attack. Their discussion lasted until nearly dawn.

No one was completely sure—records of meetings, when they were kept at all, tended to be haphazard and careless about such details as attendance and agenda— but not even the oldest kender could remember having seen City Hall's audience room crammed quite so full as it was that morning. There were currently one hundred and three Council members, and by the time Riverwind, Brightdawn, and Moonsong arrived, the room was quite literally packed to the walls.

Though the impending attack by Malys and the ogres was still weeks away, Riverwind and Brightdawn were both dressed for war. Clad in leather armor, she wore her mace on her belt. He had his sabre and a quiver of white-fletched arrows. Instead of armor, Moonsong wore a new blue gown—a gift from the kender—but like her father she had a sword at her hip. The weapon belonged to Stagheart, who was still too badly hurt to leave his sickbed.

Brightdawn smiled as she nodded toward the room full of milling, chattering kender. "If you'd told me a year ago that we'd be here today, I would have laughed," she said.

Chuckling, the three Plainsfolk strode into the surging sea of topknots and hoopaks. It was hard going—they were tossed and buffeted by the kender—but in time they reached the head of the room. Paxina, Kronn, and Catt waited for them, standing on a raised dais beneath a grinning portrait of their father. The Plainsfolk and the Thistleknots shook hands, exchanging words of greeting. Then Riverwind turned to face the crowd. He raised his hands and called for silence. It took a while for the room to settle down, but in time it was quiet enough for Riverwind to make himself heard.

"Before we begin," he proclaimed, in a loud, booming voice, "I'd like my knife back."

There was a moment's confusion as the Councillors looked around and checked their pockets. At last a hand shot up in the back holding Riverwind's bone-handled dagger. It passed up from one kender's hand to another, until at last it reached the front.

"Sorry!" a voice called out. "You must have dropped it on the way in."

With a tight smile—some things, it seemed, would never change—Riverwind tucked the knife back in his belt.

"I'm sure we all know why we're here," he declared. "The ogres attack in twenty days. When they do, we won't be able to keep them from breaching the walls. Kendermore will fall."

A murmur of consternation rippled through the crowd. Riverwind waited for it to subside.

"Are you saying we're doomed?" asked an old, bespectacled kender at the front of the crowd. Fear was plain in his voice.

"No, Merldon Metwinger," Paxina said. "We're not doomed—only Kendermore is."

Riverwind nodded firmly. "When I met Kronn and Catt in Solace, they asked me to help you fight Malystryx and the ogres. I thought that meant saving your city, but now I know that isn't possible.

"But," he added quickly, seeing hope fade from many of the Councillors' faces, "there is still a way to save your people."

"How?" asked several kender at once.

Catt stepped forward. Her broken arm still hung in its sling, but she held her back straight and her head high.

"We're leaving," she proclaimed. "We'll take the tunnels out of the Kenderwood, then travel across Ansalon to Hylo where the rest of our people live. They'll take us in."

"Leaving?" Merldon Metwinger asked. "What, all of us? That'll take forever!"

"Well," Catt replied patiently, "not quite that long. But it will take time. We'll be drawing lots to see who leaves when. We've already sent messengers ahead to Solamnia and other lands asking for help in our journey. The rest of us have to start leaving tomorrow, so we need you to spread the word about this fast. Yes, Merldon?"

The old Councillor tilted his head back, peering at her through his spectacles. His squinting eyes looked huge through the lenses. "Just how long is this going to take?" he asked.

Catt cleared her throat. "I've, uh, been working on that. Allowing time for holdups, we can't evacuate everyone in less than twenty-three days."

The room erupted with shouts of outrage, confusion, and alarm. "Twenty-three days!" the Councillors exclaimed. Fingers pointed at Riverwind. "But he said we've only got twenty!"

Paxina cupped her hands to her mouth. "Quiet down!" she hollered. "All of you, shut up!"

A sulking silence fell over the audience hall. "I don't mean to be rude," Merldon Metwinger asked, "but where are we going to get the other three days?"

"We're not," Riverwind said. "There will still be ten thousand people left in Kendermore when the ogres attack." A low rumble rose among the Councillors again, but the Plainsman quickly raised his hands. "That isn't all!" he shouted. "Listen to me!"

Reluctantly, the kender looked to him.

"We have to fight the ogres," he said. "There isn't any other choice. But my mistake, until now, has been assuming we can do it like humans and elves do—defending the city wall, as if Kendermore were Kalaman or the High

Clerist's Tower. It isn't.

"If we do it right, however, we can beat the ogres. But you need to fight like kender, not humans. We can't afford a face-to-face battle, but we can beat them other ways. If the Kender Flight goes as planned, the city will be nearly empty by the time the ogres attack. But they won't know that, and we can use that to our advantage."

The murmurs that erupted from the Councillors were more hopeful but still confused. "What are we supposed to do?" Merldon asked.

Kronn cleared his throat. "Well," he said, "actually the answer was my idea, although I didn't know it at the time. Riverwind had to point it out to me. Think about how Kendermore's laid out, Merldon—streets going every which way, zigging where they should zag, stopping suddenly for no good reason, looping around on themselves. Honestly, it's a mess. But that's where we have the advantage. We can't beat the ogres head-on, like Riverwind said, but if we can get them lost in the streets and use every dirty trick we've got, then we've got a chance at beating them."

"What we need to do is block off the right roads and channel the ogres toward the middle of town," Paxina said. "Then we have to hold them there long enough to destroy them."

"Destroy them?" asked a young woman in the middle of the crowd. "How?"

Riverwind looked out over the Councillors, his eyes glinting in the lamplight. "You have to burn Kendermore," he said. "You need to set fire to the city, then flee through the woods."

For a second, every kender in the room was too stunned to speak.

"Great jumping Trapspringer's ghost," breathed Merldon Metwinger. "That's insane."

"Exactly," Kronn replied, grinning. "Which means Kurthak won't be expecting it."

"It could work," said a short, balding Councillor.

"It has to," Paxina said emphatically. "While people are

leaving through the tunnels, everyone else has to pitch in, preparing the trap. We can't afford to have any doubts."

Shouts of support and approval rang out through the audience hall. Fists and hoopaks waved in the air.

In the front of the crowd, Merldon Metwinger pursed his lips a moment, then raised his voice above the din. "What about Malys?" he asked.

Silence fell over the room like a landslide. A resurgence of dismay abruptly snuffed out the glee that had been kindling in the Councillors' faces. The kender looked at one another uneasily, realizing they'd forgotten all about the dragon.

"We can try to flee through the Kenderwood," Merldon went on, "but if Malys sees us, we're as dead as if we stayed put. That forest out there is as dry as Balif's bones. All she'd have to do is clear her throat, and the whole thing would go up like so much tinder. When she burned Woodsedge, the walls of the tunnel beneath it *melted,* and I doubt she was using the full force of her breath there. If she chooses to burn the whole Kenderwood, the tunnels will become the world's biggest oven. Thousands will die."

"I've thought of that, also," Riverwind said. "I will take care of the dragon."

This time, the Councillors weren't the only ones to react. Behind Riverwind, his daughters gasped in astonishment.

"What?" Moonsong exclaimed.

"Father—" Brightdawn began.

He glanced over his shoulder. "After," he hissed.

Dutifully, the twins fell silent. Their faces, however, were pinched with worry as their father turned back to face the yammering Councillors.

"You can't be serious," Merldon Metwinger said. "You haven't even seen Malystryx! She's immense! I don't think you could kill her with Huma's own dragonlance."

"I don't mean to kill her," Riverwind replied. "I know I can't. But I have an idea how I can hurt her—hurt her so badly she won't care whether you get away or not. I might be able to buy you time to escape."

Before anyone—Merldon, the other Councillors, his daughters—could object, he went on. "Yesterday," he said, "Kronn and I questioned Baloth, the ogre we captured during the assault on the east wall. We asked him about Malystryx, and he told us why she's waiting so long to attack. Just before the ogres attack, she's going to lay an egg.

"Therefore," the old Plainsman finished, "a week before Year-Turning, I will go down into the tunnels. I'll travel east to Blood Watch and wait for Malystryx to leave her lair on the day of the attack. Then I'll enter her nest and destroy the egg."

Riverwind had expected uproar, but instead the kender were subdued, shocked silent by his words.

"I don't understand," Merldon Metwinger said at length. "How will that save us? If she leaves her lair, it'll be too late—she'll be on her way to the Kenderwood. By the time she gets back and finds out about the egg, we'll already be roasted."

"That would be true, for most dragons," Kronn answered, "but Malys isn't most dragons—and this isn't any ordinary egg."

"What do you mean?" Merldon asked.

Riverwind nodded patiently. "From all I know of them," he replied, "dragons lay their eggs in clutches—never singly. But Baloth was adamant: Malys has only one. That means something. Either she's found a way, somehow, to keep from laying more, or she's going to lay a full clutch, then choose to keep only the strongest, destroying the rest.

"Whatever the case, though, the fact remains that there will be only one egg . . . and it will be important to her. She'll take greater care with it than she might with a whole clutch," the old Plainsman added. "We already know Malys is a magic user, and a powerful one. You only need to look at what she's done to the Kenderwood to see that. She won't leave her nest without first forming some sort of link between herself and the egg, so she can be sure it's safe—and such a spell would be simple for her, compared to the magic it must take to kill an entire forest. The moment the egg is in any real danger, she'll know, and she'll forget about everything else. She'll return to her nest right away to try to save the egg. With that distraction, I'll buy you time to get away."

Again, the kender were silent, staring at him in wonder. "You'd do that for us?" Merldon Metwinger asked softly.

"Yes," Riverwind said. He smiled as he saw the admiration that shone in the kender's eyes. "I will try."

* * * * *

The meeting ended soon after, the Councillors chattering excitedly amongst themselves as they filed out the door. Several of them, including Merldon Metwinger, climbed up on the dais and solemnly shook Riverwind's hand. The Plainsman watched them go, smiling with satisfaction.

"Father!" said a pair of voices behind him.

Riverwind shut his eyes, taking a deep breath to steady himself, then turned to face his daughters. Moonsong and Brightdawn stood side by side, their faces darkened by accusation and betrayal.

"Would you excuse us a moment, Paxina?" he asked.

The Lord Mayor glanced from the old Plainsman to the twins, then nodded, understanding. "Kronn, Catt—let's go," she said. Gathering her purple mayoral robes around her, she left the room. Her brother and sister followed.

Moonsong and Brightdawn stared at their father in silence. Riverwind looked away, unable to meet their gaze.

"When you explained the plan to us this morning, you never mentioned anything about going to Blood Watch," Moonsong said.

Riverwind sighed. "I know. Nevertheless, I discussed it with Paxina and the others last night. Kronn has agreed to go with me, and guide me through the tunnels."

Despite her best efforts to remain calm, Brightdawn trembled visibly. "Why didn't you tell us?" she asked.

"I knew you'd try to talk me out of it," Riverwind answered. "And, what's more, you might have succeeded. I couldn't afford to take that chance."

"Couldn't afford to let us talk some sense into you?" Moonsong demanded furiously.

"Child, this is something I have to do," Riverwind answered. "That old Councillor was right—if someone doesn't do something about Malys, it doesn't matter whether they beat the ogres or not. The kender will die. I can't ask anyone else to go to Blood Watch. The danger's too great. So I'm going myself."

The twins looked at him silently; then Moonsong turned and walked out of the audience hall. Brightdawn lingered, however. The pain in her eyes was almost too much for Riverwind to bear.

"You should have told me, Father," she said softly. For a moment, she looked as if she might say more, but instead she turned away and hurried out the door.

Riverwind started after her, but a spasm of pain contorted his face and he stopped. Groaning, he stumbled to a chair and slumped down into it.

"I'm sorry," he whispered, then buried his face in his hands and wept.

* * * * *

Kendermore's last days passed much too quickly.

As Paxina had predicted, once the Kender Council knew about the plan, the rest of the city learned of it within hours. When the sun rose on the first day after the meeting at City Hall, thousands of kender poured into the streets, making their way to the tunnel entrances that riddled the city. Giffel and the other guards kept the crowds under control while Catt oversaw the drawing of lots. While there were some arguments and hurt feelings over the results, most of the kender accepted their place with good humor. And so, when the blistering sun rode high in the late autumn sky, the Kender Flight began right on schedule.

Several key Councillors, including Merldon

Metwinger, went ahead of the Flight to guide those who followed to the agreed upon gathering place—a shallow valley in the plains of Balifor, several leagues west of the edge of the Kenderwood. There, over the next three weeks, the kender would set up a ramshackle tent city and wait for the rest to follow.

For the kender, the hardest part wasn't leaving their homes—even the oldest of them still felt the yearning for the road sometimes, and the impending attack by Malystryx and the ogres only made that yearning that much stronger. And while there were many tears shed when they realized they had to leave behind most of the interesting things they owned, they were practical about that, too. "There's always more where that came from," was a kender proverb—although, of course, every kender who set out through the tunnels did so with full pockets and pouches stuffed almost to bursting.

The hardest part, it turned out, was saying goodbye to friends. The method Paxina and Catt had chosen for choosing who went first in the Flight was fair, but in many ways it was also cruel. Kender who had known each other for years had to bid each other farewell, and while Catt made every effort to move families out together, inevitably some husbands and wives, sisters and brothers, parents and children were separated. Around the tunnel entrances, the air rang with weeping and promises of "I'll see you soon."

While the Flight was going on, the rest of the city was far from idle. Kender filled the streets, not with their usual aimless bustle but with a singular reason: to prepare the trap that would catch and kill the Black-Gazer and his horde. Walls were erected, holes dug, and wood and stone carried back and forth. At the town's edge, teams of kender armed with chisels and picks chipped away at the city walls themselves, weakening the stone and mortar. It could have been a grim business, preparing the city for its destruction, but the kender enjoyed themselves, singing and humming as bit by bit they crafted a purpose from the meaningless tangle of Kendermore's streets.

On the day after Yule—a holiday the kender completely forgot about as they sought to prepare the defenses and flee the city—Riverwind and Paxina toured Kendermore, inspecting the work the kender had done. As they walked through the courtyards just inside the city walls, they had to thread their way carefully among the many places where the kender had pried up the cobblestones and were excavating earth beneath. The clatter of shovels rang all around them, and a constant flow of wheelbarrows hauled dirt away into the city.

"Where are they taking all the earth?" Riverwind asked, pausing in the middle of the courtyard to take it all in. There were hundreds of holes, all around them. It looked as if a colony of giant moles had invaded the town.

"All over the place," Paxina answered. "The bricklayers and stonemasons need mortar, and it turns out whatever Malystryx has done to the soil makes it perfect for that."

They continued to pick their way through the hole-riddled courtyard until they reached a place where the diggers had finished working. Here and there, kender sat around smoldering braziers, whittling wooden stakes into spears and setting them among the flames to harden. Runners moved from fire to fire, gathering armloads of finished stakes and carrying them down ladders into the many holes in the cobbles. Riverwind glanced into a pit and saw that its earthen floor, some fifteen feet down, was lined with dozens of stakes. Such deadfalls were an old trick, used by hunters all over Krynn. Many years ago, when he'd been a shepherd, Riverwind had dug them himself to protect his flock when hunger drove wolves and other predators down from the hills to the east of Qué-Shu.

"They've finished covering them over there," Paxina stated, pointing ahead. At the far end of the courtyard, there was no sign whatsoever that the ground was riddled with pits. To Riverwind, it looked like nothing but an ordinary, stone-paved plaza.

"How did you get the cobblestones to stay up?" he asked.

The Lord Mayor grinned. "Good question. Come over

here." She hurried ahead, making her way over toward the deceptively normal-looking part of the courtyard. When she reached its edge, she tapped her hoopak against the ground a few times, until one cobblestone answered with a hollow clack. She bent down and lifted it up, revealing a lattice of wood and rope that hung above a yawning, spiked pit. "Strong enough to keep the stones up," she declared, "and it'll hold a kender's weight, too— maybe even an ogre or two. But try charging a whole bunch across . . ." She shrugged, grinning impishly as she slid the stone back into place.

They went on, pausing briefly when they reached a place where the kender were busily hewing at a span of the wall. Riverwind marveled at the workers' precision. They had chipped away so much stone, it looked like the wall might crash down upon them if anyone sneezed. Despite its apparent fragility, however, sentries and archers still paced the battlements, watching the woods with a wary eye.

As he regarded the wall, Riverwind started to chuckle. Paxina looked at him questioningly. "What's so funny?" she asked.

The old Plainsman gestured at the wall. "I just had a vision of how surprised they'll be when this comes down," he said. "In most sieges, it's crews of sappers on the other side who try to weaken the walls."

"True," Paxina said with a grin. "Come on, let's head into the city. There's a few more things I want to show you."

They walked down a narrow, winding avenue, stopping every now and then to walk around places where the kender were digging more pits in the middle of the road. Bricklayers worked at certain intersections, hurriedly building walls to block off side streets. "It all leads into the middle of town, just like we planned," Paxina explained.

"Like a spider's web," Riverwind said, nodding with approval. "Once they get in . . ."

"They're going to have an awful time getting out again," the Lord Mayor finished. Suddenly, she grabbed his arm. "Watch it!"

Riverwind stopped and looked down. Stretched across the street right in front of him was a strong, thin cord.

"Trip wire," Paxina explained. "You've got to watch very carefully where you walk around here."

The old Plainsman stared at the nearly invisible wire. There was no way the ogres would see it when they came charging through. "What's it connected to?" he asked.

"This one? Nothing," Paxina answered. "Doesn't need to be. See, the front wave of ogres come barreling down the street, and they hit this. Boom, they go down."

"And the ones behind trample them," Riverwind said, nodding.

"You got it. Of course, there are trip wires on other streets that *are* connected to things. Believe me—you don't want to set off those. Here you would have fallen, no big deal. Hit one of the others, and . . . well, it wouldn't be pretty. Come on," she said, beckoning him forward.

Carefully, Riverwind stepped over the trip wire. Walking more slowly, his eyes never leaving the ground before his feet, he followed the Lord Mayor farther down Greentwig Avenue. At last, they came to a dead end. A wall, twenty feet high, stretched across the middle of the road between two four-storey rowhouses. Riverwind stared at the blank, forbidding edifices surrounding him, then looked back the way they'd come.

"I thought you said every street led to the center of town," he said.

"Well, that was a bit of an exaggeration," Paxina replied. "Actually, a few of them end up like this. Look up."

Riverwind followed the kender's pointing finger and regarded the roofs of the buildings. He was silent for a moment, then lowered his gaze back to Paxina. "There's nothing up there," he said.

"Not now, there isn't," the Lord Mayor replied. "Not much point until the attack comes. But when the ogres come down this street, those rooftops will be covered with kender."

"An ambush?"

"Yup. We've got them all over town."

Riverwind stared thoughtfully up at the rooftops, a smile spreading across his face. Then Paxina led him back down Greentwig, around a corner, and along another street with the unlikely name of Furrynose. Along both sides of the street, kender were busy tearing the houses apart. They threw bricks and boards onto carts, which other kender hauled away. Most of the buildings had been stripped bare, with only a skeletal frameworks left; others lacked even that, and nothing remained but foundations and fronts.

"There's streets like this one all over town, too!" Paxina shouted above the din. "We're taking the materials and using them in other places."

They moved on, turning off Furrynose onto Elbowpoke Way, where Riverwind stopped short. Ahead, dozens of small catapults, the same devices the kender used for target practice with their hoopaks, lined the street. Instead of clay discs, however, the catapults were loaded with small straw dummies. As Riverwind watched, the arms of several catapults sprang forward, hurling their payloads into the air. The dummies flew surprisingly far, soaring over walls and landing on rooftops.

"One of the Councillors, Pudgel Goosedown, came up with these," Paxina said. "He said he got the idea from the gnomes—apparently, catapults are all the rage at Mount Nevermind." As she spoke, one of the catapults misfired, slamming its dummy into a wall. "We're still trying to get the kinks worked out," she added.

Wincing, Riverwind followed her past the catapults, and on down the street.

They followed Elbowpoke Way as it wound through town, past many more deadfalls and trip wires, until finally they reached the middle of Kendermore. The kender had been very busy here. Dozens of houses had been leveled to create a large, empty quadrangle. "And this," Paxina declared, "is where it all comes together." She made a grand, sweeping motion with her arm, indicating the houses along the edges of the yard. "The day before the attack, we're going to soak all of those with oil and pitch. When the horde gets here, we'll have a good, old-fashioned bonfire. Goodbye ogres."

Riverwind nodded solemnly, struggling to take it all in. There didn't seem to be a single part of Kendermore that hadn't been turned into some sort of death trap. "I hope it works," he asked said solemnly.

"If it does," Paxina replied blithely, "boy, are we going to have a whopper of a story to tell!"

Smiling, Riverwind glanced around the courtyard. At the far side, a crowd of kender were gathered around one of the tunnel entrances, bidding one another farewell as they waited for their turn to leave the city. "And the Flight?" he asked. "I haven't seen Catt in a few days. Things are going as we hoped?"

"Better, actually," Paxina answered. "We should be down to the last ten thousand by sunrise on the day after Mark Year. Not bad, eh? Whoever's left behind will join the fun here. When the call went out for volunteers, we got more than we needed. A lot of my people really want to stick around and see the end of Kendermore."

They stood together, admiring the kender's handiwork, for a few minutes. Then Paxina cleared her throat awkwardly, breaking the silence. "So," she said. "what about you and Kronn?"

"We leave for Blood Watch tomorrow," Riverwind said.

"You'd get lost in the tunnels without Kronn," Paxina said. "I'm glad you're taking him with you. I'd go too—if I didn't have my own job to do."

Riverwind nodded. Paxina had taken charge of the defenses after the death of Brimble Redfeather. She would stay and fight, stay and die if need be.

"Are you sure you want to stay behind?"

"Yes," she replied earnestly. "Kendermore is my home. Besides," she added with a smile, "I'm not afraid."

* * * * *

When Riverwind came home that night, he found Brightdawn and Moonsong waiting for him. They stood in the front hall, side by side, their arms folded across their chests. Stagheart was behind them, still haggard and weak from his wounds.

The old Plainsman looked at his daughters and immediately understood the look in their eyes. "No," he said before they could open their mouths to speak. "You're leaving with the Kender Flight."

"That's our choice to make," Brightdawn answered curtly. "Just like it's yours to go to Blood Watch."

When Moonsong spoke, her voice was more gentle. "Father," she said, "all the healers in Kendermore are staying. Arlie told me. The people who've already left don't need us—but the ones who stay behind will. My place is with them—I can't just leave."

"You shouldn't have come in the first place," Riverwind said wearily. "You should have stayed in Qué-Shu."

"Be that as it may," Moonsong declared, "I am here."

"I will stay with her," stated Stagheart, his face a mask of pride and regret. "I failed to protect her before; I will not make that mistake again."

Riverwind sighed. "Very well," he said. "Your mother would do the same, Moonsong, if she were in your place." He turned to face Brightdawn. "And you? You're not a healer."

She gazed at him, her eyes fierce and clear. "I will go with you to Blood Watch."

The old Plainsman slumped, bowing his head. Tears burned in his eyes. "Child," he whispered, "please . . ."

"Listen to me," Brightdawn said fiercely. "Do you remember when we left Qué-Shu? I told you I didn't know what my place was in this world. I know, now—it's with you, Father."

Riverwind stood silently for a moment, trembling. Brightdawn stepped forward and rested a gentle hand on his shoulder. After a moment, he looked up at her and smiled, his eyes full.

"Goldmoon and I raised you to do what you knew in your hearts was right," he said softly. "I will not tell you otherwise now."

There were no more words. He gathered his daughters in his arms, unable to hold back his tears.

* * * * *

The hot wind ruffled Riverwind's feathered headdress as he stood with Kronn and Brightdawn in the center of town, outside an entrance to the tunnels. Before them was a crowd of kender, who had set aside their work to bid them farewell. Paxina, Catt, and Giffel stood at the front, Moonsong and Stagheart beside them. Moonsong held little Billee Juniper in her arms.

They had already said their farewells—Brightdawn holding Billee and embracing Moonsong, Kronn taking his sisters' hands and promising to return, Riverwind kissing Moonsong, Catt, and Paxina goodbye. Now the Lord Mayor bowed to them, smiling.

"Kendermore thanks you," Paxina said softly.

Gravely, Riverwind bowed to her, then turned and walked down the stairs into the tunnels. Brightdawn and Kronn followed. They did not look back.

Chapter 23

Time became meaningless for Riverwind, Kronn, and Brightdawn as they traveled toward Blood Watch. There was no day or night in the tunnels; there was only walking, constant and endless. Occasionally, they would reach a fork or intersection in the passage, and they would have to stop while Kronn consulted an old, yellowed map of the tunnels and determine which direction to take. Other times, their torches would begin to gutter out, and they would pluck new ones from the wall sconces and light them with the charred stubs of their dying brands. For the most part, however, the catacombs stretched arrow-straight ahead of them, a long throat of stone leading to the dragon's belly. Minutes melted into hours, hours pooled into days.

Then, after what seemed like years—but was actually only several long days—the tunnel began to change.

It was barely noticeable at first—a slight warping of the walls, a twisting of the floor—so no one spoke of it, each assuming it was simply a trick of the imagination. After several more miles, however, the passage's deformity grew more pronounced. The stone was cracked in some places, and in others it ran like melted wax. The stench of hot metal mixed with the old, familiar tang of brimstone. Faint wisps of black smoke hung in the air, writhing as they passed. It grew steadily warmer, and soon the three travelers were slick with sweat, panting for breath as they struggled on.

"This is Malystryx's doing," Riverwind said, his voice hoarse from hours of disuse.

"No kidding," Kronn answered. "Actually, I'm not too

surprised—we must be almost to the Hollowlands by now. She's been using her magic to shape the land above us—it only stands to reason that the tunnels would have been warped too."

"How bad do you think it'll get?" Brightdawn asked.

The kender shrugged. "You tell me. I haven't been down this way in years."

Suddenly Riverwind began to cough, choking and gasping in the smoky air. His steps slowed, then he stopped, doubling over and hacking violently. Brightdawn ran to his side and grabbed his shoulders. "Father?" she asked, her voice rising with alarm. His face was dark red, and contorted with pain with every wracking cough. "What's wrong? What can I do to help?"

He fell to one knee, wheezing. "Water . . ." he croaked, his voice tight and strained. Sweat ran down his face in rivers.

Quickly, she pulled her waterskin from her belt, unstopped it, and held it to his lips. He took a gulp of water, sputtered it out when another spasm seized him, then tried again. He swallowed several mouthfuls, and the paroxysm passed. Relaxing, he sat down heavily and took several long, deep breaths of the foul air. "Give me . . . a moment," he puffed. "I'll be fine. . . ."

Brightdawn nodded, then started to close her waterskin again. She stopped, though, when she saw that its neck was flecked with blood. She looked at Riverwind in alarm. His lips gleamed red; seeing her stare, he quickly wiped his mouth.

"Father?" Brightdawn asked quietly.

"I said I'm fine!" the old Plainsman snapped. Glowering, he heaved himself to his feet and started to stumble down the passage again. "Come on," he said. "We can't afford to waste any more time."

Brightdawn and Kronn exchanged worried glances, then followed.

* * * * *

The tunnel grew steadily worse, becoming more deformed. The air became smokier and closer, the heat like an oven. After several more leagues, the tremors began.

The first was little more than a dull rumble, shaking dust from the ceiling. They looked around, worried, but the stones around them soon stopped trembling, so they carried on. Only a few minutes later, though, a loud crack resounded through the tunnel. The floor seemed to fall away beneath their feet as the whole passage shook, and they fought to keep their balance, groping at the shuddering walls. Pieces of stone—some of them several inches across—clattered down around them. The quake lasted nearly a minute before it subsided, leaving them lying, gasping and wide-eyed, on the ground.

"Trapspringer's boots," Kronn muttered, standing shakily. "I didn't like that very much."

Riverwind looked up and down the passage as he rose. "I have a feeling things will only get worse, the closer we get to Blood Watch."

Brightdawn lay sprawled on her back, looking up above them. "Father . . ." she murmured. "Look at the ceiling!"

They looked up. Above them, the shoring timbers that lined the ceiling had buckled and splintered. The wood continued to crackle as the rocks above them bulged slowly downward.

"Run!" Riverwind shouted. Grabbing his daughter's arm and dragging her after him, he turned and dashed down the tunnel back the way they'd come. Kronn sprinted at their heels, his short legs pumping.

The ceiling groaned loudly. Then there was a terrible, snapping sound as the timbers gave way. Behind them, where they had been standing, the ceiling caved in, filling the tunnel with thundering stones. A blast of dust surged past them, caking their skin and clothes. Then, echoing dully, the crash faded to silence.

They slowed, then came to a halt and looked back, breathing heavily. Through the settling dust they saw that the tunnel was gone, choked with jagged rubble.

Kronn was the first to find his voice. "I guess that's that," he declared.

"What do we do now?" Brightdawn panted.

The kender pulled out his map and studied it for a moment. "Unless I'm wrong, we passed a way up to the surface about half a mile back." Nodding firmly, he folded the parchment up again, stuffed it in a pocket, and began to walk. "Come on," he said. "Let's get out of here before the rest of it comes down."

* * * * *

Lifesbreath, the kender had called the hills south of Blood Watch, and not without reason. Wedged between the thornbush-dotted Somber Coast and the grey, barren Hollowlands, it had been a green, vibrant place. The Heartsblood River had burbled noisily through its midst, flowing among drooping cottonwood trees. Clover and wildflowers had dotted the verdant slopes. Butterflies had danced on the breeze.

No more. The cottonwoods and butterflies were gone, the Heartsblood dried up and forgotten. The wildflowers would never bloom again. Lifesbreath had yielded to the Desolation.

Kronn stared around him, his eyes wide as he surveyed the dry, blasted wastelands. The ground, which had once rolled smoothly north to the sea, was riven with jagged cracks that hissed ash and steam. Mud and tar bubbled in wide, unclean pools. The wind was scorching, merciless. To the north, jagged, rust-colored peaks jutted skyward like serpent's teeth. And beyond, at the rim of the angry ocean, a tall spire rose toward the black, hazy sky. The top of that mountain burned brightly, like a candle atop some unholy altar. All three travelers knew, with a gnawing in their guts, that they looked upon Blood Watch.

"This is what she's doing to the Kenderwood," Kronn said numbly.

"Kronn," Riverwind said softly. He was ashen with

horror at what he beheld, but he fought to keep his voice from trembling. "We need to keep moving. We're running out of time."

The kender hesitated a moment longer, crouching down and scooping up a handful of dry, gravelly soil. He held it up and let it sift through his fingers. Then, a harsh look in his eyes, he rose and started walking north, toward the smoldering volcano. Riverwind and Brightdawn followed at a distance, leaving the kender to his thoughts.

* * * * *

The journey across the mountains was slow and gruelling, but not impossible. There were many passes among the peaks, and though he had no map to guide him, Kronn moved surely, always keeping the looming shape of Blood Watch before him. Riverwind and Brightdawn watched the slopes around them as they walked, wary of rockslides or worse, unnamable dangers. Once, they had to use Kronn's chapak as a grappling hook to climb over a house-sized boulder that had fallen in their path, but most of the journey was mercifully without event.

Finally, two days after leaving Lifesbreath, as Mark Year Day faded into night, they crested a low, jagged ridge and stopped.

They stood at the edge of a broad, bleak valley. On the far side, directly across them, loomed Blood Watch. It towered impossibly high on the edge of the red sea, dwarfing the craggy peaks that surrounded it. In the darkness that had settled over the Desolation, the fires that burned on the mountaintop outshone even the full, pale moon, lighting the land all around. Glowing red lava snaked down the sides of the spire, and a cloud of black smoke roiled above it. Ash fell like snow from the sky, swathing the land in a blanket of gray. The air stank of sulfur and soot.

"Mishakal have mercy," Brightdawn whispered, trembling at the sight of the volcano. "How do we get in there?"

Shading his eyes, Riverwind peered across the valley. After a moment, his gaze fixed on something. "There," he said and pointed.

The others followed the gesture and saw what he had spotted. A low cavern mouth nestled at the foot of the mountain. Even from nearly a league away, they could see the hulking shapes of several ogres standing before the cave.

"Six of them," Kronn said grimly. "Two each."

A shower of pebbles slid down the rocky hillside as they scrambled down into the valley. They stopped at the bottom, watching to see if the ogres had heard, but the creatures didn't move. Blood pounded in their ears, echoing the rumbling of the ground below their feet, as they glanced warily at the fiery mountaintop.

"I don't mind telling you," Kronn said unhappily, "I'm starting to feel a little bit of that fear everybody's been talking about."

The Plainsfolk regarded him a moment. Then Riverwind rested a sympathetic hand on the kender's arm. "So am I," he said.

Stealthily, they snuck across the valley floor, moving from shadow to shadow in the gathering twilight. As they went, they got a better view of the ogres. Two of them were crouched down on their haunches, apparently asleep, and the others stared into space or absently scuffed the stony ground with the toes of their boots. With nothing to guard against, they were anything but watchful. Riverwind and Kronn exchanged satisfied looks as they crept closer.

A hundred paces from the cavern mouth, they stopped and hunkered down behind a sharp outcropping of stone. Silently, Riverwind strung his bow and readied an arrow; Kronn grabbed a rock from the ground and fitted it into the sling-pouch of his chapak. Brightdawn readied her mace, keeping low.

A silent signal passed between Kronn and Riverwind. As one, they rose, the Plainsman drawing back his bowstring and the kender holding his chapak poised. Then arrow and stone flashed across the distance to the cave mouth. Two ogres dropped, pierced and pummeled.

Their death cries woke the two sleeping ogres and stirred the others to action. The four spotted Riverwind and Kronn and charged.

Riverwind feathered one of them in the chest as it ran, and it crashed to the ground, rolling to a stop in a tangle of arms and legs. Kronn's second shot hit another in the knee, slowing it, but it didn't fall. He cursed and shifted his chapak in his hand, readying it to use as an axe. Riverwind dropped his bow and yanked his sabre from its scabbard. Then the ogres were upon them.

The old Plainsman traded blows with a wart-covered brute who wielded a great iron-headed mace; Kronn faced off with a smaller beast wielding a spear. The wounded ogre loped onward, dragging its injured leg behind it.

Steel clashed, but the kender and the Plainsman drove back their foes, dodging and parrying, then lunging in to draw blood—a nick on one ogre's shoulder, a gash on the other's thigh. The ogres were strong, though. Handpicked by Kurthak the Black-Gazer to guard Malystryx's lair, they did not fall easily.

Brightdawn didn't immediately enter the fray. She continued to crouch out of sight, watching the third ogre's halting approach. It never saw her coming. As it rounded the outcropping, she leaped out in front of it, swinging her mace with both hands. Her weapon struck the ogre squarely in the face, and there was blood everywhere as its suddenly lifeless weight crashed down on top of her.

She wriggled out from beneath the corpse just in time to see her father slide his sabre through his opponent's chest. Before that ogre hit the ground, Kronn buried his chapak in his own foe's belly. It doubled over as he jerked the axe free, and he brought his weapon down on the back of his head.

Panting, the three of them paused and leaned against the outcropping while they gathered their strength. They looked around, half-expecting to see the gigantic form of the dragon watching them from above, but there was nothing. They appeared to be alone in the valley.

"That was easy enough," Kronn said wryly. He wiped his bloody axe on a dead ogre's sleeve. Then the three of them crossed the last, short distance to the cavern mouth.

It was dark in the cave, so Kronn pulled a torch from his pack, struck his axe against the rocky side of the volcano to light it, and shone the brand inside. The cavern was wide and deep, narrowing at the back to a tunnel that led into the heart of the volcano. The passage's walls were rounded and glassy, reflecting the glimmer of the torchlight. In the distance, there was a dull, ruddy lambency coming from somewhere far inside the mountain. The three companions looked at one another, resolved, then entered the cavern and started down the long, snaking tunnel.

They did not see the lithe, black-cloaked figure emerge from the shadows and steal after them.

* * * * *

The last of the Kender Flight had to be out of the city by dawn that morning. The streets lay empty, waiting, as the final kender whose lots had been drawn bade farewell to those who would stay behind, then walked down the stairs into the dark, ancient catacombs. When they were gone, Catt Thistleknot and Giffel Birdwhistle stood at the same entrance where Riverwind and his companions had departed a week before, and looked out over Kendermore.

"Strange," Catt said. "It doesn't really feel like home anymore."

Paxina faced them, ready for war. She had shed her purple mayoral robes, leaving them in the audience chamber of City Hall. In their place she wore a breastplate and greaves of boiled leather. Her arms were bare, save for a pair of metal bracers. Her face was daubed with red paint—a fanciful touch she had picked up in her youth, among the Kagonesti in Ergoth. In her hand she held her hoopak; on her hip was a sack of slingstones. She wore no other pouches.

With her were Moonsong and Stagheart, similarly clad for battle. The Plainswoman held a staff in her hands, while her companion wore his sword and bow. There was also Arlie Longfinger, who had neither armor nor weapon despite his friends' insistence.

"You take care of that arm of yours, now," the old herbalist said, squinting at Catt through his thick spectacles. The sling had finally come off just a few days ago, and she still held her arm tenderly.

Paxina glanced at the eastern horizon, which was brightening from black to deep blue. "You should go," she said. "It won't be long now."

Catt stepped forward and kissed her sister on the cheek. "I'll see you in a few days," she said.

"Sure thing," Paxina said, grinning. She pulled a dagger from her belt and cut off her cheek braids. She held the locks of hair for a moment, then handed them to her sister.

Catt nodded, understanding, and tucked the braids into a small doeskin pouch. Returning Paxina's smile, she turned and walked to the top of the stairs. Giffel took her hand, and together they descended into the tunnels.

Paxina listened to them go until the sound of their footsteps faded away. Then she turned to the others, her war-painted face hard with determination, and nodded.

"Let's get ready," she said.

* * * * *

On the second day of the new year, and Kendermore's last, Kurthak stood just within the tree line, watching the sun rise. He shifted his gaze to the city across the meadow. Apart from a few sentries atop her walls, the town slumbered complacently. The Black-Gazer's mouth curled into a malicious smile.

"Send out messengers," he said. "Wake the horde."

Tragor looked up. He was sitting on a tree stump behind Kurthak, scraping a whetstone alone the blade of his massive sword. He dropped the stone immediately, rising from his seat. "Is it time?"

"Not yet," the Black-Gazer answered. "But I want everyone ready when Malystryx gives the order. Move."

Grunting, Tragor headed off into the woods. A few minutes later he was back at Kurthak's side, and a dozen ogres ran around the edges of the meadow, spreading the word to prepare for the attack. Kurthak watched in satisfaction as his army came to life.

They gathered at the edge of the barren, parched waste that had once been the meadow surrounding Kendermore, buckling on armor of leather and bronze and slamming crude iron helmets onto their heads. Their massive fists clenched the hafts of axes and clubs, spear shafts and sword hilts. Others gathered armfuls of javelins and handed them to their fellows. They gnawed cold, gristly meat from the bones of last night's meal and took deep swigs from skins of skunky ale. Here and there they raised their voices in droning war chants, accompanied by the rumble of massive drums. Standard-bearers appeared at the tree line, raising the emblems of their war bands— crude leather flags, poles hung with bones and animal skulls, and stakes mounted with the severed, withered heads of kender, around which buzzed clouds of black, stinging, flies. A great cheer went up as these gruesome trophies appeared, and the standard-bearers shook them wildly, the sallow, foul-smelling heads knocking against one another as they swung by their topknots.

As the sun cleared the eastern horizon, a low, angry rumble began to build among the ogres, swiftly growing into a chorus of furious roars and vicious snarls. A forest of weapons and horny fists raised in the air, pumping up and down in time with the clamor. Those from the more savage war bands slashed their flesh with stone knives, smearing themselves with their own blood as they whipped themselves into a frenzy of battlelust. In many places, Kurthak's officers had to physically restrain the shrieking, frothing ogres to keep them from charging onto the field. Ogres from rival tribes growled and spat on one another. The horde—nearly ten thousand ogres in all, completely encircling the clearing and the city within—grew more and more rabid as Kurthak watched. If the signal to attack didn't come soon, he knew, the crazed brutes would turn on one another in their rage. Despite this, however, he did nothing—only waited as his horde seethed around him. Anticipation scorched the air.

Time passed. The shadows of the city walls grew steadily shorter. Then, an hour after dawn, Kurthak felt a dark stirring inside his mind. Recognizing the feeling, he fought back the instinct to resist. His eyes lost focus as the stirring became a presence, and the presence became a voice.

Black-Gazer, it said.

"Malystryx," he whispered. Tragor looked at him sharply. "Your egg?"

Is safe. Are your people ready?

"Yes."

Good. It is time.

The voice faded, but the presence remained. Kurthak looked at Tragor and nodded. "Sound the attack," he said.

With a sanguine leer, the Black-Gazer's champion pulled a long, curving horn from his belt. He raised it to his lips and blew a single, blaring note.

Chapter 24

Catt and Giffel were a league west of the city, walking through the tunnels at the end of a line of kender that stretched ahead for dozens of miles, when the call of the ogres' war horns echoed faintly down the passage behind them. Hearing the noise, many of the kender stopped and looked back. Catt was one of them.

"That's it," she whispered. "It's started."

Giffel squeezed her hand. "You can't go back," he said, and nodded down the kender-filled tunnel. "We have to get them out of here."

She looked at him, hurt, then breathed a small, helpless sigh. Swallowing tears, she turned back to the kender who had halted in their march. They were all looking at her.

"All right," she told them. "Let's keep moving. We've got a long way ahead of us."

Reluctantly, the kender began to move again. Sliding her arm around Giffel's waist, Catt followed. For a few minutes she was silent, but then she drew a breath and began to sing.

The song was an old one, older than Kendermore itself. It was a trailsong, a tune Catt's people whistled to pass the time during their wanderings. Its melody was cheerful and lively, with a brisk, steady rhythm fit for walking. Every kender alive learned it as a child, and knew it by heart:

Old Danilo Twill had a hundred bags o' gold,
And a dozen times more silver than he could ever hold,
But he lost it all at knucklebones, till he didn't have a crumb,
Still, there'll always be more where that came from.

There's always more where that came from,
So strike up the pipes and bang on the drum,
Now don't be cross, lads, and don't be glum,
'Cause there's always more where that came from.

Giffel picked up the melody, singing along with her. Then the kender in front of them joined in, snapping their fingers in time with the second verse:

Before a year was done, good old Dan was rich again,
Shipping mead, wine and grog out across the salty main,
Then all his ships went down with their holds all full o' rum,
Still, there'll always be more where that came from.

Old Dan built himself a mansion, with twenty-seven floors,
Four-and-sixty windows, and twice as many doors,
But it burned right down to the ground and he moved into
the slum,
Still, there'll always be more where that came from.

Swiftly, the trail song spread forward, through the tunnels. The kender whistled and hummed, clapped their hands and stomped their feet. Some whirred their hoopaks in the air; others took apart chapaks and played them as flutes. Dozens of melodies wove together in complex harmonies—and occasional cacophonies. Every voice embellished on the song in some way, making up new verses about Danilo Twill and his resilience in the face of misfortune. And there were thousands of voices.

So, surrounded with music, the kender left their homes behind, bound once more for the road.

Now some folk, they might say old Dan's luck is running black,
But no matter what he loses, one day soon he'll win it back,
'Cause all you need's a hoopak and a merry tune to hum,
And there'll always be more where that came from.

* * * * *

On the barren meadow outside Kendermore, the harsh, fierce tone of a hundred war horns sounded all around the city. Howling with bloodlust, the ogres charged, a black wave dotted with foam of bronze and steel. The war bands' standards flew high. The thunder of the war drums echoed the pounding of iron shod feet.

In the midst of it all, however, Tragor paused, angling his head and frowning with confusion.

Kurthak glanced at his champion, wondering. "What is it?" he asked, shouting to be heard over the din of his charging troops.

Tragor concentrated a moment longer, then shook his head. "Nothing," he said. He raised his great sword above his head, bellowing a ferocious battle-cry, then charged onward. He didn't tell Kurthak that, just for a moment, he would have sworn he'd heard the faint sound of kender singing.

* * * * *

Paxina dashed up the steps to the battlements at the city's south wall, Moonsong and Stagheart right behind her. At the top, she peered through the crenelations and saw the dark stain spreading out of the Kenderwood.

Fear swelled within her, an unfamiliar and unwelcome sensation that choked off her voice. The sweat that trickled down her face turned cold, and her mouth went dry. "So many," she breathed.

A hand touched her shoulder, its grasp at once tender and firm. Paxina glanced up and saw Moonsong. The Plainswoman's face was pale, but she smiled nevertheless. That smile was a balm, easing the dread in Paxina's mind. The Lord Mayor looked back out at the field and laughed.

Then, recklessly, she leapt up on the merlons and turned to face the eerily quiet city. She cupped her hands to her mouth and shouted as loud as she could. Along the walls and among the streets, other voices echoed her call, sounding it all over Kendermore.

"Be ready! Here they come!"

* * * * *

When the silver-haired kender jumped up on the battlements and sounded the call to arms, Kurthak laughed aloud. He and Tragor marched at the rear of the horde, thousands of raging ogres before them. Swords and hammers, axes and spears waved above the army's heads.

"Remember!" he bellowed, his voice barely audible above the din. "Take as many of them prisoner as you can! Ten thousand steel pieces to the one who captures the most slaves!" He pointed his spiked club at the silver-haired kender. "And another thousand to whoever brings me that one's scalp!"

"I'll remember that," Tragor said, leering wolfishly. "You'd best be ready to pay up when this is over, my lord."

The Black-Gazer howled with glee, then raised his cudgel high above his head. "Charge!" he cried.

Tragor winded his horn again. Other trumpeters echoed the call. The army stopped marching and broke into a run, bellowing and shrieking as though their very voices would topple Kendermore's walls. The ogres closed around the city like a noose. Their pounding feet churned the blasted ground, sending great clouds of dust billowing high into the sky.

Atop the battlements, archers and slingers began to fire. As before, when Baloth's war band had assailed the city, many ogres fell to the barrage—but many, many more held their shields high and kept running, eagerly striving to be the first to reach the walls. They struck on all sides at once, hammering against the flagstones with weapons and fists. The stones did not yield. More and more ogres caught up with their fellows, adding their weight to the onslaught. From atop the walls, the kender on the walls met the attack with more arrows and rocks. Looking up, Kurthak saw the silver-haired kender flinging stones with her hoopak; beside her, one of the Plainsmen peppered the field with arrows.

"Where are the cauldrons?" Tragor wondered suspiciously, scanning the battlements. An arrow glanced off his plumed helmet, knocking it momentarily askew; he straightened it with an irritated grunt. "They poured buckets of pitch on Baloth's band."

Kurthak squinted at the walls, his brow furrowing. Then he shook his head stubbornly. "What does it matter?" he snapped. "Fewer dead on our side this way!"

The blasted ground ran red with the blood of dead and wounded ogres, but the living far outnumbered the slain. Some of his troops heaved javelins up at the battlements; pierced by those spears, kender began to topple from the walls. The horde crushed them into the ground where they landed.

"Ladders!" Kurthak cried.

Tragor sounded a third call on his horn. Ogres picked up scaling ladders—more than a hundred of them—and started forward, into the melee. Some didn't make it, brought down by the bombardment from above, but most pressed on, until at last they were in place. They planted the bases of the ladders in the blood-dampened earth and raised them toward the battlements.

Then something curious happened. Atop the wall, the silver-haired kender who had stood on the merlons at the start of the battle called out again. "Retreat!" she shouted.

At once, the kender vanished from the battlements, yelling and screaming as they climbed down the insides of the walls. In mere moments, none remained. The ogres whooped with malevolent joy, clashing their weapons against their shields.

"What's happening?" Kurthak wondered aloud.

"They're retreating!" Tragor cried jubilantly, waving his great sword in circles above his head. "The walls are ours!"

The ladders rose upright. Ogres started to clamber up toward the abandoned battlements. They spread along the catwalk, tossing aside the bodies of kender who had died on top of the walls.

The new sound was low at first, scarcely audible above the yowling of the horde. It grew quickly louder, though, and Kurthak and Tragor glanced at each other in confusion as the ground trembled beneath their feet. Then their eyes widened when they recognized the noise. It was the grinding and cracking of stone.

"Fall back!" Kurthak shouted to his troops. "Get away from the wall!"

Too late. With a rumble that shook the earth, the city's walls groaned and gave way. The ogres on the battlements screamed as the catwalks fell from beneath their feet, then they plummeted to their deaths in the middle of the avalanche. The walls did not simply collapse, however; the kender had spent weeks preparing them, chipping away the stones at their bases so they would do the most damage to their enemies. They fell outward, on top of other attackers.

Stones pounded down on on top of ogres, crushing them by the score. Scaling ladders, pushed back from the crumbling battlements, crashed to the ground. Within seconds, a large part of Kurthak's horde disappeared beneath countless tons of rock.

Dust exploded outward from Kendermore in a billowing, gray wave. Kurthak and Tragor choked and wheezed as it broke over them, stinging their eyes and filling their throats. When it cleared, they stared in shock at the ruins. The clattering of stone mixed with the cries of injured and dying ogres. Besides the hundreds who lay buried beneath the rubble, hundreds more lay on the ground, their legs crushed, or staggered aimlessly along the edges of the wreckage, clutching broken arms and bloodied bodies. Those who had escaped stood about the periphery, staring dumbly at the heaps of shifting flagstones.

Soon, however, the stupor wore off. The ogres had toppled the walls. The city lay naked before them, inviting and defenseless. What was more, hundreds of kender stood, in the courtyards just beyond the ruined battlements, leaning on their hoopaks and grinning mockingly. It was too much for the dull-witted ogres. Howling furiously, they surged over the shattered walls, trampling their own dying comrades as they boiled into the city.

They poured into the courtyards like water through a

broken dam, weapons held high. As they ran, though, the ground gave way beneath their feet. Their bloodthirsty roars became a chorus of screams as they vanished into the earth.

The kender had dug over a thousand pits in the courtyards. Most swallowed at least one ogre, and many claimed two or more. Kendermore's attackers died by the hundreds, their massive weight breaking the fragile rope-and-wood lattices that held up the cobblestones. They fell, landing hard on the sharpened stakes that lined the bottoms of the pits. Gored, they writhed and choked as they died.

Kurthak seethed with fury at what was happening. Rage filled his mind, clouding his vision with red mist. The kender were grouped on the other side of the pits, in the shadows of the courtyards, laughing. Laughing at him.

His temper snapping, he threw his massive arms up over his head and howled. "Kill them!" he cried. "Take no prisoners! Kill them all!"

The surviving ogres—no more than five thousand of his original mass of ten—began to pick their way past the deadfalls. Hooting derisively, the kender turned and ran down the streets into the heart of the city. Kurthak drove his ogres furiously after them.

* * * * *

Riverwind and his companions had walked for hours, following the snaking passage deep into Malystryx's mountain. As they went, the reddish glow before them grew slowly stronger, flickering and gleaming as it reflected off the obsidian walls. The ground beneath them shuddered frequently, sending shards of glossy, black stone showering down from the ceiling. One piece nicked Kronn's forehead, and the cut stubbornly refused to stop bleeding. Other than that, though, their march went undisturbed. They never noticed the shadowy form that trailed silently behind them.

"I should be making a map of this," Kronn whispered. His voice sounded loud and strange.

Riverwind chuckled softly. "Next time."

At last, the light ahead grew bright enough that they could douse their torches. The air, already oppressively warm, grew steadily hotter. The three travelers wiped stinging sweat from their eyes. In the distance, they could hear the crackle of flames. Wispy smoke curled around them. Kronn reached behind his back and touched his chapak warily; beside him, Brightdawn and Riverwind rested their hands on their own weapons.

The tunnel wound around a corner. The three companions rounded it, then stopped in their tracks, staring in wonder. Brightdawn gasped softly.

The passage opened into a vast chamber, a hole in the mountain's heart. The light here was shockingly bright, the heat like a dwarven foundry. A glowing pool of magma roiled and bubbled far below, choking the air with smoke and ash. Flames danced across its surface and burst forth in violent gouts. Stones, shaken loose by faint tremors, rattled down the walls to vanish with hisses of steam into the molten rock.

On the far side of the cavern, across the soot-choked chasm, yawned a dark tunnel mouth, twin to the one where Riverwind and his companions stood. Stretching across the gulf, joining the two passages, was a crude bridge. It was made mostly of thick rope, tied fast to stone outcroppings on either end. A series of wooden planks were lashed to the span, but the companions could tell the purchase they provided was precarious at best: scorched by the baking heat from below, they looked fragile as eggshells, and there were several ominous gaps where boards had fallen away. As Riverwind watched, a glowing cinder landed on the bridge, burned brightly for a moment, then went out, leaving behind a charred, black spot where it had been.

"Whoa," Kronn said, and meant it.

Suddenly, Brightdawn made a small choking sound. Riverwind glanced at her sharply, but she said nothing, only raised a trembling finger and pointed up the cavern's far wall. The others followed her gesture, squinting against the stinging smoke. When they spied what she had seen, they caught their breaths, paling with horror.

"Sweet Mishakal," Riverwind gasped.

On a broad ledge, high above the bridge, stood a pile of dragon skulls. There were dozens of them, bleached bones and teeth glowing hideous orange in the firelight. They had been carefully arranged, one on top of the other, into a pyramid fifty feet high. Looking at it, they could count the different types: the long-fanged maw of a black dragon, the ram's horns of a brass. White and green, blue and bronze, copper, silver and gold, even a lone sea dragon skull—every breed of wyrm was represented in the gruesome shrine. At the top of the pile, staring down at them with sightless eyes, was the massive skull of a red.

"That's her mate," Kronn whispered. "Isn't it?"

Riverwind had come to the same conclusion. He nodded.

"Can you feel it?" Brightdawn asked faintly. "The power..."

The others closed their eyes, their faces pinching. Riverwind slumped against the wall of the cavern, sweat streaming down his face. "Magic," he said. "It's coming from that totem. It must be what she uses to fuel her sorcery—to shape the land."

"That thing killed the Kenderwood?" Kronn asked, his eyes glinting angrily. He studied the far wall. "Maybe I can climb up to it and knock the skulls off the ledge..."

Riverwind, however, shook his head. "No, Kronn."

The kender regarded him in disbelief. "*No?*" he exclaimed. "She laid waste to my home with that thing, Riverwind! It needs to be destroyed!"

"I said no," the Plainsman replied firmly. "We can't afford to waste time here. We have to get to Malystryx's nest."

Kronn shook his head stubbornly, his cheek braids swaying. Brightdawn laid a hand on his shoulder. "Father's right, Kronn," she said. "Destroying that totem won't bring the Kenderwood back or make you forget your fear. Your people are counting on us to destroy the egg."

In the shadows behind them, a black-swathed figure stiffened, then slowly relaxed and began to creep forward. The soft scuff of its boots against the obsidian floor, the whisper of its dark cloak, and the faint hiss of its breath were all lost in the rumbling of lava and crackle of flames that filled the cavern. If any of them had turned, they might have caught a glimpse of movement, but their eyes were all fixed on the skull totem, and so they did not notice Yovanna's approach.

"I'll go first," Kronn said, forcing his gaze back to the smoldering bridge. "Don't follow me right away."

Swallowing, he stepped off the ledge, onto the first blackened plank. Gripping the hand ropes to either side, he eased his weight onto the board. Behind him, Riverwind and Brightdawn held their breaths. The plank creaked and groaned, but it held. Kronn lowered his other foot onto it, then walked forward, stepping carefully, never too hard. When he was twenty feet out—less than a quarter of the way across the span—he glanced back at the Plainsfolk, flashing a smile full of clenched teeth. "It's not that bad," he lied. "Just don't look down."

"Thanks," Brightdawn said dryly, as she started across after him. "I'll try to remember that."

Riverwind watched, his stomach a leaden knot, as his daughter crept along behind Kronn. He wanted to follow right behind her but knew that would only put her in more jeopardy. It would be dangerous to strain the bridge with too much weight in any one place. Far below, a bubble of magma burst, sending flames blossoming upward and spattering the cavern walls with globules of molten rock that quickly dimmed from golden yellow to black-crusted red.

Swallowing repeatedly in a vain effort to moisten his parched throat, the old Plainsman finally stepped onto the bridge. By far the heaviest of the three, he winced when he heard the soft sound of splintering beneath his feet. Somehow, though, the board did not break. Gripping the hand ropes with sweaty fingers, he inched along behind Kronn and Brightdawn, toward the impossibly far tunnel at the span's other end. Waves of broiling heat washed up from below.

When they were halfway across, the bridge began to shake. The companions didn't notice at first—the movement was slight—but with each passing heartbeat the ropes swayed more and more violently until the entire span was swinging. Brightdawn cried out in alarm, and the companions stopped, grasping the ropes tightly as a massive tremor rocked the whole cavern. More planks fell from the bridge, knocked loose by the quake, and burst into flames before they vanished into the seething, churning magma.

The tremor lasted nearly a full minute, but it seemed an eternity. At last, however, the swaying grew less violent, the planks' creaking less strained. The companions relaxed, sucking in deep breaths of scalding, smoky air and leaning weakly against the hand ropes.

With a loud snap, the rope on their right gave way.

All three somehow managed to keep from falling. Kronn stumbled, and Riverwind dropped to his knees; one of the boards beneath him snapped in half, and his left leg dropped through the opening.

Brightdawn, however, remembered the lesson Catt had taught her aboard *Brinestrider*. She found her sea legs immediately, then turned around. "Father!" she shouted as Riverwind struggled to pull himself back onto the bridge. She started toward him, gripping the remaining rope with both hands. "I'm coming," she said. "Hold on—"

Then her eyes focused on something behind him, and she screamed. Kronn looked up, and Riverwind craned, trying to see what she had spotted.

A black-cloaked figure stood upon the ledge they had come from, naked steel in its gloved hand. It stood by the frayed remnants of the severed hand rope, then began to move to the other side. As they watched, Yovanna touched the edge of her dagger to the remaining hand rope and began to saw the blade back and forth.

Acting on instinct, Brightdawn dashed back across the bridge, heedless of the planks' protesting groans. Riverwind stared in mute astonishment as she charged toward him; she was past him before he knew what she was doing.

"Brightdawn!" he shouted as she ran away from him.

Yovanna continued to cut through the rope for a moment, then glanced at the onrushing Plainswoman and stepped back, her dagger poised. Brightdawn didn't slow, however; she leapt onto the ledge, at the black-cloaked figure. She grunted with pain as the knife plunged into her side, but her momentum knocked Yovanna into the wall, driving the air from both women's lungs.

Riverwind watched in horror as his daughter and Malys's thrall grappled on the ledge. Straining mightily, he pulled his leg back up through the hole in the bridge, then started back after Brightdawn.

Then another tremor struck, nearly pitching him off the bridge. The cavern lurched wildly, sending showers of scree plunging into the molten pool. Brightdawn and Yovanna stumbled sideways, toward the edge of the ledge. They teetered on the brink for a moment, then overbalanced and toppled into the void.

"No!" Riverwind bellowed.

For a moment Brightdawn was free, falling toward the hungry, waiting magma. Then she caught the lip of the ledge with her hands and held on with an iron grip. Yovanna grabbed her about the knees, arresting her own fall, and Brightdawn groaned as their combined weight began to loosen her grip on the stone. The muscles in her arms strained, and she ground her teeth with effort and agony.

Regaining his balance as the tremor subsided, Riverwind heaved himself toward the ledge, trying to reach her. "Child," he gasped helplessly, "I'm coming . . ."

Brightdawn kicked and thrashed, trying to knock Yovanna loose, but the black-cloaked figure held her tight. Yovanna's hood fell back from her head, revealing the tortured ruins of her face. Her lipless mouth twisting into a snarl, she grabbed the back of Brightdawn's tunic and began to climb.

"Please," Brightdawn sobbed. The sharp obsidian dug into her palms, drawing bright blood. "Father . . ."

Riverwind moved as quickly as he could, but he could see his daughter's grip faltering and knew he wouldn't be fast enough. Another board gave way beneath him, and he nearly fell, clutching the weakened hand rope. Tears of frustration crawled down his cheeks.

Yovanna continued to pull herself up Brightdawn's body, growling like a wild animal. Her hand clawed up, reaching for the Plainswoman's collar.

Then a tiny dart hissed through the air, striking the back of her neck. Reflexively, Yovanna swatted at it . . .

And lost her grip on Brightdawn.

As she fell, the glittering cruelty faded from Yovanna's eyes. A look of relief took its place. Then the heat of the magma ignited her robes, and she plunged, burning like a torch, into the molten rock.

Brightdawn sobbed, her fingers slipping. Recklessly, Riverwind charged the last dozen paces back along the bridge, threw himself flat on the ledge, then reached back and caught her wrists. Groaning mightily, he pulled her up, out of the abyss. They lay sprawled together on the stone for a moment, shuddering, then Riverwind pushed himself weakly to his knees. His face was ashen as he beheld his daughter's body. Yovanna's dagger was still buried to its cross-guard in her side.

The Plainsman glanced back across the bridge, seeking Kronn. The kender stood still, holding the haft of his chapak in his hands. Pieces of the weapon protruded from his pouches and pockets: while Riverwind had striven to reach his daughter, Kronn had dismantled it, turned it into a blowgun, and fired the dart that had felled Yovanna. Now he slid the haft into his belt and dashed back along the bridge to help Riverwind and Brightdawn.

She rolled onto her side, the dagger's hilt sticking up into the air, and looked at them both with bleary eyes. Her tunic was dark with blood. "I don't think I can make it . . . on my own," she hissed.

Riverwind's jaw tightened; his face might have been carved of granite. "It's all right," he said. "I'm here, child. I'll help you."

Somehow, using the remaining hand rope to guide them, he and Kronn carried her across the bridge. When they finally reached the far side, the kender and the Plainsman sank down on the stone, exhausted. For a long time, none of them could do anything but gasp for breath. Then Brightdawn stirred. "Father?" she asked in a small voice. "Why is it so cold?"

A spike of horror drove itself through Riverwind's gut, paralyzing him. Wearily, Kronn crawled over to Brightdawn and inspected the dagger lodged in her side. He dabbed at the wound, and his fingers came away with blood—and something else. Something black and oily.

He looked at Riverwind, shaking his head.

His face constricted with anguish, Riverwind lifted his daughter and rolled her over, resting her head in his lap. She was shivering, and her lips were blue. Her eyes gleamed feverishly in the fireglow.

"Oh, child," he said. "My sunrise."

"She would have killed us all, Father," Brightdawn hissed. "She would have cut the rope, and we would have fallen. I had to stop her. I had . . . to save you."

"Oh, gods." Riverwind's voice was ragged with tears. "Child, you cannot save me. You cannot." He hesitated, summoning strength from within. "I'm dying, Brightdawn."

Kronn choked suddenly and turned away.

Brightdawn smiled, however. "Then," she breathed, "you'll see me again soon . . ."

Helplessly, Riverwind bowed his head.

"Father?"

"Yes, child?"

"Do you remember, when Moonsong and I were young, how sometimes we'd cry until you came to kiss us good-night?"

He nodded. "I remember."

"You used to sing to us . . ." A shudder ran through her body, and she groaned.

"Shall I sing it for you, child?"

She nodded, smiling weakly. Her eyes fluttered closed.

Riverwind took several long, slow breaths to calm himself. Then, with grieving effort, his baritone voice rose softly, singing an old Plainsman lullaby.

> *Hush baby, sleep baby, nighttime is here*
> *And the moons circle round up above in the skies.*
> *The evening is calm and the blanket is soft,*
> *Time to rest, time to sleep, close your eyes.*
> *So hush baby, sleep baby, don't stay awake,*
> *Let your dreams carry you to a world far away.*
> *A world that is peaceful, a world filled with love,*
> *Where all children share laughter and play.*
> *So sleep till the dark fades away.*

Sometime, while he was singing, Riverwind's daughter died.

* * * * *

He held Brightdawn tight, stroking her golden hair. Kronn walked a short distance down the dark tunnel, partly to leave the Plainsman in peace, partly so he could cry alone. When he returned, Riverwind was still holding her. The Plainsman seemed very old and frail.

"Riverwind," Kronn said.

"It should have been me," Riverwind whispered. "First Swiftraven, now . . ." He bowed his head, shuddering.

The Plainsman removed Brightdawn's mace from her belt and tied it to his own. Then he dug in his pack and took out a woven blanket. His hands trembling, he folded it about his daughter's motionless form, then rose and lifted her in his arms. He walked to rim of the ledge and paused there.

"When you return to your people, Kronn," he said, "tell them how she died. Tell Moonsong."

The kender nodded sadly. "I will."

Riverwind kissed Brightdawn's forehead, then dropped her from the ledge. Her body spun slowly through the air, then vanished into the magma.

They turned and walked away, deeper into the mountain.

Chapter 25

Moonsong groaned loudly and stumbled, nearly falling, as she dashed down Tornado Alley. Stagheart, running beside her, caught her arm. She doubled over, gasping desperately for breath that wouldn't come. Her face grew deathly pale, seeming to age before Stagheart's eyes. Kender surged all around them, fleeing from the toppled walls toward the center of Kendermore.

Nervously, Stagheart looked over his shoulder. The ogres' bloodthirsty shouts were growing louder all around as they swarmed into the city. He tightened his grip on Moonsong's wrist. "What's wrong?" he asked.

"Brightdawn . . ." Moonsong sobbed, her shoulders heaving. She looked up at him, her blue eyes brimming with anguish. "Stagheart, she's dead. My sister's dead."

He swayed on his feet, his chest tightening, then forced himself to swallow the acid taste in his mouth. "You're sure?" he asked gently.

"I know!" she cried. "Stagheart. She's gone."

The roars of the ogres were very near now; the mobs of running kender were thinning.

"And your father?" Stagheart pressed urgently.

Moonsong shook her head. "I don't know. Oh, goddess. What if they've failed?" She sucked a shuddering breath through her teeth, shivering convulsively.

Stagheart could see the ogres now, at the far end of the broad, straight street. They were moving swiftly, chasing a mob of shouting kender. He drew his sabre and pulled her away. "Come on," he told her. "We have to keep moving. Paxina's waiting for us."

The sharpness of his voice reached her. Swallowing her grief, she started to run.

* * * * *

The Black-Gazer's horde spread into the streets of Kendermore, pursuing the retreating kender. Their quarry led them on, running hard to gain ground, then waiting for the ogres to catch up, always keeping maddeningly just out of reach. Each time they stopped, the kender turned around to mock their foes, pointing and laughing, their voices rising in a chorus of sweet-sounding derision.

"Do the lice ever complain about how bad you smell?" they shouted gleefully.

"What are you, nine feet tall?" asked others. "I didn't know they piled dung that high!"

"Do ogre women really like men whose teeth look like smutty corn cobs?"

"Say, you've got a great big boil right—oh, sorry, that's your face."

"Wow! A five-hundred-pound walking wart!"

"Hey, liver-brain! I've seen things living under rocks that could outwit you!"

"So, when did you find out your sister and your grandmother were the same person?"

"Great Reorx, you're ugly. One look at you would make Lord Soth cry for his mother! What are you, part troll or something?"

"Scumlickers!"

"Pigspawn!"

"Overgrown, dimwitted, bandy-legged, slack-jawed, dirt-sucking heaps of rotten goblin excrement!"

Already enraged by the deaths of their comrades, the ogres went utterly berserk. Howling with mindless fury, they charged blindly down the streets after the jeering kender. The kender ran onward, shouting a constant stream of insults as they led the ogres through the confusion of Kendermore's streets.

Gradually, deliberately, the kender broke up the horde.

They split at each fork or intersection, drawing their pursuers in every direction. The ogres surged along the tangled avenues, running as fast as their tree-trunk legs would carry them.

The kender knew where the trip wires were. They saw them as they ran, and hurdled nimbly over them. The ogres, however, could see little but their own crimson rage. They hit the wires, stumbling and falling headlong onto the cobblestones. All over Kendermore, the same thing happened. Hundreds of ogres died, their bodies crushed by the weight of those who came after them.

Many of the trip wires did no more than that; others, however, set off all sorts of booby traps. On Tallowwax Way, a tall rowhouse collapsed, crashing down on the charging ogres and choking the street with broken stone. Across town, on Applebloom Trail, countless caltrops poured from roofs and rainspouts, clattering onto the street like barbed hailstones and crippling anyone who stepped on them. On Tornado Alley, in Moonsong and Stagheart's wake, a series of wires caused the strings of two hundred carefully arranged crossbows to thrum. Scores of ogres collapsed, their bodies riddled with quarrels. All across the town, pits and snares and rockfalls slaughtered Kendermore's attackers without mercy.

On Greentwig Avenue, the ogres swarmed over their comrades' trampled corpses as they continued to chase the kender. They ran with all the speed they could muster, and even caught some of their quarry, seizing several unlucky kender and tearing them apart in mindless rage. Still the surviving kender ran, their taunts growing more vicious. As the street twisted and turned, they ducked down alleys or into narrow doorways, their numbers diminishing until only eight remained, pursued by a hundred raging ogres.

Two lagged behind, and the ogres caught them, snapping their necks with their bare hands.

Then, suddenly, they rounded a corner and reached the dead end. A brand-new, twenty-foot stone wall blocked the road, stretching between two four-storey rowhouses.

The remaining six kender didn't stop, however; in front

of them, less than a dozen yards before the wall, were several catapults. They sprinted to the devices and leapt onto their arms. As the ogres rounded the corner behind them, the kender released the catapults' catches.

The machines' arms sprung, launching the kender aloft. Behind and below them, the ogres skidded to a halt, staring in astonishment as their quarry flew high into the air, vaulting up and over the wall.

On the wall's far side, Greentwig Avenue was heaped with loose straw. The kender landed in it, rolled, then leapt up and ran onward, laughing with reckless glee. Back in the dead end, the ogres gawked at the abandoned catapults. Their prey suddenly out of reach, they snarled savagely, shaking their weapons in angry impotence.

When the low, whirring sound first began, the ogres' eyes narrowed, and they peered about in confusion. The noise seemed to come from all around them, an irritating drone that slowly grew into a loud, high-pitched scream—the shriek of dozens of hoopaks, swinging in unison.

Then the ogres' confusion gave way to panic as slingstones began to rain down on them from above. Kender appeared on the rooftops of the tall row houses, flinging rocks down into the street. The ogres dropped in waves, filling the air with cries of pain. Those who didn't fall at first tried to flee, scrambling back away from the wall in a desperate attempt to escape the ambush. More ogres kept coming around the corner from the other direction, however, trapping their fellows and leaving them exposed to the hail of stones. When the last handful of surviving ogres finally broke and ran, they left more than a hundred of their comrades' battered bodies behind.

So it went throughout the city. Kender led ogres along, dividing them, trapping them and leading them to their deaths in Kendermore's twisting, mazelike streets. But there were still hundreds of ogres, and there was no stopping them all. Whenever one fell, another stepped over its body to take its place. Though a great many died, they continued to push deeper into the city, down Strawberry Boulevard, up winding Straight Street, along Whitehare

Lane and Horsetail Avenue. Hundreds of unlucky kender perished when they stumbled as they ran or tarried too long to taunt their foes.

Inexorably, the ogres overwhelmed Kendermore, pressing inward on all sides, toward the middle of town. In the end, barely two thousand ogres remained—but they had conquered the kender capital.

Which was just what the kender wanted.

* * * * *

The glow of the magma pool faded behind Riverwind and Kronn as they marched onward, following the sinuous, obsidian tunnel. They walked for an hour in silence, pausing only long enough for the kender to light another torch when the shadows grew too deep to see. From time to time, Kronn looked up at the old Plainsman, a question on his lips, then looked away when he saw the fierce scowl that twisted Riverwind's face.

The passage began to wind upward, like a snake rising to strike. The floor's glossy surface gave their feet little to grip, slowing them considerably as they fought to keep from slipping. They gripped the walls, pressing their hands against the smooth stone to keep themselves upright. Their legs burned with pain at every faltering step, and the tunnel's slope grew ever steeper. Once Kronn's right foot slid out from beneath him, and he stumbled, grunting with pain as his knee struck the floor. He slipped back several feet, scrabbling to stop himself, before Riverwind's strong hand caught his sleeve. Straining, the Plainsman pulled Kronn back to his feet.

At last the tunnel leveled out, its slope becoming more and more gentle, until finally they could rest without fear of falling. They sank to the ground, panting as they leaned back against the walls. Riverwind groaned, holding a hand against his belly, then leaned over sideways and retched, his chest heaving violently. When the spasm passed, he sat back upright, wiping his mouth with a weak, shaking hand. He smeared blood across his lips.

"Riverwind?" Kronn asked.

The old Plainsman's eyes rolled toward the kender. A moment passed before they lit with recognition. "Kronn."

"How long have you known you are dying?" Kronn asked.

"Many months. That's why I was in Solace when you and Catt arrived—to say goodbye to my friends."

"And you still came with us?" the kender asked, astounded. "Why?"

"Because I knew no one else would," Riverwind replied softly.

After another ten minutes of walking, a light glimmered before them once more. The air grew warm, and a sound rose—a slow rhythm of rushing air, like the pumping of elephantine bellows.

Kronn doused his torch, and they crept stealthily onward through the gloom. The light before them brightened. The passage wound sharply to the left, then arrowed straight for nearly a hundred yards. At its end, they could see, it opened into another chamber.

They traveled that last hundred yards on their bellies, listening to the steady whoosh of the dragon's breath. Finally, they reached the end of the tunnel.

It opened out into a vast, vaulted cavern, even larger than the magma chamber. Orange firelight danced upon the walls, casting shifting shadows that seemed somehow alive. Looking up, they saw the wide shaft in the nest's ceiling and the telltale clawmarks in the stone at its edges. Swallowing, the kender and the Plainsman shifted their gazes down, to the floor of the cavern a hundred feet below. Riverwind sucked in a sharp breath.

Malystryx covered the floor of the cave, her wings tucked in at her sides, her head held low to the ground. Her scaly, scarlet sides moved in and out as she breathed. Her body was coiled, wrapped around something in the middle of the chamber. They couldn't see what she encircled, but they guessed.

The dragonfear that rose from her motionless form crushed Kronn and Riverwind into the ground, paralyzing them where they lay even as their minds screamed at them to flee. Madness clawed at them, and they quivered with terror and dread.

"Blessed goddess," Riverwind hissed. Kronn whimpered softly beside him.

They lay upon the ledge at the tunnel's mouth for what seemed like hours, listening to Malys's breathing, waiting for her head to snap up and her golden eyes to fix upon them. The dragon, however, took no notice of them. Her attention was elsewhere, many leagues away.

* * * * *

Malystryx's presence was a white-hot cinder in Kurthak's mind as he and Tragor strode down Elbowpoke Way, toward the center of Kendermore. The street was littered with corpses from both sides of the battle, but there were three slain ogres for every kender who lay broken upon the ground.

The dragon's voice swelled within him. *Black-Gazer*, it whispered, menacing. *What has happened?*

"My people," Kurthak answered. "Slaughtered . . ."

Slaughtered? the voice shrieked, forging a stabbing pain behind the hetman's eyes. *By the kender? How?*

"Trickery," he replied. He spat angrily on the ground.

Then you are beaten?

"No!" he snarled. He raised his spiked club, which was stained with kender blood. "We have them cornered now. We will destroy them."

"There, my lord!" Tragor said suddenly, pointing with his sword. Kurthak looked past the red-dripping blade and saw what his champion had spotted. A group of kender—he counted ten—had stepped out from a side street onto Elbowpoke Way. They froze, staring at the hetman and his champion.

Kurthak glared back at them balefully. "Wait," he said as Tragor started forward. "It could be another trap."

Obediently, his champion stopped, waiting tensely. Kurthak's brow furrowed as he regarded the kender.

Seeing the unfeigned fear on their faces, he smiled. This was no trick. The kender were caught, paralyzed by the sight of the two ogres. He charged, his club held high. Tragor ran with him.

The kender faltered, too surprised to react before the ogres struck. Kurthak brought his club down on a female kender's head, crushing her where she stood. Tragor waded into the battle a heartbeat later. He swung his sword low, cutting a male in half across the stomach. He reversed the stroke, sending another kender's head skipping away across the cobblestones. Kurthak savagely smashed a fourth. It crumpled, its back broken.

Panicking, the remaining kender tried to flee. Tragor slashed two of them in half with one sweep of his sword. Kurthak swatted a third into the air. The kender flew across the width of Elbowpoke Way, its neck flopping limply, and struck the side of a house before sliding to the ground. The two ogres turned to face their remaining opponents. Two warriors faced them, one armed with a hoopak and the other wielding a battak. Just behind them was an old, unarmed male, quivering with fright as he squinted through a pair of bottle-thick spectacles.

"Run, Arlie!" the hoopak-wielder shouted. He glanced over his shoulder at the old man. "We'll try and hold—"

Before he could finish, Tragor drove his sword through the kender's body. The other warrior charged toward Kurthak, swinging his battak. The hetman batted aside the desperate blow with his club, then lashed out in response, crushing his attacker's skull.

Arlie Longfinger backed away, terrified. Kurthak strode forward, snarling, and slammed his club down on the old herbalist's head. The Black-Gazer pounded Arlie's body until nothing remained but a lifeless pulp.

Enough, Malys's voice said within his mind. *He is dead. Where are your followers, Black-Gazer?*

His nostrils flaring angrily, Kurthak turned away from Arlie's battered corpse and stalked off down Elbowpoke Way. Tragor followed, teeth bared in a feral snarl.

Soon they caught up with a bedraggled group of a

hundred ogres, most of them wounded. The group, which was all that remained of a band three times that number, pursued one group of jeering kender.

"Hey!" the kender taunted. "Do you smear yourselves with filth on purpose, or does it just happen naturally?"

Kurthak and Tragor added their voices to the chorus of roars that erupted from the ogre band. They chased the kender around bend after bend in the road, yearning for slaughter. Then, suddenly, they rounded a corner and stepped into the cleared quadrangle in Kendermore's midst.

A pitched battle was raging, all across the yard. A thousand ogres pressed toward the quadrangle's midst from all sides, hacking and stabbing madly at a cluster of a few hundred kender. The kender fought back desperately, their weapons clashing and clattering. Many of their number lay sprawled in pools of blood, but somehow the survivors held their own, keeping the remnants of the horde at bay. In their midst stood three figures Kurthak recognized. Two were Plainsfolk—a young man and woman—and the third was the silver-haired kender who had stood atop the merlons that morning. With them were several dozen archers, who clustered around glowing braziers, arrows nocked on their bowstrings.

The kender fought valiantly, but they were clearly doomed. More and more ogres staggered into the yard, bloody and bruised from the gauntlet they had run through Kendermore's streets. Every time one of Kurthak's troops fell to the kender's whirling hoopaks, another stepped forward to take its place. The battlefront began to constrict as the ogres slowly pressed inward.

Paxina Thistleknot turned and met the Black-Gazer's hateful glare. Her lips curled into a tight, vulpine smile, then she said something to the archers.

Sensing something was wrong, Kurthak cast about wildly. He sniffed the air, his nose wrinkling. A pungent reek hung over the quadrangle, thick enough to bring tears to the hetman's good eye. Casting about, he quickly spotted the source of the smell. The walls of the tall houses and shops surrounding the yard were covered with thick, black grease.

"What is that?" he asked.

Tragor looked, frowning, then reached out, brushing the nearest wall with his fingertips. They came away smeared with grime. He rubbed them together, held them up to his nose. Then he turned back toward Kurthak. "It's pitch," he said.

"Ready!" shouted Paxina.

As one, the archers touched the tips of their arrows to the smoldering braziers. The shafts' tips, wrapped in oily rags, burst aflame. The archers pulled their bowstrings back to their cheeks, aiming high. Kurthak's eyes widened with understanding.

"Fire!" Paxina cried.

A multitude of twangs rang out. The arrows flew high, arcing above the seething battle, then dropped toward the houses at the quadrangle's edges. A blazing shaft whizzed past Tragor's head, embedding itself in the wall before him. He stared at it, blinking in surprise.

The wall exploded with fire. Tragor screamed as flames flared out around him, enveloping his body. Kurthak could do nothing but stare in horror as his champion became a living, howling torch. Tragor staggered back from the building, dropping his sword and beating wildly at the sheath of fire that surrounded him. He shrieked in agony, fell to his knees, then crashed face forward onto the ground. His burning body twitched violently, then was still.

The building he had been standing before rapidly became an inferno. It wasn't the only one. The archers' flaming arrows struck dozens of other houses, setting them alight as well. The fire spread with shocking speed, leaping from one pitch-soaked building to the next. In moments, the quadrangle was surrounded by a ring of flame.

Through the heat-shimmering air, Kurthak saw plumes of black smoke rise where other blazes were breaking out all over Kendermore. The crackling of burning wood grew deafening, drowning out the clamor of battle.

"What are they doing?" the Black-Gazer shouted. "They're burning their own city!"

The ogres panicked, searching vainly for a way out of the trap. In that moment, the tide of the battle turned. The kender in the quadrangle's midst pushed forward, slashing and stabbing. Many of the ogres died; others broke and ran, screaming as they sought to escape the conflagration.

But the kender knew their home. They knew which streets to block, which buildings to set alight. Most of them managed to escape, running out of the city ahead of the flames; others dove down tunnel entrances, scattering in all directions through the passages. For Kurthak's horde, however, there was no escape. Sheets of flame blocked their way; burning buildings collapsed, filling the streets with fiery rubble. Ogres perished by the score, overcome by fire and choking smoke.

Kurthak stood amidst it all, hewing about him with his club. He spotted a group of four taunting kender, who had just killed two ogres and were trying to escape through the smoke. They saw him as he charged toward them, and turned to run. One of them, a tow-headed boy in bright blue trousers, lagged behind his fellows: Kurthak knocked him flat, then smashed his cudgel down, spattering the young kender's blood on the cobblestones. The other three glanced back, horrified, but did not slow their pace: they ran onward, through a roiling wall of smoke. He gave chase, but when he cleared the other side of the pall, they were nowhere to be seen. He cast about, growling in frustration, but the kender were gone. Enraged he lashed out with his club at the nearest available target: a stack of water barrels, piled high against the wall of a burning blacksmith's shop. The barrels shattered, splinters of wood flying everywhere. He began to turn away, then stopped, confused. Where was the water?

Looking down, he confirmed his suspicions: the barrels had been bone-dry, empty. He kicked at the broken staves, pushing them aside, and saw the hole in the ground.

It was dark and small, too tight for him to squeeze through, but large enough to admit a kender . . . or three. It led down into the ground, its earthen stairs freshly scuffed by passing feet. He gawked at it, dumbfounded. Then his mouth dropped open with sudden comprehension. All at once, he knew—how the kender had eluded his people at Myrtledew, how they had fled the inexorable advance of the horde toward Kendermore, how, even now, they were escaping the inferno they had made of their city. He reeled, nausea twisting his stomach as he stared into the tunnel entrance.

Off to his left, a burning house collapsed, littering the ground with stone and blazing timbers. The deafening crash roused him, bringing him back to his senses. He glanced back into the quadrangle, through the billowing smoke. The remaining kender were making short work of his people, then melting away into the shadows—fleeing, he realized, into the safety of their subterranean passages. At that moment, Kurthak the Black-Gazer knew his horde was utterly beaten and that he would die here with his people if he didn't get help soon.

He sought that help in the only place left to him: his mind. Concentrating, he focused on the presence that simmered within him, seeking the other who dwelt in his thoughts. "Malystryx!" he begged, speaking the words aloud even as he thought them. "Mistress, hear me."

I am here, Black-Gazer, Malys's voice growled. *What is happening?*

"We are betrayed!" he shouted. "The kender have tricked us! They destroy their own city and flee through tunnels, under the ground! We are doomed!"

For several heartbeats, Malystryx didn't respond. Then a white-hot star exploded inside Kurthak's head as she forced her way into his brain, ripping into his memories, seeing what had happened, how the ogres had been fooled. Her disgust flooded his mind, and he doubled over, gagging.

Imbecile, her voice snapped in his mind. *They set a trap for you, and you charged right into the middle. And I had such hopes for you.*

"Help me, Mistress," the Black-Gazer begged, his throat so tight he nearly strangled on the words. "Please. . . ."

She laughed, then, a cruel, hissing sound that made ice of Kurthak's heart.

Help you? she echoed mockingly. *Whatever for? You have earned your fate, fool.*

"I have served you," Kurthak whimpered. "I've done your bidding. You owe me—"

The pain in his mind grew even stronger than before, blinding him, driving him to his knees. He squeezed his eyes shut, his voice giving way to a silent, agonized scream as the dragon tore his mind apart.

"Owe you?" he shrieked, but it was Malystryx's voice that issued from his mouth, not his own. *"I owe you nothing! You have failed, and you will pay. I will see to it! I will burn everything: the forest, the kender in their tunnels, and yes, Kurthak, you and your pathetic horde. I will burn you all until nothing remains!"*

Then, in an eyeblink, she was gone from his tattered mind. Kurthak knelt on the stones for a time, retching. Smoke and screaming surrounded him. Then, roaring with senseless rage, he lunged to his feet again and charged back into the quadrangle. He swung his spiked club wildly, lashing out on all sides. Kender and ogres alike fell around him as he cut a bloody swath across the yard. He sought neither escape nor vengeance; such things were beyond him now. Abandoned by his mistress, unable to stop his horde from falling to pieces around him, Kurthak the Black-Gazer went mad.

A wave of smoke blew in his face, stinging his eyes, but he kept on going, a juggernaut of insane wrath. He only stopped when he reached the far side of the yard and saw the burning buildings before him, barring his way. Crying out in impotent anger, he started to turn around, to charge back into the fray.

He did not see Paxina. She ran toward him on his left, his blind side. He only realized she was there when the spiked butt of her hoopak plunged into his flank. Using her own momentum, the Lord Mayor drove four feet of ironwood through his bowels.

He spun, his left arm lashing out. The back of his hand caught Paxina square in her chest, lifting her off the ground and hurling her away. She struck the ground hard, landing in a motionless heap at the foot of a burning house. He started to turn toward her, but staggered, his head spinning. Hot blood coursed from the wound in his side. His world began to grow dark.

"Malys," he wheezed. He took two faltering steps, then stumbled to his knees. "Help me."

Stagheart came out of the smoke, his sabre flashing. Kurthak tried to block the vicious slash, but he no longer had the strength to raise his club. The Plainsman's sword opened his throat. Choking, Kurthak the Black-Gazer died.

* * * * *

Malystryx's eyes flared wide, blazing with rage. Above her, Riverwind and Kronn drew back from the rim of the ledge, shaking with fear. She didn't see them; her wrath consumed her.

"No, my precious kender," she hissed in a voice as deep and dark as an ossuary. "You may think the game is done, but it is not. You will not escape. Your tunnels will not save you. My flames will find you, even far beneath the earth."

With unnerving speed, she uncoiled herself, rose on her hind legs, and leapt into the air. Her gargantuan form streaked past Kronn and Riverwind, up toward the rift in the ceiling. With a scraping of scales against stone, she pulled herself through the shaft. Her sinuous tail flicked with anger, then vanished from sight as she crawled out of her lair.

Riverwind and Kronn stared at the ceiling, watching chips of stone rattle down from the shaft and listening to the echoes of the dragon's passage fade away. Even when the cavern was silent again, they continued to gaze upward, as if waiting for the enormous crimson head to reappear. At last, though, they let out their long-held breaths, and looked down at the floor of the nest.

The egg was loathsome, a leathery abomination six feet long and nearly half as high. It nestled in the middle of the floor, half-buried in a wide bed of warm, white ash. Orange firelight flickered across its rust-red shell, though there were no flames to be seen. Riverwind and Kronn beheld it with silent revulsion.

Wordlessly, the kender unscrewed the cap on the butt of his chapak's haft. He unspooled the long silk rope from the weapon, slung the axe across his back again, and lashed one end of the line soundly around a rock outcropping at the ledge's lip. He yanked it hard, testing it, then checked the knot and nodded with satisfaction.

"It'll hold," he declared, grabbing the rope with both hands and swinging a leg over the edge.

"No," Riverwind said, catching his arm before he could go farther. "I will go first."

Kronn met the old Plainsman's firm, unwavering gaze. Seeing the resolve there, he hoisted himself back onto the ledge and handed the rope to Riverwind.

"Watch your step," he said.

Gripping the rope with strong hands, Riverwind lowered himself toward the distant cavern floor.

* * * * *

Moonsong fought her way through the smoke and the press of bodies. The ogres ignored her, trying to flee or hewing wildly at the kender. She saw Stagheart, standing over the body of the ogres' hetman. She saw Paxina's hoopak, lodged in Kurthak's gut. Then, turning, she saw the Lord Mayor sprawled on the ground like a discarded doll. The house Paxina lay beside groaned loudly, its flame-eaten walls starting to buckle. Blazing cinders rained down around the Lord Mayor's body.

Moonsong ran, dropping to her knees beside Paxina's unmoving form. As gently as she could, she turned the Lord Mayor over. Paxina's face was pale beneath the war paint and soot. Checking furtively, Moonsong found the lifebeat in the kender's throat. She whispered a prayer of thanks, not caring that Mishakal wasn't there to hear.

"Paxina?" she asked urgently. "Can you hear me?"

The Lord Mayor groaned, her eyelids fluttering open. She looked up at Moonsong and grinned weakly. "Wow," she said. "Those ogres can sure pack a wallop when they want to."

A loud creaking sounded above them. Moonsong glanced up and saw the house shift slightly, leaning over them like a smith's hammer above the anvil. Shards of pitch-soaked plaster broke off the walls, shattered against the cobbles all around them. Cold with fear, Moonsong grabbed Paxina's hands and dragged her to her feet. The Lord Mayor was still stunned by Kurthak's blow, however, and her knees buckled limply beneath her. The house continued to crumple, beams and timbers protesting loudly as they gave way.

There were tears in Moonsong's eyes as she dragged Paxina along with her. "Come on," she pleaded. "You have to help me. I can't carry you—you've got to walk."

"I can't," Paxina replied. "I can't feel my legs, Moonsong." She glanced up at the sagging building. Slate shingles slid from its roof, smashing to flinders as they struck the ground. Her eyes hardened. "You'd better leave me."

Moonsong paled, her eyes widening. "What?"

"You heard me," Paxina replied firmly. "Find Stagheart, and get out of Kendermore, through the tunnels. I'll only slow you down. Tell Kronn and Catt I'm sorry. . . ."

Moonsong ignored her. She grabbed Paxina and tried to drag her away from the burning house. The kender's weight was too much for her, though. They had scarcely gone ten feet when a loud crack split the air. Looking up, Moonsong saw the house's flaming wall begin to topple.

"Go!" Paxina shouted. Somehow, she twisted free of Moonsong's grasp. Before the Plainswoman could do anything, the kender shoved her with all her might, sending her stumbling away from the toppling building.

As she staggered, Moonsong saw Stagheart running

toward her from Kurthak's corpse. Then she tripped, crashing headlong to the ground. As she rolled to a stop, she caught a glimpse of Paxina lying on her back, a smile on her face.

"Oh, well," the Lord Mayor said, unafraid. "It was fun while it lasted."

Then the house fell on them both, and the world crashed down in fire and darkness. Moonsong smelled hair and flesh burning. Then nothing.

* * * * *

Stagheart shouted in incoherent anguish, reaching out for Moonsong as she collapsed. Then, with a deafening roar, a deluge of blazing plaster and smoldering timbers poured down on her, and she disappeared.

"No!" he roared.

Recklessly he surged forward into the burning rubble. Muscles straining, he lifted pieces of smoldering wood and heaved them aside. He burnt both his hands as he dug, but he didn't care. Tears washed Kurthak's blood from his face. He called Moonsong's name again and again.

When he lifted a charred board and saw her hand, he let out a ragged cry of relief and dread. Working quickly, he picked up debris and heaved it aside. He grabbed beams he should not have been able to lift; desperation fueled his strength, however, and he tossed them away like twigs. At last, he uncovered Moonsong's body.

Burning pitch covered half her face, searing her flesh. Sobbing, he clawed it away, not noticing as blisters rose on his fingers. Underneath the tar, Moonsong's skin was bright red. He ignored the sight of it and put aside the sweet stench of seared skin as he lifted her up and carried her out of the wreckage.

He didn't go back for Paxina; there was nothing more he could do for her. The house's upper floors, which had fallen on Moonsong, had been made of wood and plaster, but the lowest, the one that had buried the Lord Mayor, had been hewn of fitted stone. Where Paxina had been, moments before, there was only a crude cairn of jagged rubble.

Stagheart glanced around. The yard was all but empty: the ogres were all dead, and most of the kender were gone. Buildings were crashing to the ground everywhere, sending storms of cinders shooting up into the smoke-darkened sky. The heat of the burning city made it hard to breathe.

Holding Moonsong's limp form close to him, trying not to jostle her, he began to run. He sprinted through pools of blood, skirted around huge and small bodies, then came to a halt at the edge of a dark shaft that led down beneath the ground. A pile of corpses marked where the kender had made a stand, holding off the ogres while their fellows fled. Stagheart stared at them a moment with raw, red eyes, then dashed down the stairs, out of the shambles of Kendermore.

* * * * *

Of the ten thousand kender who had stayed behind to defend their city, nearly half perished in the battle. Those who fled through the tunnels emerged several leagues to the west and quickly caught up with the far greater numbers who had escaped through Kendermore's sundered walls. They struggled wearily onward through the dead forest, straining toward the distant fields of Balifor. Word of Paxina Thistleknot's death spread quickly, and the kender wept for her, but they did not slow their pace. There was still a long way to go.

Less than an hour after the last survivors escaped Kendermore, however, one young kender glanced back at the plume of black smoke rising from the city's ruins and cried out in terror. The fleeing kender stopped, turned, then echoed his exclamation with sobs and screams of their own.

In the distance, too small yet to see clearly but growing steadily larger, a red, winged form streaked across the sky.

Chapter 26

Malystryx shrieked angrily as the barren land streaked by beneath her. She flew high over the Desolation, the wind roaring in her ears. Far ahead of her lay the parched bones of the Kenderwood. A black, smoky finger stuck up from its midst, pointing defiantly toward the empty, blue sky. She stared at it balefully, knowing she looked upon the downfall of Kurthak the Black-Gazer's horde. She knew, too, that the kender were still alive.

"Not for long, miserable wretches," she sneered. "You have won nothing. I will turn your bones to ashes."

She soared onward, the Kenderwood inching steadily closer.

* * * * *

His arms burning, Riverwind lowered himself toward the floor of the cavern. Eight feet above the ground, he lost his grip and fell, landing hard and grunting with pain. He lay on his back a moment, his chest heaving, then forced himself to stand.

"You all right?" Kronn called from above, his voice echoing hollowly off the walls of the cave.

Riverwind nodded weakly. "Yes," he lied, his face contorting with agony as he clutched at his stomach.

"All right," the kender declared. "Look out below. I'm coming down."

Wrapping the rope about himself, he swung over the ledge and started to descend. He rappelled down, pushing off the cavern wall as he slid recklessly down the rope.

In less than a minute he stood on the ground beside River-wind, panting and flushed.

"Whew," he said, grinning. "I forgot how dizzy that makes me." He crouched down, clutching his knees as he cleared his head. After a moment he knelt, then plucked a small, leathery shard from the floor of the cave. He held it up as he stood, showing it to Riverwind. "Eggshell," he said, and gestured across the floor. The edges of the cave were littered with such fragments. "Just like you said— she laid a whole clutch of them, then destroyed all but one."

Together, they looked across the cavern at the ash-heap and the abomination nestled in its midst. "The strongest one," Riverwind said.

They stood still for a moment, then exchanged determined glances. Kronn reached over his shoulder and drew his chapak from his back, smiling grimly. "All right," he declared.

"Let's be done with this."

Riverwind and Kronn crept across the cavern floor. As he walked, the old Plainsman stole a furtive glance up at the ceiling. The cleft in the rock was empty. Squaring his jaw, he looked toward the egg.

It was even more repulsive up close than it had been from above. Its leathery shell gleamed dully, and it seemed to pulse as they approached. The stink of brimstone that hung about it was almost suffocating. The ash pile surrounding it rippled, and glints of light danced about it, faster with every step, bobbing like a multitude of golden will-o'-wisps.

They stopped at the edge of the ash pile. Riverwind reached to his belt, his fingers clasping about the handle of Brightdawn's flanged mace. Drawing the weapon, he stepped forward.

The instant his foot touched the ashes, the flitting motes of firelight stopped moving. With a noise like a distant blast of wind, they blazed brightly and began to coalesce. He stared in horror as they gathered together, forming a lithe, wriggling shape.

The serpent was fifty feet long, and its red-gold scales glittered as it coiled protectively around Malys's egg. Its hooded head rose above Riverwind and Kronn, baring a mouthful of long, needle-sharp fangs and hissing like water thrown on hot stones. Two bright, blood-red spots glowed malevolently in the depths of its eye sockets.

"Branchala shave me bald," Kronn swore devoutly.

In an eyeblink, the serpent's head surged down, toward Riverwind. He tried to leap away, but its jaws clamped fast around his right ankle, fangs sinking deep into his flesh. Gagging with pain, he swung Brightdawn's mace, bringing it down on the serpent's head. The blow bounced harmlessly off the monster's skull. Then the serpent raised its head again, jerking Riverwind off the ground.

The old Plainsman flailed his arms in the air, hanging upside down from the fiend's mouth. Beneath him, Kronn raised his chapak and struck at the serpent's body with all his might. Its scales turned the blow harmlessly aside. Tightening its grip on Riverwind's leg, the serpent began to shake him violently, trying to snap his spine.

Riverwind fought ferociously, battering the serpent with his daughter's mace. Each blow was strong enough to crush a man's ribs, but the serpent ignored them completely, continuing to thrash him back and forth. At last the mace fell from Riverwind's hand, landing with a puff in the bed of ashes. He continued to struggle, beating at the serpent with his bare fists.

Kronn swung his chapak again and again, trying to penetrate the serpent's scales. Every time, the axe glanced off harmlessly—until, finally, an errant swing grazed part of the serpent's soft underbelly. Burning blood dripped from the wound.

Kronn glanced at the wound, then looked up at Riverwind. The serpent was still shaking the Plainsman, who had gone limp in its jaws. Furiously the kender raised his chapak high and buried its head deep in the serpent's throat.

The first blow didn't kill the monster, nor did the

second or the third. Kronn struck the serpent's throat again and again, like a lumberjack trying to fell a tree. The monster's blood scorched Kronn's skin, but the kender ignored the pain and continued to chop at the serpent.

Kronn cleaved the monster's flesh a dozen more times, laying open its innards. At last, it stopped shaking Riverwind, then slumped over and died.

The old Plainsman lay motionless, his ankle still clamped in the serpent's jaws. Then he raised his head and looked at Kronn, his hair and clothes dusted with fine, powdery ash.

Kronn breathed a sigh of immense relief. "How bad are you hurt?" he asked.

"I don't know," Riverwind answered, staring at his wounded leg. "I can't feel anything below my knee."

Together, they pried open the serpent's viselike jaws. Blood welled from the old Plainsman's leg as the monster's fangs pulled out of his flesh, but he did not wince or moan. As soon as he was free, the serpent's shimmering body turned dull black, then crumbled into a shapeless heap of soot.

"I should have known Malys would put a ward on this place," Kronn muttered, angry with himself. "She'd want to protect her egg."

The serpent's teeth had shredded Riverwind's leather boot, then had done the same to his skin. The flow of blood, strong at first, was choked off by the rapid swelling of the wound. Working quickly, Riverwind drew his dagger and cut off his pantleg at the knee. The wound darkened, the flesh surrounding it puffing up until it was the size of a kurpa melon. At last, however, it ceased to swell, though it continued to throb angrily, oozing thin trickles of blood. Kronn stared at it, sickened, as the old Plainsman extended his hand toward him.

"Kronn," Riverwind said plaintively, "help me stand."

It was difficult—Riverwind could barely bend his knee, and his numb foot had trouble supporting his weight—but Kronn took the Plainsman's hand and pulled him upright. Plowing a furrow in the ash pile as he dragged his injured leg behind him, Riverwind limped to where Brightdawn's mace had fallen and picked it up again. Its flanged head gleamed dimly as he turned to look at the egg.

"I had thought, when the time came, that we would argue over who should do this," he told the kender solemnly. He glanced down at the discolored ruin of his leg. "Now, though, there no longer seems to be a need."

"What do you mean?" Kronn asked.

Riverwind's gaze turned stern. "Kronn, you must go."

"What?" the kender gasped.

"I want you to leave this place," the Plainsman stated. "I cannot climb with my leg like this, so I will stay and destroy the egg. There's no need for you to remain as well. Leave, Kronn. When the dragon finds me, she'll assume I'm here alone. She won't look for you."

"I can't just abandon you here." Kronn's eyes were pleading.

Riverwind smiled sadly. "And I couldn't forgive myself if I let you stay. Kronn, go to Balifor, and find your people. Your sisters are waiting for you. The kender will need your help."

"But . . ." the kender began; then his voice broke and he looked away, blinking back tears.

Riverwind paused a moment, then opened his pack and reached inside. Kronn watched him, craning his neck curiously, then caught his breath when the Plainsman produced his worn, bonewood flute.

"I want you to have this," Riverwind said.

Kronn stared at it, his mouth agape. "I can't take that."

The old Plainsman laughed suddenly, eyes sparkling. "That's something I never thought I'd hear a kender say," he said. "Please, Kronn—it should be with someone who will play it."

Reaching out, Kronn took the flute from Riverwind. He held it a moment, then tucked it safely into one of his pouches. "Thank you," he said softly.

Riverwind extended his hand, and Kronn shook it firmly. His face quietly thoughtful, the kender turned and crossed the cavern floor. He stopped when he reached the rope, then turned. The Plainsman still faced him, smiling.

"Goodbye, Riverwind," Kronn said, his voice trembling.

"Farewell, Kronn-alin. You have been a good friend."

Swallowing, Kronn turned toward the cavern wall. He slung his chapak across his back, grasped the rope with both hands, and began to climb.

Riverwind watched him ascend, his face grave. It took the kender several minutes to reach the ledge. Finally, Kronn scrambled nimbly onto the stone balcony, looked down at the cavern floor, and waved his arm above his head. Riverwind raised his hand in reply. Then Kronn was gone, walking swiftly back down the obsidian tunnel.

Sighing, the old Plainsman turned back toward the egg. He looked at it silently for nearly a minute, then crossed the warm ash pile, walking swiftly to its side. "Goddess give me strength," he whispered. "Guide my hand."

Slowly, deliberately, he raised Brightdawn's mace high above his head. He held it poised a moment, then swung downward, striking the egg's ruddy shell.

* * * * *

The Kenderwood was very close, only a few scant miles away. Malystryx glared down at it, her blood burning with hate. She could see Kendermore clearly now, still blazing brightly in the midst of the wide, lifeless meadow. Beyond it, still far in the distance, her keen eyes spotted the fleeing kender, shadows flitting westward through the skeletal woodland.

"You will not escape," she hissed at them. "I will make this forest a holocaust. You will die screaming my name."

Her wings pumping mightily, she began to rise, gaining altitude so she could swoop down on the Kenderwood and blast it with her breath. The ground fell away beneath her.

Then, suddenly, a violent shock jolted her, nearly knocking her from the sky.

She fell a thousand feet before she recovered enough to

move, then struggled to keep herself aloft. Her wings strained, the membranes snapping taut, as the Desolation spun up toward her. Finally she arrested her fall, flapping to put empty air between herself and the ground. Blood pounded in her ears, and she screamed balefully, her head snaking about to gaze upon the burning mountain, many leagues behind her.

With great effort she focused her mind, reaching toward Blood Watch. *Yovanna,* she thought. *Someone is with the egg. Protect it.*

Yovanna's mind eluded her, however. She reached out, searching, but she soon realized her servant was dead—and then she knew that the fire serpent she had set to guard her nest was dead too. The egg was unprotected.

Another shock hit her, and she dropped again. This time, however, she recovered quickly, then rose higher. A bright star of rage burning within her, she turned back the way she had come, streaking away from the tinder-dry forest. The kender fled behind her, forgotten.

*   *   *   *   *

The egg would not break. Again and again Riverwind struck it, Brightdawn's mace rising and falling as he beat a cadence of frustration upon its shell. Though its surface looked and felt like stiff leather, it was as hard as iron, refusing to crack even when he swung the bludgeon with both hands. His arms blazed with pain from the exertion, and he fought valiantly to keep from losing his balance as his benumbed leg tried to give way beneath him. The mace's flanges bent, and its head began to loosen as he pounded. A loud, thunderous boom sounded with every blow.

"Give, damn you!" he snarled through clenched teeth. He could sense Malystryx's wrath bearing down on him, growing with every hammering stroke. She would be here soon, emerging through the rift, thirsting for his blood. If the egg didn't break before then, he would fail.

He could not—would not—let that happen.

Shouting incoherently, he brought the mace up with both

hands and slammed it down with all his might. The force of the blow knocked him off his feet, sending him sprawling. The mace flew from his hand as he fell, its haft splintered. He writhed on the ground, gasping for breath, for long moments before he found the strength to turn his gaze toward the egg.

A long fissure marred the shell. Thick green ichor seeped from it, darkening the ashes where it dripped.

Riverwind stared at the crack a moment, then heaved himself upright and stumbled toward the egg. Steel rang as he jerked his sabre from its scabbard. Carefully, he wedged the sword's tip in the fissure and leaned upon it hard. The membrane within the shell resisted for a long moment, then yielded. His sabre slid into the egg.

Green, sticky albumen spewed forth, soaking his arms. It stank of brimstone and putrescence, but he fought back his rising gorge and kept his grip on the hilt of his sword. Singlemindedly, he sawed the blade back and forth, slitting open the egg along the length of its shell. Then, weakened by his efforts, the shell burst, breaking open and drenching him from the chest down in slime. The ichor poured over the ashes, soaking them. Riverwind's sabre trailed strings of albumen as he jerked it out of the egg.

Then, ulcerating out of the ruined egg like suppuration from a festering wound, the embryo slid free. It landed with a wet smack at his feet.

He stared at it, gagging with disgust. The baby dragon was nearly four feet long, from nose to tail, but it was completely helpless, not yet fully formed. Its body was shriveled and dark, shaped like a tadpole that had just begun to turn into a frog. Its legs and wings were useless stumps; its eyes were large and dark, covered by thin, ruddy membranes; its mouth gaped wide, revealing a single, barbed egg tooth. The baby wyrm twitched wretchedly, fighting to stay alive. Riverwind sank to his knees beside it, his guts wrenching with nausea.

At that moment, a deafening scream rang out from beyond the shaft in the cavern's ceiling.

*　*　*　*　*

Red fury filled Malys's mind as she dove toward Blood Watch. The last shock had wracked her body, filling her mind with pain. The egg, she knew, was destroyed. Her child was dying, helpless, and she couldn't save it.

But she could avenge.

The volcano loomed before her, incredibly close. She spread her wings wide, slowing her descent slightly. Then the stone trembled as she landed next to the entrance to her nest. Moving with crazed purpose, she climbed into the shaft and began to wriggle through it toward her lair. Scales tore from her body as she slithered, ripped loose by jagged stones, but she ignored them, pulling herself along with claws that shredded the rock like loose earth. She heaved herself forward until she saw the dim orange glow of fire-light beneath her. Snarling, she took the last fifty yards to the end of the shaft at a single lunge.

She caught herself at the lip of the shaft, talons driving like pitons into the stone. Her head snaked downward, her golden eyes flaring with rage as she stared down at the floor of her nest, far below. She saw the ash pile, stained green by the egg's juices. She saw the egg, split nearly in half and dripping with slime. She saw the embryo, quivering miserably on the ground. And then she saw the old Plainsman, kneeling beside the baby dragon's side, sword in hand. He looked up at her, his lips curling into a victorious smile.

Malystryx shrieked, shaking Blood Watch to its very roots.

* * * * *

Riverwind only heard the first few seconds of the dragon's screech, then the noise burst his eardrums, deafening him. Pain roared in his head, but he kept his eyes fixed on Malystryx. She clung to the rocks high above, her mouth open wide. An avalanche of stone showered out of the rift as the shaft behind her collapsed from the force of her rage.

I was wrong all those years ago, Riverwind thought as he stared up at her. Death's wings aren't black at all. They're red as the vanished moon.

Suddenly, the dragon's mouth snapped shut. The mountain continued to tremble beneath Riverwind for a long time. Malys glared at him, unreasoning hatred in her eyes. The dragonfear was horrifically intense, clawing at his sanity. He swayed as it beat down upon him but fought it off valiantly. Glaring up at the enormous wyrm, he reversed his grip on his sabre so its blade pointed downward, then raised it high in both hands. He held the sword poised for an instant, then drove it downward, through the helpless embryo's breast. With one last, miserable shiver, the baby dragon died. He let go of the sabre, leaving it buried in the embryo's stilled heart.

Her eyes shining ferociously, Malystryx hunched her shoulders and sucked in a long, deep breath. Not taking his eyes off her, Riverwind reached beneath his fur vest and locked his fingers around the Forever Charm. He yanked, and the medallion's chain snapped as he pulled it from around his neck. He squeezed its two interlocked circles, feeling their steel edges cut his flesh. Blood welling between his fingers, he thrust his fist above his head.

"Goldmoon," he whispered as flames surged up the dragon's throat.

* * * * *

Kronn-alin Thistleknot waited for hours, crouching low on the ridge opposite Blood Watch. The mountain shook again and again as Malystryx thundered her rage, deep within its heart. A gout of smoke spewed from the volcano's caldera, and rivers of glowing lava poured down into the valley below. Sheets of stone broke loose from its sides, smashing to pieces as they struck the ground.

Finally, around dusk, the noise and the tremors died away. Blood Watch fell silent. The dragon did not emerge.

Kronn stayed where he was a short while longer. Then he rose and walked away, toward the setting sun.

Epilogue

A cool breeze blew through Solace Vale, soughing through the branches of the vallenwoods and rustling their blue-green leaves. It was late summer, with a fortnight still to go before the Harvest Come festival, and the weather had begun to slide toward autumn. The front door of the Inn of the Last Home stood wide open, as did its stained glass windows, allowing the gentle wind to blow the taproom.

This afternoon, the tavern was more or less empty. It was market day in Solace, and the Inn's patrons had gone down to the town square to shop, gossip, and enjoy the pleasant weather. Tika and her daughters were also at the market, buying food to stock the Inn's larders.

Thus it was that—with the exception of Clemen, Borlos and Osler, who sat where they always sat, playing cards and swearing at one another—Caramon found himself left alone for a while. He took the opportunity to drag an armchair over to a spot where the breeze was particularly pleasant, sit down, and take a long, leisurely nap. He did not sleep alone, however; in his arms, he held Ulin, his grandson.

Usha's child had arrived right on time, not quite a year ago. He had been born strong and healthy, and no one—not even Palin, who'd been beside himself with joy—had been quite as proud as Caramon. In the best grandfatherly tradition, he'd spent the past year fawning over Ulin, much to Palin and Usha's chagrin. Tika often quipped that Caramon spent more time with the baby than he did with his own wife, but she was no one to talk. She spoiled Ulin rotten too.

Today, as with all market days, Caramon had volunteered to take care of the child, giving his mother and father an afternoon to themselves. And today being a particularly lazy day, both Caramon and Ulin were content to snooze quietly, listening to the orchestra of muttering leaves and twittering birds outside the Inn. They were both sound asleep, then, when the tromp of feet sounded on the stairs far below.

As the footsteps drew nearer, Clemen, Borlos and Osler set down their cards and glanced across the tavern. "Hey, big guy!" Clemen shouted across the room. "Company coming!"

Caramon answered with a cavernous snore. In his arms, Ulin made burbling sounds but didn't wake. The footsteps were close now, nearing the balcony that surrounded the Inn.

"Whose turn is it this time?" Osler asked.

"Bor's," said Clemen.

Borlos groaned, then set his cards face down on the table. He rose and walked over to Caramon, then reached out and tapped the innkeeper on the shoulder. "Wake up, you old lummox," he said, not unkindly.

Caramon's eyes blinked open, and he peered up at Borlos. "You're lucky I've got the kid here," he grumbled, nodding at the baby in his arms. "What have I told you about waking me up?"

Just to be safe, Borlos took a quick step back from the chair. "Don't matter what you'd do to me," he replied. "Tika said she'd do worse if we let you sleep when guests showed up."

Caramon's brow furrowed. "What'd she do, threaten to take away your cards?"

"Well, uh," Borlos answered, flushing with embarrassment, "actually, yeah."

Caramon snorted with mock disgust, then shook his head groggily, clearing out the cobwebs. "You said something about guests?"

"Outside," Osler called from their table. "You can hear them, can't you, big guy? Haven't up and gone deaf in your old age, have you?"

Scowling sourly, Caramon strained to listen. Hearing the footsteps—they were on the balcony now—he heaved himself to his feet, Ulin in his arms. Before he could move any farther, though, a shadow stepped into the doorway. Caramon stepped back, fighting to focus against the glaring sunlight that streamed through the door. The visitor was a young woman, clad in a Plainsfolk dress. She walked with a limp, favoring her right leg. Her face . . .

Caramon caught his breath as he finally made out the woman's features. She had been truly beautiful, once. On the right side she still was, her strong face framed by long, golden hair shot with strands of silver. The left side, however, was a horror. From forehead to chin, and on down her neck, her skin was red and puckered—a large, glistening scar. Her left eye was seared shut, her left ear a gnarled stub. The golden hair had been scorched away on that side, laying bare her burn-ravaged scalp.

Behind him, Borlos swore softly and hurried back to join the other card players. Caramon took no notice; for a time, he could do little but stare.

"Moonsong?" he breathed.

The right side of her mouth curled into a smile. "Caramon." She nodded at Ulin. "Your grandson?"

"What?" he asked, stunned. "Oh. Yes." He continued to look at her, not believing what he saw. "Moonsong . . . what happened?"

"In good time," she replied. "We will tell you."

Caramon's brow lowered. "We?"

A second woman stepped into the Inn, leaning on a plain staff. She was older, but her face still retained the beauty that once had been Moonsong's. Caramon recognized her immediately, a sharp ache in his heart.

"Goldmoon," he said.

The older woman regarded him kindly. "My friend," she said. "It is good to see you."

For a moment, Caramon couldn't think of anything to say. "Why—why are you here?" he asked lamely.

"We come bearing news you should hear," Goldmoon

replied. "My husband is dead—and Brightdawn, Swiftra-ven, and thousands of brave kender with him."

* * * * *

Folk who came to the tavern at the Inn of the Last Home that night found it dark and locked. Handpainted signs were posted at the front door and at the bottom of the long flight of stairs that wound around the vallenwood tree.

Closed tonight in memory of Riverwind of Qué-Shu. Guests, please use the back door to go to your rooms. We will reopen tomorrow.
— Tika and Caramon Majere

Inside, the taproom was almost empty. Clemen, Borlos and Osler had gone home shortly after Tika and her daughters returned. Little Ulin had started to cry when he woke and saw Moonsong's scarred face, and Laura and Dezra had offered to take him home. The girls stayed at Palin and Usha's house that night, knowing their parents would want to be alone.

A few lonely candles glowed in the tavern, casting dancing shadows on the walls. Caramon and Tika sat at a table by the darkened fireplace, across from Goldmoon and Moonsong. The old Plainswoman sat quietly, her eyes shining in the flickering light, as her daughter told of Riverwind's last quest and the fall of Kendermore. As she spoke, Caramon bowed his head sorrowfully. Tears crawled down Tika's cheeks.

"When the house collapsed on top of me, Stagheart pulled me from the rubble. We escaped into the tunnels," Moonsong said. She paused, taking a sip from a glass of wine Caramon had poured for her. "The fire left me as you see me now. I would surely have died, but the kender saw to my wounds and carried me away through the forest. I remember nothing of that journey, save the kender's cries when they saw Malystryx on the wing. They were terri-fied. But she turned back when she was nearly upon us, and I knew Father had succeeded.

"The next thing I remember, I awoke in Balifor, in the kender camp. We had made it safely out of the Kender-wood. Stagheart was with me—he had stayed at my bed-side for days, waiting for me to wake. Later, Catt came to visit me. I didn't understand her pity when she looked at me . . . not until I asked her to bring me a mirror, and I saw what I had become. . . ."

Moonsong's voice broke, the right side of her face creas-ing with bitterness. She looked up at the ceiling, blinking rapidly. Goldmoon rested a gentle hand on her arm. For a time, the Inn was silent, then Moonsong shook her head, angry with herself, and lowered her anguished gaze back to Caramon and Tika.

"Stagheart didn't look at me that way, though," she said softly. "Looking in his eyes, I could almost believe I was whole again—at least in my body. Nothing can make me forget the hole inside me where Brightdawn used to be.

"We stayed in the camp for two weeks. I must have been visited by a dozen healers. They treated me with poultices and salves, herbal draughts and vapors. Slowly I recovered, but I knew it would still be some time before I was well enough to walk.

"Then one day I heard shouting outside my tent. At first, I thought the dragon had returned—we were not far from the Kenderwood, and I feared she would fall upon us and burn us for spite. But I soon realized the kender were crying out not in fear or panic, but with joy. I asked Stagheart to go find out what was happening. I thought, maybe, that somehow Father had survived, and had finally caught up with us.

"It wasn't Father, though; it was Kronn, and he was alone. He came to visit me in my tent and told me what had happened at Blood Watch. We had won, and Father and Brightdawn had bought our victory with their lives.

"The kender threw a party that night. They danced and sang until dawn. I didn't feel like celebrating, though. Then, in the morning, I had visitors: Kronn, Catt, and Giffel. They thanked us for what we had done—not just

Stagheart and I, but Brightdawn and Swiftraven. Then they gave me this."

Moonsong reached into her pack, which rested under the table. After a moment, she pulled a smooth, white object from it and set it on the table. It was a small bust, carved from bleached wood in Riverwind's likeness. It captured the old Plainsman's stern face and kind eyes perfectly. Caramon felt a rush of hot tears as he looked upon the sculpture.

"Kronn crafted this from one of the Kenderwood's dead trees," Moonsong stated, her voice thick with tears. "Mother and I would like to take it to the Last Heroes' Tomb."

"Of course," Caramon said. "We can do it tonight when we're done here. I'll take you there."

Moonsong tried to smile, then lapsed into silence, staring at the bust. It stared back at her, proud and serious.

After a while, Tika cleared her throat. "What happened after that?" she asked. "What became of the kender?"

The young Plainswoman blinked, startled out of her reverie, then nodded and went on. "They did what kender do," she said. "After Kronn returned, they didn't stay put much longer. Before another week passed, most of them packed and set out on the road. Most, but not all—Kronn stayed behind, with a thousand of the kender who had fought at Kendermore. Catt pleaded with him to come along, but he refused. 'The ogres took many of our people as slaves,' he said. 'We're going to try to free them. And then there's Malys—she's beaten for now, but she won't be stopped. Someone needs to keep an eye on her, though, and make sure she doesn't make too much of a nuisance of herself. And maybe, one day, someone will defeat her for good. When that happens, I want to be here.'

"So we left him there and set out on the road. The morning we left, Catt and Giffel were married. They led the Kender Flight north, and Stagheart and I went with them. I still wasn't well enough to walk, so they carried me along with the other wounded."

Moonsong paused, sighing. "It wasn't an easy journey.

You can imagine what people's reactions were, when they saw thousands of kender headed for their villages. We were driven out, even attacked. We went on up the coast, but everywhere it was the same.

"Along the way, of course, our numbers dwindled.

"Then, when we were traveling through a mountain pass just beyond the Great Moors, we heard what sounded like an army coming the other way. The kender were afraid, thinking someone had sent soldiers to stop us from going on. Giffel went to scout ahead so he could sound an alarm in case of trouble.

"It wasn't trouble at all, though; in fact, it was just the opposite. One of the messengers Father had sent out before the Flight began—a young kender named Blister Nimblefingers—had made it to the Knights of Solamnia. The Knights had sent a brigade to escort the Flight to Coastlund, where there were ships waiting to ferry them across the straits to Hylo, the kender homeland in Northern Ergoth.

"Stagheart and I remained with the Flight until we reached Estwilde," Moonsong concluded. "By then, my wounds had healed enough for me to walk, so we left the kender and headed south through the hills, then across the New Sea. We returned to Qué-Shu in the springtime, bearing word of what had happened."

"But I already knew," Goldmoon said softly.

Caramon and Tika looked at her, surprised. "How?" Tika asked.

The old Plainswoman reached into the neck of her pale blue tunic and pulled out a small, silver-steel medallion shaped in the form of two teardrops, joined end to end. "I gave this to Riverwind the day he left our village for Kendermore," she said. "On the day after Mark Year—the day he died—a sudden impulse drew me to the Temple of Mishakal. I went inside and found this upon the altar."

Caramon and Tika stared at the Forever Charm in mute wonder. A silence settled over the tavern. After a while, the old Plainswoman tucked the medallion back beneath her tunic.

"We would have come to Solace sooner," she said apologetically, "but there was much to do. Among my people, the time of mourning for a chieftain lasts a full month. There were feasts, ritual hunts, funeral games to oversee. And there was also the wedding of my daughter and Stagheart of Qué-Teh."

"Wedding?" Caramon blurted, astonished.

Moonsong nodded. "We were married on the first day of summer."

"Where's your husband, then?" Tika asked.

"He remains in Qué-Shu, leading the tribes while Mother is away," Moonsong answered. "He is also war leader now. Wanderer has left Qué-Shu. When he learned that Father and Brightdawn were dead, he took Cloud-hawk, his boy, and rode out of our village. I do not think they will return soon."

"And so I have lost two children, and my husband as well," Goldmoon said quietly. For the first time since she had entered the Inn, a glimmer of sadness disturbed the serenity of her eyes. "But the strange thing is, that is not the heaviest burden to bear. What causes me the most grief is that Riverwind told no one he was dying until the end was near."

Something inside Caramon gave way. He broke down, sobbing raggedly and covering his face with his shaking hands. "Oh, gods," he groaned, his voice raw with pain. He cried quietly for a moment, then looked at the old Plainswoman with sore, red eyes. "Goldmoon," he murmured. "He told us just before he left."

She turned very pale, staring at him. Unable to meet her stricken gaze any longer, Caramon rose suddenly and walked out of the tavern, into the depths of the Inn.

Tika's face was damp with tears. She reached across the table and took the old Plainswoman's hand. "I'm sorry," she said.

"Do not be," Goldmoon answered. "If I were to blame someone, it would be Riverwind, not you—but I cannot do that either. In my heart, I know why he didn't tell me. He was protecting me, as he had tried to do all his life."

Soon after, Caramon returned. He moved slowly, wearily, as he crossed to the table where his wife and the Plainswomen were. He did not sit; instead, he held something out to Goldmoon. It was a small, silver scrolltube.

"Riverwind gave this to me before he left Solace," Caramon said softly. "He wanted me to give it to you after . . . after he was gone."

Goldmoon looked at the scroll tube, then took it from his hand. "Thank you, my friend," she said.

Grimacing, Caramon turned and brushed Tika's shoulder. She touched Goldmoon's arm, then stood and walked with her husband out of the room. A moment later Moonsong rose and followed them, leaving her mother alone in the tavern.

Goldmoon held the tube silently, watching the candlelight gleam brightly on its surface. Then, taking a deep breath, she opened it and pulled out the scroll within. She unrolled the parchment gently, her hands trembling. The writing upon it was spare, precise.

Kan-tokah, it read. *Forgive me. I will wait for you.*

She stared at the words long into the night.

DRAGONS OF SUMMER FLAME
MARGARET WEIS AND TRACY HICKMAN

The best-selling conclusion to the stories told in the Chronicles and Legends Trilogies. The War of the Lance is long over. The seasons come and go. The pendulum of the world swings. Now it is summer. A hot, parched summer such as no one on Krynn has ever known before.

Distraught by a grievous loss, the young mage Palin Majere seeks to enter the Abyss in search of his lost uncle, the infamous archmage Raistlin.

The Dark Queen has found new champions. Devoted followers, loyal to the death, the Knights of Takhisis follow the Vision to victory. A dark paladin, Steel Brightblade, rides to attack the High Clerist's Tower, the fortress his father died defending.

On a small island, the mysterious Irda capture an ancient artifact and use it to ensure their own safety. Usha, child of the Irda, arrives in Palanthas claiming that she is Raistlin's daughter.

The summer will be deadly. Perhaps it will be the last summer Ansalon will ever know.

THE CHAOS WAR
MARGARET WEIS AND DON PERRIN

This series brings to life the background stories and events of the conflagration known as The Chaos War, as told in the *New York Times* best-selling novel *Dragons of Summer Flame*.

The Doom Brigade
Margaret Weis and Don Perrin

An intrepid group of draconian engineers must unite with the dwarves, their despised enemies, when the Chaos WAr erupts.

The Last Thane
Douglas Niles

The Choas War rages across the surface of Ansalon, but what's going on deep under the mountains in the kingdom of Thorbardin? Anarchy, betrayal, and bloodshed.

June 1998

Tears of the Night Sky
Linda P. Baker

A quest of Paladine becomes a test of faith for Crysania, the blind cleric. She is aided by a magical tiger-companion, who is beholden to the mysterious dark elf wizard Dalamar.

October 1998